LIGHT MY FIRE

A SEX ROCK MAFIA NOVEL

JESSICA RUBEN

Visit my website at www.jessicarubenauthor.com
Cover Designer: Sarah Hansen, Okay Creations
Editor: Jovana Shirley, Unforeseen Editing, www.unforeseenediting.com
Editor: Nicole Bailey, Proof Before You Publish
Proofing: Sarah P, All Encompassing Books
Publicity: Autumn Ganz at Wordsmith Publicity

ISBN paperback 978-1-7334751-1-2
ISBN e-book 978-1-7334751-0-5

To Leigh Raines, a talented author and friend I simply couldn't live without.

BLURB

He saved me from war.
Fed me when I was in too much pain to eat.
Smuggled me and my family into America when it became too
dangerous to stay.
But, Nico didn't flee with us.

While I began elementary school in the United States,
He was building the greatest and toughest Mafia of the century.
The Mafia Shqiptare.

Nico is now King of all underground trades.
Sexy. Aggressive. Brilliant.

After years of nothing but silence, he's back in my life,
Ready to do *whatever* it takes to bring me into his universe.
He isn't leaving until he takes me with him.

PROLOGUE

Kosovo, 1998

JAKUP SITS WITH HIS LEGS CROSSED, CIGAR SMOKE LEAKING FROM HIS pencil-thin lips as he howls, "We cannot fold! The KLA will win this war in the end. It has to." His voice reverberates through the home like thunder.

My hands clutch themselves together like magnets.

The top of my wooden staircase has a direct view of the living room. Hiding behind a large green plant mother recently brought inside, I watch the conversation unfold.

My father leans forward in his chair. "Serb police need to all be gunned down, once and for all. Over thirty of our children were killed this week. In the streets! They're animals, Jakup. We need independence. We need freedom. These atrocities cannot stand." Father's voice shakes with emotion. "But when will the US intervene? All they talk about is Monica Lewinsky, and meanwhile, the stakes here"—he points to the ground with a firm finger—"are rising."

I shift, the words *children ... gunned ... killed* bang against my head.

Father must hear my stressful thoughts because he calls up, "Elira, come down now."

Mother told me to stay upstairs today. "You're only ten," she said. "Your place is by my side."

But mother is not home; she's at the market, gathering food with my older brother, Agron. And as Father always says, I'm his right hand when mama isn't home.

Step by step, I move downstairs. Nerves envelop me, but thankfully, my legs do as they're told.

Over the last three months, men have been coming and going from our home, using our farm to train. We've been cooking the biggest meals.

"Like there's a party every day," mama said.

We're freedom fighters and members of the KLA, the Kosovo Liberation Army. My father along with Jakup are the two main party leaders. Albanians in Kosovo want to be free from Serbian rule. We want to govern ourselves. And my papa is going to bring us there.

"Jakup, this is my daughter, Elira."

I sit on the chair beside his, sitting tall and strong, just like he taught me.

Rubbing my back with his warm hand, his touch says, *Don't be nervous.*

I turn to him and nod. I'm not scared.

Jakup puts out a hand, and I do the same, hoping I look adult.

He laughs. "I can see it in your eyes; you're smart. You'll go places one day. And your father and I will clear the path for—"

The front door is kicked open. Gunfire. I turn my head to hide in my father's chest, but he throws me beneath the table. I curl up by a wooden leg, ducking my head low. Shots ring loud. Stomping and then yelling coming from the kitchen, too.

There's a war in the house! Can they see me? Will they get me? My entire body shakes. *Do I stay, or do I run?*

Suddenly, a hand grabs my leg like a vise, dragging me out from beneath my wooden cave. I want to scream and kick, but nothing comes from my mouth. My legs are lead. My voice is gone; it's vanished.

I'm forced to stand when a gun is brought to my temple. It's hard and cold. Wetness leaks beneath the pink flowery dress my mama sewed last week, dripping down my leg like a broken faucet. Suddenly, mama is before me. My father is lying on the floor, his head shattered. My brain turns to chaos and buzzes with light. Something within me floats from my chest.

Has God come to take my soul?

The gun is pressed harder against my head. He's screaming, "Where are the men hiding, Blerina?"

She doesn't reply, sweat soaking the front of her black hair.

He chuckles darkly. "Tell me, or I'll blow your daughter to bits."

Her mouth opens and shuts before her green eyes turn resolute. She stands taller, steadfast in her beliefs. My throat stings because my mind knows. The most important men in the resistance meet and train here. Their deaths could mean the end of our freedom, which everyone tells me is more important than the lives we've lost. She will never fold. My heart sinks, knowing my end is here and now.

Children in the streets ...

Children in the streets ...

My body will be among them.

BOOM!

My mother screams. I'm on the ground with a huge man on top of me. Blood and bone against my skin. From the corner of my eye, I see Nico, huge and looming, shooting his gun.

BOOM. BOOM. BOOM.

I don't take a breath as the chaos re-erupts around me.

Silence and stench. The room spins. I'm nailed onto the floor, something unmovable crushing me under.

Mama is down on her haunches, pushing the weight off my body and lifting me in her strong arms. She walks up the steps.

Am I a corpse, watching from above?

Her tears drip onto my face, telling me I'm alive.

Methodically, she turns on the bath before stripping me of my dress and underwear. I put my thumb in my mouth, a soothing habit I broke years ago. She places me in the bath and scrubs my skin until it's raw. I don't dare move.

The steam tells me the water is hot, but I can barely feel it. After a few minutes, she pulls me out, wrapping me in my towel, still damp from last night. Pink pajamas are slipped over my head. It's still morning, but we continue our nightly rituals until I'm tucked into bed.

"Now, don't move, Elira. Rest until I return."

"Don't leave me!" I finally cry as she reaches the door. My voice is loud, but it doesn't sound like mine. It's rough and too high-pitched.

Her eyes widen, like I just made a big mistake. I cover my lips with my hands.

Did the Serbs hear me? Are they back?

Before she can exit, my door swings open, and my mouth poises to scream. It's Nico, taking up my entire doorway.

"I'll stay with her, Blerina."

Mama trembles, folding herself into her own arms. He's eighteen but much bigger than she is. Nico is the biggest.

"Nabergjan is next on the Serb radar. This wasn't just a single hit but the start of terror in our village." He folds his heavy arms across his chest. A gun hangs around his waist, and I know there's a knife on him, too.

I hold my breath, listening.

"I will find arrangements for you to take Elira and Agron out as soon as possible. Your work is done." His voice is measured as he gives his decree.

"But—"

"Don't argue with me. It's for your safety." He cracks his knuckles. "Bring Elira tea. Now."

She nods in obedience. Father always said Nico is young but brighter and crueler than the rest. When Nico speaks, everyone listens and follows his orders. He fights for our freedom like the other men, but he is different, too. He's unlike the others in the way he carries himself—with so much strength and determination. Nothing can get in his way.

Mama's pale lips quiver, like she wants to say more. She leaves.

He comes next to me when I ask, "Why is she g-going down?" My voice is a whisper as I clutch on to him.

His white shirt is damp. Instinctively, I tuck my head into his chest. It's instant relief.

He pulls me closer, allowing me to take him in. "She's got to clean up the mess downstairs. You saw your father, didn't you? And Jakup?" His voice is firm and honest.

I look up into his deep, dark eyes. For me, Nico brings only truth. He holds my shoulder, like I'm a friend he's trying to comfort. From his touch, my heartbeat slows.

"They're dead now. But don't worry. I will find and kill the Serbs who got away. You have my word." He pauses, eyes narrowing into slits. "I'll never let them get away with this." His voice is harder than I've ever heard it.

A knock at the door. I freeze, but it's only my mother entering with a cup in her hands. Mint leaves float at the top, sugar already melted. She leaves it on my bedside table, and Nico gestures for her to leave. I should say I want my Mama, but I don't. He's all I need.

He stands, and I whisper-beg, "D-don't leave me."

The cup looks like a toy in his hands. "I will not leave your side. Not yet."

I sit up, my legs still beneath the covers. Gazing at him, not breathing, I watch as he gently blows the steam. He lifts the cup to my lips, and I slowly drink. It's hot and sweet. When it's finished, he leaves the bed to place it on the small table by my window.

How can the sun be shining when my father is dead?

I move inside my covers, feeling physically comatose from my internal pain. My feelings and thoughts are scattered like dead bodies in the streets. Life's leftovers for anyone to poach.

He sets himself next to me, the sheet a division between us. We're separate, but I can feel his body heat. He hugs me to his broad chest. I nestle my head beneath his chin as his hands move around my body like a vise. I like when he holds me like this. There's no way I can move, but why would I want to? He's hard, but nothing can hurt me when I'm in here. Slowly, I feel myself settling into safety. The warm tea has coated my stomach, softening the pain.

I try to calm my body, remembering yesterday. Nico chased me around the house and threw me over his shoulder and tickled me until tears dripped down my face. Before dinner, he told me about democracy. We reviewed my English words. *Bed. Chair. Pajamas. Slippers. Toothbrush.*

Nico is sort of like my father but not. He's kind of like a brother or a teacher but not that either. He's the man I love. Some girls know their favorite color. I know the man I will marry one day. Still, he's always out of reach. Too old. Too handsome. Too powerful. But one day, I won't be a child anymore. And I'll show him I'm worthy to be by his side, as his queen.

Mother tells me, when I was born, he came with his father to bring some fruit to celebrate my birth. I had been crying, seemingly inconsolable, and he asked to hold me. The moment I went into his arms, I calmed.

"She likes you," his father said.

After his family was killed by Serb forces, he came around to help my father with the KLA.

He whispers, "You were so brave, Elira."

He kisses the top of my hair, still damp. It reaches down my back in black waves. Sometimes, it gets knotted at the bottom, but I normally keep it in one long braid. Mother forgot to fix it after my bath. Anxiety returns to my chest. I lift my face, so I can see Nico's eyes. They're darker than night.

"My hair," I start. "It's always braided when I rest. Mama forgot!"

"Sit up. I used to do this for Elsa when she was small."

He separates my hair into three sections and begins to braid. When he's done, I lie back down, feeling better.

His skin is tanned from spending days in the hot sun. My white hands are pale compared to his. I trace the planes and angles of his face, memorizing his hard-looking, prominent cheekbones and straight black hair. I should feel shy to touch him in this way, but I don't. He never gave me permission to, but I have it. If I didn't, he would stop me. Nico isn't a man who ever lets things happen without his permission.

Just last week, Zamir didn't follow Nico's protocol when finding a Serb officer on the street. Nico had him beaten, threatening to never let him near the KLA again. Some people were scared, saying Nico shouldn't hurt one of our own. Others said Nico did right; he can't have a team who doesn't listen to their commander. Plus, Zamir's actions could have resulted in many people's deaths.

He shuts his eyes, a smirk filling his lips as I draw.

Women always giggle and smile around Nico, even when he doesn't try to make them laugh. Especially Bardha. Her huge breasts are always pulling against her shirt. And she tries to stay outside to get bronze on her face even though she should be helping in the kitchen. She talks about Nico. How "big" he is and how "good" he is in bed, but I don't see why that's special. Everyone can see how big he is. And, of course, he's good in bed. Aren't we all good when we sleep? So, why does she say it like it's a secret?

A few weeks ago, me and Bardha were rolling out dough for the lunch pies.

I asked her, "Why do you laugh when Nico is near? Why does your voice get squeaky like a mouse in the attic when he speaks with you?"

But she just rolled her eyes and told me I couldn't understand —yet.

"Nico is the kind of man who doesn't just talk about change. He makes change," she said. "Just last week, he organized ten of our men against fifty Serbian police, and Nico won! He leads like no one else. He's going to be the one to win our independence. I can feel it."

"Is he nice to you?" My hands balled into fists as I silently prayed the answer was no.

"No." She shook her head and smiled as though my question were silly. "Nico is a warrior. He fears no man on this earth. He is not the eldest, and yet he has earned the greatest respect because of the battles he's won on our streets. He has no great family lineage, but he has the confidence of a king. A man like Nico will never be nice. But that doesn't mean he isn't good ... in other ways." She winked.

Before I could respond that Nico was nice to *me*, she kissed my cheek and walked away. For days, I thought about what I could say to her. I still haven't had the chance. I'm not sure I ever will. Without Papa, nothing can be the same.

From my chest, the words, "I'm not safe here anymore," bubble out from my mouth.

His eyes flit open. "You will always be safe. I swear it. And my oath is my bond, Elira."

"What if those men come back for me?" The reality of this hits me, and panic begins to build.

"They can't. Those men are now in hell, where they belong. When you move into the afterlife, there is no return. And the ones who ran, I will find." A sneer mars his face.

Into his chest, I ask, "What if their children come for me?" My heart beats faster. Revenge is the natural order.

"I'll kill them, too." He shifts, so he can hold me closer. "Don't you know I will kill anyone who tries to hurt you?"

"Uh-huh." I nod quickly, eyes wide.

He's scary right now, eyes with such undisguised hatred and maliciousness that, for a moment, my voice fails me. This is the Nico men fear. I want to give myself up to crying convulsively, but Nico's strength holds my emotions up like a pillar. I won't cry. Not in front of him.

"Okay." I swallow hard, maintaining eye contact.

He holds the back of my head, as though to make sure I listen intently. "You are allowed to grieve for your father, and you should. You are allowed to be afraid, too. Giving yourself time to hurt will make you resilient. If you don't, the pain will eat at you and weaken you. When mourning is over, you must emerge to be the strong girl I know you to be."

"How do you know I'm strong?" I want reassurance. I want him to tell me who I am and what I'll be because his word is everything.

"What happened last week when you took the pie from the oven and burned yourself?"

"I rinsed my arm with cold water and put cream on."

"I watched how you dealt with the pain. Other girls or boys would scream or cry. Not you."

It was painful, but I didn't want to cause trouble or add to my mother's load. I burned my arm badly, but I know it will heal.

"And when you saw Alek's mother fallen, with a wound in the street, what did you do?"

"I-I got help."

"Right. You saw she needed aid, knew you couldn't bring her in yourself, and got someone strong to lift her. That's exactly right. Smart and intelligent people see a problem and do not cower. They find an answer. That's what you have always done. You are different from other girls, Elira. Better. I saw it from the moment you were born." He smiles, tapping my head. "But if you want to grow your strength, you'll make sure to deal with all problems as they come. Understand?"

I'm suddenly breathless. The loss of my papa, our home's protector, begins to leak into my consciousness. "I can't go downstairs. Papa is gone now. What will we do?"

The enormity of his death has only slightly touched the surface of my mind. It's too much for me to handle. I want to hide. Scream and cry. Instead, I sit frozen and still. His isn't the first death I've seen, but it's the first one that will permanently change my life.

He exhales, mood softening. "Your father is in heaven now, but you will continue with your mother and Agron. I see big things in your future." His voice is resolute.

"Big things?"

"Yes." He shifts his body, tucking an arm behind his head. "Remember what I told you about America?"

In the English he taught me, I tell him, "America is free and B-big Mac hamburg and gold in street."

He lets out a small laugh. "That's right. It's time to get you there.

Now that your father is no longer alive, I don't want you staying in Kosovo."

"But ... how? Isn't it hard to get into America?"

"Yes. But I know someone who will bring you there. I wanted you to leave sooner, but your mother wouldn't leave without your father."

"And what about you?" Worry fills my chest. I've heard of the country, but I can barely imagine the things I've heard.

"My place is here. I must finish this war."

My pillow turns damp with tears. *Am I crying?*

"Just sleep now. I will take care of everything."

"My feet are cold." I crouch my legs up.

Nico stands, taking another blanket from my closet. He covers me.

My voice shivers. "I'm scared, Nico." Heat seeps into my body quickly, but I still shiver like it's ten below.

He smooths the hair from my forehead. "A rose is afraid to open its petals until light coaxes it open."

"You're light," I whisper, my body growing heavier by the second. It's only moments more before I fall off to sleep.

THE NEXT THREE DAYS, I refuse to leave my closet. I hide behind my hanging clothes with my back against the hard wall. Nico tells Mama it's okay, to let me sit until I'm ready to come out, but she is worried. *Doesn't she understand I cannot be seen?* Those men know where we live. They will come back. Each day, Nico swears I am safe but doesn't force me out. Instead, he tells me to sit and cry until I'm ready to emerge. He's giving me one week.

Nico knocks three times before entering the closet—our secret code. Sweat beads between his brows. I want to put my nose into his shirt and take in more of him. He's fresh dirt, grass, and soap. His scent makes me a good kind of dizzy.

"How are you, kid?" He squats low, bringing his large hands together.

"I'm hungry," I whisper, slightly embarrassed. Turns out, I'd rather be safe than full.

He grunts in annoyance. "Agron was supposed to come up an hour ago. Did he not?"

Not wanting to get my brother in trouble, I only shrug. "He must be busy."

He shuts his eyes in annoyance. "Your brother needs to learn to follow orders. He has many personalities, that Agron. You never know who you'll get."

Standing wordlessly, he leaves. I try not to cry at his hasty departure.

Nico returns, knocking again before opening the door. I'm sure it annoys him, but he does it anyway. My eyes widen in surprise as he steps in with a plate full of food.

"Fried potatoes and sour cream. Green tomatoes and fresh bread. Flija. Spinach pie." Piece by piece, like I am one of the baby lambs on our farm, he feeds me.

"How did you find this?" I chew.

He doesn't answer but lifts more for me to take.

"Is this yours?" I swallow, but the food sits like a lump in my throat.

Agron forgot to save me food, and Nico gave me his to eat.

My eyes fill with tears. "No. You need this. I don't."

"Shh. When you're full, I'm satisfied."

"Are you going to marry me when I'm older?" It's my secret wish —not so secret anymore.

He laughs and pats my head. "We'll see, kid. We have a long time before thoughts of that."

I flush, embarrassed. Nico carries me into the white bathroom and stands by the door, so I can wash up and use the toilet before placing me back inside my closet, nestled into fresh-smelling clothes.

That night, I sleep deeply.

"Elira, you cannot stay in here anymore." Mama is here, on her knees, trying to coax me out.

I tell her, "Only Nico."

"Nico is training the men, my sweet pea. Talk to me. Tell me. Open your heart."

"I miss Papa," I finally wail. The moment I say it, it's as though a dam is broken. I cry harder than I thought possible, shaking in her arms.

Clutching me against her chest, she says, "Yes, as do I. But this is the price we must pay. There are things in this world larger than we are. There will be time to mourn for him but not yet."

"I was going to die," I stutter out. "He was going to shoot me—"

"You were. God has other plans for you, it seems. Now, come out. Let me feed you at the kitchen table. The sunlight will be good."

Holding hands, we trek downstairs. The house is quiet and creaky. The sun is barely up, and the men haven't arrived to eat. I sit on the wooden chair with my feet curled into my chest. She gives me two boiled eggs. Fresh bread with butter. I eat hungrily.

Faster, faster—before they come.

Mama sits beside me. "Elira, I know how much you love Nico. But I worry for you. He is a man, and you're still a child."

"So?" My voice is loud and defensive. I can feel the heat crawling into my face.

"Don't speak. Just listen." Her words are firm. "When you were born, you wouldn't stop crying. Nico came over—"

"And he held me, and I stopped my tears. I know this story." I sulk.

"Nico has always had a soft spot for you. A place he has for no one else. But I do not want you to become attached to him. He is dangerous. He is always in the front line of all things. You must keep some distance between the two of you."

"Why?" I demand.

"Because you are a good girl. A smart girl. A man like Nico isn't for you. Not now and not later. You will grow up and find a man worthy. A doctor maybe. Not a man with violence in his veins. He's a man who likes power. He's grown accustomed to it, it seems." Her eyes cloud.

I shake my head, refusing to listen. "Nico isn't violent with me."

"Listen to me, Elira. The things he has done, I cannot repeat. I don't like him being near you, but what choice do I have? Now that Father and Jakup are gone, what he says goes. But if you create some space—"

"You can't make him stay away!" I yell, my voice shaking.

"No, I can't," she says admittedly. "But I want you to pull away. Don't look at him with adoration. Don't allow him in your room. It isn't appropriate anymore," she pleads. "You'll be eleven soon, too old to have a man who is not your brother or f-father alone with you." Tears fill her eyes at the mention of Papa. She opens and closes her mouth as though there is more to say, but nothing comes out. Her words are gone.

She lifts my plate in her hands and walks to the sink. Her back shakes as she turns on the water, head dropping low. Without another word, I run upstairs and into my closet. Shutting the door, I sit down in the corner. They can't find me here.

In the middle of the night, I'm awoken. It's Nico.

"Come on, kid. Time to go to America."

"Huh?" I'm confused, mouth dry.

"Yes. You will go with your mom and brother by horseback now to Montenegro. From there, someone will bring you to a place called Pennsylvania. You'll be safe there."

"I can't leave!" I scream, punching his hard, muscled chest as he drags me out.

He covers my mouth with his heavy hand. "You must. The arrangements came together very fast. I know it's short notice, but it's the safest way."

He lifts me over his massive shoulder and takes me downstairs. I want to yell, but fear has paralyzed my voice once again.

He whispers, "Don't be afraid. Soon, you will be free."

"When will I see you?" I plead.

Agron holds me tightly, keeping me away from Nico. *I want to stay!*

"One day, we will meet again. I swear it."

My brother clutches me atop his horse. And we're off.

1

PRESENT DAY

PULLING UP THE FAMILY EXPENSES SHEET FROM MY DESKTOP COMPUTER, I deduct fifty dollars for the pain meds and a week of wages due to mom's sciatica. These setbacks suck. I drop my head into my hands, leaning my elbows on my wooden desk. I need a miracle.

Should I look for a different job?

The problem is, Mr. Weber pays me under the table in cash so that I can avoid taxes. Sure, it's shady. But I'm desperate, and working as a waitress is flexible work. Other restaurants might give me a few extra dollars an hour, but that money, which would be paid on the books, would go to taxes mom and I can't afford.

A knock on my window, and I freeze. Turning my head toward the sound, I notice a dark head lurking behind glass. If I were in a movie, I'd shriek. No doubt, the intruder is a dumbass college kid, trying to scare a town resident—nicknamed townie by the students at Green University.

We live off Green's campus, and the area is constantly patrolled by police—for good reason. The difference between the people who live in this town and the college students who study here is incredibly wide. To simplify, the students see us as impoverished rats, and we see them as entitled assholes. The fact that I'm both student and resident has made things pretty awkward on occasion. It goes something like this.

Typical college kid: The streets are so dirty and dangerous. Someone needs to do something about the townie problem here!
Me: Fuck you.

It wasn't always this bad between us, but since the plant shut down and people lost their jobs, the area has continued to disintegrate while the school thrives. It's an odd blend of ignoring each other's existence, as we're in completely different orbits, and outright animosity and hatred. Hence this dipshit who thinks he can break into my home to scare me. The torture gets worse when the fraternities have freshman pledges. They always make them torment us for fun. Last year, they threw water balloons on any town people they saw walking. My mother had just gotten her hair done when a red balloon came crashing over her head.

Another knock against my glass, and I stand tall, taking a blue ballpoint pen from my drawer and gripping it in my right hand. I doubt I'm strong enough to stab him, but hopefully, it'll be enough to scare the shit out of him. I laugh darkly.

Oh, sorry, Officer! I thought he was trying to break in. How was I supposed to know he was an innocent college kid?

Flipping on the light by my desk, I'm ready.

"Entitled asshole," I grumble, smirking. I hope I scare him so badly that he falls off the sill.

Getting closer, I pull up the window with my left hand, pen raised in my right, high and ready to—

"Oh shit!" I drop the pen and slide the glass all the way up.

Agron climbs through, headfirst. My hands shake in relief that it's him. I haven't seen my brother in three months, his whereabouts essentially unknown, despite hundreds of attempts to locate him. My mother and I begged him to stay home until he saved enough money to rent his own place, but he claimed he'd found a roommate and an apartment and a big new job.

"Bigger things are calling me," he said.

His cheeks are flushed, and his brown hair is ratty and long. He's wearing a dark T-shirt and dirty denim, complete with holes. I try not to cringe from his scent—unclean. I can't even say hello. All my words are stuck in the back of my throat, clogging all airways. I'm in shock at the state he's in. Big job? Bigger things? I don't think so. I swallow, my mouth desert dry.

His first words are, "Elira, I need you." Lifting his shaking hands in prayer, his mouth gapes open. "So glad you're home; you know how it is; shit has been crazy but needed to see you." His words are a flood.

"Where have you been?" I accusingly look him up and down.

"Mom is poisoning you against me now? Is that it?"

Six feet of man comes closer, body language suddenly aggressive. His breath, sour, turns my stomach. Hands, which used to help me cook ramen noodles and make peanut butter sandwiches, are now balled into furious fists. Eyes, which used to look at me with love and adoration, are now red-rimmed.

I step backward, naked feet shuffling against worn gray carpeting. My head tells me this feeling of *he's going to hurt me* isn't possible, but my hands lift in front of my chest, acting out of an innate sense of preservation. A large man moves aggressively toward you, you step back. Unnatural space comes between us.

My brain says, *Agron has never gotten violent, not with you.* Still, fear slinks itself into my legs.

If he notices my retreat, he doesn't say.

I steel my nerves and open my lips. "A-are you kidding me, Agron? Coming into my bedroom like some robber, looking dirty and deranged." I want to ask him if he's on drugs right now, but I'm worried that would only incite him. "Why don't you take a hot shower? I'll get you something to eat, and then we'll talk. I've got some chicken from last night. Roasted in the oven, how you like." My voice sounds strong and in control, but deep down, I'm scared to death.

It's Agron, but a version of him I can't stand to see. He's more animal right now than man.

"I don't look pretty enough for you?" He chuckles darkly. "P.S. you look like shit yourself." His voice is nasty. Dropping onto my bed like it's his own—which, technically, it once was—he crosses his feet and places his hands behind his head.

I can't help but notice that even his sneakers are ravaged with holes and caked with dirt.

Coming to the United States for a chance at survival and a life of peace, mom sacrificed every day—and still does—to give us a shot at the American dream. She worked at the factory in twelve-hour shifts, managing to cook and clean when she came home. Our clothes were always fresh, stomachs never empty, and our circumstances were stable. Life wasn't luxurious, but it was good. And compared to what had happened to our family who stayed back in Kosovo, America was essentially heaven.

Agron lies with his head back, staring at the ceiling. Dark circles rim his green eyes in a mean shade of purple. He's in a nasty and broody mood, and if mom saw the state he's in, she'd be mortified. All her hard work to give him better. More.

We spent the last few months in emotional agony, not knowing where he was. And then to find him ... wasted.

I move toward my bedroom door, locking it from the inside. Mom doesn't need to see him this way.

He laughs after hearing the click. "You don't think Mama wants to see me? Big, strong man I've turned out to be?" He lifts a brow, his voice full of cynicism.

We've always been able to read each other easily. Too easily.

I let out a sarcastic laugh. "You mean, see you looking so strong, clean, and healthy? She'd be thrilled."

It only takes a second for my emotions to bend to anger. Agron made shitty choices, and he has to deal with the result. This is real life—not a fairy tale where boy goes out on his own, only to become a millionaire through luck. *And he has the audacity to come into this house and insult me? Put his dirty feet on the bed I clean and wash religiously twice a week? Screw him!*

"Well, let's see." I tap my foot on the floor. "Our mom breaks her back at her cleaning job. Instead of following in her footsteps, which would clearly help us in the short-term, I'm at Green, praying that when I graduate, I can get a higher-paying job to get us out of this house we live in and pay off my college debt. School takes roughly thirty hours a week between classes I need to attend and studying, and the rest of my time is spent working as a waitress, serving peers who think that because they've got money to spend and I don't, I'm not worth much. So, excuse me for not getting my hair done for you in advance with all the extra cash and time I've got lying around." I grit my teeth.

He sits up, square face dripping with guilt before contorting to anger. "Fuck that factory for closing and ruining all our lives!" He stands up, placing his hands against my white wall and pushing against it. "Look," he exclaims, spinning back toward me, "I know how hard you guys work." He opens his large hands to me. "I've got some big ideas. Once I get out of this ... predicament I'm in, I'm going to start a business. I've got the whole plan up here." He taps his temple. "Then, you'll never have to work again. Or mom." He pauses and smirks, like he's about to give me a huge piece of information. "Nico is here now. He left the UK and now lives in Manhattan full-time."

A full tremor racks my body. "Last I heard, Nico was the boss of the Mafia Shqiptare. Are you i-insane?"

Agron growls. "Have some respect. Nico got us out of Kosovo, and he's a very, very powerful man. He's since grown out of Kosovo and greater Albania." Agron's chest puffs up with pride. "Nico not only survived the war, but he also now controls the underground in several countries. He—"

"Do me a favor, and don't tell me more. The Mafia Shqiptare is dangerous as all hell. They make the Italian families look like child's play. That much I know is true. There's nothing else I need or want to know." I put my hands on my hips, finished with this conversation.

Still, my heart pounds, *Nico is here. Nico. Nico.* His name ricochets off my insides, leaving an acidic burn in its wake.

I always thought Nico would contact me. He was everything to me back in Kosovo, but after I left, he deleted me from his life. Not a visit. No phone calls. Not even a measly letter after the hundreds I sent him. Through small bits of gossip through my mother and aunt in Albania, I understood that Nico left to Albania after Kosovo was freed. Using his connections from the Kosovo Liberation Army, he grew the Albanian Mafia, also known as the Mafia Shqiptare. While I was still in high school, I heard he was expanding the cocaine trade in the UK.

I wanted so badly to ask my mom and aunt for more details, but I was nervous. What if my mother figured out how I felt about him after all these years? Would she shout? Tell me I had no business even thinking of a man with that much dangerous power? The thought that my mother would somehow figure out my feelings for him was impossible. So, I did what any teenage girl does when nursing a crush that needed to be kept secret from her family. I never asked about his whereabouts while secretly dreaming of him at night. I dreamed of him so often that his face became hazy. Like a photograph I touched too many times, all of his features are now blurred. But I remember the way he made me feel. Cherished beyond words.

Before high school graduation, I faced the truth. What I felt for Nico was one-sided. I was a child when I knew him, my memories likely blown up. I was simply a sweet baby for him to coddle in the midst of war. It was time for me to let him go.

My brother leans against the window, a hand-rolled cigarette between his fingers. He lights up with a black Zippo, and his brows knit thoughtfully as he exhales into the night. "Nico was always powerful. But he was young when we knew him. Today, he's a man with control over everyone and everything."

I shake my head, swallowing hard. "Just last week, I saw an article in the paper claiming they seized control of the entire UK drug trade."

Agron's face is steel. "Yes, Elira. He's willing to do whatever it takes, as am I."

"Don't talk that way," I chide, clenching my fists. "Just stop and think, Agron. That life isn't for us. We aren't in the middle of war anymore. You don't have to be part of an army."

He snarls, "That life is me." He stands and begins to pace.

In my bedroom, he's like a tiger in a cage. He always said the house and the life we lived was too small for him. I still wish with all my heart he'd find a way to settle into something stable.

"I know that you're both killing yourselves, and I hate it," he yells, slamming his hands down on my desk.

"So, just stop this!" My words come out like a plea. "Come home. Get yourself straightened out. Get a job and go to school like I am. Forget Nico. One day—"

He raises his hand and drops it, cutting the air. "No!" he barks. "School isn't for me. What, to be a cog in the bullshit American dream machine that tells you, 'Step inside, friends! All you've got to do is put in the hard work, and then you'll step out a millionaire'? In this world, there's only one way for people like us to go—down. Unless we find a way to make our own rules. Rules that work for who we are. Yes, I'm American. But I'm also not American. We saw things and did things that changed the fabric of *our* insides." He stresses the word *our*, as though we are one and the same.

"Don't lump me in with you. I'm not like you," I huff, praying that my words will become truth.

"Elira"—he laughs—"you and I are exactly the same. We're on different paths, but I have no doubt that eventually you'll be led to my side. You aren't like these American kids we know. How could you be after the things you've seen and done?"

"Who are you?" I scream. "It's like I don't even know wh—"

"You know me, and I know me." He stands up to his full height, but his body language moves away from threatening. "The question is, do you know you?"

I open and close my mouth. I should continue arguing with him. Tell him that there's no way I'm going to that side. "Mama didn't leave Kosovo to have her children back in a web of underground dealings."

He blows air through his nose. "I know that I look like shit. I hate it, too. But I'm on my way up."

I stare into his light-green eyes, the same as mine. Agron was always smart. Smarter than the types he's gotten mixed up with. I still have faith in his goodness even though I shouldn't. He's given me no reason to believe in him. And yet, I do. He and I are siblings by blood. Even without that, we have experiences that tie us. Our escape from Kosovo. Immigration to America and seeking asylum. A new school system. Learning English. We were all the other had as we adjusted to the American way.

"I owe some people," he continues, voice stronger. "And if I don't get some cash—" His voice cuts off, but I know what he's implying. He's here for money.

"We're barely making ends meet as it is. You can't just come and take."

His breaths turn staccato. He's desperate, and it's written.

"I'd do it for you. You know this. If you needed something, I'd go to hell and back to make it happen. I just need a little to tide me over. Just for a bit, and then I'll get my shit together. Nico and I have a meeting coming up, and I've got a plan. But I can't die before that day."

I stomp my foot on the ground. "I worked hard to make this money. And we *need* it, damn it."

He steps closer. I can see his temper flaring up, like the tick of a clock before a grenade explodes. But then he breathes in deeply, in and out, as though to calm himself.

"Things are going to get better. I swear. I've got plans. Big ones. You'll see. Do me this solid, and I'll pay you back tenfold. Once I link up with Nico—"

I counter, "How do you even know Nico will bring you in?"

"Of course he will. Why not? I will pledge allegiance to him. Our father was the founder of the KLA."

"No, Agron. Don't," I plead.

But his mind is made. My stomach drops low, like heavy cement has been poured inside. He sees the change in me and hugs me close.

"I love you, Elira. I know shit hasn't been good, but I'm going to make it up to you. And mom."

I feel a prick come to my eyes. I swallow saliva, wanting to burst into tears. They don't fall but sit over my pupils like a sheer curtain. I don't want to give him this money, but what choice do I have? Mafia future aside, he owes someone.

In a whisper, he finally asks, "Do you have cash?"

He requests money in the same way he used to ask if I had his toy. If I saw his sneakers before heading out to a basketball game in the park. If I needed help with my math homework.

I plead, "Can't you just move back in with us?" It's a last-ditch effort, but I'm not above begging at this point. "I'll take care of you while you figure things out."

"I can't leave this life behind. I've made promises, and I'm close to so much more. There's no turning back. Just a few more months, and then my new path is going to open. You'll see."

His eyes shine, and I see him—my brother, filled with hope. I just wish his plan weren't a dark one.

I step into my small closet and pull out the silver lock box I keep behind my heavy winter sweaters. I fiddle with the code—Agron's birthday—and it opens with a pop. Inside this small box rests my meager savings. Each week for the last one hundred and one weeks, I put five bucks in here. Everything else I make goes straight into household expenses or textbooks and gas. There's five hundred and five dollars in cash, saved for a rainy day. I swallow hard, fisting the money I worked for.

"Elira?" he loudly whispers, hurrying me.

The money feels soft in my hands.

He moves behind me. "Don't worry. I'll be paying you back."

Hope blazes in the eyes we share, reminding me that Agron wouldn't lie. He'll pay me back. On an exhale, I give it to him. My hands shake as the bills disappear into the back pocket of his dirty jeans.

Hurriedly, he says, "I promise. Tenfold."

He lifts the window back up and leaves into the night.

2

ONE MONTH LATER

UNDER THE BRIGHT UTILITY LIGHTS OF THE ESPRESS YOURSELF DINER, I move my beige dishrag in circles, rubbing the linoleum in a semi-trance as Eddie Vedder croons on the sound system.

"Earth to Elira," Natalie calls from across the counter. I lift my head. Her 36-DDs pour out of the white uniform all of us waitresses are forced to wear. She's got the kind of body that turns even the most conservative outfit into something lascivious. Not that this uniform is conservative by any means. Actually, it's so thin and tight that it's essentially a cheap Halloween costume.

Now that I've paused cleaning, a wave of self-pity so strong washes over me. My chest, tightening like bowstrings, has me unable to take a solid breath. I grip the rag so hard, my forearm shakes.

Mom's sciatica is acting up again, and I know in my gut that it's become unmanageable. My savings is gone, and Agron hasn't been in touch to pay me back.

And then Natalie is next to me, placing a soft hand over mine and stilling my movements.

My gut wants to scream, *Don't touch me. If I stop moving, I'll have to think.* I bite my tongue before exhaling slowly through my mouth, attempting to regain control.

"What is it?" Her words are whispered, face angled down toward mine.

Turning, I press my feet into the floor, doing my best not to drop into her arms and cry. *Leave me alone. Mind your own fucking business. Get out of my face.*

But then she blinks, her soul transparent through her eyes. She's sad for me, and I feel like an asshole for wanting to yell.

Natalie is the silver lining in my life—the best friend it took me nineteen years to meet. Like me, she's in her fourth year at Green University. She's working part-time through school to make some extra cash. From the first day I worked here, she was the one who took me under her wing. Our friendship might be only a few years old, but from the moment we met, we clicked. Our connection runs deep. Natalie is the last person on earth I want to alienate.

"Agron came over last month and looked worse than I've ever seen him, asking for money." I pause, gathering my bearings. "I gave it to him, of course. And my mom's back problems are getting worse. I have a feeling she'll need surgery. It's so bad that she can't work. And we've got no financial cushion. Seriously, if things don't start looking up, I might have to cut back on classroom hours so I can work more."

She opens her mouth to speak, but I beat her to it. "I know, I swore I wouldn't help him after he initially left, but the reality is, I can't say no. He's my brother." I can't hide the pain in my voice. I know he's taking advantage of me, but I also feel like there are no other options. Familial duty is greater than anything else even if it means me getting hurt.

"You shouldn't help him if it means hurting yourself."

"My brother is part of me." I touch the center of my chest. "Helping him is the same thing as helping myself. I know it's difficult to understand, but it's what it is." I lick my lips and go back to buffing the counter.

"Has your mom gotten a scan?" Her voice is softer.

"She's refusing." I shrug. "Keeps saying she's okay and just needs a few more days to rest."

"Did you tell Agron?" She bites her thin bottom lip.

"There wasn't time. He came through my window like a burglar, looking like shit and smelling worse. I gave him money, and he left." I continue to clean, sweat trickling between my breasts and beading around my hairline. I probably look like hell, mascara fallen below my eyes and mixing with my cheap drugstore foundation.

"Do you think it's drugs? Because Jim used to act that way with me, too. And he had a terrible drug prob—"

"Can we not talk about this anymore?" I switch my motion to counterclockwise, and a lock of hair frees itself from my pony, brushing against my eyes. I'd stop to fix it, but what difference does it make now?

Again, her hand moves to mine, stilling my movements. "Maybe it's bad timing to mention this, but we're going out tonight."

I pause quickly enough to see her smile has turned mischievous.

"Out?" I shake my head, immediately backing off. "No way. I'm going to have to take on an extra shift from six to nine, and—"

"A new band, Heretic Pope, is playing at Alpha Sig," she interrupts, trying not to squeal in delight. As a dual major in music and journalism, Natalie always has her ear to the ground for new bands. "They have a phenomenal sound. Listen to them on YouTube. They've already got over a million views for their song, 'Verona Sweat.'" She's giddy with excitement, practically bouncing on her toes. Only Natalie can fly between emotions this quickly.

"And Jack Gallagher has one of the most unique voices you'll ever hear. I've heard he's hot as all hell. I've never seen him, but I'm dying to." She claps. "I know you're miserable, but what better way to let out steam than to hear someone new? Plus, it's our last year at school. We have to make each night count."

I can feel the crease between my brows deepening. The only part of her diatribe that's echoing in my ears is that stupid frat. "Alpha Sig? You know I hate those guys, and they hate me back."

Two months ago, a group of them came into the diner. Seeing me in my uniform gave Rome, the fraternity president, the idea that I was for sale. Unfortunately for him, I don't take too kindly to men thinking my ass is up for grabs. Maybe I shouldn't have spilled his leftover fries and ketchup onto the front of his khakis. Oh, who am I kidding? I'd do it over again if I could. Pig.

"Yeah, well"—she smiles—"things change. Janice gave Rome a blow job. So, they're welcoming us over tonight with open arms. So, the plan is, you finish work at nine. Go home and change. Then, I'll swing by and pick you up, and we'll head to Alpha Sig!"

"Wait." I lift my hand up. "Welcome us with open arms? Janice and Rome? How the hell did this happen?" My voice sounds annoyed and angry. Still, I'm curious.

All three of us go to Green University together, but we don't hang out with the Greek scene. They're mostly entitled assholes who, for some unknown reason, believe they've got dicks made of gold.

"Apparently, they met in the tattoo parlor waiting room together. At Rock Ink."

"Wait. Janice got a tat?" My day seems to be full of surprises.

Natalie nods, as though this isn't news. "Remember, she wanted a rose on her ass?"

I let out a snort, nodding. "Oh, yeah."

Two weeks ago, Janice told us the reasons a black rose on her right butt cheek was a great idea. Something about a deeper meaning and a hidden spot. I thought she was joking around, but apparently, she was dead serious.

"This would only happen to Janice."

"Right?" Natalie is exasperated, dropping a hand on her curvy hip. "The girl opens her damn eyes in the morning, and things just *happen* to her. If I went to get a rose tatted on my ass, I'd probably end up with hepatitis. But Janice goes, gets her tat—which looks great, by the way—and gives a blow job, and *boom*, the door is open for us to see this new band."

"Bing, bing, bing!" I try not to laugh out loud. Pointing out the obvious, I add, "And when those Alpha Sig guys see me, they're going to throw my ass out."

"You and your tiny ass will be totally protected because we're with Janice, and Janice is with the president." You'd think she just solved world hunger with the way she's nodding.

"What type of music?" I'm hoping they play something loud and hard. I've got lots of pent-up anger I'd like to expel.

"They're a mix of metal and grunge, but they're sexier, deeper, and totally new. Maybe a little Dave Matthews meets Nirvana."

"Really?" I exclaim, my excitement obvious. She's got that look of winning in her eyes. "Wait. Are you just saying that because you know I love those bands?"

"Why can't you just be positive for once in your damn life?" She laughs, bothering me about the fact that I'm not exactly Ms. Sunshine.

I raise my brows, still not completely believing her.

She puts a hand on her hip. "Ugh, you'll see when you come tonight. It's that bone-deep, soulful lyrics, but then *BOOM*. The crash." She claps her hands together, excitement thrumming.

I don't think I've ever seen her this excited. I try not to show it, but I'm excited, too.

Sure, I'm underwater in more ways than one. But a night out won't change anything. I exhale, and her smile grows. She won.

"Will the crowd be Greek life?"

"I pray to God it won't be. The guys, yeah, because it's their house. But I can't imagine any Alpha Phi girls wanting to listen."

Natalie typically prefers a dark crowd that's kinky and outlaw and all *fuck you, world!* with ripped clothes and piercings and heavy tats. Her parents are fancy lawyers in New York City, and she despises them. She'd be lying if she denied the fact that one of the reasons she likes looking different is because it tortures their sensibilities. Still, she's gorgeous, no matter how much she tries to alter herself. Her style is part of her insistence that she's an individual who can do with her facade as she chooses. A ring through one eyebrow, one through her nose, countless piercings through her ears, and a beautiful tattoo of a black lace veil spread over her right shoulder are all meant to prove *my body is my own; no one controls me but me.*

I reorganize the sugar packets at the bar, letting myself focus on the band tonight. There is something undeniable in the air when music gets loud and hard. I'm freed from the bonds of life as I know it. Stress and anxiety and *what about tomorrow* is crushed beneath the heavy sound. It's liberating.

The silver bell on top of the door chimes. A group of girls—sorority sisters if I could take a guess—enter. One glance at the blonde's shirt confirms it. Bold Greek letters in pink.

Natalie nudges me. "You want the table?"

She's trying to do me a solid. I can use every extra buck they throw my way. Natalie only works here for petty cash she's too proud to ask her parents for, whereas I need the money for living purposes. She doesn't have to throw extra work my way, but she does, and I love her for it.

Before I can respond, Mr. Weber steps over to us, white buttons on his black shirt straining to burst, thin beige hair like oily wheat spread across his white scalp. "What is this, coffee talk?" He spits out his words with an exaggerated smile, leaving me unsure if he's being friendly or just nasty.

Natalie steps off quickly, not wanting to incite him. Just last week, he pinched her so hard in the arm "as a joke," and he left a bruise. We could quit, or we could stay and deal with his bullshit. So far, we've both stayed.

The sorority girls settle in a booth in the back, laughing loudly before pulling out their phones.

I take long strides into the kitchen, put down the dishrag, and grab my notepad and pen. Taking six menus from the counter, I put my big-girl panties on and make my way toward them. Weber's eyes are glued to me as I walk. I do my best to ignore him.

Placing the menus on the table, I smile. They look me up and down, judgment in their gazes. I stand up a little taller, daring blonde number one to keep looking at me like I stole her boyfriend before sucking him off in the back of his fancy BMW. This uniform really has a way of attracting the worst kind of attention. "I'll be back in a moment—unless you know what you'd like?"

One of them clears her throat and spits out her order.

SOME PEOPLE outside Tobeho have family farms or sprawling estates that have remained in their family for generations. I have 304 East Main Street, a thousand-square foot home with rickety floorboards, dingy walls, and bricks that are falling off the house's facade. Real fancy, I know. It's still better than living in one of the trailer parks on either end of the town.

I twist the doorknob, and it immediately opens without any resistance. I'm annoyed at the fact that my mother didn't lock it, but still, a sense of relaxation comes with my exhale as I unzip my jacket and hang it on the coat rack behind the front door. Pulling off my short black boots, I neatly place them against the wall. My home is carpeted in a soft, hazy brown. The cream floral wallpaper is peeling and crusty with the smell of fried onion and spices embedded within from years of heavy cooking. My mom was insistent on giving Agron and me the freshest possible food. Homemade bread and jam was always a staple. Those memories are now set into the bones of the house. It's home.

I find my mom in our eight-by-twelve living room, lying on the black recliner in front of the television. Today is another day of skipped work, her sciatica wreaking havoc on her ability to move. Her skin, suddenly too loose for her face, hangs like a soft white curtain over thin birdlike bones.

I bend down, kissing her forehead, saying, "Hey, Mom," before taking out a large blanket from the wicker basket beside the chair. I drape the cover over her, a soft red chenille I bought for Mother's Day four years ago.

She sighs, comforted, and I smile.

"Mom, how many times do I have to tell you to keep the door locked?"

Mom is so strong; she hates being told what to do. But sometimes, she needs to hear what she needs to hear. And I'm not going to tiptoe around it.

"It's dangerous to leave it open. This town isn't exactly Pleasantville, if you haven't noticed."

"Well, hello to you, too." She shifts, grouchy, and immediately winces. "If anyone wants to break in and kill me, I'll tell them, *Thanks for coming and putting me out of my misery.*" She laughs, pointing to the kitchen counter. "They could use one of those knives we ordered from that catalog a few years back."

"None of that's funny, mom." I step closer to her, fluffing her flat hair.

It's always been cut in an eighties do, parted down the middle with her bangs and short side layers curled back and typically frozen in place with hair spray. I used to beg her to change her haircut, but it's what she likes, and in some weird way, I've grown to love it.

"Well, I'm laughing." She tries to shrug, but the movement is difficult.

Knowing the answer but asking anyway, I turn to my mom. "How are you feeling today? Better?" Taking two glasses from the wooden cabinet above the sink, I fill them with ice from the freezer and water from the tap.

She grunts. "Like hell."

"Don't sugarcoat anything for me, mom," I say sarcastically, reentering the living room.

I bring the glass of cold water to her lips. Even moving her arms is a difficult task when her back is frozen. She takes one measly sip before turning her head away. I place it on the small table next to her hand, and she shuts her eyes.

"Did Mrs. Perez stop over to help you eat lunch?"

"Yes." Her eyes are still closed.

"Can you look at me? I want to make sure you weren't hungry today."

"You know I can't eat when I'm like this."

"You can't starve yourself." I walk back to the door and open my bag, taking out a turkey sandwich and fries I brought from work. "Come on, mom. I'll help you."

With a trembling body, she lets me feed her. When the food is gone, I give her some more pain medication with water to swallow it down.

"You're a good girl, Elira. I'm so proud."

"I'm me because of you, mom. Now, rest."

She squeezes my hand and shuts her eyes again.

"I'm going to assume they haven't fired you yet?"

"Thanks for the vote of confidence," she grumbles.

"Well, you've taken more days off than you're allowed. Just this week, you've passed your allotted days off. If they fire you, we'll get something else. But if that's coming, I want to plan—"

"Elira, they haven't fired me. For whatever reason, it's like I'm untouchable in that place. I'm half-convinced that if I stopped showing up to work entirely, they'd still hand me my paycheck."

Hesitantly, I tell her, "All right then."

"Now, leave me alone," she says sourly but with love. "I'm tired."

Sliding into my bedroom, I strip off my clothes from work and get into the shower, scrubbing off the smells of cooked food from my body. The world has rules. Things have already been set in motion. But tonight, surrounded by music, I'll be free.

When going to a show, I dress to get into my zone. Black bra with decent support. Thin white T-shirt, cropped above my belly button. Black studded belt around low-slung jeans, loose and boyfriend-style. Black combat boots with a sneaky platform no one can see. The lift is necessary when you're five foot three, but so is support when you are headbanging in a crowd. I don't want to be stepped on or hurt. I want to be free.

Coal-black liner is strategically placed around my large green eyes, and golden bronzer is brushed beneath the hollow of my cheekbones. It takes about ten minutes to blow-dry my long black hair. Natalie keeps telling me that her friend Janelle, a hairstylist in New York City, could do some colorful and tasteful streaks if I wanted.

Maybe some purple would look cool at the ends, but I've never been daring with my physical appearance.

After brushing some shine oil through my strands, I sneak back into the living room, not wanting to make any noise if she's fallen asleep. Getting close to her, I see she has. I kiss her again, silently swearing to be safe before leaving home. For a moment, I feel guilty. *What if she needs me?* She isn't her strong, regular self when her back goes out. But I force myself out the door.

Natalie is waiting, blowing smoke out her window. "Get in," she calls out.

"I need this night," I tell myself on repeat. "Mom will be okay."

WE'RE HOLDING cups full of shitty beer from the keg, sweating. The frat house is a shithole, filled to the brim with drunk and smiling college kids.

"They really need to open up a window or spring for a new AC. Half these frat guys are loaded with money. They should ask their dads or whatever." Janice's skin is splotched red from the heat. Considering I'm just as pale, I can only imagine how I look right now.

Eyes zeroed in at Janice's damp cleavage, Natalie drawls, "Looking hot, my friend."

Janice slaps her in the arm in mock anger, laughing. "Anyone have a tissue or something?"

I put my hand in my purse and pull out a Kleenex. She takes it, pressing it between her breasts.

The neon Coors Light sign, likely stolen by some freshman pledges, shines above us as we continue to sip our beers, casting a weird green glow over Natalie. She looks like a sexy witch with her skin tinged olive from the light and her long purple hair styled pin-straight. She purses her full red lips, pencil-made.

Janice moans, "I hate these guys." Looking around the room, her eyes move through the crowd. "I'm sick of random, messy hook-ups with drunk frat boys. I need someone stable." She looks at my glass, close to empty. "Speaking of needing things, we need refills before the keg empties." Janice twists her body, trying to find the best route, when a stack of pizza boxes lands on a table near where we're standing.

Someone lifts a steaming meat-greased slice straight from the box. My stomach grumbles as the smell wafts around us. God, I'm starving. I was supposed to eat that sandwich I gave to my mom.

Janice adjusts her boobs within the black fishnet top she's wearing. "We should head downstairs soon before it gets too full."

A random body moves behind mine, pushing me closer to my friends. "I wonder if Jack is hot."

"Girl," Natalie starts, staring directly at me, "did you not watch the YouTube video of them playing? I couldn't see him, but it's obvious he's hot as fuck!"

"You're crazy," Janice chimes. "With his head bowed and long, dirty hair in his face, I could barely tell. You're such an exaggerator. He must be a troll." She nods decidedly. "I mean, what front man in a band would ever hide his face unless he's horrible? I'm going with acne scarring."

"That voice can't be attached to anything but perfection. Plus, Lorraine from my Econ class says she's hung out with him before and that he's the hottest guy she's ever laid eyes on." Natalie drains her beer. "Not that she's ever spoken to him. She's got a big mouth with the girls, but she can barely let out a peep in front of a guy."

Janice moves a hand into her silky hair, twirling it into a bun to lift it from her neck. "Whatever. Hot, not hot, I'd do him. But, seriously, who would have thought would be so difficult to find a good man in college?"

Natalie chuckles when she says, "What about the president?"

"Tiny dick." Janice shrugs. "But at least I got us in here. Oh"—she pauses, taking a drink—"I think I should pierce my nipples. I saw this porn last night where—"

"Please, stop. For God's sake ..." I shake my head.

Janice smirks. "Nipple piercings are sexy. Natalie, tell little Miss

Goody Two-shoes that nipple piercings are hot." She raises a brow to Natalie, and I wonder why she's looking at her all secretively.

Natalie points to her nipples. "Pierced."

"What?" I exclaim. "How could I not know that?"

Strangely, I feel like I've been lied to. Shouldn't best friends know these things about each other?

"Surprised?" Natalie's smile is downright dirty. "It's always fun to see the shock in people's faces. That's half the fun. Like yours right now. Priceless."

"Just when you think you know someone." I playfully roll my eyes, trying not to look hurt. "How does Janice know about this, and I don't?"

Natalie shrugs her shoulders. "I got them done when she did her nose piercing. You want to see?" Her lips twist in a wry smile as she holds on to the bottom of her shirt.

"Nope," I reply calmly, smiling. If I get too excited, she's likely to flash the entire house.

A speaker crackles, and we know the show is about to start.

We push ourselves through the crowd to get into the basement where the band is set to play. A large wooden stage is set up, complete with a sound system.

Heretic Pope consists of four guys—a drummer, lead singer, bassist, and guitarist. They're all in torn jeans and worn T-shirts with names of obscure bands I've never heard of. Jack's face is lowered and hidden behind a curtain of mid-length dishwater-blond hair. The drums begin to pound, and I can feel the heat start to pulse in my veins. I love this part.

Not even an introduction. Just distorted riffs and a mean, angry pace. It's an organized instrumental pandemonium. His voice begins to growl over the chaos of bodies. It's dark and low, blurring between guttural moans and melody. And those remarkable guitar chords and driving bass lines practically force my body to move. It usually doesn't come this soon, but I'll take it.

The guitar in Jack's hands, slick black, is electric. His hair is unbelievably sexy. A messy, chin-length screen. It's like he's under a hypnotic spell, deep in concentration. I wish he'd show his face. All I can see is a gorgeous body in relaxed-fit Levi's and a snug white T-shirt with the name Foes of Heaven written in bold letters. I make a mental note to look that up, assuming it's a band friend of theirs. Jack is skinny but broad with defined pecs and a tapered waist. Tattoos peek from beneath his short sleeves. Riotous stars in black.

The music grows to a frenzy. Then, at once, his head tilts toward the ceiling, and I see him. It's like a collective gasp hits the entire space before girls start to scream. Because Jack is *incredible*. Dark blond hair soaked with sweat. Skin glistening. Mouth parted as he sings and presses his body against the microphone.

> *I lay down, feeling low.*
> *I stand up to get high.*
> *Anything to keep this going.*
> *Rolling, the mirror shows my damage,*
> *Water to the face*
> *Nerves fry.*

> *But you wouldn't know who rolls.*
> *But you wouldn't know who rolls deep,*
> *Who rolls deeper.*

> *I'm looking at her now,*
> *Twisted in the bedroom sheets.*
> *In a haze, I drop to my knees.*
> *For her, I'd stay low.*
> *She's falling,*
> *She's falling mystified.*

> *But you wouldn't know who rolls.*
> *But you wouldn't know who rolls deep.*
> *Who rolls deeper.*

SOMEONE TURNED on some kind of light system because blue glides over his chiseled face. A smirk lines his full lips as he leans into the silver mic, eyes screwed shut as he sings with his entire body. It only takes moments for my brain to realize that this man has what it takes. I turn to Natalie and Janice, who are jumping with the crowd as the music changes to anger. The drummer's got a mop of dark curls, and his eyes are wild, deranged. He's playing like a beast, slamming the set so hard that I'm surprised it hasn't cracked in two. This band is unreal. They might be playing in a frat house at a college, but one day, they'll be in Madison Square Garden.

Some heavy metal music is cruel. Full of doom and conjured from nonconformity and despising corruption and lies from family and country and God. This is nothing like that. The music is severe but lyrics truthful. Jack's voice spells blood in liquid letters, but it's also full of soul. He's not doing what he should; he's doing what he feels. He's singing now, wrenching all doom and beauty from his voice, about a boy who's being bullied and contemplates suicide. It isn't even over, and I want to ask him to start again because I want to *understand*. Everyone is headbanging, knocking into each other.

I can feel a sheen of sweat rising into my skin, tattooing the moment onto my insides. It's so good to be lost in the crowd, all burdens gone and nothing but enjoyment and freedom ahead.

A girl with green hair screams, "I'll have your babies!"

One of the frat guys jumps onto the stage. He dives off into the crowd, screaming, "Hell fucking yeah!"

But do they hear what I hear? That this sound is totally unique from all the bands who came before? Jack has a different kind of depth and intensity. I can't help but clench my fists in excitement as I mosh with the rest of the crowd. It's like a tornado has erupted as bodies spin, banging against each other. I'm pushed left and right, and I love it.

Bruising and pain are the cost of release. Nothing in the world is free.

The pounding of the drums moves up through my toes. But that guitar. And that *voice*. Holy hell, he's even sexier from this angle.

He pauses playing with the band when his eyes click with mine. The world seems to stop. His pale pupils widen. The music rages, and everyone's still moving, but suddenly, I'm not. I've moved onto a different plane, lost to his water-blue gaze. His fingers keep moving across the guitar. He's wild and hot, but his aura is so calm.

My entire body vibrates with awareness as my heart stutters. *Ohhhh*, pings in my chest. I'm struck.

Before I can register what's happening, his eyes are shut again, and he's groaning into the mic.

A furious riff to end the song, and we're all panting as a collective, waiting with bated breath for the next song.

Song after song, and the entire crowd is plugged into this moment. It's one of those shows where the entire room is flooded with the feeling of *now*. *Collective*. Jumping, thrashing heads.

My dark mane is soaked in sweat. The good girl who lives for her family is gone. In her place is a woman who yearns to feel and escape. I'm so lost in the music and in my own world. His face fades until all I can do is hear and feel, thrashing.

Someone careens into me, and I'm down on the cement floor. My eyes widen, and I'm poised to scream. And then Natalie's hand is out, and she pulls me back up, laughing. Wrapping an arm around my shoulders, she jumps with me. We're stronger together.

Jack plays a ballad, singing about sleeping and not wanting to wake up. Everyone listens in rapt attention. We're swaying, hearts still pounding. The next song is back to danger. The high-low giving us musical whiplash.

There are no words to soften the end. Music just turns off, and, "What the fuck?" fills the air as people scatter, squinting, lighting cigarettes, and beelining back upstairs to the beer. The band begins dismantling, and three of us girls nod to each other like, *Yeeeaaahhh!* This is easily the best band I've ever seen live or heard, period. Never have I heard music that speaks as theirs does. It just digs deeper somehow.

A calm sets over me, post-storm. Everything in life is important and necessary but, at the same time, out of my control. And maybe it's okay that I can't control much. Maybe things can just happen as they come, and I shouldn't fight it. Eventually, my mom will get better and go back to work. Agron will figure out his own path. I have to believe this. Until then, I'm going to continue working at the diner and studying. I'm no one if not my mother's daughter. And there's a greater purpose waiting for me. I settle back into myself, loving this feeling of understanding that always comes after a great show.

Janice's laugh brings me back to the moment. She's chatting with the president, clearly ready and willing to hang out with him again. He's preppy-looking with those perfect all-American features—straight nose and lips, light dusting of freckles under his eyes and over his nose. I remember dropping food onto his lap, the ketchup plopping onto his khakis, followed by his shock and outrage. I bite my cheek, trying not to laugh at the memory.

With his back straightened out, he tells Janice, "We got the good liquor upstairs. Let's go." Turning his head, he sees me. Recognition passes through him. He glares.

"Sorry, Rome," Janice says in a singsong voice. "You'll have to play nice with Elira if you want us to stay." She wraps her arms around his neck and looks up at him. She's pouty and seductive. "And you do want me to *stay*, don't you?" The word *stay* is filled with sexual promises.

He turns his face and looks at me, hard. Steam lets loose from his nose. Finally, our staredown is over, and he takes Janice's hand to leave the basement. Men are so predictable. People part as he walks forward, and we follow up two flights and walk down the corridor, finally entering a large bedroom. A queen-size bed sits nestled into a corner, frat-boy complete with shiny black sheets. A black pleather L-shaped couch faces the center of the room with a glass coffee table in front of it. The room's walls are filled with posters of half-naked women on motorcycles and stolen street signs. Classy.

I sit down on the couch, damp thighs sticking to the faux leather. Natalie practically drops into my lap when a gigantic bottle of Stoli

Vodka appears in front of us. A guy with a neat buzz cut lifts the bottle and pours shots into red Solo cups. With his posture, he looks like he could be a Marine. Handing one to me, he tries to make eyes, but I ignore him. The last thing I need in my life right now is a pain-in-the-ass frat boy. I take my drink from his hands and quickly shoot it back. The hiss from the burn feels so good.

Marine Guy tries to make small talk, asking if I like my classes. I try to be nice, but it's obvious I'm uninterested. I don't mean to be a bitch, but sometimes, a girl has to be clear about her intentions. Checking my phone, I see a text from my brother. Natalie hands me another shot of vodka. I take it before stepping outside of the room and reading his message.

Agron: Where are you?
Elira: Where are YOU?

I huff. How dare he ask me my whereabouts when he's been AWOL for a month.

Agron: I left something for you at home.
Elira: You went into the house? Did mom see you?

My heart pounds. If he looks the way I saw him last, she'd have a heart attack.

Agron: Yes.
Elira: And???
Agron: A lot has changed since the last time you saw me. Don't worry. I've cleaned up. She saw me and cried happy tears.
Elira: So, you're back now?

I hold the phone tightly in my hand. Three dots appear, and I know he's typing. I bite my lip, waiting.

Agron: Not sure. Got lots of things coming up ...

For reasons I don't want to examine, this news worries me. I drop my phone back into my bag. I need to go home. What the hell did Agron leave for me? I hope it's the money. But if it's the money, does that mean he connected with Nico? My heart beats a little faster.

Turning around, I bump into what feels like a hard wall—

"Argh!" A muscular chest starts to shake, as though from laughter.

It's him. Jack Gallagher. Sparkling blue eyes smile down at me. His blond hair is sexy and mussed, like he's run his hands through it a million times. With his strong jaw and cheekbones, he resembles a Viking warrior. I typically don't go for blond men, but the bottom line is, hot is hot. My skin flushes fiercely. Heat rides from my stomach straight up over my neck and cheeks. He's even more beautiful up close.

"Hey." He sounds nicer than I would have guessed from the way he sings. His smile is appreciative and calm.

"Hi." I move my hair to the side, a nervous habit, and look back up at him.

He leans against the white wall, long, denim-clad legs crossed in front of him. "You come to this house often?"

It's a cheesy line, but I don't mind.

I deadpan, "Oh, yeah. Me and Alpha Sig are like this." I twist two fingers together, as though we were as thick as thieves. My sarcasm is obvious.

"I hate these assholes, too." He smirks. "But the band wanted to play here tonight. Went pretty well." Again, that gorgeous smile. Straight white teeth and full pink lips.

"Oh, you're in the band?" I open my eyes wide, all innocent-like.

His face is momentarily stunned in a look that says, *Is this girl for real?*

I laugh. He totally thought I was serious.

He points at me in disbelief. "You're funny."

He tries not to laugh but can't seem to help himself. The sound reverberates deep within my belly. I'm being a smart-ass, but I can't help it. Someone steps into the hallway, lighting up a cigarette.

Jack looks up and nods with a, "Yo," to the smoker.

The guy steps over. "Hey, man."

He exhales over his shoulder, conscious not to get it in my face. I cock my head to the side, trying to place him. Curly, dark hair. Trimmed black beard. Small but shining eyes. He's wearing an old band T-shirt, a group I've never heard of. That's when it hits me. He's the—

"Drummer." He smiles, and a dimple indents his right cheek. It's incredibly cute against the tough look he's sporting. I like it.

"I knew that." I shrug, pulling out a piece of gum from my bag. "Took me a second, but you beat me." I unwrap the gum and pop it into my mouth. Oh, good. It's mint.

"Gotta be faster if you wanna win." His voice is completely flirtatious. "Got another piece?"

"Sure." I offer him the pack. He takes one out before handing it back to me.

Jack shoots a look in the drummer's direction that says, *Back off.* "Want to go inside?" He gestures to the room's door.

Ignoring Jack, the drummer puts out his hand. "Scott Sands."

I take it, and we shake, all serious-like. I give as good as I get, squinting my eyes and acting like I'm interviewing at a white-shoe law firm. He breaks first, laughing, and I follow suit.

"Well, Scott Sands, I'm not going to lie. Your sound. It blew me away." I risk a look at Jack, embarrassed by my fangirling. Luckily, he looks pleased.

"Well now, I've gotta tell you, I like hearing that." Scott smiles, stepping closer. "A lot."

Suddenly, a heavy, callous hand takes mine. I look up.

"Let's go." Jack licks his full lips, and I do my best to not melt.

My phone buzzes as we walk into the room, and I unzip my bag to pull it out.

Agron: Don't be out too long. Package for you is on your bed.

I let out a grumble over the text as we step into the enveloping crowd. It looks like the room has gotten a lot busier in the last few minutes.

Jack backs me up against the wall. He's crowding my space so that he's all I can see. My belly flutters from him, but my brain tells me that more important things await.

I sigh. "I should go." I want to keep cool and not act disappointed. I want to curse my brother before punching him in the face.

"Already?" He scrunches his brows.

"Yeah. I—" I stop, unsure of what to even say. Society would say it's too much information to give a stranger, but I decide to go for it. "I've got a brother who is out of his mind and owes me money. He claims he left me something on my bed, and I need to see if he paid me back."

"This is probably a weird sort of Karma then. Because I owe my sister, like, two hundred bucks." He grins.

"I seriously hope you're joking." I pop my gum.

"Dead serious. Needed some new band equipment. But she knows when I make it big, I'll pay her back. Plus, she's got a seriously rich husband, so it doesn't matter that much to her."

"Lucky you." I snort.

He tilts his head to the side. "How about I take you home?"

I look at him closely to evaluate the state he's in.

"I'm sober," he adds, answering my silent question.

"You're telling me, you played tonight, and you didn't take anything?" I squint to get a better look into his eyes. *Is he full of shit?* I might not be a party animal, but I've been to enough shows to know that drugs are a huge part of the scene.

"Got a long history. Kicked that habit a few years back."

"That's good." I look elsewhere, trying not to show how badly I'm crushing on him. He's got all the sex appeal of a sweaty, badass rocker, minus the drugs.

"Yeah." He whispers, "So, I noticed you while we were playing."

I can't help but look up into his face. His eyes are slits, slanted and almost wolflike.

"Noticed you dancing, getting completely into the music. Crazy hot." The smile is gone. In its place is need.

I hum, doing my best not to jump on him in the middle of the party. Turns out, sexual chemistry is a real thing. Something tangible crackles in the air between us. He's daring me to make this happen. My pride says no way. I like privacy, and I'm not one to give people a free show. But Natalie's reminder that this is our last year at Green and to make it count tells me to just go for it.

The flare of his nostrils has me licking my lips. Suddenly, he's leaning forward, arm against the wall and caging me in. I lift my face, wanting him. Wanting him to just take me over, mind and body. I nod, silently saying yes.

Centimeters from my lips, he grumbles, "You still sure you need to leave?" His nose moves against my hair, taking a deep inhale.

A shiver moves down my spine.

"I should take you out of here," he whispers, "get you alone." Callous hands frame my face, fingers tracing lines above my eyebrows and down my straight nose, lining my lips next. "Nothing with the crazy brother will change in a few hours ..."

My phone buzzes again, the sound distinct and breaking the moment. Still, neither of us moves. We're just locked in this stare.

Again, the phone buzzes.

I blink, cursing as my shaking hand plunges into my deep purse. It could be my mom.

Agron: Are you home yet?

"Motherfucker," I whisper under my breath, scowling.

Jack laughs, as though my outburst was funny. "I get it. Let's go." He takes my hand to leave the party.

I stop. When his head turns back, I tell him, "I need to tell my friends I'm leaving."

He replies, "Yeah."

I let go of his hand and turn, immediately spotting Natalie on the other end of the room. She's pressed up against the wall, legs wrapped around Marine Guy.

I move through clusters of people holding Solo cups filled with beer and tap her shoulder, ignoring the fact that she's in the process of being dry-humped. Removing her red mouth from his, she smiles drunkenly at me. His lips immediately plaster themselves to the side of her pale neck; this man isn't one to be deterred. Natalie laughs from his enthusiasm, gripping his shaved head in her hands. She's happy.

"I'm going to head home." I look back and spot Jack laughing with Scott.

He's so hot. I should be enjoying myself with him right now. I press my lips together, wanting to strangle Agron.

Suddenly, Natalie pushes the guy off her. "One of the brothers can give you a ride. Don't walk at this hour."

Friends to the end.

"I got someone." I smile. "I'm cool."

"Love you. Text me when you're home."

"Will do. I'll message Janice, too."

"Don't bother. She and Tiny Dick are getting it on." She raises her brows before grabbing Marine Guy's shirt and forcibly bringing him to her mouth.

I shake my head as I walk back to Jack.

Together, we leave the room and head downstairs. People tap Jack on the back, congratulating him for a great show. He's unfazed but cool to anyone who pays him the compliment.

He opens the front door for me, and I step out. The air feels crisp and cool, our pathway moonlit.

"So, you mentioned something about the band and ... fucking incredible?" There's a twinkle in his eye.

He's flirting with me, and I love it.

Pulling a set of keys out of his back pocket, he walks me to the passenger side of an old black Toyota Camry. "Yes, it's true. You were unbelievable."

He opens the door. "Your chariot awaits." His voice is a flourish, complete with a British accent.

I don't want to laugh, but I can't help myself. He's being silly, which is completely unexpected. Feeling brave, I rise onto my toes and wrap my arms around his neck. His mouth quickly descends on mine. My moan can't be stopped. His heavy hands press me closer to his lean body. We kiss just long enough to realize what I'm missing out on.

"Ready?" He places small kisses over my neck.

"Yeah. No. Yeah." My voice is raspy.

I can feel his chuckle against my skin.

He stands tall, stretching out as I slide into the seat. "Let's hit it."

He shuts my door and with shaking hands, I buckle up.

With eyes glossed over, I look around his car. I like it. It's beat up and old with a Christmas tree scent dangling from the rearview mirror. It's authentic somehow. There's a vibe, like good shit has happened in here. Or maybe it's just the feeling Jack gives off.

"So, believe it or not, I didn't catch your name." He turns on his phone, finding a playlist. Audioslave's "Like a Stone" plays as the engine rumbles.

"Elira Berisha."

"Wow." He smiles appreciatively. "Exotic."

I roll my eyes. "I'm Albanian. From Kosovo."

Jack blurts, "You're gorgeous." He blinks, clearing his throat, like he's slightly embarrassed to have told me that. "Off-campus, on Fifth?"

He's assuming I live with most of the upperclassmen who no longer live on campus. "Nope. I'm actually at 304 East Main, on the corner of Broadway."

His eyes widen, moving between me and the parking lot as he pulls out. "Townie? I never woulda guessed, but I gotta say, Elira, I like it."

I laugh out loud. "Why would you like it? I'm a townie who goes to college here. Nothing much to like or not like. Actually, scratch that. Definitely more to not like with the amount we steal from the rich kids, eh?" I raise my brows, testing him.

I know how much shit the students talk about townies because I hear it all the time with my own ears. They have no clue I'm from here, and so when they speak, they don't hold back. I'm not ashamed to admit, I've got a serious chip on my shoulder. Okay, fine. More like a boulder. "I've got an entire stash of computers I've stolen from the library under my bed."

Now, it's his turn to laugh. "Can I get in on that business? Could use the cash." He winks like he knows I'm talking shit. After a few beats, he blurts, "You're different."

Changing the subject, I ask, "Where are you from?" I pull a red lollipop out from my purse, attempting to act nonchalant. There is so much I want to know. The band, where he hangs out, how he started, and where he's going.

"Upstate New York."

"Cool. Is it a similar place to this?"

"If by similar, you mean poor and shitty, the answer is a great big yes. Your family worked in the factories, I'm guessing?" I lick my lips, surprised at his question.

Most of the students at Green are so isolated in the college bubble; they act as though they have no idea there is a world outside of college athletics and Greek life.

"My mom, yeah. When it closed, the entire town went to shit." I pull down my window, hoping the fresh air will clear the heaviness that's descended in the car. I swirl my tongue around the lollipop and stare outside.

Loads of college kids are drunkenly walking up and down the street, moving from one party to another. Slowly, I risk a glance at Jack, wondering if the way he looked at me before will now change with my admission. Not that he's driving a Porsche or anything, but I know that Tobeho is definitely the lower end of low.

He grips the steering wheel. "It's crazy how bad Tobeho has gotten over the last few years. I've been here at Green for almost four years, and the town has declined. All those dead factories, full of squatters. Although there are great acoustics in the factories. We recorded in there." He smirks like he's just joking, but the truth is, those huge, empty factories are scary and full of drug addicts.

Fifteen years ago, Tobeho wasn't exactly thriving, but still, it was growing. People were employed. John Mahoney Steinert Company made jeans and suits in three giant plants, employing roughly two thousand five hundred. In 2000, the layoffs began until, finally, it closed its wash plant, distribution center, and cutting center. By 2003, the last people were laid off. In the years since, the town disintegrated. Where the bank used to be is now a broken-down building where the homeless crash. Even the town supermarket is closed. To shop, people drive to the town over. But still, Green University stands on the highest hill, shining with money and opportunity. The dichotomy is mind-blowing—in a really bad way.

"So," I start, clearing my throat. In an interviewer voice, I ask, "Jack, how's it, being the front man?"

"Hard work. Lots of blood." He shrugs casually, the rock god persona shining through.

I hum. "Tell me more about this blood ..." I hope to sound casual. Meanwhile, my heart is pumping. How much will he tell me?

"The music is punk and metal. Hard sound is our energy source."

"It was flowing tonight." I inch closer. "And the rest of the guys?"

"Scott, our drummer, is crazy talented. A good man. Eric and Rob are brothers. Eric has a darker sound. The bassist." His eyes skim mine before turning back to the road.

"And you?"

He licks his lips, thinking thoughtfully. "I write lyrics first. Music follows. More authentic that way."

"How does it feel to be a sex symbol in the rock industry?" I continue my mock interview, and he smirks, full of confidence. He knows how hot he is.

A strand of hair drops into his eyes. "You're cute."

"Oh no." I shake my head and purse my lips.

"No? What's wrong with cute?"

"Cute is reserved for your friend's little sister. I'm not cute."

"You're hot as fuck." He raises a brow. "Better?"

I can't stop my smile. "Much." I don't want this conversation to end. "What's your major?" I hold my breath, hoping he keeps talking.

"Engineering."

I snap, "I don't believe you." I've never been good at biting my tongue.

"What do you think my major is?"

"Music. Or, like, something in the arts."

"Wrong. Electrical engineering. Take a look in my backseat."

I swerve around to see engineering and mathematics textbooks. I'm shocked.

"Man's got a brain. Surprised?"

I tilt my head to the side in curiosity.

But his eyes ... they're all-knowing. Intelligent.

He stops at the Stop sign.

"Aw"—I rub his arm—"cute and smart. A good combo."

His laughter is loud. "I'm cute, huh?"

I shrug, not wanting to tell him that he isn't even close to cute. He's ridiculously hot and sexy, and I have to cross my legs to keep myself in check. But I don't want to give in. I'm not afraid to admit that I fear rejection, especially from a man like Jack.

He pulls onto my street. "Which one's yours?"

Moving my purse back over my shoulder, I tell him, "Third on the left."

He drives forward, pulling up to my sidewalk and putting the car in park.

I unclick my belt, turning toward him. "Thanks for the ride." My voice comes out throaty.

"My pleasure. You live with family?"

"Yeah. My mom."

"You guys close?"

"Yes. Very."

"You're lucky."

"You aren't close to your mom?" I look down, noticing the floor of his car is super clean.

"Hell no. My parents split up when I was younger, so I ping-ponged between them. Both of them remarried people I hated. I was pretty angry for a while, but now, I guess I should thank them. All the fucking up they did was good for the music."

He gives me a sexy smirk, acting casual about something that's anything but. He pulls out a piece of gum from a pack on his dashboard.

"That seriously sucks."

"Yeah." He chuckles. "But it is what it is."

My hand moves to the door handle when I realize he didn't take my number. "So, are you going call me?" A little forward, even for me.

"Nah. I'm more of a *let's see if fate brings us back together* type."

I roll my eyes. I know a brush-off when I see one. And, now, I'm extra glad I didn't tell him how hot I think he is.

I open the door without another word when he says, "Hey." His big hand touches my back. "Wait. I'm serious. I have a weird thing about letting things just happen naturally." His eyes soften, like he's trying to make me understand.

Is this a fucking joke?

"Well, in that case, see you. Maybe."

Stepping outside, I slam the door shut behind me. Walking through my overgrown grass, I get to my front door. With my hand on the doorknob, I turn back. Jack is intently watching me, lips slightly parted. Beautiful.

I unlock my front door. I find my mom still awake on the living room recliner.

"Hey." I walk to where she's sitting, squeezing myself on her chair. She shifts to see me better, but I move myself so that she doesn't have to.

Her voice is scratchy when she says, "Agron came."

"I heard. How was he?" My voice is full of hope. I want to hear about a miracle, that he's cleaned up and doing better. I want to know that she didn't see him at rock bottom, like I had.

"You know your brother. Heart of gold but always searching for more. He's never satisfied. He sees himself as the man of the house, and he desperately wants to provide for us. But I'm afraid of where that desperation has taken him." She holds my hand in hers. "Elira, I know you have a very loyal and dutiful heart. But I'm asking you now to take a step back."

I stay silent, waiting for her to continue.

"Agron has been getting himself into a web of trouble. Since he left home, he's been involved in lots of illegal things, including drugs. Stealing from gangs in the area, too." I open my mouth to argue, but she lifts a hand in the air. "Don't try to convince me otherwise. I know what I know. I have friends, and the town isn't big."

I drop my head. She tries again to shift her legs, and this time, I help her to sit up. I fluff a pillow at her back and slightly bend her knees. Clearly, her pain is extreme, but my mother has always been tough.

"He came here earlier and casually mentioned the Mafia Shqiptare." She pauses for a moment, barely breathing. "And we both know nothing is more dangerous than them. I have reason to believe Agron might have gotten into trouble with one of the small gangs around here. Maybe he needs the Shqipe to help him ..." Her eyes move upward in thought. "Albanians are a different breed, as we know. Much darker. Much harder. Nico runs the Albanian Mafia. If Agron wants to work for him, you must swear to stay away."

"Stay away? But, mom, Agron is my brother. If he needs me—"

"I don't want you having anything to do with Nico." Her voice is firm. "He's a menace. And he isn't for you."

"Why do you hate him this much? I don't understand—"

"Do you remember when Papa slapped you across the face for talking back to him? He split your lip."

My breathing slows as I remember that moment. I was filled with so much shame.

"Nico saw you the next day at the market," she continues. "But what you don't know is that he came over that night after you were asleep. He put his hand around Papa's neck. Threatened him. Told him if he ever hurt you again, he would kill Papa with his own bare hands."

"And?" I shake my head. "He probably thought he was protecting me—"

"What do you mean, and?" she yells. "Nico is a monster. You were a baby, and he thought you needed protection from your own father? The man who'd helped to give you life? Nico is a killer."

"Mom—"

"Don't." She shakes with emotion. "There's more I can tell you, but I won't because it isn't necessary. You'll stay away from that man."

"You used to tell me, 'Until you have a husband, your allegiance must be to Agron.' You always showed us that nothing comes before family. If Agron works for the Shqipe—"

"Nico is where I draw the line!" Her words are final, and frankly, I wouldn't dare speak up against her right now.

"I understand, Mama." I stand, gently fluffing her matted hair. "Don't get yourself upset."

As she settles down, her eyes soften. "That's my daughter." She puts her hand on my leg, voice filled with emotion. "Such a good girl. You were always the strong one. The smart one."

In vain, I ask, "Why did Agron have to do this?"

"Just promise me," she stresses. "No Nico."

I pause, unsure of what to do. I force my head to nod.

She begins to shift, the pain from her back obviously causing distress. I help her settle back down in a position that's more comfortable before standing up and turning off the lights. I wish she could sleep in her own bed, but until her back settles a bit, this is the most comfortable spot for her to lie.

Opening my bedroom door, I drop onto my single bed. A thick envelope sits on my pillow. I open it, counting each crisp bill. It's ten times what I gave him. I clutch the cash in my hands, so relieved that I tremble. I'm glad to see his word is still his bond even if the money obviously came from a shady place. I wonder how he got this and who he now owes. I'm happy, but I'm not a moron. This is Agron. There's no way he got this money without screwing someone over.

Regardless of where it came from, this cash will help. I lie on my bed, wanting to turn my thoughts to Jack. Instead, I keep imagining Nico. His face is hazy, but the warmth and comfort he made me feel is embedded in my bones.

I get myself up and walk into my bathroom, turning on the sink.

As the water warms, I undress. Nude, I use makeup remover pads to take the black liner off my eyes and makeup off my skin. When I'm finally scrubbed clean, I look at myself in the mirror. It's as though a costume has been removed. My face is pale white, eyes a light green, skin almost translucent. I'm only twenty-one, but my eyes are old.

A hollowness seeps into my chest. The things I've seen and done have chipped parts of my psyche. I might have been a child in Kosovo, but I saw and remember enough that it continues to have an impact on my life. Losing my papa in front of my eyes? Barely a week goes by without something to remind me of that day. It's hard work, acting like I'm the same as all the regular college kids around me, and it takes a shitload of energy to smile and act carefree. It isn't until the evening when my energy expenditure comes to a stop, and all I want to do is collapse. It's exhausting.

I do my best to fill the empty space up with the American ideals I've been taught to want. And in many ways, I do want them. I want to work hard in school, so I can get a great job to earn money. I want to buy a big house with a backyard. A nice car. The problem is, I know that all of these things are just filler, and filler always dissolves. Particularly after the atrocities I saw back in Kosovo, there is no amount of stuff that would erase the past. But if that's the case, where can I go from here?

I walk back to my room, sliding on an old pair of sweatpants from my bedside. They're riddled in holes and gray from overwash, but they're by far the coziest pajamas in the world. Just touching them evokes relaxation. After sliding them on, I jump back into my bed and lie in thoughtful silence.

Agron. What will become of him?

3

THE SKY ISN'T CLEAR. SHUFFLING DOWN THE QUIET GRAY STREET, I LOOK at the familiar, shoddy landmarks. Along this stretch of Main Street, there are a few bars and a tattoo parlor. All other commercial buildings are vacant. Still, I know every crack in these concrete sidewalks. It's home.

A few bums circle a tall silver trash can in front of Safety Net, a small-time pawn shop.

A man in torn clothes slurs, "Some change?" He pulls out a hand-rolled cigarette from his ratty shirt pocket. A scar leaks down his face. Homeless and full of grime.

Janice would be grabbing her pepper spray right now. She'd be on high alert. But I'm not her.

I stuff my hand into the front pocket of my book bag, finding some loose change at the bottom. "How are you, Jerome?"

I hand him some coins, and he finally looks up at me, taking them with grace.

The bums here aren't random drifters. They belong to Tobeho and worked in the factories alongside my mom and everyone else. After the layoffs and subsequent closures, some people were able to swim, bob along the water's surface and find other ways to work and make money. Others, like Jerome, sank. Can't blame them.

He squints, a dirty hand raised above his eyes to create shade. He doesn't seem to notice there is no sun out today. "Ah, it's you, Elira?" He stands straighter. "Barely recognized ya. How's school goin' with those rich fucks?" He laughs, his throat scratchy from years of cigarettes.

The early morning townies all know that I go to Green. It seems to be a source of pride for them.

"Just focusing on my studies."

"They don't need to teach you shit. You're the teacher!"

I laugh.

"And your mom? Always was a looker. Like you." His compliment has me smiling.

"Full of flattery." I start walking away, calling out, "Gotta get to class."

He calls back, "Thatta girl! Go teach 'em all a little respect while you're up there."

I turn my head, yelling, "You bet."

I step onto campus for my first class of my last year at school. It's so beautiful here. Some people love to read the kind of books that bring them to another universe. I don't need books for that because I actually live in what feels like two separate worlds. For all my complaining about the students, I feel extremely lucky to have the opportunity to study here at Green. With that being said, I need to get a good job upon graduation.

I don't see myself as a townie in Tobeho forever. I love this place, but I know I need to get my mom and me out of here. In nine to ten months, I plan on moving to New York City with a kick-ass job as a financial analyst at a hedge fund. I have my sights set on Goldman Sachs or Fidelity. Interviews are coming up, and I will ace them.

I pull up a tulip from beneath a tree, bringing it under my nose. The campus architecture is a blend of modern and medieval, which sounds crazy but is actually really impressive. By far, my favorite building at Green is the Raines Library. The rotunda has a swirling, iron-railed staircase topped by a stained-glass skylight that gives the space an amber glow. It's a great spot to study and also to be alone. It's just got a feeling of *anything is possible.*

My first class is in the business school, where my major lives. I step into the aisle of the lecture hall and make my way into the back row. Only one other person is sitting in this area. A man slumped into his seat, like he'd rather be anywhere else. Dark hat down low with a wide brim that shields his face. Loose black sweatshirt and baggy sweatpants. Chewing the end of a pen in his mouth.

What a scrub, I think. Sure, I like to go out and listen to bands and party as much as anyone else. But coming into class, I do my best to look clean and alert. It's a respect thing. I take a seat.

"Elira?" Blue eyes widen, surprised.

I'm utterly floored. Scrub boy is Jack!

Leaning on my desk, I ask, "You're taking Economics?"

"It would seem that I am. And here we are. Meeting again. By accident." He taps the pen on his desk.

"You're really into this accidental thing, huh?" I roll my eyes.

He stands up and moves into the seat next to me. "Yeah, I guess I am." His turquoise eyes are shining.

The class settles in as the professor enters the room. I do my best to focus on the course, my eyes glued to the Smart Board. Jack spreads his legs apart, leaning back into the chair until his thigh is flush against mine. The fact that these parts of ours are touching has warmth rushing through my limbs. I'm not a very touchy type of person. I'm very sensitive, and I don't like to hug or get too close to people physically or emotionally. And, now, the hottest guy on campus has his leg against mine. It's intimate, but I don't want to move away.

The lecture is over. I pack up my bag, slowly putting each book inside. I'm hoping he'll finally ask for my number.

"Do you have another class now?" His question has warmth oozing from my stomach.

I casually reply, "I'm free for about forty minutes." As though I'm not dying of excitement inside, I add a shrug.

We leave together, his hat still pulled low. I can only see the tip of his Roman nose and the slice of his chiseled jaw.

We walk silently together, passing students entering and leaving other classrooms. I keep my hands wrapped around the straps of my backpack, needing to keep them tethered to something. I blindly follow him until we wind up at an on-campus coffee shop. The place is filled with college students taking their first coffee of the day.

"What do you want? I'll order." He turns to me, a small smile filling his lips.

"Small black." I want to keep it simple.

"Why don't you grab a seat for us?"

"Sure." I step out of the line and scan the room to find an empty table in the back.

The red velvet chairs are obscenely oversized, so I sit on the edge to avoid getting lost in its depth. A few minutes later, he's across from me. Pulls off his dark hat. Slicks his dishwater-blond hair backward with two heavy hands. Azure eyes, red-rimmed, are sexy as hell. I don't want to blatantly stare, but I can't help myself.

He takes a sip of his coffee, leg bouncing up and down, when my phone pings with a text message.

Agron: I need you to come into NYC next weekend.
Me: ???
Agron: The Shqipe is having a party.

Jack seems to notice my concern. He furrows his brows. "Everything cool?"

"Yeah. Just my brother. Driving me crazy lately." I drop the phone back in my bag, needing to put this information far away from the center of my mind.

The lead singer in the hottest band I've ever heard just bought me a coffee. I want to live in this moment.

"What does he need?" He leans forward, elbows to his knees, getting closer.

I can see flecks of silver in his blue eyes.

"Nothing too important." My smile is tight because I just want to get off the subject of Agron.

Luckily, he gets the memo because the rest of our conversation flows, skipping between music and classes. Nothing is too deep, but it's warm and comfortable. We're making fun of the frat guys the other night when he leans back into the chair. His shirt presses against his chest, and I can see the outline of a strong, lean body. "You've got a big family, eh?"

I press my lips together. "I used to, but everyone either died or scattered after the war. My mom and brother are all I have really. And an aunt in Albania."

"The brother who was texting and the mom you live with are here?"

I nod. "Looks like you got me all figured out."

"Not nearly as much as I'd like to. Truth is, I've thought of you a lot since I met you." His face is suddenly serious.

I stare into his eyes, so sad-looking.

"So"—I take a sip—"when did you learn to play?"

His eyes shine. "Nana." He says his grandmother's name with love. "She taught me to play guitar when I was five. She's always been really musical. Gave lessons to the kids in town."

"So, when's the big break coming?" I smile.

"Scott knows the son of some big executive out in California. I'm praying a deal will happen in the next few months." He knocks on the wooden table between us.

I wrap my arms around my stomach, excited and nervous for him. "You've got the talent, and the band is totally killer. There's no doubt really."

"Luck is what we need." He leans forward in his chair, clasping his large hands together. "The thing is, music is my life. It's in my blood. I can't do anything but this. I won't."

"You won't have to." I speak the truth. Talent like his isn't ordinary. Someone important will notice, and then that will be that.

His eyes search mine for something. He's looking for connection and understanding. I drop my eyes, not wanting to confirm his stare. I'm not sure why I feel that slight resistance, but I do.

"And you, Elira?" He licks his lips before leaning back, and I take in a breath.

"What about me?"

"Well, I know you're from Kosovo. Do you ever go to visit?"

I shake my head. "My memories aren't positive."

"Really? Why?" His eyes swim with confusion.

"Well, there was a war." My voice is curt.

His eyes widen in surprise. "War? When?" He opens his hands to me.

His ignorance has me cringing. It astounds me that I lived through a war that NATO ultimately had to intervene in, calling it a "humanitarian crisis," and yet people in America are blissfully unaware. Maybe I'm expecting too much, but why shouldn't I? The Yugoslav forces had a campaign of terror against us. It was nothing short of a mass murder intended to drive us to death. My dad fought and died for freedom, and yet Jack probably doesn't even know where Kosovo is on the map! Just the thought makes my stomach turn in anger.

Jack seems cool as hell, but like all the others before him, he just can't grasp who I am at my core. Sure, I'm American, and I love this country. But my Albanian roots are important, too. And without understanding that piece of me, I can't be understood at all.

I exhale slowly, my disappointment obvious. I don't want to be annoyed because it isn't his fault that he doesn't get it. But it's still aggravating.

I sit up taller. "There was a war over Kosovo. The president of Serbia at the time refused to recognize the rights of the majority in Kosovo, who were Albanians. He wanted to replace the Albanian language and culture with Serbian establishments. The Serbian government destroyed villages and massacred us. Women and children—everyone was under attack, and most were killed." Ignorance is a major turnoff, and I'm frustrated.

"I see." He presses his lips together, nodding.

But herein lies *the* problem. Anytime I want to get close to a man, he just doesn't really get me or where I come from. The best I can hope for is an appreciation for my background or maybe even empathy but never actual understanding. My mother and my father —God bless his soul—raised me differently than the way an American man like Jack was raised. There's a separate value system and even ethical differences between the cultures that separate me from native-born Americans. My mother works so hard to give me a good life, and one day, when she's old, I'll do the same for her. My job will be to care for her and to keep her comfortable. There are surface differences, too. The language we speak that Jack can't understand. The jokes. The foods we eat. It's the priorities that have been instilled in me since birth that aren't aligned with his.

I rise, lifting my phone from my bag, checking the time. I want to get out of here. "I've got class." My voice is brusque.

"Listen"—he stands, blocking my path—"I'm sorry that I'm uninformed. I'll read about it."

He looks genuinely sorry, but my blood is still running too hot to care.

I purse my lips. "Keywords: *Kosovar Albanians* and *ethnic cleansing.*"

His eyes widen, and he whispers, "All right."

I made him feel bad, but whatever.

My eyes turn toward the window. I want to disappear from this conversation. The entire campus is so green. There are cherry tree blossoms and lilacs everywhere, and the smell, even from inside the coffee shop, is so fresh. It's time to go outside.

"Elira?"

I turn back to Jack. He's gorgeous and nice. But I just can't do this right now.

I try to walk around him, but he follows behind, asking, "Let me have your number?" His voice is anxious.

I might not have known him long, but I can tell that he's not used to feeling this way.

I give it to him but without waiting for him to get out his phone.

Walking out of the coffee shop, I keep my head high. I'm being a bitch, but the truth is, I'm not about being fake.

I walk up the steps toward my next class, calling Agron.

"Yo," Agron answers.

"Hey. What are you talking about, New York City?" I'm in a foul mood.

"You've gotta come."

I huff. *I'm so sick of men right now!*

A few students shuffle past me, laughing happily without a care in the world. It's official; nothing is more annoying than watching happy people when you're in a shitty mood.

"Listen," he says, voice suddenly serious, "I spoke on the phone with one of the guys in the Shqipe. He invited me to a party in the city this weekend. I want you to come with me. I can go on my own, of course"—he pauses to cough—"but maybe it would be better if I had you with me."

I want to scream, tell him that I can't have his problems be mine.

Agron seems to take my silence as a negative because he continues, "Elira, I need you. Don't you understand? My way in with those guys is to pull at our shared history. And you're part of that."

Seeking shade, I pause beneath a large tree. I press my lips together, gearing up to talk some sense into him. "I want you to realize that you're asking me to support your induction to the Mafia Shqiptare. Not write a recommendation letter for a job. You're asking me to help you become involved with the most dangerous gang in the world. Not simply the most powerful on the East Coast. Not even just America. The world! Do you understand? Drugs. Guns. Girls. All of it. Potentially prison. Agron, tell me you're using your head. If you start this, you'll likely just be one of their lower-rung guys, doing the dirty work. You won't be walking in as a boss."

"This is my destiny, Elira. I'm not afraid of anything that might come. I have plans for our family, and it's time for me to man up. I've got a few things going—" He stops abruptly, as though he was about to mention something he shouldn't. "This is the path that has been set for me." His voice is hard and full of finality. "Either you help me or you don't. Either you're with me or you're not." His voice is a threat, the words *or else* hanging in the air.

A fire rages in the pit of my stomach. I don't want to lose him. I feel backed against the wall, but the choice is here. Either I help Agron or I lose him completely.

Licking my lips, I firmly tell him, "This is the last time I'm helping you."

The lie is so obvious; it's laughable. This isn't the last time, and we both know it.

"I love you, okay?" His voice seems to rattle across the line, and in that moment, my stomach sinks. He's in trouble, and I know it. "I-I'll text you all the details later." He hangs up first.

Looking up at the sky, I think, *My day has really taken a shitty turn.*

And then I ask God to help my older brother. He's a good man, but he's made some really bad choices.

I find my way to Advanced Statistics with my head in turmoil, but I welcome the distraction of class. I want to forget that my brother is planning on becoming Mafia or that I might see Nico for the first time since I left Kosovo.

A memory assaults me as I walk into the mathematics building.

I was washing dishes between meals.

Our home was a center for the resistance, and the green woods in the back were where the men hid, trained, and gathered weapons to fight. The kitchen was where they'd eat.

Mama and I, along with other men's wives and sisters, would cook all day to fill what seemed like insatiable appetites.

One morning, I was standing on a chair in front of the sink, washing dishes. Mama always told me to move slowly. The dishes got slippery when wet, and we didn't want any of them to break.

"Careful and thorough," was what she always told me.

Two other girls were rolling out bread dough. They were making jokes and laughing.

Suddenly, Nico burst into the kitchen, dirty and sweaty with huge black boots on his feet. His hair was soaked with sweat, eyes not their usual clear black. Even at my young age, I sensed the violence in them. Blood pooled above his brow, dripping onto his cheekbone like oily paint. His white T-shirt was torn savagely from the neck.

"Everyone, get out," he barked. I bent to jump off my chair when he said, "Elira, stay."

The other women didn't need to be asked twice. They left the room so quickly that not even dust rose from their wakes. I stood there, chest gaped in nerves as he brought his cotton shirt up above his head, wincing with the movement, before dropping it onto the floor by his feet.

I had never seen Nico without his clothes. He was very muscled and tan with broad shoulders and heavy arms. When he moved beside me, his side touched mine. I froze, unsure what to do.

I can remember the heavy beat of my heart. My immobilizing shyness.

Nico placed his huge hands into the soapy dish water. He scrubbed his forearms, corded and veiny, and his darkened face. He wasn't speaking, and neither did I. How could I have? What words did my childish head know to speak? My eyes flitted between the white kitchen door and the huge man beside me. Wanting to be useful, I lifted a cup and filled it with water. He took it from my palms, greedily drinking it down. His Adam's Apple moved with each swallow.

I watched. Nico was much larger than Papa or Agron. He washed himself like no one was beside him. A man, who was not my brother or father, was shirtless ... beside me! What would Mama say? Maybe for another man, she'd raise hell. But this was Nico. No one told Nico what to do.

I stared. He was sweating. Bloody and dark. I didn't know what to make of it.

Silently, I handed him the small towel I had been using to dry dishes. He patted his body, and I watched open-mouthed. Embarrassed to be staring, I moved my gaze into the sink. The water was red. I wanted to yell, but I didn't.

Nico told me, "Thank you, zemer." His term of endearment warmed me from the inside out.

My face turned red as he kissed the palms of my hands. Nico was no longer frightening. I felt like hope was all around me. A desire to live life. A desire to love.

"What will you make us to eat tonight?" He leaned onto the side of the wooden counter, the muscles in his sides trim.

"S-spinach pie," I managed to stutter out.

He winked. "Make sure you save me the corner."

I couldn't help but smile. "I always cook it a few minutes longer for you."

"And I always finish it, don't I?" He patted me on the head before lifting his soiled shirt from the floor. And then he was gone.

I BURST through the diner's back doors, the smell of grease and meat immediately coating me. Glancing up at the clock above the stove as I move through the kitchen, I see it's three fifty-five p.m. I've got five minutes to change into my outfit in the restroom before clocking in.

Natalie is already here, wiping down the counter. The ends of her hair are electric blue today.

I'm tying the white apron around my waist when she says, "I can't get over how hot he is," and nods to her right.

Jack is sitting casually at the diner's counter, taking a bite of his burger.

I try not to gasp. "He's here?"

"Oh, yeah," she sighs. "And I'm totally offering him a slice of cake after his burger." She points to the desserts lining the counter and smiles. "We've got strawberry cream." She suggestively raises her brows up and down.

"I can't believe he came here, of all places, to eat." I pull the tie out of my hair and redo my low pony. I need to keep my hands steady. "We had class together this morning and then got some coffee before Statistics. And, now, he's here."

I'm not sure if I want to jump up and down with excitement because a super-hot musician seems to be pursuing me or scream for him to get out. Sure, the whole *not knowing about the Kosovo conflict* upset me. And the chances of us going anywhere after a short fling are slim to none. But he did feel bad about it. And he was nice.

Natalie shakes her head, saying, "Lucky bitch. You have naturally bee-stung lips, and"—she gives me the stink-eye—"now, the hottest guy on campus wants to fuck you. And to think, you almost didn't come out on Friday." A hand moves to her hip, like she's waiting for a thank-you.

"I doubt he wants to fuck me."

"Girl, don't be dense. Guys don't just take girls to coffee for their own health. Anyway, the drummer was hot, too. Find a way to get us together, and I'll call it even."

Immediately, I reply, "Done."

"I wonder how Jack is in bed," she whispers, moving closer to me and knocking her arm with mine.

Together, we stargaze. His hat is off, dirty-blond hair tucked behind his ears.

I exhale, watching him put down his food to scribble on a red notebook. I'm glad he hasn't seen me yet. I need a few minutes to calm down and study him. He might never really understand who I am and my history, but he's just so sexy in that rocker, *I don't give a fuck* way that it's difficult to care right now.

Natalie organizes a stack of napkins, a wry smirk on her lips. "The Marine was actually a rabbit." I questioningly look at her, and she continues, "You know, he just pounded away …"

We both burst out into laughter, and I pretend to understand. I always play it off that I'm a real freak behind closed doors, just stingy when it comes to the details of my own exploits. Luckily, neither of my friends has ever questioned me for any facts substantiating what I allude to. At least, not yet. Between Natalie and Janice, they fill in all the blanks themselves. It's not that I don't want to have sex. I fooled around with guys in high school and even lost my virginity my freshman year of college, but it was definitely not an experience I want to repeat. Pain aside, it was awkward to be with a guy I barely knew outside of class. The social pressure to "lose it" had definitely been weighing on me, and I just wanted the encounter behind me. What a mistake I made.

Afterward, I told myself I didn't want to have sex again until I was ready. I'm choosy, and I want someone who can understand me completely—this includes my past and the woman I want to be. And I want him to love me, and I want to love him in return. It's my right as a woman to decide who I let or don't let into my body regardless of social norms and expectations. Casual sex is just not for me. I don't want to publicize that though because I don't want to come off as judgmental toward a woman who chooses to be freer in her sexuality. Instead, I just stay mum.

"Do me a favor." Natalie interrupts, her voice suddenly serious. "Close the deal with Jack before you lose your chance. And then let's have lunch, so I can hear every dirty detail." She rubs her hands together, plotting.

I roll my eyes.

She accusingly points at me. "Don't pull your quiet routine. Not this time and not with this guy." She expectantly stares at me, like she can't understand my hesitance.

"Whatever. Nothing's even happened yet. By the way"—I clear my throat, ready to change the subject—"I'm going into the city next weekend. Can you cover me here? Agron invited me to his friend's party."

"Sure. But only if you swear to give me every detail on Jack."

I throw a pink sugar packet at her chest, and she laughs.

"Wait"—and she pauses—"Agron?" She says his name like a curse. "Don't tell me you're doing him another favor. Elira, we've been over this. You're in a pattern where he asks for a favor, you say no, and then you cave. I'm taking Psychology 101 right now, and seriously, you're in the middle of a very abusive relationship. It's called emotional blackmail." She sadly nods her head, as though this one class has turned her into Dr. Phil. "He asks something of you. You say no. He threatens to never see you again, and blah, blah, blah until you give in."

"He said it's important." I look at the door, hoping someone will come in to eat and interrupt this gossip session. Unfortunately, I don't even see anyone walking on the sidewalk. "And anyway," I continue, "he paid me back the money I'd lent him. I didn't want to say yes this time, but he—"

Like a gift, a new customer walks in and seats herself on the left side, my section.

"Hallelujah," I whisper under my breath, strutting forward to take the table.

Before I can get to her, Jack calls out, "Waitress!"

I pivot toward the counter, where he's sitting. He slides his black hat backward on his head.

"Yes?" I reply in a singsong voice, stopping close to him.

Despite looking as though he rummaged through the donations bin and picked up the rattiest clothes he could find, his scent is clean laundry.

"Look at you in this outfit." His gaze scans from my toes up to my eyes.

I point to my eyes. "I think you meant to tell me I have the most beautiful eyes." I lift my brow.

"That, too." He laughs. "So, you work here ..." His voice trails off, as though he's unsure if he's asking a question or making a statement.

Suddenly, it dawns on me that maybe he's not here for me at all. Maybe he just came to eat, and this whole thing is another coincidence.

"I do work here." I tilt my head to the side, trying to figure out his angle.

"That's cool." His grin is slightly shy, tipping the scales in favor of him knowing my place of work.

I can't help the relief that sets in my chest. I guess I did want him to seek me out.

"I'm sorry for being ignorant about Kosovo. I might have done some reading, and I wanted to find you." The tips of his ears turn pink.

I relax, shrugging. "No, it's okay. I was rude about it. More than rude even. I shouldn't have been. It's not your fault you didn't know. I mean, it's not like it's part of any school curriculum or whatever." I look to the customer and see that Natalie has taken care of her.

Silence moves between us, but it's not cold.

"Look," he starts, fidgeting in his seat, "I want to invite you out this weekend. We've got a pretty big gig in New York City. We're using Scott's van, and it'll be packed with equipment and stuff." He pauses, like he isn't sure what to say.

"Yeah?" I ask, waiting for him to continue.

"If you don't mind squeezing between instruments and bodies, you should come. With me. To watch us, I mean."

I laugh at the coincidence. "Believe it or not, I was planning to go to the city Saturday night. My brother has this party, and he invited me to go." I bite my lower lip.

"That's cool. Even if you can't watch us play, there's still room in the van."

"I could definitely use the ride."

"Cool. I'll text you."

"You got my number?" I blush, feeling like a complete jerk with the way I gave him my digits earlier.

"I've got a good memory." He winks. "It's already in my phone."

And then he stands up to leave. A single ten-dollar tip sits on the table. I take it, sliding the money into my pocket. Fate is crazy.

The evening rush begins, and the next few hours fly by. Before I know it, it's time for my break. After using the restroom, I pull out my phone and type out a quick text to Agron.

Me: Where am I supposed to meet you?
Agron: 79th and Park Ave. Wear something nice. 9 p.m.
Me: Are you kidding me?
Agron: Not a joke. The dress code is to look Shqipe-worthy. Got it?

Under my breath, I mutter, "Jerk."

∾

"Natalie?"

Our shift is over.

We're changing back to street clothes in the white-tiled handicapped restroom, moving as quickly as we can, when I say, "Can I borrow a dress for Saturday night?"

I hate asking for help of any kind, but spending money on a dress I wouldn't wear more than once is wasteful.

"Of course," she replies nonchalantly, pulling her head through a black sweater. She pulls her hair up into a sloppy bun. "Come over now and take whatever you want."

"By the way, I'm driving in with the band."

"No shit!" she exclaims. "In that case, we'd better make sure you look good enough to eat."

We drive over to her apartment in her black Jetta, chatting about her pending interview with an online music magazine. She's in the process of gathering the best work she's written so far, but she wants to put something special together for Heretic Pope. It's so awesome that she's following her dream like this. I'm not even sure what my dream of dreams is. All I know is that I didn't risk my life escaping Kosovo to be anything other than a professional.

After parking, we take the elevator up to her super-comfortable and perfectly designed apartment. Natalie has a way of throwing random things together but making it look edited. There's a circular table off to the right made of burl wood and topped by a freaky-looking white skull statue. Her living room is complete with a purple couch and white love seat. A flat screen TV and black faux marble coffee table sit in the center of the room. And yet, even with all these seemingly random pieces, it looks incredible. I always wonder what it is that makes her apartment look so cohesive, but I still can't figure it out.

Entering her white-and-blue cloud-like bedroom, we step to her closet and sift through a stack of dresses. I try on four and finally settle on a short black number that accentuates my boobs and legs.

"A little makeup, and you'll be puuuurfect."

Job complete, Natalie lifts her phone, skimming through. Suddenly, anger replaces her calm demeanor.

"What are you looking at? Whatever it is, you look like you're ready to grab a knife." I shimmy out of the dress and put on my clothes before folding the dress neatly on her fluffy white bed.

"Seriously, social media is ruining my life," she grumbles, still scrolling. "This girl Daniela, who I went to high school with, her social media account has one purpose: to make her life look better than everyone else's. She and her boyfriend, Vincent, will make you want to gag with their perfection. He's the hottest guy I've ever seen in that rough, sexy way, and she's, like, this impeccably coiffed redhead and always with a Chanel bag." She takes a look at her chipped black nails before staring back at me. "Fuck them."

I shrug. "I can't even deal with social media. Biggest time suck. And why would you even follow people you hate?"

"Ew!" she shrieks. "I'd never follow her. I just stalk her—occasionally."

I pointedly look at her. It's obvious her stalking is nothing close to occasional. She purses her lips, not even trying to deny anything, before pulling off a set of black bracelets from her wrist and dropping them by her bedside.

"She sounds horrible," I add.

"I lived it. Daniela wasn't just horrible. She was hell."

"Where does she go to college?"

Girls like that always interest me. Maybe it's because we're so different, but I'm always curious about how life is for someone when money is literally no object. Is life easier and more comfortable, or is it just the same shit with better shoes?

"Columbia." Natalie rolls her eyes. "She's smart, too. But, of course, she had to stay in New York City so she can live lavishly, right? God forbid she got stuck going to school near ... townies."

She winks as I grab a throw pillow, knocking her in the head. Her laughter can probably be heard down the hall.

∾

The van is gray, and it has no windows. Driving into Manhattan, we probably look like the Beverly Hillbillies, complete with smoke pouring out of the back. But Jack is squeezed in next to me between a few pieces of the drum set. And it's dark. And he's talking to me between kisses, as though the rest of the band, plus two other girls, isn't even here. I don't know what is happening between us, but it's so thick and real that it's practically tangible. The most surprising thing I've learned is that Jack Gallagher is nice. Genuine. Maybe he could really understand me. *Maybe.*

Scott shouts, "Mudhoney played in this fucking spot, guys! Mudhoney!"

Cheers ensue, the boys whistling. Jack lifts his mouth from mine to clap and hoot.

He places his arm around my shoulders. "It's a small spot." His voice is hushed, like he wants to tell me something no one else knows. "But legendary. It's a dream for us to play here. Don't tell him, but Scott has been freaking the fuck out."

"And now, Heretic Pope is joining the ranks!" Rob screams. Throwing a piece of candy at Scott's head, he shouts, "Hell fuckin' yeah!"

Scott ducks, and the van swerves. The car's jerk has Jack unceremoniously landing on top of me. We all laugh, feeling invincible. It feels like nothing bad can happen here. The thrill of being with a band that's going places has my blood pulsing. Looking into Jack's face, I know he feels it, too. He gathers me into his lean, strong arms, his lips insistent and hot. I open my mouth, wanting more of this. I hum into his mouth, and he pulls back.

His face darkens before he presses his forehead against mine. "More later."

The guys start talking about California, and I zone out of the conversation.

Small tinges of stress begin to move through me like a weak current. *Will I see Nico tonight?* I knew him as a child. He was like a big brother—that's it. My sadness over the fact that he never called me or reached out over the years is stupid. I made our friendship bigger in my mind. After all, I was a kid in war-torn Kosovo. Things weren't exactly normal back there. And I clung to him.

I was just a child.

My hands feel jittery, so I shake them out.

Jack seems to notice something is off when he asks, "Hey, you cool?" He puts a warm hand on mine.

Jack is safe. He's an American in all the ways one would expect. Strong, confident, and optimistic. Things might not have always been easy for him in his life, but they've been … easy. I want easy, too.

Maybe I shouldn't go to this party. I mean, Agron can fend for himself. He doesn't need me. And I definitely don't need to see Nico —if he's even there. And then, because my life couldn't get more confusing, my phone rings, and it's Agron's name flashing on the screen. I hit Silent. It rings again.

Jack looks down in confusion. "Why are you being shady? Who's calling?" His voice is accusing, which is highly annoying.

Possessive much?

"It's my brother." I click Answer.

"You close?" I can just picture him chewing on his nails. A nasty habit he's had since forever.

"Yeah," I reply, trying to stay cool.

Agron is anxious and nervous—rightfully so.

"I'll meet you in the lobby. I'll be there in about thirty seconds." He clears his throat before switching to Albanian. "Is your ride okay? Maybe I should have brought you myself."

I reply in our mother tongue. "Yeah, it's fine." I hang up first.

Jack raises his brows, seemingly impressed. "Sexy," he whispers. "Wanna teach me a few words?"

"Maybe." I try not to cringe from his request.

Since I turned thirteen, guys have been asking me to teach them Albanian words. It's annoying as hell, especially because none of them can ever pronounce a syllable.

He presses his lips against my neck, kissing me, asking, "How do I say hello?"

"*Përshëndetje.*"

He laughs out loud. "You're kidding, right?"

I shake my head. "Nope. It's not an easy language. Thirty-six letters in our alphabet."

"That's ten more than English," he exclaims. "Pretty intense. How did you learn English?"

"I had a ... friend. He used to teach me words and phrases. And then I watched lots of television."

He waits for me to elaborate, but I don't. I turn to look out the window, wanting the conversation to end.

Luckily, Scott pulls over. "We've reached the corner of 79th and Park Avenue. Princess, your party awaits."

Jack lifts my purse up off the floor. "This party looks pretty fancy, eh? That's some address."

I detect a little unease in Jack's face. Not insecurity, but something like it.

I whisper in his ear, "It's nothing."

He pulls me onto his lap for another searing kiss, meant to stay on my mouth long after our lips have parted. The lights in the van are on now, and the group starts cheering and whistling over our display. I pull back, embarrassed.

Jack whispers, "Maybe"—kiss—"if you want"—kiss—"you can come downtown when you're done. We're crashing at Scott's friend's place after the show. I'm sure there's room on the floor. With me."

His breath moves into my ear, and I shudder.

Slowly, my hands make their way into his hair. It's an absolute mess. Stringy, *I don't give a fuck* hair. I've been pulling on it for what seems like the entire car ride.

I try to comb it out with my fingers, but he shakes his head, saying, "I like it like this."

"I'm sure all the girls watching you tonight will, too." I can't stop the snark in my voice.

He tilts his head to the side, eyes glassy. He likes that I sounded jealous.

Scott yells, "Get your ass out of the car, Elira. We gotta go."

"I'm leaving. I'm leaving."

Jack's hand moves back to my ass, and I swat it away, ducking low to avoid hitting my head on the car's ceiling.

Hopping out, I adjust the dress and my boobs. I'll definitely need to stop in the restroom before seeing anyone. Reapply my lipstick and make sure I'm not in shambles. I walk toward the front door of the building, and a man in a black uniform bows his head and opens it for me. Stepping inside onto the black-and-white-checkered marble floor, I'm stunned. The lobby walls are painted in shining black lacquer. A huge oil painting of a brown-and-white dog is on the right side of the room, gilded in gold. On the opposite end stands a black marble fireplace. In the center of the lobby is a small seating area, complete with a tufted couch in navy velvet. Every detail of the lobby spells *money lives here*.

I swallow hard. This building isn't normal. Whoever lives here is seriously loaded. I shouldn't be surprised. The Mafia Shqiptare rivals Xerxes the Great in money. Still, it's shocking to see so much wealth in a small lobby.

With all the strength I can muster, I move straight to the front desk. "Is there a ladies' room I can use?"

"No." His voice is firm, leaving no room for negotiation. I see a twitch in his eye.

"Are you positive?" I can barely contain the annoyance in my voice. It's so obvious he's lying.

"There is one available for unit owners only. You, unfortunately, are not a unit owner. And therefore, I cannot give you a key."

I want to slap the smugness off his face. He is staring at me like I'm nothing more than shit on the bottom of his shoe.

"I'm a guest." I grit my teeth and straighten my back.

It's not even that big of a deal; I can go upstairs and use the bathroom at the party. But I'd rather clean myself up before going upstairs. If Nico is there, I want to look my best. Not that it matters, but it's a reunion of sorts, and I'd rather look good than not good. And this jerk is making a simple situation difficult because he wants to show his power. It's a restroom, for God's sake!

I open my mouth to speak again when a group of men bursts

through the large double doors. The concierge runs out from behind his large desk, fumbling with his cap and asking if any of the men need anything. They strut by, ignoring our presence. I want to see who they are, but I can see nothing other than a flurry of tall, dark suits moving directly into the elevator.

After they're gone, the concierge is visibly sweating. I can use his nerves to my advantage. If he's afraid of them, I might be able to make him afraid enough of me to hand over the keys to the restroom.

"I'm with them."

"Them?" he repeats, eyes widening.

"Yes," I reply deliberately. "I'm heading upstairs. To those men. But before I go, I need that restroom key." I raise my brows before continuing, "I'm sure they wouldn't be happy to hear their guest wasn't treated well."

Ruffling through the desk drawer, he pulls out a silver key ring. He hands it to me with shaking fingers. "It's behind the pillar."

Plucking the key out of his palm, I turn and strut across the marble floor, heels click-clacking as I walk.

The lobby restroom is just as opulent as you'd expect. The walls are black and mirror-like in their shine, floor a black marble.

I open my purse and set it on a small table, level to the sink. Looking up, I groan at my reflection. "Jack seriously did a number on me."

A smile fills my now makeup-less face. I pull out my small compact and press the powder against my T-zone. Everything I use is a drugstore find, but after years of experimenting, I think I've finally figured out the best pieces of makeup from each cheap brand. I do wish for the expensive and beautiful pieces in shiny casing, but this works for me—until I get a high-paying job, that is.

I reapply my Wet n Wild kohl eyeliner next, lining the inside and outside of my eyes. I know I've got a slightly gothic edge to my look. It's not that I'm aiming for it, but my features lend itself to that. I'm pale, and my hair is dyed black. Plus, my name is Elira, and people confuse that with Elvira, the vampy character in that 1980s sitcom *Elvira: Mistress of the Dark*. Natalie thinks it's hilarious when people mix up my name. I just think it's annoying as hell. It doesn't hurt her case when autocorrect always switches Elira to Elvira. I feel like I should write a letter to Apple, letting them know that there is a name Elira, not Elvira!

On a positive, my green eyes are really bright tonight. I turn on the faucet to warm, and I dip my fingers into the water and then onto my hair, combing out the tangled strands. I still look a little flushed, but I think it's working for me.

Lastly, I lift my black dress up around my waist, adjusting my underwear higher to avoid any visible panty lines. After pulling the dress back down, I stuff my hands into my neckline and lift my boobs within my black Victoria's Secret bra. They aren't big by any means, but they're good and perky, and the bra has a great underwire and light padding.

With my last deep breath, I tell myself that everything will be just fine. Nico is an old friend. If I were to see him again, it would be nice. Sure, he runs the Shqipe. But he was plenty dangerous when I knew him, and I wasn't worried then. It'll be fine. I'll be there for my brother. That's what's important tonight.

Stepping out of the restroom, I find Agron on the lobby couch. Leaning forward, he's bracing his elbows on his knees. With a creased brow, he seems to be in deep, unpleasant thought.

"Agron?" I keep my voice quiet, trying not to startle him from his trance.

He pops his head up with a huge smile, as though nothing were awry, which, of course, makes me nervous. I take a moment to do a once-over. He looks much better than the last time I saw him, although his pale green eyes are still bloodshot. He's handsome. A little thinner than he should be, considering his height, but there is some color in his cheeks, and his skin is no longer sallow. His black hair is clean-cut and short. But the suit he's wearing is probably the biggest surprise. I stare at his feet, and he's wearing what looks like a fresh pair of leather loafers.

"How—"

"I had to splurge on this stuff." He points to himself before standing up. "Otherwise, they'd never take me seriously. Gotta spend money to make money, right?" He shifts his thin shoulders.

"Spend whose money exactly?" I shake my head. "I don't even know what to say to you right now."

His eyes scan my body. "What about your dress? I'm sure you spent a pretty penny," he sneers.

"Actually, no. I borrowed this dress from a friend. And you, Agron?" I cross my arms in front of my chest.

He blinks quickly a few times, one of Agron's nervous tics. "I'm stressed, all right? Give me a break. I need tonight to go well."

I open my mouth, ready to continue, when he says, "Do me a favor, Elira. Just don't be your usual self." He puts his hands in his pockets, adjusting them.

"Excuse me?"

"Don't play dumb," he snaps. "It's a bad look on a girl as smart as you are. I'm talking about your usual sarcastic, cynical, smart-ass—"

"Come on," I argue. "I'm never ... rude."

"Sure you're not," he replies mockingly.

"How about, 'Hey, Elira. You look gorgeous. Ready to step into the party you came all the way from Pennsylvania to attend, for my sake'?"

He huffs, pointing a finger at my forehead. "That's what I'm talking about. You have to act like I'm important. Like you wouldn't want to cross me. That means, show a little respect. You can start with not asking me how I pay for my clothes."

I look up at the ceiling, trying to calm down. "I won't mess it up for you, okay?" I focus back on my brother, knowing that, above all, I'm here to support him. "I'll be peachy sweet and meek." I give him my best smile. I'm a good actress after all.

"Let's just hope you can do a better job when we're upstairs." He cracks his knuckles, the nerves radiating off him in dark waves.

"Chill, okay? I got this. I won't mess it up for you. I'm here, aren't I?"

The fact that my brother is committing himself to a life of crime should be making my head spin, but it doesn't. Agron is an adult, and he can make his own choices. The Mafia wasn't technically organized like this back when we were kids, but all the pieces were there. None of this—the crime, the killing, the money—is new to either of us. Life is a power struggle between light and dark. If Agron wants to take part in that war, that's on him. All I can do is pray for his safety. My mom asking me not to support him rings in my ears, but I can't listen to her. She's always harbored a grudge on Nico.

"Whose place is this anyway?"

"The Shqipe owns it. They throw parties here often—or so I've heard." Agron shrugs, as though owning a penthouse apartment on Park Avenue was as simple as buying candy on the street.

I clench my hands, feeling the key in my palm. "Oh." I make eye contact with the concierge and walk back toward him. "Your key."

He clears his throat. "I'm not sure how much you know, but those men in the penthouse aren't exactly the playful type. You seem like a nice enough young girl ..." His voice trails off as he intently looks at me. He's trying to communicate, without words, that they're dangerous.

I want to tell him these types of men just don't scare me. They never have.

Instead, I just nod. "Thanks for your concern." My voice is softer. "I'll be sure to come straight downstairs if I need to."

"That's right." He slightly relaxes. "Now, about that key. It's against policy to let anyone who isn't an owner to use it. I wasn't trying—"

"I know," I interrupt. "I won't say anything, all right?" I swallow, feeling slightly guilty for deceiving him.

He nods, and I turn back to my brother.

Taking Agron's hand, I squeeze it in solidarity. "Let's go."

We enter the elevator, and Agron pushes the top button for the penthouse.

4

THE APARTMENT IS EXTREMELY LUXURIOUS, AND EVEN THAT IS AN understatement. If I were another woman in my position, I might be afraid to break something. I might worry that I don't fit in with this rich crowd. Luckily, I'm not that girl. I might not have their money or status, but I'm proud of who I am and who I'm becoming.

A server steps in front of us with a silver tray filled with bite-sized hamburgers.

"Burger?" He smiles, bringing it closer to us.

I look onto the large plate, picking one up along with a napkin. "Thank you," I say, putting the piece in my mouth. I hum from how good it tastes.

Mom and I always make our food as freshly as we can, but it's not always easy when time is limited. Fine dining like this? Never. If I have to do this for my brother, I'll make the most of it. That means, I'm going to drink the best liquor and eat everything that comes my way.

Swallowing, I glance around at the beautiful framed art in the apartment's entrance. *Wow. This is incredible.* Agron takes my cue and walks us into the living room. I can feel the tension in the way he holds my hand.

"Loosen your grip," I whisper-yell, trying to break free from his tight hold.

He nods, sweat beading on his brow.

If he can't even handle a simple party, how does he think he'll be able to handle living "the life"?

The living room itself is an open-floor plan with three separate seating areas, and it's gigantic. Floor-to-ceiling glass windows cover the entire northern portion of the room, showcasing sparkling New York City lights.

"The view," I say out loud, unable to help myself.

Agron whistles in agreement.

We spot the bar in the left corner of the room and walk toward it. I move as if we belong here. With these types of men, it's necessary to act entitled. Showing any type of insecurity is never an option, not even in a simple task like walking.

The intricately carved wooden bar is built into the corner of the room and stocked with crystal glasses, sparkling like diamonds and showcased along the shelves. Beneath them are rows of different liquor bottles. I recognize the names, but I've never tried them.

The bartender moves toward me, and I go with my usual. "Tequila soda, please."

She has long, dark hair, styled down in waves, and wears a black bustier top, boobs on display. Not that I have any right to judge. My uniform at the diner isn't exactly prim.

"Which kind? We've got Don Julio, Patrón, and Cassamigos." She mixes someone else's drink in a cocktail shaker, high breasts jiggling, before pouring it into a martini glass.

Agron says, "Get the Patrón."

I want to argue and tell him I'm perfectly capable of figuring out what kind of tequila I want. But I swallow my words, knowing that I need to be amenable this evening, for his sake. I shut my eyes, pull on my sweet-girl persona, and then reopen my eyes with a sugary smile.

Knowing he won, Agron lifts his chin to the bartender. Leaning forward to get closer to her, he orders two Patróns with a splash of soda. "Extra limes, please."

She smiles seductively, head slightly bowed. It's not until she hands me my drink that I notice how beautiful she is. Tiny turned-up nose, extra-full lips, and large blue almond-shaped eyes. I swallow hard, finally looking around the room. It's as though the hottest women of Eastern Europe were dropped off here after a modeling gig. Oh, who am I kidding? Modeling, my ass. These girls are definitely working tonight, and it's not for a photographer in the fucking Maldives. High-class hookers. They're like feminine robots in designer clothes. Fake tits. Faces molded. Hair extensions. Six-inch heels, complete with Louboutin red soles. All the dresses are different colors but fit the bill—short, tight, and essentially painted on. I know these Mafia guys believe that everything in this life can be bought and sold at a price. I'd be appalled by the situation, but it's clear in the way they're walking that they want to be here.

Thank you, Daddy!

Agron glances down at me. "You look beautiful, by the way." His smile is genuine as he lifts the glass to his mouth.

He isn't perfect, and he drives me insane most of the time, but he knows when a woman needs a compliment. I'll give him that.

"Thanks." I click my tongue, trying not to act like I give a shit. "I guess you look okay, too."

He laughs.

"So, when's the man of the hour showing up?" I glance around the room again, trying to see if I can spot Nico.

I wish my memory were clearer. Back then, he had black hair and matching eyes, but so do ninety percent of the men in this room.

Agron takes another sip. "Nico will show up if he wants, when he wants. Do you remember him well?" His voice is lower.

"I can't remember his face. But I do remember...other stuff." My reply is noncommittal.

I still have trouble admitting my memories to myself. I can't decipher what it all meant. To him, I was a baby. To me, he was everything.

"What about you?"

"Of course I do. I wasn't a child in those days, like you were. I was under his command, of course. He taught me to shoot a gun. How to run in a zigzag. He taught all of us." He takes another large sip of his drink, eyes narrowed.

I look around me, and everyone is busy in their own conversations. "What do you think you'll be doing for them?"

"There's lots of entry work." He looks around to make sure we have some privacy. "Say an Albanian wants to be smuggled into America for twelve-K. He'll pay a certain amount up front and then owe the rest later. Some people don't want to finish paying, right? I might be the one to persuade them that paying is the better option. Stuff like that." He scratches the back of his head. "I think."

"I'm assuming that's what you'd do if you were lucky." I take another sip, trying to maintain my calm.

The work he's describing wouldn't be difficult because, typically, the people who are smuggled here are just hard-working, regular Albanians who want a better life. They aren't thugs.

"I'll do whatever I've got to do. Hopefully, it won't take too long to rise up." He puffs out his chest.

I can't fault Agron for turning out this way. He was a teenager in Albania when the war broke out. He saw the deaths of friends and family with his own eyes. Some men came out of the war and just wanted to hide. Others, like Agron, occasionally stood up but only if they could lean on another stronger man to lead them. And a few, like Nico, live their lives with strength, determination, and an iron will. He didn't wait to be asked to do something, nor did he blame others for his actions and choices. He was always man enough to take responsibility for himself and others. A true leader.

"Agron," a deep voice calls out.

A man walks toward us, immediately shaking Agron's hand, as though they're friends. He's in a fitted navy suit, complete with a blue pocket square, and looks to be the same age as my brother. He's average height by Albanian standards, shorter compared to Agron. With his black hair slicked back, he looks like the stereotypical Albanian mobster. Maybe it should make me worried—to speak to a man who must have at least one gun on him. It doesn't.

"My sister, Elira," Agron introduces me formally. "Blerim."

Blerim's eyes slightly widen as he steps forward, kissing both of my cheeks. I try not to cringe from his sharp cologne. Everything about him is so obvious and expected.

Luckily, it only takes a moment for them to begin talking about the new Knicks starting lineup. Anyway, I want to use the bathroom again. I was so concerned about looking good that I forgot to actually pee.

"Agron," I interrupt with a sweet smile. "I'm going to use the bathroom."

He nods calmly, already involved in his conversation as I step away. I walk back toward the entrance and find a cream-carpeted hallway to the left. At the first door I see, I place my hand on the silver door handle and pause. Maybe it wasn't smart of me to wander. This isn't a frat house but the apartment of someone very important and dangerous. My bladder pounds a little harder, reminding me what I'm here for. The bathroom.

"Ugh, whatever." I swing the door open before I can question myself again.

The lights are off. The entire room is cast in a dark glow, illuminated by a sliver of light coming from the window, allowing me to see only a handful of details at a time. An enormous bed with a canopy sits on one end, complete with curling posts. Decadent yet masculine.

My hands move to the wall to find a light switch, but then I freeze in place when I hear a rustle and a moan. There's a man here, standing against the wall opposite the bed. His shirt is off. A woman is on her knees before him, as though in hero worship. It's slow motion as her head bobs up and down, humming in a measured deep rhythm. My entire brain and body are suddenly immobilized as I hear the sound of saliva mixing with suction. It smells like musk, mixed with a sharp vanilla and something woodsy. It's masculine and sensual. I'm not sure why I know this particular scent, but I do. Something within my stomach flutters in understanding, but I don't know why.

The man's head straightens. In the dark, I can only see his

angular face with planes so sharp that they look as though they were carved in marble. His eyes though. They're black and laser-focused on ... me. His mouth parts; he's about to scream at me to get the fuck out! But nothing leaves his mouth. I'm struck dumb.

Another hum from the woman on the floor. The blood in my body congregates at my center; like a magnetic energy, it pulses.

His chest is perfectly defined. I can make out the shadow of a dark tattoo on his right shoulder, dipping down onto a muscular pec. Lifting both hands, he places them on the back of her head, impaling himself inside her and then bringing himself out slow, like leaking molasses. She's up and down. He's in and out. Watching this is a shameless type of torture. I'm mortified by what I'm seeing, but my blood won't quit. It thrums hot. I might not be very sexually experienced, but I'm not a prude. I've used my hand and had an orgasm. I'm not even touching myself right now, and I can honestly say that I'm so heated up, I could probably finish with slight pressure. Sweat breaks out on my forehead.

My conscience knocks on my brain, telling me to move my ass out! This is insane and wrong and all kinds of screwed up. But I literally can't tear my eyes away.

Fuck it. This is happening.

What would it be like to be on my knees like this for a man this commanding? I want to be the kind of woman who can bring that deep grumble into this man's voice.

He grips her hair before swiveling his narrow hips and pushing forward, deeper. She moans, seemingly in delight.

Jesus.

Sweat drips between my breasts. My throat is so dry.

He speaks, "You like my cock?" His face is still straight, seemingly locked on mine.

I blink. My head nods.

The girl on the floor replies, "Mmmnnn."

She has no clue I'm in here, watching. If she did, would he even let her stop? I imagine his fingers tightening in her hair. I lick my lips, wetting them. Throwing his head back, he groans in what sounds like bliss.

His voice rumbles, "That's good, baby. So good. You want this, don't you?"

I hear the slight Albanian accent in his voice, and it turns me on like nothing else. My face flushes red. *I want more*, I silently beg.

He seems to understand my thoughts because he starts to fuck her mouth faster. His breaths quicken, attention still nailed solely on my face. I couldn't move even if I tried. He's trembling. I imagine the beads of sweat that are dripping down his temples. He's huge and strong, and his body is impossibly beautiful. I should leave.

Teeth gritted, he barks, "Don't move. Stay right where you are."

His words nail me to the floor. The depth behind his voice is warm but threatening, and I'm powerless to disobey. The man commands attention and respect. He's a force.

And then, suddenly, like a switch, my brain flips back on. I pivot and fly out the door like my ass is on fire.

With my heart in my throat and my panties soaked, I lean my back against the wall, panting. "What in the fuck was that?"

I take several deep breaths, clenching and then unclenching my fists. Sticking my hands into my purse, I pull out a stick of Orbit Sweet Mint gum, unwrapping it with shaking fingers. Sliding it into my mouth, I exhale, the chewing motion somehow calming. I adjust my skirt and leave the hallway.

Reentering the living room, I do my best to camouflage my shaky legs with a confident smile. I spot a server in a white uniform holding a silver tray of what looks like miniature tacos.

Walking over to her, I ask, "Any idea where there's a bathroom?" I chew my gum, trying to get my body back under control. I'm still completely stunned.

She points toward the entrance, her long blonde hair loosely curled and eyes a bright blue. "Powder room is by the front door, on the left." Her accent is Russian, voice sultry.

I shut my eyes for a moment because, obviously, I'm a moron. Why I would think I could walk into the living quarters of a stranger's penthouse apartment is beyond me. I can be so dense. Finally finding it, I open the door, gawking at the crystal chandelier hanging from the ceiling, painted silver. I let my hands graze the walls, which are papered in navy fabric. It's all so beautiful and masculine. Finally finishing my business, I wash my hands with my head bowed. I can't even look up into the mirror. I'm ashamed by what just happened. How could I stand there and ... watch?

I am so affected by what I saw, my body still trembles. I'm turned on beyond belief but also incredibly shocked and embarrassed. I need to get the hell out of this godforsaken place.

Drying my hands on a gold-colored hand towel strategically placed beside the sink, I grumble, "Oh shit."

What if that man leaves the room and sees me here?

The light in the hallway was on. He might have been darkened to me, but I might have been totally visible to him!

What if what I did somehow affects Agron? My brother would never forgive me.

On the other hand, this is the Mafia, not the Priesthood. I had a weird run-in with one of the guys, who might have been a nobody. Whoever he was, I'll never see him again after tonight. I might share a history with the Shqipe by virtue of my being Albanian, but my future is on a different path.

I step out of the bathroom and go back into the party to find my brother. I swore to support him during this party, and I will follow through.

Immediately spotting Agron against the bar, I walk to his side. He's still in what looks like a casual conversation with Blerim.

Agron smiles in relief as I move beside him. "Did you get lost in the toilet?" he speaks jokingly, but the lines around his eyes tell me he was worried about my whereabouts.

I nod, silently communicating all is well. "A little detour, but I found it."

Blerim pulls a silver iPhone from his back pocket. Glancing at his screen, he reads something. Lifting his head, he nervously looks at me and stands up straighter, as though he's showing respect. I squint my eyes, confused, but then decide not to read into it. My emotions at the moment aren't reliable. My insides continue to quiver from what happened, and I'm hypersensitive.

Agron expectantly turns toward the bar. I know he's waiting for Nico or someone of importance to appear. As he impatiently taps his foot, I put a hand on his back to silently tell him to calm down. Looking tense isn't a good idea. Not here.

Blerim pushes back his dark hair, telling Agron, "Come with me. There's an errand we can run together." He returns the phone to his back pocket before removing a pack of Marlboros from inside his jacket. Pulling out a cigarette from the carton and dropping it into his mouth, he lights it up.

"Errand?" Agron repeats, parrot-like.

"The car will be in front of the building in a few minutes." His voice is hard.

Agron opens and shuts his mouth a few times. It's obvious he wants to ask a question, but even I know that the conversation is over. It must be disappointing that he won't be meeting up with Nico. Maybe it's better this way.

I squeeze Agron's arm. My brother is bright, but he has a bad habit of acting or speaking before thinking. If he wants to become inducted, he'll have to pay his dues, starting now.

"Nice to meet you." I smile to Blerim, ready to leave, but he immediately drops his head and puts out his hand to mine for a shake, as though not to offend.

I'm weirded out. Agron is so annoyed over the turn in events that he doesn't seem to notice this obvious shift.

"Elira," Blerim says, blowing smoke upward, "you aren't leaving."

"What?" The pit of my stomach feels suddenly empty. And scared.

"You will stay."

"Stay?" It seems my brother and I have turned into parrots.

I turn to Agron, confused.

I open my mouth to speak, but Agron beats me. "Just chill and enjoy." He laughs condescendingly, as though I were nothing but his baby sister, needing to be coddled. "Have another drink and relax. They want you to stay, so stay."

He kisses me on both cheeks and says good-bye. *What the fuck?*

I stand in place for a moment, unsure. The women are here for the lifestyle, men to show off their exploits. The Albanian Mafia is nothing if not in-your-face money and glamour. Granted, this apartment is classy and not gaudy in the least. But the crowd is anything but. Why does someone need me to stay here? None of the possibilities feel decent.

What if it's Nico? my mind asks.

Well, if it's him, he should come out himself and tell me to stay! I'm not a whore who must obey the Shqipe's commands.

My decision is made. There is no way in hell I'm going to sit and wait. I'm not a prisoner or a girl on call. And I'm not trying to get involved in this life either. This is my brother's battle, and he's no longer here. My work here? It's done.

I make my way toward the front door, passing through a group of scantily clad women giggling around a huge guy with a big smile. My heart pounds as I move, but I ignore it. I just want to get out of here. If Agron asks, I'll say no one came, and after thirty minutes, I left.

The entire elevator ride down, I'm worried that someone is going to stop me. When I make it out onto the sidewalk, the relief I feel is huge. Freedom. I walk east, pulling out my phone so I can find the subway map. I want to go downtown and see the guys play, turn my night around. I head toward Lexington Avenue and then north to 77th Street. After figuring out which is the northwest corner for the Downtown 6, I cross the street and take the concrete steps underground.

After buying a one-way ticket from the kiosk, I see a group of maybe ten people on the platform who look about my age. I've come into Manhattan with friends before, but I've never taken the subways at night. My sense of self-preservation tells me that I'll be safer with this bunch, especially being dressed as I am. I don't look obnoxious, but my outfit is definitely sexy. I slink closer to where they stand, hoping I can just blend in with them. Luckily, they don't seem to notice or care. The 6 train arrives, along with an explosion of air. My hair goes flying upward and into my face, sticking to my recently applied lip gloss. When the subway doors open, I exhale, following the group of friends inside.

After combing my now-crazy strands with my fingers, I hang on to the center pole and try to locate a map on the train's wall. Even though my phone gave me directions, I want to confirm where I'm going. As the train moves into an even speed, I walk my way to another pole and immediately spot a poster detailing the trains and their stops. I follow the green line for the 6 train and find Spring Street, just as I hoped.

THE STREETS SHOULD BE dark at this hour. Between apartment building windows and commercial storefronts, the dark sky is lit. Nothing can compete with New York City lights. I walk up and down Forsyth Street, eyes flitting between the map on my phone and the numbers on the buildings.

I mumble, "Where the hell is this place?"

I stop at an unmarked door. It's brown wood, scraped up and full of graffiti sprays. It's almost as though someone were testing out the can before actually using it. Hesitantly, I put my hand on the knob and twist. Inside sits a huge bouncer on a small stool, a red curtain between him and whatever is inside.

"Is this the Bottom-Feeder?" I ask distrustfully.

"ID." He snaps his gum, eyes at half-mast. A large pink birthmark spans from the side of his nose to his ear. The wall behind him is littered with signed photographs of Kurt Cobain, Eddie Vedder, and Dave Grohl.

WOW. I can't even believe how calm Jack was about this place.

I open my purse, taking out my old black wallet. After showing him the card, I stuff it back into my bag and open the heavy red curtain, stepping into the bar. The first thing I take in is the smell of beer and old wooden walls, not unlike the bars near home. But knowing who played here in the past definitely elevates the place.

Heretic Pope is onstage, red lights blaring above them. The bar isn't full, but the people who are here seem to be loving the sound. A row of short skirts, hands raised above them, are flush against the stage. They must be gawking at Jack, and I don't blame them. His eyes are screwed shut, head bowed and hands hanging on the mic.

I've seen her hanging around,
The black hole she lives within.
Her hands touch the dirt,
And I join.
All of her dreams come onto me.
They come to me.
The dark sky,
The dark she brings,
Come to me.
They come to me ...

He's amazing. His white T-shirt hugs his chest, hair mussed in that just-fucked way. I want to push myself to the edge of the stage. Make my presence known and claim him. But first, a drink. After that party tonight, I feel like I need to shake myself back into reality and remind myself that the world I saw tonight has nothing to do with me. I might share a language and a history, but my future doesn't coincide with the Albanian Mafia.

After ordering a tequila with soda and handing the bartender my credit card, I lean against the bar, watching Jack. Eyes screwed shut, he's singing with all his heart, alternating between that slow ballad and that perfect groan. She brings my drink, and I sign the receipt before thanking her.

With that first sip, guilt, like a dirty snake, slinks into my insides, making me feel ill. The truth is, it's not like Jack and I have discussed exclusivity. And it's not like I technically did anything wrong by watching that couple. But the entire scene was just ... totally fucked up. A normal person would see a guy getting a blow job and run.

That man, whoever he was, had a hold on me like nothing I've ever experienced in my adult life, and yet—

Suddenly, the band stops playing. I hold on to my ice-cold glass, feeling insecure and nervous. I'm not ready for Jack to see me. Maybe I should have walked a bit more before coming inside. The guys leave their instruments onstage, stepping off with sweat glistening on their faces. Women immediately swarm them. Jack moves to the bar with his friends, a harem trying to get his attention. He's laughing with Scott as a girl whispers in his ear. His dishwater-blond hair hangs loose in his face. She pushes it away. Surprisingly, I'm not jealous in the least. I feel a sense of pride. Not that we've come so far together or anything like that, but they're so talented. They really deserve this break.

I put my hand in my bag and feel for my emergency pack of Parliament Lights. I grip the carton in my palm. I want to have a smoke and unwind before I see Jack again, face-to-face. I'm not ready for him. Not yet.

Gripping my purse and keeping my head down, I stride back through the red curtain, letting the bouncer know I'll be back. Stepping back outside into the bright night, I walk around the block and pause in a dark corner. I kick a piece of lone trash as I lean against the alley wall, adjusting my dress and taking out a cigarette. My white lighter is where it should be—in the small zipper pocket.

After this cigarette, I think, *I'm going to get back to my life.* That includes exploring whatever is happening with Jack, completing school, and acing my job interviews.

But, in the few minutes it takes to smoke this cigarette, I'll let myself stress about what happened tonight. And when I'm done, I'll be ready to move forward.

Feeling confident in my plan, I flick on my lighter with my thumb and put it to the tip of my cigarette. It lights up amber. The first drag is perfect. Since I don't smoke much, that first inhale always moves straight into my head. So good. As I exhale, I think about Nico and what he must be like now. As the head of the Mafia Shqiptare, he must be extremely dangerous. Then again, wasn't he basically that same way back in Kosovo?

A black Bentley pulls up in front of where I stand.

I squint my eyes as I exhale smoke, unable to see within the darkly tinted windows. "Who the hell is tha—"

A sharp sting bites my arm, and a dark haze takes me over.

5

I WAKE UP WITH THE HEADACHE FROM HELL. MY STOMACH ROLLS AS recognition moves through me. I'm in the backseat of a moving car. It feels like pillows are on either side of me. I blink but see nothing but darkness. My eyes are covered. The smell of leather and the stop-and-go movement have my head in a pound and spin. The vehicle comes to a complete stop, and my stomach decides to heave. Vomit leaves my lips, spilling over my clothes and arms like burned acid.

I want to pound my fists and scream, *Get me the fuck out of here!* But I can't move. My limbs are immobile and voice stuck in the pit of my stomach. My tongue is lead, body sluggish, and nothing is moving as it should.

Suddenly, the door opens. Cool night air comes rushing over me.

"Oh shit," a man says angrily. "He's going to freak out! She puked."

The smell of my own vomit, combined with what's to come, has me gagging again. I need to stand up and run. But I can't. Tears flood my eyes as my head throbs. Why won't my voice work or my body? I need to scream for help! I open and close my mouth, but my tongue is nothing but dead weight.

"We have to clean her up." His accent is Albanian, voice cold and devoid of emotion.

Chills run through me so deeply that even my bones shudder. My fear is a real, tangible thing. I've been taken by the Mafia Shqiptare.

I've dreamed of countless scenarios where I'm pulled out of my small closet or my bed or beside my kitchen sink, stolen, raped, and abused before being left for dead. It was the ending of so many women I knew in Kosovo. Is it mine, too?

Wetness slips down my face as I think of my mother, who did everything she could to give me a better life. I love her. I hope I was a good daughter. Will Agron be able to care for her in the ways she needs? A son might be considered more valuable, but a son can never care in the way a daughter does.

The tears smear down my face like dripping pain, pooling behind my ears.

God, why?

Someone lifts me in his arms and walks. The pounding in my head increases with each step, and a new emotion takes over. I need to stop crying and get a grip. I can't let this happen to me. The drugs will wear off eventually. And when they do, I plan to fight. Until then, I'll pretend that I'm just a useless and scared girl.

I'm placed on something soft. A mattress? I hear people shuffling around. A door slams shut. My brain tells me there is only one possible reason for me to be on a bed right now. I want to scream, but I don't. It's time for me to figure out my plan. I open and close my fists, tears of relief spilling down my cheeks. My body is beginning to respond. But still, I play dead. Once my hands work, I'll tear the cover from my eyes.

A crawling sensation moves from my toes, upward. The pessimist on my shoulder reminds me that I'm at their mercy. From the sound of it, countless men have me outnumbered in this room. On the other hand, they're speaking my native tongue. I might not know these particular guys, but I *know* them. I know how these types think and act. They might believe themselves to be badasses, but in the end, they're humans. They have the same mothers and fathers just as I do.

We've eaten the same food. Had similar upbringing. These men aren't absolute strangers to me ... right?

Still, they're the worst of their kind. They are thugs in the most deviant of ways, and I'm nothing but a young girl in their hands. I have to appeal to them as people. I will speak to them only in Albanian. I could make them feel as though I were a sister of theirs. And no one would ever want to rape their sister, right?

My arms twitch, sweat pouring from my head and burning my eyes despite the cold numbness I feel in my bones. As a child, I heard the word *rape* countless times. I overheard women saying it beneath their breaths and in whispers. It's what the Serbs would do with the women they found after they killed their brothers and husbands but before they killed the women themselves.

"Killing brings out lust," my mother used to say. "After men fight, always hide from them."

Someone grumbles, "We need to clean her up. Problem is, he'll go berserk if any of us see her naked."

I hear the click of a lighter before the scent of cigarette smoke moves into my nose.

I bite my tongue, the tears continuing to stream.

"Yeah, but I'm like a doctor." A new, higher-pitched voice cackles. "I won't touch any parts that are unnecessary. Trust me. Just a little looking. Some cleaning." The smarm in his voice has my heart pounding.

The rest of the men chuckle at his comment.

A joke? Please let it be a joke.

"Just drop her into the shower and turn on the spray," someone chimes in. He speaks like I'm nothing but a nuisance. "When he comes in, he'll know what to do."

Someone adds, "There's no way I'm going to put her in the shower. I won't risk that. Afrim, wipe her down."

Suddenly, I feel a warm towel pressing against my face, neck, and arms.

"Don't worry," the man says in Albanian, voice calm. "No one's going to hurt you."

I don't risk moving but manage to wriggle my toes. More tears arrive as I see that my body is finally able to move again.

"Don't be afraid."

I tremble, lying on the bed, continuing to act virtually comatose, as chatter ensues. I need a plan before I stand up and run. The element of surprise has to mean something. I wriggle my fingers and try to move my arms. They all twitch.

One man's voice rises above the chatter. "You believe they bumped into each other? Bergdorf Goodman. Natasha saw Olga using my credit card, buying me a fucking tie!"

The men laugh so loudly that I'm momentarily stunned.

"I do believe that would happen to you." Someone chuckles. "You gotta keep your wife separated from your girlfriend by at least a few zip codes. Everyone knows that. Speaking of zip codes, I was at that fancy restaurant downtown last night."

The group quiets again.

"ABC Kitchen. And this guy who's sitting right next to me, wearing a black toupee on his little egg-shaped head, falls off his chair, breaks his fucking nose, and dies of a heart attack! His hair was flopped over like this."

Another bout of laughter erupts. It's as though they've forgotten about me. I need to find a way out of here!

A raspy voice replies, "What did you do? Did the ambulance come?"

"What did I do? I gave back my steak and ordered the salmon. I've got high cholesterol myself." He pauses for a moment. "This asshole asks what I did. I'm not about to get on my knees and pump his heart. The only thing left to do was eat my goddamn fish. Which wasn't too bad."

The group starts laughing again, and I don't know what the hell is going on.

Are they about to rape me? Kill me? And they're talking about restaurants?

I hear a door opening.

"Where is she?" A deep voice. It's not loud but extremely commanding.

Another man speaks up, explaining the chain of events. He doesn't lie, giving a detailed play-by-play of what happened to me. I listen as closely as I can, hoping to pick up any details about my whereabouts. He says nothing I don't already know.

"Get out," the deep voice orders.

I hear feet scuffling and then the door shutting. I don't dare to move. Large hands bring me to a sitting position, so my back is against what I assume is a headboard. My entire body is frozen in fear. What feels like pills are placed into my mouth before a glass is brought to my lips.

"Swallow."

Chills move up and down my spine. I know this voice.

His tone tells me to do what I was told, but I've never been good at that. With all my might, I spit the pills out and pray it pops out his eye. If he's about to hurt me, I won't go down without a fight.

He chuckles darkly as I fume.

"It's just Motrin." His voice is still calm. I'm not rattling him—at all. "No need to get feisty." That time, he spoke in Albanian.

"Let's try it again. Your headache is going to get worse if you don't take this."

Two more pills are thrust between my lips, and the cold cup is again brought to my mouth. I want to drink badly. My mouth is so dry. But what's inside? And are these pills really Motrin? I shake my head. I'm scared of him but also unwilling to give in to my basic needs so soon. I'd rather starve or dehydrate than give in to this monster.

Suddenly, strong arms move beneath my knees and around my back. I'm lifted up and brought into his chest as he moves. I scream and flail my limbs, trying to get free. The dead girl routine is done. His body is hard as granite; there's no getting out of his hold. He just laughs, as if my attempts at freedom are nothing to him.

I'm placed on my ass on top of a hard, cold floor.

"Stop moving," he commands. "You're on marble, and you don't need a concussion."

My breaths are coming out heavily as he uncovers my eyes. The world is a blur, but I don't dare move. When my vision clears, I see I'm sitting in a shower, facing a white marble wall with streaks of gray. I still cannot see my captor but know he's behind me. The pounding in my head intensifies, but I try to turn myself around and punch him in the face. Either my reflexes are incredibly slow or he's extremely fast because before I can turn around, he places me in a choke hold. Whoever he is, he doesn't want me to see him.

"Come in," he shouts, gripping my chest between his arm and elbow.

I want to fight, but all he does is increase the pressure. I'm not in any pain, but his movement is enough to scare the shit out of me.

"L-let me go," I beg.

He doesn't reply.

What feels like moments later, a new body is beside me.

Nude stiletto pumps and long legs, and then a Russian accent tells me, "Let me help you."

The man behind me loosens his hold, steadies me, and then releases.

"Raise your arms," she requests somewhat clinically.

I hear a door opening and shutting before she says, voice calm, "We're alone. I will help you undress and clean."

"I h-have to leave." The words leave my lips like a prayer. My body shakes, and my headache is worsening by the second.

She clucks her tongue. "No, darling. No leaving. Only cleaning. Now, raise your arms."

"M-my head—" I want to continue to speak, but the pounding in my body becomes so intense that I feel like I'm going to pass out from the pain. It feels like I'm on my period, but the pain is compounded by a million. Cramps rack my body, and my stomach rolls.

Black spots swim in my vision when she places pills on my tongue. "Just for the headache. Take it."

The glass is back on my lips, and I immediately swallow. Anything is better than this.

I collapse back into her surprisingly strong arms, my blood throbbing in agony.

"You need a bowl." She's strictly business.

Holding me up from beneath my arms, she helps me to the toilet, holding my hair as I puke. It hurts so bad.

When I'm done, I hang my head inside the toilet, unable to move.

"Your headache is going to settle now. Watch." She takes my bare right foot and, using her fingers, applies pressure in the center of my arch. Like magic, the pain in my head stills.

She continues to rub at my feet, putting pressure at different spots. Whoever she is, I am so thankful. Little by little, the pain dissipates.

"Now, it's time to inhale and exhale lightly. Don't be afraid to breathe."

I listen to her, slowly inhaling and exhaling. It helps. When I'm finally back under control, I turn around to her.

"Hello," she tells me, perfectly defined lips smiling. Her blonde hair is cut in a shiny, sleek bob and looks freshly blow-dried. "That was bad, huh? But the medicine is working. Let's wait a little more before we wash you."

"Who are you?" I want to be distrustful, but I also want to weep in her arms from relief.

"I'm a doctor. I was called in to ensure your safety."

"Safety?" I'm shocked.

"Yes. Believe it or not, he doesn't aim to hurt you."

I blink. "Who is he?"

She chuckles. "You will know soon enough. For now, let's just get you washed. The fact that you aren't in the basement at one of their warehouses means it can't be too bad."

I pointedly look at her. Am I supposed to be happy right now? What the fuck is this? "And you're what, the doctor on call when people get roughed up?" The attitude in my voice surprises me.

She shrugs. "Something like that. I'm sure you realize you're in the hands of the Mafia Shqiptare, yes? My husband is part of the family."

"Lucky you," I reply sarcastically.

She laughs, helping me stand. I want to ask if she's Natasha or Olga, but decide to shut my mouth. The last thing I want to do is piss off the one person who could help me escape.

"I know you think you can shower yourself, but after what you were given, you could fall. I've been given orders to deliver you back onto that bed in one clean piece."

I look to the door, and she immediately notices.

"Why do you have to make this difficult? The sooner you get cleaned, the sooner you'll sort out whatever this issue is. If you try to escape, your punishment will only grow. Trust me." Her knowing eyes have me swallowing hard.

She unzips the back of my dress, but I defiantly hold it up with my hands. There is no way I'm letting her watch me shower. The entire thing is glass and, therefore, see-through.

"Pretend we're at a gym." She shrugs. "I'm not going to hurt you. I'll help you inside and turn on the spray. You'll sit on that bench and use the products inside. Don't stand up. The temperature will be hot, and that could be dangerous. When you're done, I'll bring you a towel and help you back into the bedroom. There are some clothes in there for you. Are we clear?"

I nod, feeling slightly better by her plan. She hands me a towel, and I use it to cover my body as my dress slides to the floor. If we know each other's names, maybe she'll see me as more of a person and less of a prisoner.

"I'm Elira," I tell her, trying to sweeten my voice.

It seems my sweet-girl routine goes nowhere because she snorts. "I know who you are."

"And your name is?" I ask with eyes wide, hoping to befriend her.

Without wasting a beat, she replies, "Elena. But my name won't get you anywhere."

Her perfectly manicured hand takes mine and helps me step inside. Just as planned, she turns on the shower, adjusting the shower head to spray where I'm sitting. I take a seat. The marble is freezing but instantly warms under the hot spray. After she turns her body around, I do as she said and clean myself up, telling myself that a shower is a good thing. It'll give me the strength I need to fight my way out of here. I lift a black shampoo bottle. It says *Oribe*. Weird name. I open it up and inhale. Oh. My. God. It smells heavenly. I scrub my hair and rinse, happy to see the matching conditioner is here. These products are better than anything I've ever used. After using the face wash to scrub my skin clean, I soap my entire body. It's odd to sit while showering, but I do feel pretty shaky. It's probably best this way.

"I'm finished," I call out.

She opens the door and leans inside to turn off the water. Producing a towel in her hands, she wraps me in the fluffiest and hottest white towel I've ever had the pleasure of using. Did they put it in the oven or something? God.

"I must say, the Shqipe treats prisoners pretty damn well."

She laughs. "You aren't exactly a typical prisoner, clearly."

Walking me over to the bedroom door, I stop. "No surprises yet, right? Just changing clothes?" I bite the bottom of my lip.

"Yes." She nods. "Once you're changed, he'll come in and speak with you."

He? Who is he, damn it? I want to ask, but instead, I say, "Can you stay here with me?"

Her full lips turn down. "No." She shakes her head. "I'm not going to lie to you and tell you I'll stay when I won't. I'll make sure you change into clothes, and then, like I said, he'll come in. That's all I know."

I nod my head, appreciating her honesty. My brain reminds me that I have no plan, and I need to come up with one, stat.

I step tentatively into the bedroom. If I needed confirmation that I was in an apartment of a member of the Mafia Shqiptare, this bedroom is it. The ceiling is maybe fifteen feet high, walls complete with intricate moldings. A fireplace faces the bed, decked out with a black-and-white marble mantel.

"Holy shit," I say out loud, scanning the room's details.

Despite the old-world bones of the room, the furniture is all modern and sleek. The contrast is stunning. A bed, low to the floor, is tufted in black leather. Wooden side tables, finished with shine. Even the floor lamps are really modern. They're chrome and look like over-size searchlights, kind of like you'd find in a lighthouse or something. Maybe they're antique. All I know for sure is, this is crazy expensive.

The woman gestures to the bed, and I step forward. The clothes set out for me on the comforter are nice. And by nice, I mean, likely worth more than my entire wardrobe. My hands touch a pair of blue lace panties in a size small and matching bra in a 36B—both La Perla. Either whoever took me owns a clothing store or he's been watching me for a while because they are both exactly my size. I pull off the tags and look behind me. She's staring at her phone, so I drop the towel and quickly put the undergarments on. Next, I lift a pair of designer denim, a price tag of three hundred twenty-five dollars hanging off the belt loop!

"Holy shit," I mumble under my breath, pulling off the tag— Victoria Beckham.

One leg and then the other, I slide the pants up. They're soft and giving but straight leg. Not surprisingly, they fit perfectly. Next is a black crew-neck sweater in the softest material I've ever felt. It must be cashmere. A pair of black leather ballet flats are here, too, in a size eight. I slide them on.

Walking to the window, I turn my head to find Elena with her back turned to me. Hope fills my chest. I pull back the lush silver curtain and grip the bottom of the window to lift it.

I can get out of here! I can escape! I just need to—

It's locked. Bolted shut.

Shit!

"Come. There's nowhere to run."

I turn to her, my heart dropping.

"Don't look so sad. Trust me. If they wanted to hurt you, you wouldn't be here. Just take it easy, okay?" She holds a brush and a hair tie in her hands, offering them to me.

I walk around the beautiful white bed and take the items, brushing out my long black hair and securing it in a long braid. Do I want to cry? Yes. But I won't.

"Where are we?" Who knows how long I was out in the back of that car? Is it possible it was days?

"What I can tell you is ..." She pauses, as though changing her mind.

I wait for her to speak, but she simply presses her lips together before turning away.

"I'm under orders only to take care of you right now. My work is done. Good luck to you, Elira." She has the decency to drop her head as she walks out, but then bells ring in mine.

Get out of here!

I'm curious to see whom the man is that she keeps mentioning, but my curiosity stops when it comes to my life on the line.

I hold the door handle, counting to ten for good measure. Swinging it open, I come face-to-face with a hard chest, encased in a fresh white button-down shirt.

"Hello, Elira." The voice is dark and almost gravelly.

It doesn't take my head or my heart even a millisecond to know exactly whose voice this belongs to. I immediately squeeze my eyes shut.

It's him, my mind tells me.

Tears fill inside my lids as my heart patters. I know I should look up, but I can't. If I don't see him, he can't see me. Every part of my body yells at me to run, and every part of my brain tells me, *Look up*.

I knew him so well once.

I ball my damp hands into fists, willing myself to make a move. He smells just as I remember and as a man should, like soap and clean sweat.

He chuckles, that deep sound moving through me like a torrent. "Don't tell me you're afraid. I thought you'd be tougher than that," he challenges.

Oh, hell no!

I flick my eyes open, refusing to show any kind of weakness, and defiantly raise my head. Enormous arms are holding either side of the doorframe, sleeves of his shirt rolled to his elbows. I raise my head higher. Oh God. He's straight-up massive. Well over six feet, for sure. I see his face, and my knees literally go weak.

His eyes are pools of brown so dark, they're practically black. He has some dark stubble lining his strong, square jaw, as though he hasn't shaved in a few days. His neck is strong, thick, and powerful.

I'm completely drawn to his physicality. He isn't beautiful or handsome. Nico is too rugged to be described with those words. He's dangerous, chiseled, and raw. He is physically everything a man should be. Tall, broad, and lethal.

He leans his huge body against the doorframe, and my stomach clenches. The way he's staring at me, swallowing all of my features at once with his eyes, it's enough to melt me.

I want to blame the warm shower I just took or the cashmere sweater, but the truth is, my whole body feels hot, and I have the self-awareness to know that it's straight from the man in front of me. I want to jump into his arms. I want to scream at him for not contacting me, slamming my fists into his chest and cursing. I have a million questions, all beginning with, *Why?*

I blink, and a shiver runs down my spine.

The rational part of my brain shouts, *You're fucking insane, Elira! How can you heat up over a man who stole you? This isn't a boy at a frat party. This is a man, in all sense of the word. The boss of the Mafia Shqiptare!*

And—*oh shit.*

His black eyes narrow, straight white teeth clenching. A jitter moves through my body.

You're not here to rekindle a friendship. You've been taken against your will. You were drugged. Dragged. Forced into this ... place. You've got to get the hell out of here!

My eyes flit past him, but he immediately notices because his callous hand grips my wrist, knowing I've got plans to bolt.

Terror should be choking me right now. Instead, the ballsy girl within my chest yells, "You stole me? Fuck you!"

I try to yank my hand away, but his heavy grip only tightens. He isn't letting me go, but his refusal only fuels my determination. I try to fling my body side to side. I try to spit in his face, but his left hand pushes my head down, so my saliva winds up on the floor. Next, I lift a knee in an attempt to get him in the balls. He pulls his body backward, so I can't reach him.

"Motherfucker," I shout, sweating, my voice turning ragged.

I scream again, my damp braid flying in every direction.

This time, he lets go of my wrist but grips my shoulders, shaking me. "Stop it, Elira. Enough."

Like a woman on a rampage, I lift a hand and slap him straight across the face. The sound is so loud, it's shocking. Never in my life have I actually hit someone before. My jaw drops. His eyes widen before he starts to chuckle, slow and deep. He's laughing at me!

"You've got fire. Most women in your position would be crying in a corner. I can't say I'm surprised." The look in his eyes tells me he's giving me a compliment.

I try not to cringe at the red mark splattered across his cheek.

I grit my teeth and dig my feet into the floor. That's when he brings me straight into his broad chest. It's not a hug but a move meant to keep me frozen. He's hard—everywhere. I can feel the outline of his dick against my leg, and I suck in a hard breath.

Oh shit.

He whispers into my ear, "Don't ever forget whose world you're in —mine." His words are menacing, but his body is so hot and hard. "My world, my rules," he breathes, a minty heat. "The next time I send a request for you to wait, you stay right where you are. You don't move a muscle."

Shit. It was him who wanted to speak with me. Well, he could have come out himself and said hello. Not tell one of his underlings to make me wait there, all alone. I open my mouth, ready to give him a comeback, when his phone vibrates.

He lets me go and pulls a phone from the back of his pants pocket. Before answering, he lifts a finger to my face. "Don't. Fucking. Move."

He turns away from me and lifts the phone to his ear, snapping, "Do you think this is a game?" He paces the carpeted hallway, taking five steps away from me, pivoting, and then taking five steps toward me. His voice barely moves above standard volume as he strides forward and back, listening to whoever is on the other end of the line. "I will have my boys on your ass within twenty-four hours if that shipment doesn't make it. Just complete your end of the bargain." I can see his chest vibrating with rage as he listens to whoever is on the other end of the line. "I'm a man of my word, and I always deliver on my promises. Do you hear me? Good. Now, get my shit over here before I have a reason to rip your fucking head off."

If I were the person on the other end of the line, I'd be pissing myself right now. Hell, I'm not even the recipient of Nico's wrath, and I feel the nerves fluttering in my own stomach. Still, he's so sexy that every hormone in my body tunes into him. There's nothing all-American about this man. No picket fence in his future. No two-point-five kids or a dog. Nico is dark. He's also written into my history. Changed the course of my life. I shiver.

He slides the phone into his back pocket before cracking his knuckles. His vibe changes from maniac to gentleman in a nanosecond.

I swallow hard and think, *What. The. Fuck?*

He stares at me.

My eyes reply, *Why did you take me? Why didn't you just reach out to me? I would have come.*

With a different type of man, playing the scared, innocent girl might be the route. But not with this one. I always had the mouth I have, and Nico knew it better than anyone. I was a good girl, but I always had trouble with my temper. With the way Nico's looking at me now, I can tell he expects some bite. Hell, he seems to want it with the expectant gleam in his eyes. I do my best to stand taller, but inside, I feel like I'm shrinking. I'm scared. Nervous. Turned on.

"Let's go." He tips his head toward the hallway.

I look behind me at the bedroom and then in front of me, where all I can see is a dimly lit hallway.

I've been kidnapped, I think.

I'm in an unfamiliar space. Sure, he's gorgeous, and I used to know him well. But I don't know anything about him now. I hate to admit it, but I'm afraid to leave this room.

"Go where?" I demand, my voice shaking. "And w-what am I doing here?" My voice comes out stronger than it has any right to be. "I haven't seen you in years, and now, you steal me, drug me, and drag me to your ... whatever this place is." I'm opening my big mouth to this utterly powerful man who could have me killed and buried with a snap of his fingers. Am I insane?

He looks amused. "We'll sit in my kitchen. Eat something. And I'll tell you what will happen."

There is no room for negotiation, but I refuse to let that stand.

"Listen, I have to get out of here." My voice comes out between a beg and a cry. Every fantasy I've ever harbored for this man makes me feel like an utter idiot. I need to go home. Tears threaten to escape.

"No." He raises his dark brows, stepping into the doorway and blocking my path. His black molasses eyes flash with an emotion I cannot catch.

"Yes!" I stress. "I want to go home. You don't have to hurt me or force me to stay here. If you need to talk to me, talk. And then I'll leave."

He steps closer to me, menacing. "You aren't going anywhere until I say so. Do you understand me?" His voice is cold and final.

Common sense tells me, for the sake of self-preservation, it's time to shut up and listen. This man is the last human on earth anyone with a brain would mess with. But, as usual, my mouth doesn't get the memo.

"I have nothing to do with you and this life. I just want to go home." An awkward breath breaks free from my lips before I ask, "Please?"

He tilts his head sideways and laughs. "You think you have nothing to do with this life? Your father ran the Kosovo Liberation Army. You've been watching this entire story unfold from the start. Don't act like this life is something you've never seen." He shakes his head side to side, eyeing me like he knows something I don't know.

"M-my friends and family will come looking for me." My voice breaks.

He stands up taller, a smirk lining his lips. "The boy you came with thinks you are with your brother. Agron is tied up at the moment. And your mother and best friend assume you're here in New York. No one is worried."

I blink. How does he know all of that?

I feel frantic, palms sweaty. "What are you, stalking me?"

A tic moves his throat. His face is so harsh, but the look in his gaze is anything but. I know that look. It's that old warmth he reserved just for me, but something new is there, too. A strange sensation fills my chest. A spot within that I didn't even realize was scarred pulses like a phantom pain. This man I loved with all my heart when I was just a child is back in front of me now. Why?

Suddenly, memories that grew foggy over time come back tenfold. His scent. His hands. His power. Desire, hot and slick, pools low in my belly.

Before I can question my mental stability, he laughs.

"I make it my business to know everything about everyone I work with."

"Huh?" I'm confused over what he's responding to.

"You asked if I stalked you?" He smirks again, as if he knows where my head went.

I shut my eyes, embarrassed. Oh, fuck that. I'm not letting him take over my emotions. I refocus and take a slow, deep breath. This man stole me. History or no history, I'm essentially his prisoner right now. I can't be fantasizing about him!

"We don't work together, and we never will. Maybe I understood this life once. But I'm American now. I'm done with my past." I steel myself.

"Sure you are. Come," he states plainly, as though he's done with the conversation. He turns to move but then pauses, looking back at me. "And don't even try to run. This entire place is fortified. And even with all the security I've got, if you were to get away, I'd scour the ends of the earth to find you," he threatens.

I'm completely struck in a way I've never felt before. I don't trust it.

I follow him through the wide, carpeted hallway. The walls are painted a light, dusty gray. My thoughts are rampant. A small headache starts up in my skull as a memory flings itself to the forefront of my mind.

I was four. Father was on a business trip. My mother was weeping, and my fever wouldn't settle. Agron watched us from the corner of my room. My bed was soaked with sweat. Nico lifted me from the bed, asking why he hadn't been called. He ordered my mother to change me out of my drenched pajamas and to change the sheets. She did as she had been told before calling him back. He brought me downstairs, my head resting on his chest. All I could process was the feeling of safety. Placing me near the sink, he turned on the cold water and let it run against my toes. He brought the water into his large hands and rinsed my legs and arms, one limb at a time. When he pressed a wet towel against my head, I shook like a dry leaf.

"I did that already, Nico. It isn't working," my mother cried.

Nico gave her a look that silenced her. He had her bring more towels. He stood over me, rinsing my hot body until I passed out.

The next morning, I woke up in my own bed, feeling weak but no longer sick.

In fact, I remember feeling famished. Nico was near me, sleeping in a chair beside the bed. I thought he'd saved my life.

Maybe my memory is faulty. Maybe I was delusional. Is this really the same man?

He walks ahead of me now, moving as though he's hardwired for confidence and strength. No matter what, he'll prevail.

My thoughts are paused when I'm brought into a huge kitchen, the scent of food from home hitting my nose, reminding me of how hungry I am. It has been years since my mom or I cooked authentic Albanian cuisine. We're just so busy. Days spent cooking are behind us.

The kitchen itself is all white and gray marble with stainless steel appliances. The oven is painted a shiny blue. It's gorgeous.

Nico nods his head toward a circular glass table, and I take a seat. He glides into the chair in front of me when two women enter the kitchen. They're wearing maid uniforms, except black pants and button-down shirts instead of dresses. White aprons are tied to their backs. It's only moments before clean glass plates are set in front of us along with silverware. The women barely raise their heads as they fill the table with plates of food. Fresh bread is set beside a bowl of tarator—a yogurt and cucumber dish mixed with salt, olive oil, garlic, and herbs. It was my father's favorite summer food. After his death, my mother couldn't bring herself to see it anymore, much less make it. Kackavall, a fried cheese dish, is set down next. And then Albanian-style meze, which is a selection of hard-boiled eggs, cured meat, and cooked vegetable salads.

"I'm sure you're starving. Elena told me you were sick to your stomach. That wouldn't have happened if you'd just taken the medicine I gave you." He gestures for me to take food, body language serious, hard, and not to be messed with.

I fill my plate. He follows suit. We sit in silence, passing the dishes between us. Silently, I take a sip of the drink beside me, a wineglass filled to the rim. It's a delicious white. I've never had wine from anything but a box, and yet my palate knows this shit is good.

"So," he starts, "I have you here in my home."

"Yes," I reply, my smart mouth open. "You had your goons steal me, remember?"

He chuckles at my attitude. "True. But that's because you didn't follow directions. You were supposed to wait. But you ran."

"Yeah, well, I have nothing to do with all of this." I lift my hand, waving it in the air and gesturing around me.

He hums. "You're in college. Studying finance."

"That's right." Now, it's my turn to nod my head. I've worked my ass off to get to where I am, and I'm proud.

"You were always good with numbers."

I swallow hard. He is finally admitting to our shared history. "Yes, I was. I am."

He places a hand over his heart, absently rubbing. "It's your brother," he says matter-of-factly. "But you probably knew that already."

My stomach drops. Agron.

"It seems he's been stealing from some of my associates." His voice is completely devoid of any feeling. "He was dealing for them and keeping a little bit of product for himself. Sometimes, he used it; other times, he sold it. But after a while, people began to notice. He ran to the Shqipe for help."

I want to blink, but I cannot move.

"I gave him the money to pay those debts. And now, I'm the one he owes. I figured I could use him to do some small-time work, get my money back that way." He takes a sip of his wine, completely unfazed. "And then I hear, Agron wants a firm spot in my world. Gave one of my men a whole story that the Mafia Shqiptare is where he's meant to be.

"As we both know, your brother has always been a loose cannon. Arguably, untrustworthy. I knew him when he was a kid, but I'm a firm believer that people don't change." He stops speaking, continuing to dig into his food.

Meanwhile, I'm worried mine is going to come back up. Hearing this about my brother isn't a surprise, but it's painful nonetheless.

I take another sip of my wine, hoping it will calm me or at least give the illusion I'm relaxed. Unfortunately, my hand trembles, and the glass shakes, giving me away. Nico notices, of course.

He clears his throat, putting his fork down. "There is something I need from you. And if you give me what I want, I'll protect your brother from the other gangs by giving him a spot in the Shqipe. You do not have to agree to the arrangement. But if you do, there is no end to it until I decide it's over." He settles into a forward-lean position, big arms resting on the glass table and shirtsleeves pulled up to the center of his strong, corded forearms. Everything about him, from his body language to his words, spells dominance.

I open and then shut my mouth.

Nico looks me up and down, his gaze stormy and hot.

Is Nico going to ask me for sex? It wouldn't be unheard of in these crazy circles. But I have a limit, and whoring myself out for the sake of my brother is a no-go. No. Impossible. Never.

"What I need is simple," he continues casually, the look in his eyes extinguished. "There is a new family I'm aiming to do business with. They're the type who like to work with men who are ... settled down. I know how loyal you are to your word. We share a language and customs. You will act as my wife when I request it."

"I have school." I lick my lips. I can't let go of my future. Not for Agron and not for anyone. I won't!

"You can go back for your studies"—he nods—"finish your degree. But when I call, you must come."

"This arrangement," I start, pointing between himself and me, "it's just for public purposes, r-right? Nothing private you're expecting or illegal?" I can't help my stutter. I want to stay strong in the face of all of this, but it's getting difficult.

Nico looks over my shoulder, and I turn my head, finding no one behind me. When I refocus on him, he's fuming. He knows what I'm insinuating.

He grits his teeth. "You aren't my whore, Elira. And I'm not going to ask you to do my dirty work either." His eyes are hard.

Is he offended?

"Take my proposal at face value." He finishes his drink. His huge hand places the delicate crystal glass on the table. "There is no hidden agenda. You pretend to be my wife, come when I call you, and act as I expect, and in return, I will bring your brother into my fold, making sure that no outsider kills him. If you walk away, he's on his own."

"He wants to work for you. He will do a good job for you." I swallow hard.

He cocks his head to the side, like he's calling bullshit. "Agron's best asset is that he is related to you."

I shift, but the weight of my body feels like it's doubled. "And if he's within the Shqipe, the other groups won't be able to touch him?"

"That's right."

Quiet descends upon our discussion, but my mind shrieks. The skeptical part of me is on questioning overdrive. "What kind of events would be required of me?"

He takes another bite of food. "We'd travel. Dinners. Things like that."

I wait to hear more, things along the lines of dungeons and sex slave, but thankfully, it doesn't come. "So, all I have to do is pretend we're married?"

He nods. "Yes. Exactly."

"But what about when this business thing you need me for is complete? What will happen to Agron then?"

His lips quirk up. "You're very loyal, Elira."

"He's my brother." What else can I say? I want and need Agron to stay safe and alive. This is clearly his best shot.

"We'll cross that bridge when it comes. I would take this offer then if you are so keen on making sure he stays out of trouble."

"You'll swear to that?"

"My oath is my bond."

I know he's telling the truth. For people like us, honor is everything.

I wait for him to elaborate some more, but he doesn't. Surprisingly, I feel my nose twitch. I was expecting him to mention something, anything, about *before*. About what we had. But he doesn't. And I'm not about to either. I just want to get the hell out of here. I want to go back in time and tell myself not to have that damn cigarette. I wish I'd flagged Jack down when he was circled by those girls and claimed him for myself. Instead, I made one fucking choice, and now, here I am, in front of Nico, my life on crazy ground.

"It's late." Nico shifts in his chair. "You'll stay tonight and think. Tomorrow morning, give me your answer. Regardless of what you choose, I'll have my car bring you back to school." He stands up, twisting the fancy gold watch around his wrist. "When you're finished eating, Maria will bring you back to your room."

"I want to leave tonight." Some of my bravado from before is gone. Beneath the strong girl is plain me—a college kid from Tobeho. Here is the last place I want to stay.

"Until I have your answer, you aren't allowed to take one step out of my sight." He stands up to his full menacing height, and in this moment, he truly scares me. He doesn't give a shit about what we had —that much is clear.

I force myself upright, refusing to cower.

Seemingly satisfied, he walks away.

"What an asshole," I curse under my breath.

He snaps, "What did you call me?" His stubborn jaw gives him a stony expression.

My stomach drops to my knees.

"Something to remember." He saunters back to where I sit. "I will not be seen with a woman who doesn't look polished or well-raised. I know who you are and where you come from. Act like the woman you ought to be or forget the deal." And with those final cutting words, he's gone.

I gasp. What a dick!

He exits, and I inhale the rest of the food.

So good.

The truth is, I can't even remember the last time I ate this well. That, plus the stress I'm under, has me ravenous. Natalie is one of those blessed *I'm too nervous to eat* types. Unfortunately, I'm more of a *where the hell is that cookie dough* type. So long as I'm chewing, I can delay my thoughts. When there isn't even a morsel left on the plate, I see an older lady waiting for me. I assume she's Maria.

"I'm finished," I tell her politely, squeezing my hands together.

"Follow me," she says brusquely.

She is wearing black pants and white shirt, dark hair in a tight bun, slicked back with gel. I'd say she is around my mother's age.

While she isn't friendly in the least, I wouldn't be me if I didn't at least try to get some information from her.

"So, Maria, how long have you worked here?" I slow down my pace, wanting to be with her as long as possible.

"Six years," she replies easily.

My ears perk up. She's willing to speak!

"Is Nico a good boss?" It's a very forward question, but I don't have more than another handful of steps left to go before I'm back in jail—also known as the bedroom.

"He is very fair." She continues to walk at a slow pace. "The way I grew up in Mexico, this life is not new to me. Nico is ..."

I lean in, waiting for more.

"Nico has high expectations. If you meet them, he is content. If you don't, well, that's a different story." She shrugs her shoulders, as if to say, *It is what it is.*

"And does he have a girlfriend?" The question leaves my mouth before I have time to think. I want to backtrack. "Not that it matters, of course."

She smiles knowingly. "Nico has many women but no *woman.*"

I stop walking down the hallway. I know once I'm back in that room, there will be no way out. I want to know where I am. "A-are we in the Bronx?"

There are Albanian neighborhoods on either side of East Fordham Road—Pelham Parkway on one side and the Belmont section on the other. My mother has some friends who immigrated to both of those ends. She loves to visit them because she can pick up copies of *Illyria,* the Albanian newspaper.

"You're in Manhattan. You'll see where you are when you leave."

I glance down at my black ballet flats. I need to ask her more, but I'm not even sure where to go from here.

She puts a hand on my shoulder. "Nico is not a nice man. He is very hard. Very strong. Very commanding. But if you do right by him, he will always treat you fairly."

"Okay then."

She opens the bedroom door. A set of lace and silk pajama shorts and a matching camisole sit on the bed. "Thank you, Maria."

"There is water for you on the nightstand and two pills. Nico requests you take them right away." The door closes behind her.

I'm all alone, I think. I raise my head to the ceiling corners. *Are there cameras?* None that I can see.

So, I do what any normal girl would do in this situation. I start tearing the room apart, trying to find something, anything. What I'm looking for, I don't have a clue. A key? A photograph? I'll take anything.

I slide my hands beneath the mattress, which might be ten times the thickness of mine at home. Damn, it's heavy! Crawling beneath the bed, there's barely even a speck of dust. I open up the drawers in the dresser cabinets, and they are empty but lined with navy paper that smells like fresh linen. I'm sweating by the time I reach the bathroom, opening up anything that will open.

When I'm done, I reenter the bedroom and plop on the carpeted floor. The only thing I've learned from my search is that whoever cleans this room is immaculate. I stand up, walking back to the door. I press down on the handle for good measure, but I can't open it. Locked. I recheck the window. It's bolted.

With my hands on my hips, I pivot, staring at the beautiful pajamas left for me. It dawns on me that if I wear them, it could mean that I've accepted his offer. Will I? Must I? I drop my head in my hands, wanting to cry. Tears threaten, tickling my nose. How much sacrifice must I make for my brother? I know my mother doesn't want me in this life. But what option do I have? And it's not like Nico said he'd hurt me, kill me, or even physically use me.

I'm angry. Furious! I don't need or want this shit right now! I want to be a normal American college kid. I want to do well in school and go out with Natalie and date Jack. I don't want to be wrapped up in the fucking Albanian Mafia! The tears fall, and I don't even bother to stop them.

Nico isn't a stranger. I knew him once—and not just his face or his name. Sure, I knew his full lips and slashing dark eyebrows. Even as a kid, I recognized his physical dominance, which has clearly grown with time and age. Nico was strong then, but he seems to be reinforced and hardened now. I also always knew that he was the type of man others could only try to mirror. His outside is all strength and fearlessness and intellect. The type who'd run into a burning building if there was something inside larger than himself to save. And within, Nico is absolute honor and the purest of love. And if others didn't see it back then, it's because he didn't allow just anyone to look inside him. Maybe it was because I was just a child and he wasn't afraid of letting me in. But I was there and I saw him. Really, really saw him. I know who he is. Or at least, I used to know. *Is he the same man now?*

For years, I dreamed of him coming into my bedroom and taking me away. Not that my life was horrible or painful, but life with Nico ... I thought it was my destiny. He'd lift me in those arms of his, apologizing for not coming sooner. I had the whole scenario planned out in my head with ten years' worth of dreams to support its validity. Instead, he drugged and stole me. Gave me an ultimatum, of all things, to pretend to be his wife! To pretend to be the one thing I used to dream of.

Life makes no sense anymore. Sadness, like a torrent, swirls in my head. I don't know how this choice will affect my future. The tension within myself coils.

I have to put my feelings aside. This is a business arrangement where I'd spend time with him, and in exchange, he'd protect my brother. It' be nothing more. Maybe I shouldn't think about it any deeper than that. I would go to dinners with him. Call him honey maybe? Take a vacation? I've barely ever gone anywhere before. Maybe it would be nice to go away. Maybe it doesn't have to be complicated. Eventually, he wouldn't need me to be his wife anymore. And by then, Agron would be firmly embedded within the Shqipe. He'd have proven himself and be a full-fledged member. It'd be okay.

I touch the beautiful, silky sleepwear, noticing my nails are short and undone. I'm sure he'd expect me to be presentable in the way an Albanian man likes. And believe me, I know their type. Tits and ass.

Makeup and the works. Not girls who listen to heavy-metal grunge and work in shitty diners. This life of his couldn't be further from the woman I am.

I have to ask myself, *Why is he asking me, of all people, to do this?*

The silk is so delicate. It's something I'd never wear. I lift up the camisole, chucking it into the corner. I'd rather sleep nude than sit in clothes bought for me by a thug. I laugh, loving how throwing his shit gives me some control. So, I do just that. I strip myself, balling each expensive piece and strewing it around the room. Nude, I decide to take the medicine because I don't want another headache. I might want to kill Nico right now, but I'm not willing to hurt myself. Finally, I climb into the *God only knows how many million thread count* sheets, curling atop the most comfortable mattress I've ever lain on. It only takes a few minutes for me to fall blissfully under. But not before I curse out my brother and Nico.

"Fuck them," I grumble into the pillow.

6

I WAKE UP WITH A START, THINKING, *WHERE THE HELL AM I?*

"Shit," I groan, throwing an arm over my eyes.

When I finally sit up, I pause and scan the room. Unfortunately, none of it was a dream.

I have to give him my answer this morning, but first, I'm going to enjoy that shower again. And this time, without an audience. I look beneath the covers and am reminded that I'm completely nude. I stand up, bringing the sheets with me. Not that anyone is here for me to hide from, but if there is a camera somewhere, I'd rather not give a free show.

The shower is hot and perfect. When I'm finished, I remove a towel from a drawer below the sink. It's perfectly warm. Hot even. How is this possible? After wrapping myself, I squat down to take a closer look. That's when I notice the temperature field to the left. Holy shit, it's a towel-warming drawer! Seriously, whoever made that thing up is genius.

Next, I remove the blow-dryer and brush. Since I pulled the room apart last night, I know where everything is. When I'm done, I put the jeans and sweater back on. I make a mental note to ask where my dress went. It isn't mine, and I'll need to get it dry-cleaned before I give it back. I can only pray it's salvageable.

Moving to the bedroom door, I'm pleasantly surprised to see it isn't locked. I'm about to step out when a huge guy steps in front of me. I let out a yelp.

"Don't worry," he says in Albanian. "I'll just bring you to the kitchen."

In English, I tell him, "I can make my own way. It's down one hall to get to the kitchen. I don't need an escort."

Nico must really think I would bolt. It makes me feel good to know that he recognizes I'm not some docile woman.

"Boss's orders," he replies again in Albanian, shrugging casually. He isn't being aggressive.

I want to argue, but then again, what's the point?

I roll my eyes but follow him down. When I get to the kitchen, I find the table filled with all kinds of fresh breakfast items. It's a buffet fit for a king. Waffles, pancakes, fruits, yogurts, and fresh cheeses. My eyes widen while my mouth starts watering.

"Coffee?"

I raise my head, and there he is, sitting at the marble counter with a newspaper in his hands. He's so ridiculously hot; it stops my breath. He's casual in a pair of dark jeans and a black T-shirt. His hair is wet and spiky, like he just got out of the shower. I knew he was gorgeous last night, but now and in the light of day, I'm floored. The strange thing is, I know it's not just his looks causing this reaction in me. He's everything I know in my heart he still is despite the fact that I haven't seen him in years. I had a million questions last night about the man he is today. But my gut knows him.

Nico raises his brows, waiting for an answer. He lifts the mug, shaking it side to side.

"Yes." My voice comes out scratchy. "Yes," I repeat, clearer.

I shuffle my feet, wishing I'd had access to my makeup this morning before seeing him. He looks freaking amazing, and I look exhausted, as though I was stolen and drugged. Oh, yeah, I was actually stolen and drugged. This whole situation is just too fucked up.

He pours a mug full from a silver carafe. It steams. He slides it across the counter to where I stand. Either he knows I take my coffee plain and black or he doesn't want to be bothered to ask. Regardless, this is good. I'll say no to a lot of things but never coffee. I help myself to the seat next to him when he points to the kitchen table behind us.

"Scrambled eggs and cucumber tomato salad. Take."

He doesn't have to ask me twice. If this is prisoner fare, I wouldn't mind being jailed from time to time. My mom and I always eat well enough, and now that I work at the diner, it's not like I ever go hungry. But this isn't just food. It's gourmet. I happily fill up my plate, not caring about how it might look. I'm a woman. I eat. Surprise!

I sit back down and take my first sip of coffee when he clears his throat.

"As much as I hate to interrupt your breakfast"—his eyes move from my full plate to my eyes—"I'm waiting for your answer."

He pulls a cigarette from his pack of Marlboros, lighting up. I hate how sexy he looks, smoking. Licking his lips and relaxing.

I clear my throat. "What will I need to know about you, husband? Details of how we met maybe?" I take a bite of a warm butter croissant and try to focus on that instead of him.

He inhales his smoke deeply and exhales slowly, looking like Marlon Brando in one of those 1950s films. The way he holds the cigarette with his thumb and forefinger. I try to focus on my food to keep myself from gawking.

"Nothing," he replies, licking his lips. "I'll answer any questions that have to do with us. But if you're in a situation where you must say something, tell the truth. We met back in Kosovo. I knew your family. And then we reunited here, years later."

Now, it's my turn to quirk a brow. "Oh, we knew each other, did we? How interesting. And here I was, thinking you had amnesia."

He laughs, shaking his head. "I remember. You were a cute kid back then. Not sure what happened since."

My jaw drops from his insult, but then he grins, a playful, full-on, sexy-as-hell smile. He looks so much younger right now.

He shifts his body and takes another sip of his coffee. "There's one more thing."

"Yeah?" I sit up. Is this where the ball drops? *Sex slaves, dungeons, and—*

"There can be no other man in your life. In the world I'm in, loyalty is everything. If you're going to act as my wife, there cannot be an implication that you are stepping out of our marriage."

"Well ..." I pause, my mouth opening and closing like a fish.

Jack's face flashes before my eyes. I exhale. This sucks. This really, really sucks. Sure, we didn't get that far. But maybe I would have liked to explore that.

I swallow hard as he says, "If you can't agree—"

"You have my word." My family comes first, and Agron's safety is my priority.

He nods before standing up. "I'll reach out to you."

I'm unsure if he's going to shake my hand or what. He steps so close to me until there are only centimeters between us. I can smell his soapy scent. Nico kisses one of my cheeks and then the other. It's whisper soft and slow. He smells so warm.

"Maria will meet you here and give you details on how you're returning home." And then he's gone.

I finish my plate and coffee when Maria comes back into the kitchen.

"The car is waiting for you out front."

I hop off the chair. "Do you know where my clothes are? The ones I came in."

She hands me a large silver-gray bag that looks like a soft leather shopping tote. "It's all been dry-cleaned."

I clutch it to my chest in relief. "Thank you so much." I peek inside, and everything is here—from my shoes and Natalie's dress to my purse. I rummage around to find my wallet and phone, safely intact beneath the clothes, and think, *Thank God.* "Do you want the bag back? I can put everything in a plastic bag."

She chuckles. "No, sweetheart. It's yours now."

I take a look at the tag inside—Goyard. I've never heard of it.

The car ride back to campus is uneventful but extremely comfortable. When I'm a huge banker in New York City, making a million dollars a year, I'll have to buy myself a Mercedes like this one.

As far as this situation with Nico goes, I plan on living my normal life, and when he calls me, it will be nothing more than a small detour in my otherwise straight-as-an-arrow life. I can handle this.

What about my mother though? Should I tell her? I already know what her answer will be, and telling her would only add to her stress. Plus, her back pain is already triggered by stressful events.

A few months ago, when Agron left the house? Her back went out. When the plant shut down and she wasn't sure what she would do for work? Her back went out then, too. The last thing she needs to know about is my involvement with Nico and the Mafia Shqiptare.

I get home to find my mother drinking tea in the kitchen. For a moment, I question whether I should withhold this information. I hate lying, especially to my mother. But when I see her rubbing her back, I decide my initial thoughts are the right ones.

"Hey, Mama!" I exclaim.

She moves her hands to the table, forcing a smile. She's wearing a set of freshly pressed pink scrubs, the uniform for The Campus Cleaning Company, so she must be going to work today.

"How are you? And your back?" I take a seat beside her.

"It's great," she lies.

Like mother, like daughter, I think.

"Going to do the afternoon shift today."

"Are you sure you're up to it?"

"I'm all good. Told you, I just needed some time. And I even lost a few pounds. A small gift for my suffering." She shifts in her seat, clenching her teeth while refusing to show pain. "How was New York?" She makes no eye contact when she asks, instead lifting the paper in front of her eyes.

Luckily for me, her preoccupation with her own lie is a simple cover for mine.

"It was fun. Great even. I've got lots of studying to do today, so if you need me, I'll be in my room." I stand up to leave.

"I put some meat and potatoes in the Crock-Pot for dinner."

"Great."

THE NEXT TWO weeks are spent studying, working, and occasionally hanging out with Natalie along with Jack and the band. Everything is smooth and simple. Jack hasn't mentioned the fact that I didn't show up or call him in New York. If he's disappointed, he doesn't show it.

Jack and I have been occasionally hanging out after our class together, just getting to know each other as friends. All I can do is pray he never makes a move because then I'd have to end what we've got going on. As of now, I can tell Nico with a straight face that I did nothing against his wishes. I'm allowed to have friends. Luckily, Jack is a lot less assertive than I first thought. Right now, he's safely in the friend zone where I can have my cake and eat it, too.

The best part of hanging out with Jack is that when we're together, I don't have to worry about the ever-looming Nico. I can just enjoy myself and act like a regular college kid. In other words, when I'm with Jack, it's time spent not stressing about Nico and when or if he'll call me.

The problem is, the moment—and I mean, *the moment*—Jack walks out of my sight, Nico barges into my brain. I shouldn't compare the two men because one has zero to do with the other. Nico is the king of the Mafia Shqiptare, a completely unattainable and danger-ous-as-all-hell man who I should run far, far away from. And Jack is the man for my college world—a cool, calm, and sexy musician. I'd be lying if I said that Jack makes my heart race in the way Nico does. Mafia aside, Nico knows me in a way Jack never could. He knows my history and my family. He knows parts of me I've never shared with anyone. And it's frightening to admit, but there are parts of my heart that only Nico can ever own. Anyway, Jack isn't pushing to be anything more than friends, and of course, neither am I.

It's Friday afternoon, which is a really busy time for both Jack and me. Either I'm working at the diner or studying and doing homework in the library, and he's always with the band. But last night, when he texted me to come listen to them practice, I jumped at the chance. I've been listening to their songs on the internet nonstop, and I'm totally in awe of them. I just know, deep in my gut, that they'll be huge one of these days.

Right now, I'm sitting on the floor of one of the studios in the music department and completing a Statistics assignment while the band is working out the kinks in a new song Jack wrote. It's taking me a lot longer than it should to complete the assignment because it's so interesting to watch; the whole process of completing a song is surprisingly tedious. I'm happy though. At this moment, listening to the band feels so surreal. The whole trouble with Nico feels like nothing more than a bad dream, and my life is just as it should be. Simple, American, organized, and—

My phone buzzes, and I jump like I've been stung, hands turning sweaty. Is it him?

"Oh shit!" I shuffle through my gigantic new bag, cursing the fact that I can't find the phone. "Where is the fucking phone?"

Where the hell is it? I push through countless receipts from Target, my Kindle, an empty water bottle, my wallet, a tube of glossy lip oil, and finally find the phone. I glance at the screen and see *Agron*.

"Fuck," I curse, hanging my head. It's not Nico.

When I look up, the guys are all staring at me in silence.

"What has you so spooked? Shit. You'd think you were waiting for a call from the President of the United States. Level 10 anxiety." Scott shakes his head, laughing, his dark curls falling into his face.

"Spooked?" I chuckle as though his comment is funny while trying to settle my breathing. "Just—"

"Your brother." Jack pops the gum in his mouth.

He's annoyed. Hell, I'm annoyed, too. Anytime Jack and I are together, we can expect at least one call or text from Agron. But only because Agron is freaking out about my situation, losing his mind over my role as Nico's fake wife. I haven't given Jack any details about

Nico, of course, because, frankly, it's none of his business. He isn't my boyfriend.

I clear my throat, and the guys expectantly stare at me.

"Yeah." I scratch the back of my neck. "Just ... I need a few minutes." I stand up from the corner I was sitting in, wiping the back of my jeans, and leave their practice room without a backward glance.

I've got a parallel life happening right now that can't be ignored. And while I've done a good job of keeping thoughts of Nico at bay, every dream and moment that isn't spent actively ignoring him, he's in my thoughts. I should be thrilled that he hasn't contacted me yet. Instead, I'm just waiting with bated breath for him to just tell me what and where and when he needs me.

I can't remember a time when my nerves were more frayed. My stomach is so twisted in anxiety that it's become a black hole for food. Nothing I eat fills me up. I look down, expecting to see a bowling ball for a stomach. Luckily, it's still my same flat abdomen.

I lift my phone and dial Agron.

"Did he call you yet?" he asks in a rush.

"You're seriously crazy. Stop calling me. I'll let you know when he reaches out."

"I fucking hate how he has you under his thumb right now. Makes me sick. If he tries to touch you—"

"He hasn't even called," I huff, wishing I'd never told Agron about the deal. I couldn't *not* tell him though. What if there were a party and both Agron and I were there—him as a member and me as Nico's "wife"?

"Motherfucker thinks he can threaten my sister and use me as bait? Makes me sick!" he shouts into the phone.

"I'm doing it for you. To keep you safe—"

"I don't need you to do this, Elira. I can take care of myself. I can prove myself without my sister helping."

"Oh, is that right? You owe people, Agron. There's no other choice right now!"

He curses. "The second he calls you, I need to know."

I whisper-yell, "He could have hurt me when he took me. But he didn't, right?" I look left and right to make sure I'm alone. The last thing I need is for one of the guys in the band to overhear this conversation.

"The only thing keeping me sane right now is the fact that I know you're strong. If he ever touches you though, I'll shoot him in the face. Fuck the Shqipe!" I can hear his heavy breaths over the line. "I'll get him back for this, Elira."

"For the love of God, Agron, calm yourself. And never say those words. Do you have a death wish?" I look up at the ceiling, trying to stay calm. "Don't you realize I'm doing this for you? Keep yourself straight with your eye on the prize. You wanted to join them, right? Forget how you got in the door. Focus on the fact that you got your wish. Do right by the Shqipe. Eventually, I'll be out of this, and you'll be part of the family. Win-win." My heart palpitates.

Quietly, he says, "I just need to know you'll let me know when he calls you." His voice is eerily calm.

Without replying, I hang up the phone and lean my head against the wall. I used to see loyalty as a virtue. Now, I see that the kind I have for my brother is more like handcuffs and chains. Agron can never see past his own feet.

I hear the band laughing. That's where I should be right now. I haven't had a smoke in a few weeks, but I'm pissed off and shaky, and I feel like having one. I step out of the building and into a small pathway behind the music center. I pull out a cigarette from my emergency pack and light up. When I'm done, I drop it onto the floor, stepping on it with my sneaker.

I'm sufficiently calm. Well, sort of calm. I go back into the practice room and gather my things. I just want to go to my place and take a shower. After saying my awkward good-bye to Jack, I make my way back home. My phone buzzes again. This time, it's Natalie texting me, asking where I am. I tell her, and within a few minutes, she's next to me on the steps leading off campus.

"Where the hell have you been?" she asks accusingly.

We've been on different work schedules lately, which has sucked. Work is our time to catch up.

I rub my face. "I have so much to tell you. You seriously can't imagine."

I wasn't sure at first if I wanted to spill, but now that I see her, I can't possibly stay mum. I need my best friend right now. Badly.

"Wait." She stops walking, and I do, too. "What is this bag? Is it Goyard?"

"Oh, yeah." I look down at it. "I think that's what the tag said."

"Elira," she huffs. "That is, like, over a thousand dollars."

"Are you kidding me? It looks like a skinny leather shopping bag!" I pull it off me, examining how something this simple could be so expensive. Shit.

She laughs out loud. "It's true, my friend. How did you get it?"

"It's a long story," I grumble.

"I'm ready when you are," she states accusingly.

As we walk, I tell her every single detail from Nico being the love of my life as a child to how he smuggled me out of Albania. Then, how he disappeared on me once I got to America. Agron's connection to the Mafia Shqiptare. The party. Being stolen in New York City and the eventual business offer that followed.

For once in her life, Natalie seems completely speechless. Unfortunately, her quiet only lasts a few seconds. "So, you get to be the pretend wife of one of the most powerful men in the world?"

"Yes."

She jumps up and down. "We need to celebrate! This is incredible. Holy shit. I wonder where he'll take you. You'd better bring me along. And can we go to the bar for drinks? I feel like a celebration is in order," she sings.

I stop walking. "Wow. I think you need to slow down. Did you not hear what I told you?"

"Oh, I heard you all right. And the situation feels pretty clear to me. He loved you when you were a kid, as a kid. But now, you're an adult, and he's an adult. You are his solace and always were! It's so fucking romantic."

I shake my head. "This isn't a soap opera or one of those romance novels you're obsessed with where the dangerous bad boy falls in love. It's life."

"Life, schmife," she rhymes.

We get to McGrady's, a bar off-campus. Natalie and I prefer this spot because it's old and shitty, and we can get completely drunk off our asses for under ten bucks. The waitresses here are also really cool, always sliding free drinks our way. But we hook them up when they come to the diner, so I don't feel bad about taking.

"The Shqipe isn't some make-believe group," I admonish. "Do you understand what they do?"

Natalie is awesome and all about the living and loving free, but she was raised in upper-class Manhattan with two parents who each have prestigious jobs. They went to college and graduate school and make sure the maintenance and mortgage and taxes are always paid on time. She herself went to the best private schools in New York City. She grew up firm and confident. Normally, I'm in awe of her strength. But right now, I can feel the disconnect between us. To her, the Mafia is a fictional group on a hot Netflix show. To me, it's a real, tangible entity.

When I open up the bar's wooden door, the smell of stale beer assaults me. Drake sings "God's Plan" over the speakers. How fitting. I internally roll my eyes.

She counters, "Sure, I know what the Mafia does." She takes a seat at one of the wooden booths in the back, and I slide in across from her. "They kill people and deal drugs and all that. Sell organs maybe? A kidney or whatever. By the way, you know you don't need more than one kidney." She pushes her tongue into her cheek.

My eyes widen, and she starts cracking up. Seriously, what kind of best friend do I have?

She continues, "Look, I know this shit is crazy. I mean, the man is willing to do whatever it takes to get what he wants. You ran away from him at the party, and he stole you back. But if you already accepted his proposition, why not go ahead and enjoy it? Seriously, I don't even see the downside. You're young enough to enjoy this without affecting chances of marriage and kids and all that. And anyway, you have to protect your shithead brother. Oh, I'd love to see what the Mafia life is like! As a bystander, of course. Like a fly on the wall. A beautiful fly, not the kind you want to swat. I'd take fake wife, too, if it was offered to me."

Candice, one of the bartenders, stops over to our table. "What do you ladies want today? Pretty early to be drinking, no?"

She skeptically looks between us, and I don't blame her. The only patrons here right now are the old drunkards who spend their days wallowing in sorrows.

Natalie peps up, smiling. "Do you have champagne or something? We're in a celebratory mood."

She quirks up a brow, and I can't help but chuckle. I don't want to laugh because nothing about this is funny, but Natalie is lightening the situation some, and part of me wants to let her.

"I got something good." Candice smiles, walking away. A few moments later, she returns with a cold bottle of champagne tucked beneath her arm.

"Where'd you find this?" Natalie says excitedly as Candice sets two flutes in front of us.

"For the special customers." She pops the cork and pours us each a full glass. The bubbles spring to the top. "Enjoy, ladies."

Natalie lifts her glass as Candice steps away. "I know that you're overwhelmed. Let's just get shit-faced right now. When you can't see straight sober, getting drunk will help you see things clearly!"

So, we do just that. I drink two glasses of champagne, one after the other. It doesn't take long for the room to sway.

"Seeing straight now?" Natalie giggles, leaning forward against our table. "How dangerous is Nico? And how hot is he?"

"He's ridiculously gorgeous." I imagine his body. So powerful. When I bring my gaze back to her, she's smirking. "He'd never hurt me. But he-he hurt others. I know he did. But he had to. The Kosovo Liberation Army was a guerrilla force. They rebelled against Serbian domination. In the end, even though the Serbs displaced over ninety percent of our population, the KLA managed to win our freedom. Nico won it for us. They did what they had to do to gain independence. Violence was just ... the way."

"I don't know," she starts, sitting back. "On one hand, I'm afraid for you. But on the other, I'm like ... hell yes! He doesn't expect you to do anything illegal, right?"

I shake my head. "No. But no other men—"

"Oh, that sucks. Jack was cool." She raises her cup. "Good-bye, Jack!"

"You're crazy," I mumble, knocking our glasses before taking a huge gulp.

"What I'm confused about is—and don't take this the wrong way —why you out of all the other potential women? I mean, sure, you're gorgeous and smart. But a man like him probably always does things with thought and calculation. Why you? Why Elira?"

"I've asked myself that, too. There are tons of Albanian girls who'd give their right tit to be his arm candy and pretend to be his wife. Why steal and drug me and then put his foot on my throat by using Agron?"

"Let me think." She pauses, taking another sip of her champagne. "You'd be his fake wife. Not real." Natalie glances up to the ceiling, as though a big idea is forming. "So, if it ever came to it, a person who isn't his wife might be forced to testify against him in court." Her eyes come back to me, sparkling. "For all you know, he's being watched. And if you're seen with him, then you'll be watched, too. This worries me."

"I'd never speak out against him. I just wouldn't." My jaw drops open as the truth hits me. "I guess that's why he wanted me to be the wife!" It's like a eureka moment. "In Albanian culture, when you give someone your *besa*—or your trust—it's like a code of honor. By agreeing to not give details of what I hear and see, he knows I wouldn't tell a court what I saw or heard. Other girls might swear it, but he trusts me. He trusts my word because ... he knows me. Another woman, he couldn't be so sure."

"And let me guess. You were tough as nails with him?"

I nod.

"So, you proved to him what you're made of. You showed your strength, and you showed your loyalty by how far you'd go for your brother. Who else could he trust as his acting wife? Of course you'll hear tons of illegal shit while you're at his side. Another woman would gab. She'd get scared and fold. Or both. But not you."

"Oh God." I drop my head in my hands, groaning. "You're a genius, Nat."

She pours us the last of the champagne.

"This is why we should always talk. Because we come up with the best ideas together." She shrugs her shoulders.

"Okay, so now what?" I bite my bottom lip.

"Now what?" she repeats my question as though it is the dumbest thing she's ever heard. "You pretend to be his wife and enjoy the shit out of it—that's what. You've already agreed, and your brother's safety is on the line. There's no taking it back. And if you had to ever testify, my mom would counsel you. My only request is that, secretly, you tell me every dirty detail. I want to know about the guns, the drama, and of course, his dick size."

My laughter could probably be heard from a mile away! I'm about to reply when my phone buzzes on the table. My eyes, like laser beams, zero in.

"It's him!" I squeal. My hands shake as I lift the phone, reading the texts.

Nico: My credit card is on file for you at Bergdorf. Go shopping.
Nico: Dinner Saturday night.
Me: You can pick me up from 525 Fifth Street, Apt 6E

I gave him Natalie's address. If my mom saw him, she'd freak. I hate lying to her. But telling her would only bring her unnecessary anxiety. Anyway, it's not a lie. More like an omission.

My stomach drops low, eyes widening. I'm shocked. I'm scared. Hell, I'm excited. Did I really just tell him to pick me up? I can't deny the fact that he's gorgeous and powerful and rich and I'm about to play make-believe with the kingpin of the Mafia Shqiptare!

"Give me." Natalie grabs the phone out of my hands like a starved animal searching for food. She reads the texts, mouth smiling so widely that I'm afraid she might break her face, and then she finally shrieks, "Holy shit. Holy fucking shit! We're going shopping!"

I find myself yelling with my best friend in excitement. We both stand up, jumping up and down together like we just won the lotto. The bartenders are laughing, not understanding what is going on, and frankly, neither do I. All I know is, I'm about to embark on a crazy journey.

7
_____

To save money on parking, Natalie and I decided to take the bus to New York City. The entire ride was spent with each of us listening to music through our earbuds and staring out the window. I'm comfortable in a pair of loose, wide-leg jeans and a white T-shirt tucked in. I also found this cool silver-and-gold-studded belt that I decided to wear for this momentous shopping occasion. If we're shopping at these fancy places, I figured I should try to look laid-back but fashionable. Natalie is dressed in a black jersey dress that she calls her potato sack dress. It's so unsexy that it's sexy, showing off her shoulder tattoo and the outline of her amazing, curvy body.

Entering the famous department store Bergdorf Goodman, I feel like I've been dropped into an alternate universe, complete with the fanciest shit money can buy. Luckily, Natalie is my guide.

She navigates us through the store. "It's like my mom's backyard."

She swiftly walks us through sections of designer diamonds until we step into an elevator where we're whisked to the fifth floor—5F Contemporary Collection.

The elevator door opens to three life-size mannequins in trendy clothes. Designer names are written on the store walls in spray paint. I haven't heard of any of these brand names, but according to Natalie, whoever makes it to this floor of Bergdorf's is hot. I barely have my bearings before Natalie is lifting size six clothes off racks with surprising ease.

"I used to hate wearing this shit. But, man, it's going to look incredible on you." She pinches my butt, and I yelp.

A salesgirl wearing black pants, a white shirt, and diamond studs in her ears as large as her earlobes finds us and immediately takes the clothes from Natalie's hands.

"I'll start a room for you," she says with a tight smile and nose in the air, as though she's doing us the biggest favor on earth by doing her job.

"Great"—Natalie looks at her name tag—"Sarah. We're going to finish the floor, and then we'll meet you. By the way, this is my friend Elira. Her boyfriend put his credit card on file for her."

"Nico Shihu," I add, trying to be somewhat helpful.

Natalie nods. "He told her to buy anything. And I mean, anything. You work on commission, right?"

Sarah's eyes widen. "Oh, of course. Yes, no problem, I'll just put these down and wait for you. Or would you rather I come back to pick up the rest of the clothes you're trying?"

"Come back," Natalie orders before Sarah scurries away. "What a bitch," Natalie whispers louder than I would have. "Anyway, find more options."

Natalie continues browsing, and I finally get myself in the game. I pull out a few cute-looking cocktail dresses, unsure of how they'll look.

"Do you think it's a dress type of place?"

"Anything goes in New York. I'd go with sexy, comfortable, and classy. You don't know who you're meeting, so you want an outfit that's flexible."

"Right. Flexible."

When we're done, we walk over to the dressing room area. Sarah greets us and opens the door with her key.

It's fully carpeted, mirrored, and gigantic. And by gigantic, I mean, it could fit a twin-size bed and a desk. I drop my purse into the corner of the room and shimmy out of my clothes. I put on the first outfit, relieved when the skirt easily zips up. Standing on my tippy-toes and staring at myself in the mirror, I try to imagine how the outfit would look with heels.

"Let me grab you a pair," Natalie says. Lo and behold, she pulls out three pairs of strappy stilettos that were hiding beneath the beautiful chair in the corner.

"How did you know those were there?"

She laughs. "Tricks of the trade, my friend."

She lifts them up, checking the soles. "Size eight." She hands them over.

"Amazing," I gush, sliding my feet in.

"This is the one." Natalie nods her head in approval. "And the shoes are perfect. We'll go down to the shoe floor and get something similar."

I turn left and right, straightening my back and imagining how another person would see me. The brown-black-and-cream leopard-print skirt is ruched chiffon and hits my ankles but has a super high slit up to my thigh. I tuck the black lacy camisole into the skirt. I feel ... classy and sexy at once. Hell, I love it.

"I'm afraid to look at the price tags."

"Ignore those pesky little things." She stands up. "Take it off. We're buying it."

"Seriously? You don't think I should try on anything else?"

"Hell no. You look super hot, and best of all, you look like a classier, more refined version of who you already are. You want to have fun with the man, not change who you are for him."

"You're the best, you know that?"

We leave the room to find Sarah standing by the door. She takes my soon-to-be clothes to the register.

Natalie throws an arm over my shoulders as we walk. "Best part is, you can use all of this stuff after the dinner, too. The skirt would look great in the daytime with a black cotton tank. And the camisole will look beautiful under a suit one day when you're on Wall Street."

"I freaking love you." I lean my head on her shoulder.

I know how hard it is to find a true friend, and I'm so grateful to have found one. I've gone through so many friends in my twenty-one years of life, and somehow, they've always turned into nightmares. It took me time to realize that the problem was my expectations. The way I treated my friends with love, loyalty, and respect was never reciprocated. The result was a constant feeling of being let down. I knew I had two choices: lower what I would like out of a friendship and deal with backstabbing and surface-only relationships or just hold out for something real even if that meant some loneliness in the short-term. I chose to wait it out. And then I met Natalie. She is loving and honorable in the way that I am. And our friendship is something I'd never take for granted.

She stops in her tracks. "You'll need a bag!"

"I have a bag." I shrug, lifting my new purse off my shoulder.

"Elira, listen." She spins me around and holds me by the shoulders. "This man is loaded. His credit card is on file. You need to look the part. You might as well get some good shit out of it. I mean, you're not getting paid in dollars. So, get paid in shoes and bags and clothes."

"I don't want to act like an escort, for God's sake."

"He said sex isn't on the menu. But it's still your time. And your time is valuable, is it not? You could be working at the diner, making money for your rent or for clothes you'd need for interviews. Instead, you're on his arm. Shouldn't you be compensated?"

"I guess ..." My voice trails off.

I hate to say it, but she's making sense.

"I'm right. So, he said to get an outfit, and that includes shoes and a bag. Hell, that also includes a fresh bra and underwear. Let's do that, too."

"You think he'll check the bill and get mad?"

"And what if he does?" She cocks her head to the side.

"I guess ... nothing. He'd just tell me to cool it off next time. I can't imagine him telling me to return it ..." I'm still hesitant.

"Think of this like a work expense account. You need shit for your job as his pretend wife. So, what would his wife wear, huh? Not a Guess purse from five years ago. And not Gap underwear."

"Hey, don't dis the underwear!" I say, half-joking but finding myself somewhat convinced.

I can't imagine Nico being cheap. It's just not easy for me to take from him. I like to make my own way in life.

"Babe, I checked out the Albanians on social media." She smirks like she knows a secret.

"You did what?" I stop in my tracks.

"Yeah." She nods excitedly. "They even have a hashtag—Hellbanians. I think they're mostly the dealers in the Mafia. But they're all about the cars and the cash and the bling. They've got all these pics with hot girls. Kim Kardashian look-alike types."

"Jesus ..." I exhale slowly as we reach the elevator.

"We'll buy something classic and gorgeous that will last you. Something really fucking expensive, too. Chanel. I despise it for myself, but it's what you'll want in this city when you work here. Let's just buy these clothes on this floor, and then we'll head over to the Chanel boutique. It's on the first floor."

"When would I need a Chanel bag?"

"When you go out on a Saturday night—that's when. It's the style. It's the expectation. You aren't going to be a Tobeho girl forever. One day, you'll be an executive at Goldman. Trust me. I know these things."

I swallow hard, looking around at the other women shopping here. I'm shocked to see most of them have Chanel purses or other bags that look equally as expensive.

"Fine." I exhale, feeling defeated. "Call me convinced."

"I like this flexible side to you," she exclaims, happily surprised. "I thought it would take hours of persuasion."

"Show me that stupid hashtag. And don't get used to me being amenable," I sass. "You know my true colors."

"Black and gray with a side of thunder, just how I love you."

She wraps her arm over my shoulders, and I smile.

Today was spent primping. Natalie helped re-dye my naturally mousy-brown hair to black and iron it flat. It's shiny and pin-straight. The outfit looks amazing, too. My makeup looks effortless, but the truth is, it was painstaking. Black liner lifted on the ends like a cat. Lots of bronzer to chisel out my cheekbones and to turn my pasty-white skin into something that looks alive.

Unfortunately, there aren't enough cigarettes on earth to calm my nerves. Natalie forbid me from smoking once I showered and did my hair because she said it isn't classy to smell like cigarettes.

She walks over to her dresser and pulls out her favorite pair of diamond studs. "My mom bought them for me when I graduated the eighth grade. I never wear them, obviously, but tonight feels like a good time to wear them."

"Oh, no." I shake my head.

"Oh, yes," she replies, smiling.

I put them in my ears, and she looks at me approvingly.

"So, we never discussed Jack." She plops back onto her bed and scrolls through her phone.

"What about him?"

"Well, Nico forbid other men, and yet you and Jack are still seeing each other..."

"I mean, we made out the night we met and in the van to New York City, but that's all. He's great, and I like spending time with him."

"Does Jack know that you have no intentions for more?" She raises her brows. "Because Scott told me the other night that Jack's totally into you."

"Scott?" I turn around, smiling.

Natalie flushes. "Yep. God bless the man. He's the best sex I've ever had. And cool, too. We're never going anywhere serious, but it's fun."

I shrug. "I don't know what Jack knows or what he thinks. But a few coffees and listening to him practice ... oh shit. It does sound more serious when I say it out loud."

"You should just tell him." She lies back on her bed, adding a few pillows behind her to prop herself up.

"What should I say?"

"Just that you are seeing someone else. An old friend."

"Come on—"

"I'm just saying, Jack is a decent guy. And he's definitely going places in life. If you want something with him for real one day, after all this Nico shit is over, you're going to have to come up with some kind of story to put him off until then. Otherwise, you'll end up lying constantly about where you are and where you're going ..."

"I'll figure out something. Can't I just friend-zone him for the time being?"

Natalie wants to say more, but the doorbell rings. My heart pauses. What the fuck am I doing? I can't go through with this!

Natalie excitedly points to the door. "I'll get it!"

"Wait! No!" I whisper-yell, but she ignores me.

I hear her say hello, followed by his deep voice reply.

Should I go outside to the living room? Make him wait a minute? Oh, who am I kidding? I can't leave Nico alone with her!

I exhale and open the bedroom door. At once, Nico and Natalie turn toward me. He's so insanely handsome. My brain and heart both skip. Dark gray suit. White shirt. Eyes that melt me in a million ways. I should say hello and step forward. Instead, I can do nothing more than take shallow breaths.

Natalie clears her throat, breaking the ice. "Nico's here!" she says in a singsong voice, holding back a smile.

"Natalie was kind enough to let me in."

She nods, turning to me before looking back at him. "Yes, I am kind enough. Since you're, you know, all dangerous. Probably carrying a gun. Not that it's a bad thing. I mean, guns can be okay. When you need it. Which you clearly do, in your line of work. Well. Anyway ..."

Nico meets my stare, nailing me in place. "You ready?" Turning to the front door, he opens it.

In silence, we take the elevator down. My hands are shaking, so I keep them clasped together. The moment we step onto the sidewalk, a huge black Mercedes-Benz pulls up. The driver's door opens, and a man steps out. He's big, bald, and muscular, wearing a black suit. He opens the door to the backseat.

"Definitely better to step into a car with my bearings as opposed to being drugged." I sit inside and move toward the window.

"That's true," Nico says, the door shutting behind him. "But you should know, Elira, if there's something I want or need, I do what I need to do to get it as quickly as possible."

"Is there a reason you went from being nice and decent to being a complete ass in a matter of three seconds?"

"I'm not being an ass. But I'll always tell you the truth. Remember?" He raises his dark brows. "It's the man I always was, and it's the man I still am."

I swallow hard. "So"—I clear my throat—"is there any particular way I need to act?"

"Be just as you are. A college student. You take your classes and then return home. To me." His voice is so possessive that chills break out on my arms.

I check my watch. We've already been in the car for an hour. The sky is dark. Moon full. "So, where are we going for dinner?"

"Staten Island."

I look at him like he's crazy. "Are you joking? If that's the case, I should have hit up a tanning bed." I snort.

The only thing I know about Staten Island is that the people are all about fake tanning and hair. And they're more Italian than actual Italians. My mom was obsessed with that reality show about Staten Island mob wives, and I watched a few episodes with her—under protest, of course. The Gambino family, one of the biggest Italian Mafia families in the country, also lives there. Just a few months ago, the boss was fatally shot in front of his home. It was in all the papers. I wonder if this dinner is somehow connected to that.

Oh shit.

He shakes his head at me, laughing at my facial expression. "There's a restaurant. It's owned by a man I'd like to do business with. His wife is as old as your mother. I'm sure she'll fall in love with you."

"And if she hates me, does that mean we'd get 'divorced'?" I make quotation marks with my fingers.

"I won't get rid of you too easily. But I do believe in some forms of punishment." He smirks.

I tilt my head to the side. "And what if she invites me, as your wife, to a party in three years? What if, by then, you have an actual real wife?" The comment has my heart strangely squeezing.

"I'll tell her I got sick of you and traded you in for a better, newer version."

My jaw drops, and he starts to laugh. He's playing with me!

His huge body turns toward mine. I can see the muscles in his thighs pressing against the cloth of his pants. I undo the straps of my shoes and kick them off, curling my feet beneath my legs on the soft leather seat. I never understood when people made the comment, *Leather as soft as butter,* but I do now. He sees me getting comfortable, and he does the same. Surprise of all surprises, he removes his fancy loafers, too. It makes me feel like I can speak to him openly and honestly, so I do.

"Why didn't you reach out to me earlier? We were ... friends."

"You were a child. It wouldn't have been appropriate." He moves an errant hair from my face, not saying anything more.

I shut my eyes as he touches me, unable to see his eyes while feeling his hand. It's too much. I picture Nico at eighteen, his heart already hardened yet soft for me. I open my eyes, coming back to the present moment.

His gaze skims my body. "I like what you're wearing."

"I wasn't sure if—"

"I want you to make sure you have every single item you need, understand?"

The rest of the ride goes smoothly. We talk about basic things, like the courses I'm taking and my major. He listens intently to what I have to say, chiming in at all the right moments. It's comfortable. Easy.

The car pulls into a big parking lot. The place looks like a diner with the short roof and neon lights.

"This is it?" I don't mean to sound snotty, but I was expecting something a little ... more.

"Yes. The food is phenomenal. Don't make eye contact with anyone who isn't at our table. Don't be the one to bring up any topics of conversation, either. Almost all the patrons here are highly connected."

Suddenly, it hits me that I'm about to have dinner with someone from an Italian crime family. And the man I'm with is arguably even more dangerous. I'm not ready for this!

The door swings open, and Nico steps out, saying something about the mild weather. But I hesitate, looking between the window and the open car door. I should say no. It's not like me to be wishy-washy, but this is scary as hell.

"You coming out?" he asks.

I'm suddenly so terrified that I can't reply.

Nico slides back in next to me. "Elira," he says my name so gently. "It's just dinner. All they want to see is a loving, happy couple. A man who's settled with a good Albanian woman by his side. That's all. You won't have to lie outright. We've known each other since we were children. That's all there is to know." He takes my hand, rubbing his finger in circles between my thumb and forefinger.

"Okay," I whisper. "And what about newer topics? Like where we live?"

"My home is where you were—79th and Park Avenue."

"You had me in your apartment?" I try not to gawk.

"Of course. Where else would I take you?" He squints at me in confusion.

"I don't know. A private dungeon? I was your prisoner," I spit.

"Why do you sound angry that I put you in my house? Was the bed not comfortable? Would you have rather been sleeping on a concrete floor?"

"It would have made things less confusing," I practically shout. And then I think about what I just said and start to laugh. "Okay, fine."

He mutters something to himself, looking up at the roof.

"And we should be loving and affectionate?"

"Yes. You aren't a girlfriend. We're having dinner with my friends, who are now, by default, yours, too. Sal and Gina. You should feel little worry when you're with your husband. Which reminds me."

He pulls out a black box from his pocket. Opening it slowly, he takes my hand and slides the biggest round diamond I've ever seen onto the ring finger of my left hand. It's set on a thin gold band. No small diamonds. Nothing on the side. Just one huge fuck-you rock. I open and shut my mouth, speechless.

"It suits you." He licks his lips, our eyes locking.

The moment feels so right, but it's also wrong. This isn't how it's supposed to go.

"I couldn't—"

"You must."

"But ... this?" I look down at the diamond that shimmers, even in the dark car. "How big is it?" I turn my hand left and right, watching the play of light. Even though it's gigantic, it's surprisingly classy.

"Big enough for you to say, *Thank you, Nico. Should I take my top off now or later?*"

I give him the middle finger, trying not to laugh but failing. I know firsthand, life could be worse than wearing a huge diamond for a dinner.

"Okay."

"Ready?" He steps out again, holding out his hand. This time, I take it.

The restaurant looks like an old-school Italian hangout. It's all wooden and dim with red tablecloths. Surprisingly, there's a singer in the corner, crooning in Italian. I hold one of Nico's hands with both of mine. Keeping my back straightened, I try not to come off like a scared kid. The reality is though, I'm hanging on to him like a lifeline.

My father wasn't with us in America, but I remember how my

parents were when they thought no one was watching. Loving and affectionate. I lean into Nico, taking advantage of the story he's written for us. I'm not very touchy-feely, but I'm letting myself be that girl right now. It's both strange and wonderful to let a man be my anchor.

He turns me toward him and bends down his head, eyes flickering somewhere behind me. "I'm going to kiss you now."

I blink. Is this for real, or has the show started? My body buzzes in confusion, thoughts from all parts of the spectrum hitting me at once.

"Don't overthink," he whispers in my ear.

And then his lips are on mine. Warm and delicious. I melt, my knees buckling. Thankfully, his arms are around me, holding me steady. I want to kiss him back, give as well as I take, but Nico is in complete control. He tastes so good. He smells like heaven. Suddenly, he pulls back, eyes sparkling. Laughing at me?

"Look at you two," a man says behind me.

"Hey, Sal." Nico turns me around, and I step to his side.

The men shake hands amicably. Sal is a heavyset older man in a pair of dark slacks, a button-down shirt, and a checkered blue tie. Very formal, but he looks old enough to pull it off. I'd say he's in his early seventies.

His wife is exactly as I would have guessed. Probably in her sixties. Huge boobs encased in a black shirt. Nails an inch too long, painted pink. Bleached hair side-swept and puffed. She's the mob boss's wife in all senses of the word.

"You must be Nico's wife." She smiles happily. "So beautiful." Her Staten Island accent is so strong, syllables missing and the letter *W* inserted all over the place.

We're escorted to a table on the right side of the restaurant. I sit down next to Nico and across from Gina, placing the napkin over my legs. I might not be rich, but I've got class.

"The food here is amazing," she gushes. "Sal already ordered everything for us." She says the word *already* like awl-red-ee. "We know the owners," she says jokingly.

Clearly, this is her restaurant.

She shifts in her seat. "Do you drink wine?"

I turn to Nico, and he pulls me into his arm. "Yes. We'll drink wine tonight."

Within a matter of seconds of being seated, plates of antipasta are brought out. "Two kinds of mozzarella," the waiter states, pointing at two separate plates. "The burrata with eggplant and tomatoes and the buffalo with ham." Two more plates are dropped down. "The eggplant rollatini and the beef carpaccio."

Nico nods to the waiter, fully confident and composed. I don't dare touch my food until he does first. Suddenly, Nico lifts my plate into his hands and starts filling it. When he's done, he sets it back in front of me.

"Does he always take care of you like this?" Gina whispers under her breath, eyes locking on Nico. "He's incredibly handsome. Jesus. Where did you find him?"

"In Kosovo." My voice comes out more emotional than intended. But it's the truth.

She seems to sense that because she smiles thoughtfully. "I met mine in church." She nudges Sal. "I was only sixteen, and he was twenty-eight. But he saw me and wanted me. And what men like them want, men like them get."

"No shit," I mutter under my breath.

Her eyes widen, like she heard me.

Oh no. I need to backtrack!

She tilts her head back in laughter, clapping her hands together. "I like you!"

The relief I feel is enormous. Nico squeezes my thigh, like I'm doing well.

Sal does most of the talking while Nico listens. I follow his lead, doing the same with Gina. Luckily, the food is incredible. I practically lick my plate clean as I listen to her, nodding and replying when appropriate.

"Enjoy food while you're still young," she chides. "Eventually, you won't be able to eat that way."

"I'm sure you're right." I imagine my mother's friends, who all claim to have been a size two once and are now pushing size eighteen.

"I've had a tummy tuck. Butt lift. Breast implants. And I'm doing my face next week," she speaks under her breath, as though it were a big secret.

"Really?" I reply, seemingly surprised. "You look amazing."

"We have four kids. By the end, my tits were down to my belly button, and my ass sagged to the back of my knees."

She starts guffawing, and I can't help but laugh myself.

"God bless 'em, though. Ant is gettin' married next month. Great girl. Italian and Catholic, of course. Know her family from church. She's not as beautiful as you are. But with a little makeup and a nose job, I think I can fix her up."

I have no words, so I only nod and take another drink from my wine, which is incredibly good. It feels like I've been drinking so much, but every time I look down, the glass is refilled again! Being rich means never having to pour yourself a drink.

It seems that I'm not the only one who has gotten drunk because the laughter between the four of us grows, and the jokes keep getting dirtier.

Just as Nico said, this dinner seems to be for social purposes. I don't hear anything discussed that's illegal, and that helps to keep me calm. Sal tells us a story about the old days in Italy and getting caught by the police with his pants down around his ankles. He's charming.

Nico sits back, his arm around my chair. I turn toward him, the liquor giving me courage to look longer than I'd normally feel comfortable. His chiseled jaw with some scruff around the edges. Straight Roman nose. Those lips.

He whispers in my ear, "You're staring."

Gina and Sal, along with the other patrons, begin to sing; it seems like a song they're all familiar with.

Gina tells me, "The restaurant's singer is from Italy. He's unbeliev-able. He sings all the music we grew up with."

The room is swaying, singing with all their emotion. The entire restaurant is obviously Italian.

I get closer to Nico, and he puts a heavy arm around my shoulders. I'm acting. This is all an act. Nico doesn't love me. I'm not his wife. I'm just someone he used to know. Someone he can trust.

The song finishes, and the restaurant settles back down.

"Does the music break out like this often?" I ask, drinking more wine. The glass is still full. Figures.

"Oh, yes. Fun, no?" She lifts a glass of ice water and takes a huge gulp.

I should have some, too. I search to the left and right of my plate but only find a cup in front of Nico. Husbands and wives can share, right? I drink from his glass, and he squeezes my thigh.

Four huge white dessert plates are set on our table. I have no room in my stomach for more food but pick at everything anyhow. Berries with fresh cream. Cookies. Nico mentions a restaurant in Venice that this place reminds him of. I listen to every word out of his mouth with bated breath. I want to know all about his time and life after he left Kosovo. In some ways, I know everything about this man. In others, I know nothing.

The lights of the restaurant flicker on, and I squint my eyes. Huh? Looking around, I notice we're the only patrons still here.

Nico rises out of his chair as Sal puts a cream suede jacket on Gina's shoulders.

They're whispering to each other when Nico tells me, "You should have brought a coat."

"Okay," I reply in earnest, making sure the other couple aren't listening. "The thing is," I whisper, "I don't really like to shop. And plus, it's hard to come into New York with school and work."

His dark eyes bore into mine. "I'll take care of it."

He gently kisses my forehead. Like a brother? Like a father? I can't keep up. Are we still acting?

When I turn around, Sal and Gina have that look on their faces, like, *Aw, how sweet.* I blush while my stomach sinks. They have no idea.

Together, we leave.

Our Mercedes pulls up to the sidewalk in front of the restaurant.

Gina hugs me as the men shake hands.

"Let's talk Monday morning," Sal tells Nico. "I think we've got something good between us."

With perfect timing, Nico's driver steps out of the black Mercedes, opening the car door. With one last good-bye, we step inside. I slide into the seat to the end of the bench.

Nico sits beside me, legs crossed casually in front of him as he reads something on his phone.

Is that all there is?

He clears his throat. "You did good tonight."

"Thank God for the little things in life," I reply sarcastically, looking out the window as though I couldn't care less. Act is done, right?

Without moving my head, my eyes dart to Nico. A smirk lines his face. He thinks I'm funny!

He sits up with his back straight and erect, legs placed apart. "Tell me how it was for you, coming to America."

"Really?" I tangle my hands together. This is one of the annoying questions guys ask me, trying to act like they care. But this question out of Nico's mouth is different.

"Yes." He shifts in his seat. "I want to know everything about what happened, from the moment you left home."

He moves next to me, invading my territory. I want to jerk back, draw a line between us, but there is no place to go.

"And face me when you speak," he orders. He isn't cruel or loud. But he is demanding.

A dozen times, I try to speak, but my voice only holds short, disconnected whispers.

Finally, he places a heavy hand over my lips. "Stop thinking. Just tell me. You don't have to cover your truth with me." He lets go and waits.

I drop my head, my own version of assent. He lifts my chin up and nods. The story comes out like a rush. So many things I've held inside for so many years. But who to tell? My mother and brother have their own stories and pain. I've never felt like I could bring it up with them, lest they're reminded of what they themselves endured.

But with Nico, I'm not afraid. He's so strong; I know he can handle everything.

I begin with the logistics of how I got to the US. "The horse ride to Montenegro was agonizing. I sat in front of Agron, who took care of me so well." Tears drip down my face. "My brother gave me his food. Kept a gun on his chest to protect us. He was hungry, but I was the one who ate. So many people were running to catch up with us ..."

Nico sits patiently, waiting for me to continue.

"Agron is many things, good and bad. But I owe him my life during that trip." I swallow before continuing, "When we got to Montenegro, we connected with my mother's family and stayed at her uncle's house. I tried running back to you. I was worried for you." I chuckle sadly. "There was a forest behind his house with so many trees. Each morning, I would venture out deeper, trying to see if I could come up with a way to come home. But then, things got more dangerous. Village people began using the forest to hide. I'd bump into them during the day. Ultimately, Mama and Agron came with me, and we hid there with the others."

"Keep going," he whispers, gently urging me on.

"Remember my cousin Valmir? He left the woods one day to tell his mother about dinner. The Serbs saw him and sh-shot him. We kept hearing stories about the Serbs burning people alive. In the woods, we'd hear shots and bombs ..." My entire body begins to shake.

I have never repeated these memories. They've been sitting in my heart for so many years. Nico curls me into his chest, shushing me gently.

"Within ten days, a man came for us. He smuggled us into a crate in the back of a plane and took us to the US." My voice trembles. "You set it up, right?" I lift my face to his. "You arranged to get us out?"

"Yes," he whispers.

"Who paid the smuggler the rest of the money once we got to Tobeho?"

Typically, an illegal immigrant would pay a portion up front and the rest upon landing. I know from my mother that when we left, we had nothing.

"I was doing some small-time money laundering at the time. There was a man who owed me. He paid me back by paying your fee."

Tears fill my eyes. "But why did we end up in Tobeho? Is there a reason?" It's a question I've always wondered. I did ask my mother once, but she told me it wasn't my concern.

"There is food on the table, I have a job that pays, and you have a roof over your head. No more questions," she said.

He nods thoughtfully. "The factory work was good in Tobeho. Your mother didn't speak any English at that time. I figured Tobeho was also a good location, equal distance between two big cities—New York City and Philadelphia."

His hand brushes against my collarbone. I shiver.

"And was it hard to get your papers?"

"No. We were refugees, seeking asylum. And America had finally decided to intervene in Kosovo. The whole process went more smoothly than I would have thought."

"Good."

"You did good for us," I tell him. "Thank you, Nico."

"For you," he reminds me. I look out the window, but he grabs my chin, forcing me to look into his eyes. "Say it. I did it for you."

"You did it for me," I repeat. "I-I was like your little sister. You ... you cared for me."

The way he's staring at me now, with complete focus, has my heart leaping from my chest. It's desire and lust and something else I can feel, but my head refuses to name. His fingers slide over my shoulders, thumbs lightly grazing my nipples. I shut my eyes, the sensation causing a ripple through my blood.

My back arches up to him of its own accord. An offering not from me, but from something greater than I am. He continues to move his hands, rubbing against my breasts and arms. I'm quivering. Literally shaking. His touch is whisper soft, but I can feel him over every crevice.

In my ear, he asks, "Are you still my little sister?"

Suddenly, I'm pulled beneath him. His huge body looms above me, and his rough hand grips my vulnerable waist, shirt untucked and skirt crumpled. My mind is like an evening tide, coming forward before receding. My body is stiff, and yet my insides run completely liquid. I'm so turned on, trying not to pant, as he rises above me in the darkness of the backseat.

He's a killer. He helped you live. He's a thief. He stole for you. He's a dangerous, dangerous man.

His hands trail up and down my bare thighs, inching beneath my skirt. This man has watched me throw up from illness. He's held me in his arms when I was ill and shaking. Given me his food. Protected me from harm. Made me laugh, even when nothing about our lives was funny. But what ... what was it then? What is this now? I want him so badly, but I can't combine all of my feelings into a single coherent thought. I'm here and at his mercy.

"There's so much to tell you," he says, voice thick. He rests his body beside mine on the seat, leaning on his side and facing me as he continues to touch me. His warm breath is black honey at my neck, filled with so many promises and words unsaid. "You must be tired." He stills, exhaling. "Rest."

I dream of wide-open doors. The fields of my youth. Agron chasing me between high trees in the forest. Nico holding a rifle at the kitchen table, laughing at something my father said.

Suddenly, I feel suspended in the air. Cradled into something warm. I'm being carried forward. I open my eyes just enough to see what's happening.

I croak, "Nico?" Tucking my head into his neck, I smell the man I know.

"You're home."

I can hear a door shut as I'm placed on what feels like my comforter.

"You need to lock the fucking door," he says angrily.

"Mmhmm." I want to pull him down to me, tell him to stay, but he's completely unmovable, as though his body has turned to stone. My eyes pop open.

"I'm going to have your locks fixed. New keys sent over." He locks my bedroom door and then shakes it. It takes only a few seconds for him to pop off the handle!

Holy shit.

"What the hell is going on?" I sit up, confused and scratching the back of my head. I need water, and I'm exhausted, but he seems to be operating as though he's already had his morning coffee and a bath. "Did you just break my door?"

"I hate how you live here. It's unsafe." He strides from wall to wall of my bedroom.

"I like my home. I know it's not fancy, but the mortgage is paid up, and my mother and I are comfortable."

"Oh, yeah?" he says, menacingly, stepping back toward my bed. "Well, get used to the idea of leaving. Because there's no way in hell I'm allowing this shithole to be your place of residence even a moment longer. I always knew it was bad, but the inside is worse than I imagined."

"Is that right?" How dare he insult the place my mother and I have worked so hard to keep!

"You want to stay here, in this town that's weakening by the day? Let me buy you a new home. You're graduating anyway, thank God."

"No," I say through my teeth. "You aren't forcing me to move, and you aren't buying us a new house. I'm not your whore."

He moves so quickly to my side that I'm shocked frozen. His hand moves around my neck. He doesn't choke me, but I can feel his strength. It's obscene.

"If you were my whore ..." He chuckles darkly, fingers caressing my throat.

My blood turns to blackstrap molasses as my breaths shorten.

"If you were my whore," he repeats, unbuttoning his crisp white shirt with his free hand, "I'd have you down on your knees right now, sucking my cock. But you've seen that once already, haven't you? I think you liked it."

My world pauses in shock. *It was Nico.*

He smiles darkly, shirt hanging open as his muscles flex. I swear, my eyes pop out of their sockets.

"If you were my whore, I would have had your legs spread open that night in my house when I had you taken from that alley, smoking a cigarette."

His skin looks damp, eyes wild. He unbuckles his heavy belt, and his pants drop to the floor. The smell of Nico aroused and wanting is something I have never experienced or even thought to experience. It's heady and dark as rum. My mouth waters.

He pulls my neck into his chest, locking me against his body. His right hand pulls down his boxer briefs and grips his shaft. I suck in a hard breath, watching his length grow thick and flushed. That first stroke has me gasping. All these years, I've fantasized about Nico. And now, here he is, in the flesh.

"Don't move," he demands, pushing my head down toward his hip so that my head is pressed against his stomach.

I'm close enough to see every perfect detail, but he holds me firmly, keeping me just out of reach. His hand moves up and down his own hard length, alternating between slow, deep strokes and rougher ones. For a moment, fear plunges into my bloodstream. Is he going to force me?

My panties are soaked. I want this man so badly, and yet my terror increases. His thighs are so strong and powerful, his cock perfection. My entire being flushes crimson, quaking.

"I know you so well," he hisses down low in his throat. "You have always liked to watch me. As a child, you watched my every move and now as an adult."

In this moment, Nico is the deadly Mafia boss who people fear. But he doesn't do anything more than keep me tethered to him. I could shut my eyes. But I won't. Because I can't.

I imagine the woman the other night, on her knees before him. Did it end after she gave him head, or did he take her roughly against the wall to finish? Were her tits huge or small, or were they medium-sized, like mine? What does he like more?

His grip tightens around his thick shaft, and he groans, "Elira." It's my name on his lips.

My blood courses like choppy, wild tides.

It's me here with him now, no one else. The other woman flees my brain. I'd say his name, but I can't speak. I can only hear heavy breaths surrounding us. Are they mine? Ours? Yes, we're panting. I want to scream as his groans grow harsher. All the blood drains down through my body and centers at my core. The pulse is painful, the ache completely crazy. I'm restrained, in his complete control. His hand continues to jerk himself, the pace slow, hard, and lazy.

"When I finally fuck you," he says through his teeth, "you'll be begging for it."

The snarky part of my brain is on complete shutdown. The only thing my body does is breathe and liquefy. I'm up on my knees, throat clasped to his chiseled stomach as his dick pulses in his heavy hand.

"Fuuuucccckkkk," he growls, long and slow.

I could try to move. But I don't. I wonder what his cock must feel like. Is it as velvety as it looks? So thick. It's flushed and hot. I've dreamed of this. So many nights.

His body trembles, but still, he doesn't let me go. Not an inch of slack. I want to take over, touch him, but his control is not to be undone. I am a voyeur in this scene.

"Who do you belong to?" he asks.

"You," I whisper, a beg trailing behind my voice.

I want to discover all of the things I've only allowed myself to imagine. I want to taste his hard cock and feel it against my own palm. What would it be like to have him above me, inside me, behind me? I'm melting. Sweating. I can see the wet beads trail down his abdomen, cut like marble.

"Soon," he grumbles, "I'm going to lick every inch of your gorgeous body. I'm going to drink you in."

I manage to look up. His eyes are shut tight. I want to shift my body, try to relieve the ache, but his eyes flit open—

"Don't you fucking move without my permission!"

God help me.

"I bet your pussy is drenched. Slide one finger inside for me. Don't touch your clit until I say so."

My breath freezes within my lungs. "P-please," I beg, my hand moving beneath my skirt.

"No. Fuck, Elira, I can smell you from here. So fucking good. Made for me."

Finally, he begins to unravel, breathing wild. My inner thighs are soaked. My finger moves in and out of my heat. The skirt is too tight. I want to rip it off! Without his strong body holding me up, I'd collapse from pleasure.

"Now," he groans.

I touch my clit, and my entire world erupts in a melted shimmer. He moans his release, finishing all over me.

I'm whimpering as he steps away, long strides into my bathroom. I hear the water turn on and then off. He returns, rummaging through my drawers like they're his own and handing me my pajamas. They're the old gray ones, full of holes. He stares at them unhappily before handing them over.

"Use the bathroom to clean up and change. Give me your clothes when you're done."

In a daze, I stand and do as he said. When I return, he takes the skirt and top from my hands.

And then he's gone.

Holy shit.

8

TWO WEEKS PASS, AND I HEAR NOTHING FROM NICO. I'M NOT SURE whether to be relieved as hell or if I feel utterly let down. We had an incredible dinner with the Italians, and I had more fun than maybe I'd ever had. But the ending to our night was insane, and there is no other way to explain it. It was emotionally taxing, opening up to him the way I did. And then the physical component just took the entire experience into fucked up, crazy territory.

After he left, I fell asleep almost immediately. And then I woke up with the huge diamond, which I nicknamed The Rock, still on my hand. The Rock is now hidden in the lockbox in the back of my closet. A few times a day, I go to make sure she's still there.

According to Google, it's five carats. I spent a good amount of time putting the size next to the pictured size. I don't know anything about the quality, but being as big as it is, I'm guessing it's at least a few hundred thousand dollars. A normal girl would call him, let him know that he needs to pick up his ring. But I don't. I'm ... ashamed over what happened between us, and my *I don't give a fuck if you call or not* attitude is my defense. Plus, a twisted part of me wants him to call me even if it's just to get the ring back; it's my leverage to see him again.

Yes, I'm crazy, and my emotions are all over the map. I've been in love with Nico all my life. But now, I'm not a kid, and neither is he. And I'm on path A, which I'll call the Straight Arrow Line, and he's on path Z, which I'll call the Mafia Badassery Illegal line. A and Z don't intersect. They can't. Still, Nico is forcing a connection between us right now. It's shaky and untrustworthy. I'll call the connector line Agron. My brother is literally the link between us. God.

I'm cleaning the counter at the diner, my head awash in theories, when Natalie comes next to me.

"You still have to speak with Jack. You shouldn't just freeze him out, Elira. That's immature. Your date with Nico was better than expected. Focus on him and just drop Jack. Otherwise, you're going to get yourself into trouble, my friend."

I press my lips together, trying to focus on staying calm. Coming from someone else, I'd say the comment was judgmental. But I know Natalie just wants me to do the right thing. And anyway, she's right.

I focus back on her. "I just don't even know what to say to Jack. There's nothing concrete between us. He hasn't called me since I walked out of his practice session, and I haven't contacted him either. Maybe I can just ignore him until it goes away?" Not my most mature moment, but definitely the path of least resistance.

Natalie knows that Nico and I fooled around after an amazing night, but nothing more.

"That's a bad idea. We both know it." She adjusts the gold chain around her neck. "Speak of the devil." She laughs, pointing to the door.

Jack walks in with his bandmates, and I groan.

"And look at that. They're sitting at one of your tables! Good luck, you little wimp," she says in a singsong voice.

I want to laugh, but I also want to kill her.

I get cups and a pitcher of tap water from the kitchen and bring them with me to their table. Jack looks up, smiling so hard, like he is thrilled to see me.

"What's up, guys?" I pull out my pad, smiling like all is well in the world. "What can I get you all?"

Jack pushes his hair back before arching the brim of his baseball hat. "We do want to eat. But we also wanted to come in to tell you in person."

"Tell me what?"

Natalie wraps an arm around my shoulders. "Hi, Scott," she says flirtatiously.

"Elira," Jack starts, "I'm sorry I've been missing in action lately."

Natalie squeezes my back, and I bite my cheek, trying not to whimper.

"But the reason is, we were in California last week."

I raise my brows, unsure of where he's going with this conversation.

"We've been signed by Sony!" he exclaims.

Natalie and I are speechless before we start with our, "Oh my God! This is unreal!"

The guys stand up, and we do a group hug. All our arms are tangled around each other. They've been signed! We start jumping up and down together as a unit. Closing my eyes, I'm cheering with the group. It's exciting and amazing, and their feelings of euphoria are straight-up contagious. When we stop, we're all panting happily. The entire restaurant doesn't look bothered, but they're staring at us, definitely curious.

Our manager looks over at us like he's ready to throw the lot of us out.

"We were signed by Sony!" Scott yells across the room.

The other patrons clap and holler. I can see our manager's face turning red with annoyance, but how could he kick us out now?

"We have to celebrate," I say, feeling flushed.

"Hell yeah," Scott adds.

"Let's go to McGrady's and get completely shit-faced tonight." Natalie claps. "But first, why don't we feed you all?"

They take their seats, and I take their orders, my hands literally shaking as I write it all down on my small notepad. When I'm done, I smile at Jack, who has stars in his eyes. He's gazing at me with so much happiness and excitement. I smile back because, with all my heart, I'm happy for him. I'm also sad for myself.

I could be yours, his eyes seem to tell me.

I can't reply. I'm stuck in this fucked up scenario with a man I'm crazy about but, for all intents and purposes, I should run from.

I leave their table to bring the order to the kitchen. When it's taped up, I go into the restroom for a break.

Staring at myself in the mirror, I ask, *What the hell is going on here?*

And Nico hasn't even contacted me. He says I'm not his whore, but I'm literally at his mercy. I have to discuss this with him. I need solid dates and times. I can't just go and come and have a fucking orgasm! I slam my hand down against the white sink—ouch! Whatever. Time is up. Let me get done with work, and then I'll figure it out.

With trembling hands, I reenter the kitchen and pick up their food. When I place their fully loaded burgers and fries on the table, Jack rubs his hands together like he can't wait to dig in.

Before I leave, he puts his hand on mine. "Thank you. And sorry again for not calling."

He's so genuine. I can't even reply. A mixture of guilt and sadness stirs my gut. We could have had something, but it never would have gone anywhere. There's just something missing between us. He squints his eyes, noticing the change within me. But there's no way I'm ruining this moment for him by telling him the truth.

I shrug. "No worries. I'm so happy for you guys. Really."

He winks, digging into his burger, and I move back to the counter.

"You just got a *get out of jail free* card." She nudges me.

"I know." I nod. "I can just let everything be as it is. He's probably moving out to California. I've got my life on the East Coast. I can let his pace of life just end it all."

"Maybe you're right." She leans her elbows against the counter. "I guess you can just let this thing you guys have fade away. We all make plans, and then fate comes in and decides what will be."

"Poetic." I give her the side-eye, and she playfully slaps my shoulder.

One of my tables, a family of four, raises their hand to get my attention. The man mouths, *Check, please.*

I nod, so he knows I got the message.

"But tonight," Natalie adds, "we're having good ol' college fun. Complete with cheap drinks and debauchery."

"Deal." I wink, heading over to the table.

McGRADY'S IS PACKED to the brim, but we couldn't care less. Natalie and I are with the band, and Janice is planning to join us when she's done with one of her assignments. We've all been so busy. I haven't seen her since we first heard Jack play.

Jack wraps an arm over my shoulders as he talks with the guys about their plans. He's already informed me they're leaving in two weeks' time. He is so happy with the news, and frankly, so am I. Watching someone live out their dream is indescribable. I can only wish that for everyone.

Jack will be missing finals, but he's already spoken with the department head of his major, and she hooked him up with take-home exams to graduate on time.

I should feel so good about being by his side, a soon-to-be huge musician. The girls at the bar are seething with jealousy, whispering to their friends. Luckily for me, I'm immune to girls who try to intimidate me with their shit-talking. If I had a penny for every girl who'd been a total bitch out of misplaced jealousy, I'd be a millionaire.

I'm quiet tonight. I assume Jack thinks I'm not talking much because I'm sad about his impending departure. I don't try to prove him wrong.

Shots of tequila are offered to me, and I take two without blinking an eye. I just want to forget everything tonight. It's not long before everything falls away. I'm just a shell of myself. The girl I was back in Kosovo and the woman I'm trying to be is fully decimated by a few shots of tequila. *BOOM.*

Janice walks in, and I run over to her, practically tripping over my own feet. We hug and jump up and down as though we'd been separated for years.

"You need a drink," I yell, dragging her to the bar and pushing people out of our way.

It doesn't take long for her to catch up to where I am.

"Interstate Love Song" by the Stone Temple Pilots comes on the speakers, and my eyes widen. "I love this song," I exclaim.

Scott winks and begins to play air drums. Eric bobs his head with his air guitar along with his brother, Rob. Jack brings me into his chest and starts to sing, only in my ear. Chills, like tight pebbles, rise above my skin. That voice. Jesus Christ, the man has talent. His is incredible, sounding so much like Scott Weiland that it's uncanny.

Nico's face flashes in my mind's eye, and my chest tightens. Maybe I should tell Nico that I don't want to be his wife. My feelings for him are almost too intense. They're bad for me. I don't want a love like that in my life that's dangerous and crazy. I want a love like this one could be—beautiful and kind. It would just be so easy if I could go with this option.

"Don't go, Jack," I whimper, wishing he could stay in my life a little longer. Maybe I'm selfish. Maybe I just need him to help distract me. But still, I need him here right now.

He puts his nose into my hair, hugging me back into his chest. "We'll meet again, Elira. I know we will. We haven't gotten to explore what's between us. But someday, we will."

I want to believe him. I wish I could hang on to what he is and who he represents—an ideal American future without the heaviness of my past. Can I ignore who I used to be and still be happy?

Our group begins to shout, "Shots, shots, shots!"

Jack throws his arm around my shoulders again, keeping me close. It's so easy here.

The rest of the night is a haze of fun.

I find myself in my own bed, my ripped, tight black jeans still buttoned and suffocating my midsection. I shuffle out of bed and throw open the bathroom door. After dropping onto my knees and puking into the toilet, I look down at my body in confusion. How the hell did I end up back home? A million gold bangles glint against my wrist.

When my body stops heaving and I have nothing but my lungs left to puke, I move to the sink next to the toilet and wash my face. I look like death, complete with black rings around my violently red eyes. I brush my teeth, trying not to gag. Finally, I run over my face with makeup remover wipes. My eyes sting so badly. Rummaging through my medicine cabinet, I find an oily makeup remover pad and use that for my eyes instead. Definitely softer. I groan. Even my teeth are killing me. When the makeup has been cleaned off, I check myself out. Roadkill.

I reenter the bedroom and let out a silent gasp that hurts my lungs. A shirtless Jack is sprawled over my bedspread.

Whaaaaat?!

My bedside clock says 7:02 a.m. Mom should be gone already for work. Should I just run out and hope he gets the point or wake him? God, this is awkward.

Before I can decide my plan, Jack speaks, "Hey." His voice is ragged. "Give me a few minutes to wash up. Mind if I use your shower?"

"No problem at all."

He drags himself out of my bed. He's pale with sinewy, lean muscle. His shoulders are broad, but he doesn't have much meat. Unlike Nico, who personifies strength. I lean my head against the wall and shut my eyes. What the hell happened last night? When he's in the bathroom, I take the few minutes of privacy to go through my phone.

Natalie: Holy fuck, where are you?
Natalie: Answer me.
Natalie: Are you fucking Jack right now? What if Nico finds out?
END THIS!

I shut my eyes, wishing I could disappear. Instead, my night comes back like a tornado. Shots. Jack stumbling home with me. Making nachos in my kitchen. Trying to be quiet while stuffing our faces with Tostitos and queso. We were cracking up about something, loud as elephants. Thank God my mom sleeps like the dead.

We got to my room. He kissed my neck. I thought of Nico. Nico's hands. I told Jack no. And he stopped.

I open my eyes, wondering what the fuck I'm doing right now. Guilt wraps around my neck like a snake.

I need to do something about this situation with Jack and cut the cord. Delaying the inevitable is just making it all the more awkward and harder for me. I know that what I have with Nico is technically not real, but at the same time, it's the most real thing I've ever had. Having another man in the picture is wrong.

I shuffle out of the bedroom and go into the kitchen to put on some coffee. That'll make things better. After pouring the water and scooping the grinds into the filter, I flip the switch to on. I turn around and trip, almost landing face-first onto my floor. Looking down, I see one of my platform Steve Madden boots that I wore last night.

It was all innocent and fun between us.

What if Nico finds out? my mind whispers.

Whatever! I didn't do anything wrong.

Nico gave you the most incredible orgasm of your life. He's the one you've been dreaming of all your life.

I brought another man home. A friend! I did nothing wrong!

Jack walks in, looking freshly showered and dressed in last night's clothes, which aren't different from what he usually wears. White T-shirt with some obscure band on the front and jeans that look a million years old. Hot and grungy.

"You made coffee?" He looks hopeful.

Shit.

Of course he looks hopeful. He slept in your bed!

I clear my throat, interrupting my brain. "Yeah. Just you know ..." My voice trails off. What the hell should I say?

Tell him the truth! Well, most of it.

"The thing is"—I shuffle my feet—"you're leaving. So, I'd rather just keep things between us as friends." It isn't the total truth, but it's good enough.

Finally!

"You sure?" He leans against one of my kitchen cabinets. His voice sounds pained. "We can still have fun before I go. I can fly you out some-time, too ..." His blond hair is soaked, dripping down his shirt. He looks more like a sad puppy right now than a badass rocker. Jack is emotional.

I step closer. "Yeah. I'm just not the type to hook up casually. I know it's weird to most people that I'm not into sex without strings. But it's the way I am."

"No, I get it. It's the thing I like about you. You're different, Elira. You're different than these other girls."

"Thanks." I smile.

He raises his finger. "But don't think you're off the hook. One day, we'll find each other again, yeah?"

"How about we leave that to fate?" I chuckle.

"Good idea." He winks, eyes moving toward my front door.

"You sure you don't want some breakfast? Eggs or something? Coffee is already on." I wrap one foot behind the other, praying he says no. I want to be nice by asking, but I don't want him to agree.

"Nah. I got practice soon, too. If you're around, feel free to drop in." He pushes his wet hair back.

"Cool." I try to smile, relieved that he isn't going to sit.

He nods, like all is well. Any woman with a brain would be able to tell that he's let down, but I'm just going to play it off like I don't realize that fact. What else is there to do?

He walks toward the door and touches the handle. "See ya." And then he's gone.

THE RAIN COMES DOWN in sheets. I spend the entire day studying in my bedroom for Economics and trying to put together the best possible résumé. Interviewers are coming to campus in a few months, and I have to make sure everything is in order.

When the downpour is over, moonlight, faint and blue, streams through my window. I stand up and lean against the frame, my mind a complete whirl as I try to imagine what Nico is doing right now. I want to find a way to separate my dreams and fantasies from what is real. When I see him or think of him, it's difficult to separate the man I knew from the man I know. The more I try to make sense of what's happening, the wilder it all gets. I also feel so much guilt for sleeping next to Jack. I know that nothing happened, but still, it was wrong. Should I mention anything about it to Nico?

Truth is, I'm sure he already knows. Hell, it's likely. He already has my clothing sizes. That couldn't have happened by accident. It dawns on me that I'm probably being followed. Well! When I said I'd pretend to be his wife, I didn't give him the authority to have me stalked. And anyway, I did nothing wrong and therefore have nothing to fear. I hold my head high because *I did nothing wrong*. And yet, I cry.

Suddenly, I see a car pull up in front of my house. It shuts off its lights. That's odd. I leave my bedroom to find my mom lounging on our couch, watching reality TV.

To her back, I say, "Hey, Mom. Are you expecting anyone?" I wipe my face with the back of my hand, gathering myself.

"Nope." She flips the channel, oblivious.

"I saw a car pull up. I want to check." Reentering my bedroom, I take out a pair of knock-off UGG slippers and a soft, long-sleeved white cotton shirt, pulling it up over my head.

Leaving the house, I see the shiny, huge car glinting in the evening light. Is it Nico? It must be. If not him, someone from his world. No reason to delay the inevitable. I strut to the car, and the window pulls down. It's his driver, the big, bald suit. His face is handsome, although there's a hardness in his eyes.

"Looks like last night was fun, eh?" He smirks, and I want to slap him across the face and stomp my foot on the ground like an angry kid.

Nico knows, damn it!

I straighten my face. "Actually, it was a fun night." I purse my lips and lift my back. I don't have to answer to this guy. Who the hell is he to me? No one.

"I'm sure." He chuckles. "Saw you stumbling in around two a.m. Nice catch you brought home. Looked like he sleeps on the streets. I'm sure he was glad to have a warm bed to sleep in. And food to eat. Although I'm sure he could have used a steak instead of Tostitos."

My jaw drops. What in the fuck? "Not that it's your business, but he's a musician!"

"Oh, even better."

"Nico has you following me, is that right?" I put a hand on my hip, glaring. "What, you climbed up my goddamn window?"

"Something like that. It's called binoculars, college girl."

Oh shit. What did he see? There was nothing going on, but maybe it looked bad. Fuck, shit, fuck, fuck, fuck!

"Call Nico right now," I tell him in my most commanding voice. "I need to speak with him."

The man doesn't move a muscle. His eyes are smiling, like he's waiting for me to notice something.

"Why are you staring at me like that?" I accuse.

"You have no clue who I am, do you?" He tilts his head.

"Should I?" I step up, looking closer.

Big, bald suit has blue eyes. That smile though. It's familiar ...

"It's me. Alek."

My jaw literally drops open as I lean into the window, yelling, "Holy shit! It's you!"

He starts to laugh. Alek was in Agron's class back in Kosovo. They were always great friends, and I was the tagalong little sister. My hair was extremely long and soft, and Alek had asked my brother if he could feel my hair for a penny. But when Nico found out that Alek was paying to touch me, he went crazy. Punched my brother in his mouth and threatened Alek. Suffice it to say, Alek never touched my hair again.

"You work for Nico?"

"Yes. Always have, remember?"

I think back, but it all seems sort of blurry.

"So, you ... drive him?"

He chuckles. "Among other things." He pulls out a cigarette and lights up.

I'm still in shock. I can scarcely believe this. Talk about a blast from the past.

"Come on in, Elira. I want to take you out for dinner."

"Master's orders?" I ask mockingly, noticing the creases in his face. Clearly, he's lived hard.

Leaning forward onto the wheel, he says, "You do realize who you are and who I am, don't you?" Blowing smoke out the window but careful not to get it in my face, he continues, "You're currently in the hands of Mafia Shqiptare. It's not a joke, sweetheart. Nico never takes a step without constant protection and surveillance." Another deep inhale and exhale. "And now, you're shown as his wife. You think he'll let you la-di-da around school?"

The man has a point. A good point. Shit.

I look down at my feet. "I'm in slippers. Let me go change, and then we'll go."

"No need to get fancy. I heard there's a hibachi restaurant close by."

"Yeah, we go there for birthdays and stuff. It's casual. Just give me a few minutes."

I run back up into my house and change into a pair of jeans and a black T-shirt. Before I leave, my mom asks where I'm headed.

"Just out," I reply. "Love you."

I walk around the car and drop in the seat next to Alek. "So fancy." I touch the beautiful wooden console.

"Yeah. It's comfortable." He laughs.

"Did you tell Nico you're taking me to dinner?"

His face sharpens as he turns to me. "Nico knows everything, Elira."

"Oh shit." I look down at my feet. "So, I guess he already knows about Jack last night?" I'm still holding on to some hope that I can convince Alek not to say anything. I mean, there is nothing to tell!

Alek nods solemnly. "I tell Nico everything. No matter how much I like you, my allegiance is always to him. You'd be smart to remember that."

I screw my eyes shut. I'm so fucked.

He starts to drive, and I stare out the window, watching fellow college kids with backpacks and large coffees walking around without a care.

"You're the one he chose to follow me around?"

"That's right. Lucky you."

I look back at the boy I used to know. His smile is teasing.

We pull into the parking lot of the restaurant. When we enter, the smell of fried shrimp wafts through the air. Each rectangular family-style table is flanked by a chef clothed in white, who will cook fish, chicken, meat, or vegetables at the customer's request. They stand in front of tables, doing tricks with the chopped food. Pieces of shrimp are thrown into their hats and in the pockets of their shirts while the patrons cheer. It's tacky but fun. I used to come here for birthdays with my mom and Agron when we were little. Most recently, I came with Natalie and Janice for Janice's birthday. We got wasted on sake. Janice decided she'd make a great sous chef and took the chef's hat, trying to flip some shrimp inside the top. We laughed for hours.

Alek grumbles, "This food gives me the worst stomachache, but I love it. I'll need to stop for some Tums when we're through."

The hostess seats us at a table with only two seats left. I order vegetables with chicken, and Alek orders the steak, chicken, and shrimp. Go figure.

"So, tell me everything." I smile sweetly, hoping he'll talk about Nico.

"Cut to the chase, eh?" He snorts, sipping the complimentary ice water on the table. "Well, I stayed with Nico in Kosovo. My parents both died, and he became who I lived for. Not for nothing though. I was a kid then. He clothed and protected me. Armed me, too. When the war was over and the Serbs fled, the Kosovar people were looking for revenge. They wanted their rights wronged. People looked to Nico, but he said his time there was done. He left to the UK, and I followed him. After a few months, he pulled on his connections with the Kosovo Liberation Army and began opening businesses. I guess I was helpful in my own way."

"Eventually, you became a man though."

"That's right."

"And now?"

"Now, Nico's got more going on than you can imagine. You know the pizza chain, Table Manners?"

"Sure." I nod. "There's one in the town next over. I used to go during high school."

"That's Nico's."

"No shit!" I exclaim. "Wow."

He puts his plate forward, and the chef fills it with meat and vegetables straight off the grill.

"So, is he much tougher now than he was back in Kosovo?"

Alek laughs out loud. "Nico has always been tough."

"Yeah, but—"

"Always, Elira. Not with you. But to the rest of us, no one is worse to cross. You fuck with Nico? He'll bring down the storm from hell. He broke my jaw for touching your hair, for God's sake."

"Oh. Right." My voice is small, but he pointedly glares at me.

Oh God. I haven't even begun to rekindle my friendship with Nico, and I might have already fucked it up because of this Jack thing. My heart pounds.

Alek seems to notice my distress because he throws a heavy arm around my shoulders. "Don't worry about a thing. He still wants you watched. He still wanted me to take you out and make you comfortable."

I look down at my plate of food, unsure if I want to stuff my face from the stress or if eating will just have me retching. Just the thought of not seeing Nico again is enough to make me want to cry. And I'm not a crier. I've spent years pining for him. And now that he's back, I'm not ready to let him go. I'm just ... not.

We spend the rest of the night joking around, remembering the old days. Teachers we had. Kids we knew.

After the bill is paid, Alek drives me home. The car stops in front of my house.

I unbuckle my belt, turning toward Alek. "I know Nico must be fuming, thinking I hooked up with Jack. What can I do about this? Because I'm telling you, nothing happened with him. We literally both fell asleep with our clothes on. And I'm not sure if I should call Nico or—"

His face darkens, changing before my eyes. I'm out of my depth and, suddenly, under suspicion. "I won't sugarcoat it. You're in fuckin' trouble. Stumbling home with that guy. Nico isn't going to do anything rash, but he isn't happy."

"This is bad ..." My voice is wary.

"Well, not much to do about it now."

"And my brother?"

"What about him?" His eyes move between me and the street.

"Have you been with him at all? Is Nico going to take this out on him?"

"That's not your business, Elira. Now, come give me a hug before the next guy takes his shift."

I stretch myself over the console, praying my tears hold up. I need to cry but not in front of Alek.

"See that car?" He points to a black Lincoln town car parked across the street. "Raoul will switch off with me. He's all right."

"Got it."

"Oh, yeah, before I forget." He opens his window and lights up a smoke. "You're coming with us to St. Barts this weekend—as his wife, of course. Tell your friend, too. The hot one with the long hair and the tats. Natalie, is it? Nico wants you to have a friend with you. Make sure she knows the drill." His eyes sparkle.

"You're kidding." I bring my bag closer to my body, both nervous and shocked.

"I think what you wanted to say was, *What time are you picking me up?*"

"You're funny." I roll my eyes, trying not to show how afraid I am. "How about my classes?"

"School is closed Friday and Monday. Or did you forget?"

I look out the window, pressing my lips together. A trip? I'm not ready for this!

"I'll be here at six a.m. on Friday." His voice is final.

I steel myself enough to turn back toward him. "Don't I need flight information? And I don't have a passport—"

He laughs. "Now, you're the funny one. You don't need shit when you're with Nico. He takes care of everything."

"How about clothes?"

Jokingly, he mumbles, "What about the words *it's all taken care of* do you not get? Oh, and we fly private. No flight information other than to say, be there when Nico wants to leave."

My eyes bug. "Y-yeah. Okay. I'll see if Nat is free."

NAT IS FREE.

Actually, she screamed her head off in the middle of the diner when I asked her to come with me to St. Barts. Apparently, turquoise water, incredible restaurants, and the hottest DJs of all time are enough to have her not give a shit about the fact that we'll be traveling with the Albanian Mafia.

The last two days have been uneventful, except for the fact that Alek follows me around everywhere I go. I know he does his best to make me think I have my usual private life, but still, he's there. And seeing him reminds me of Nico, whom I still haven't spoken with since our date. Meanwhile, he has become a fixture in my dreams. I wake up some mornings, and I can smell traces of him on my skin. Natalie tells me that he's deeply embedded in my subconscious, and that's what I'm feeling. But whatever the reason, he has imprinted on me.

Here I am now, waiting in my living room at three fifty-five a.m. with nothing other than a small bag filled with toiletries and my heart filled with anxiety.

I went to Natalie's apartment yesterday under the guise of helping her choose some outfits for the trip. I got there, only to find her suitcase filled to the brim with clothes. I spent twenty minutes shifting my body on different sections of the suitcase while she attempted to close the zipper.

I didn't tell my mom details about the trip. She thinks that Natalie invited me to go away to St. Barts. I did my best to give her as much truth as possible, just omitting the part about Nico and the Shqiptare. I did tell Agron though. He was fuming, making me swear that I would have my own room on the trip. I tried explaining for the millionth time that Nico wasn't hurting me or forcing me to do anything against my will, but Agron is so hardheaded. He thinks that he should be invited to come along on the trip, as protection for me. I don't need protecting.

A car pulls up, a huge white Range Rover. My heart? It halts. He's here.

Oh shit. I can't do this.

The Rock is on my hand. It's heavier than hell.

On shaky legs, I force my body to stand up. I grip my purse. Somehow, I make it through the front door. I'm normally strong and confident. The way I'm acting right now just isn't me. That's when Natalie comes barreling into my arms.

"We're together. Don't be scared, babe." She wraps a skinny arm around my shoulders, walking me toward the car.

"How can you be excited about this?" I ask her.

"Oh, you mean because it's a Mafia thing and we have no clue how it'll be or who we'll meet or even where we're staying?" Her eyes widen, sparkling with enthusiasm.

"Exactly."

"Well, my friend"—she exhales—"those are all the reasons I'm excited."

Alek takes my bag and drops it in the trunk before handing me a bag from the local bagel shop. "For you two to eat."

I peer inside to see two wrapped bagels and two cups of coffee.

"You're amazing," Natalie gushes. "A good ol' fashioned fairy godfather." She bites into her egg and cheese bagel and moans.

We all laugh, and it breaks the ice some. I want to ask him if Nico will be on our flight, but I'm too chickenshit to ask. Instead, I eat my food and sit in silence, staring out the window.

Luckily, Natalie and Alek seem to get along famously. They laugh about the dumbest shit, and I couldn't be more relieved to be left out of the conversation. When Natalie notices my ring, she lifts my hand to get a better look.

"The life." I shrug.

"God."

We drive straight onto the tarmac and walk up a flight of outdoor steps to reach the jet's door. It's everything one would imagine it to be —I think. I've never even been on a normal plane, but I've seen them in the movies. This looks nothing like those; it's so much more luxurious. For one, the seats aren't set in tight horizontal rows. Instead, it's set up like a gorgeous living room with plush tan leather seats and glossy wood everywhere. There's even a bar and a large screen television.

Natalie points to the back of the jet. "I bet there's a bedroom in the back. Behind that door."

Alek is already comfortable in one of the front seats, but Natalie keeps walking until she drops into a window seat in the rear. I uneasily make my way down the aisle, taking the cushiony chair next to hers. I set myself up with my Kindle and attach my headphones to my phone, so I can listen to music. Natalie orders a cocktail from the stewardess. I decline a drink, although I'm sure I could use one.

Natalie skims through a stack of gossip magazines while we presumably wait for the others to arrive. I keep staring out the window, nerves taking over my insides.

"Take it from me." She taps my thigh. "When things get stressful, find a way to have fun. There's nothing else to do." Smirking, she says, "Come on, Elvira. At the very least, it'll be fun to finally see if vampires can tan."

I can't help but laugh out loud. "Thanks a lot."

"You're welcome." She winks.

A chill moves through me. It's so cliché, but I swear, I feel him before I see him. When I lift my head, Nico is rolling a small black suitcase and walking onto the flight with an entire entourage of seven men behind him. He's wearing a white linen shirt and khakis along with a black baseball hat, pulled down low. I can see the stubble across his defined jaw. Christ, he's sexy. One of the guys tells him something, and his lips curl up in a grin.

I'm barely breathing, and meanwhile, he hasn't even acknowledged me. Is he waiting for me to stand and greet him? I sit tight in my seat, unsure of what I'm supposed to do. Unfortunately, a set of three dark-haired stewardesses beat me to it, all walking up to him and asking if he needs a cold towel or a drink. They're giggling, for God's sake! How unprofessional! I adjust my shirt and pull out a Chapstick from my purse. Rock music continues to play in my ears. It's not helping my stress level.

The stewardesses leave his side, and he lifts his suitcase overhead. His shirt rides up, showcasing sliced, rock-hard abs. Natalie grabs my arm, so I turn to her.

She silently mouths, *Holy shit!* And then fans herself.

I can only nod in agreement. Because Nico is pure strength and rawness. He's got this dominant charisma that he's been honing in on since his youth.

The men laugh loudly, ordering drinks. I assume we're all here and ready to take off when a group of women board the flight. Twelve of them. All tall, coiffed, and dressed in skimpy summer dresses or skintight shorts.

Surprisingly, I see Elena, the doctor who helped me when I was kidnapped, walk on a few minutes after them. She's obviously different from the rest of the women though, and it's clear as day. For one, she isn't dressed like they are. She's in fitted khaki pants, but they aren't painted on. Her shoes are beautiful red loafers. And her white peasant-style top is a sexy and casual off-the-shoulder style, but it's not revealing. Her hair is like I remember—cropped short and beautifully highlighted blonde.

One of the men moves through the aisle to take her in his arms, greeting her with a chaste kiss. She puts her arms around his neck. He nods at something she says. I can't tear my eyes away. They're ... in love. An engagement ring—given for real—glints on her left ring finger, flushed against a beautiful diamond wedding band. It's perfect. I look down at The Rock, shimmering in all its glory. It's real, but it's fake. I decide that I hate it.

My Gap jeans and white T-shirt have me feeling dowdy. I fiddle with my necklace, a thin gold chain, despising this feeling running through me. I'm better than this, but I can't seem to control this feeling of less-than. It's Nico's fault. He turns me into a crazy person!

Natalie has on a black bra and an off-the-shoulder lime-green sweater with ripped jeans. It's casual but also really cool. She's got her own style, and she owns it. I, on the other hand, have always dressed for comfort and ease.

Natalie seems to notice my stress because she whispers, "You're still the most beautiful here. And natural. Be proud. You have done everything right in your life. Enjoy this time."

I try to smile at her, but my lips won't move. I feel like, all my life, I've been strong and in control. And, suddenly, everything is unraveling.

That's when Nico moves in front of us. "Hey," he says, staring at me for a few moments too long. His gaze is accusing, as though he were shouting at me, *You fucked a man who isn't me!*

I swallow hard. I try with my eyes to convey that I'm innocent. I didn't touch Jack! No words come during our staredown. My stomach clenches.

I don't know what to say. This whole thing is brand-new territory. Not only because our situation is insane and confusing, but also because I've never been in a relationship before. Nico and I had an amazing night together, sure, but then he left me without even a call! Yes, I could have reached out to him. But I was scared. He's the kingpin of the Albanian Mafia, for Christ's sake. And I'm just ... me. Not that me is a bad thing. It's a great thing. But still!

His face is set in a stern line as he folds his arms across his chest. I quickly avert my eyes away from his body, not wanting to be caught ogling.

I swallow hard, trying to force my lips into a smile. "Hi."

His eyes glance down to my hand. "Nice ring." His jaw clenches.

"Yeah, I, uh," I look around to make sure no one is close and then whisper, "meant to bring it to give it back. To you. I didn't know if—"

He shakes his head, silencing me. "On this trip, you're my wife. Do you understand me?" A tic moves through his jaw. "Wear it at all times."

He's angry as hell. At me! Shit.

Is he going to renege on our deal? Throw me off the flight? Retaliate for what he thinks I did with Jack? And then Agron pops into my head. Did I fuck things up for him? *Oh God.*

I look out the window, trying not to beg Nico to be calm about this situation. Meanwhile, my heart is jackhammering in my chest. I should just tell him outright that nothing happened. I shouldn't have brought Jack home with me. I know I shouldn't have, damn it. Not because Nico had specifically told me so, but because he and I had connected, physically and emotionally.

I bite my lip, trying to calm my head. I need to lighten this situation. Instead of telling him the truth—that I'm sorry and nothing happened—I say, "Okay then." I glance again around the plane, wanting to change the subject. "Is anyone else coming, like, a comedian?" I squeak. I'm trying to be friendly and funny but failing. I'm also trying to change the subject, but I'm failing at that, too. A comedian? Shit. Could I be any lamer?

He looks at me as though I were missing a screw in my brain. "This trip is work, Elira. Business. That's why you're here." His eyes disapprovingly move from my black Nike sneakers up to my face. "I realize, for a college kid like you, everything is fun and games. But now that you're here"—he gestures around the plane—"in my world? Well, you'd better start opening your eyes and following orders. I don't tolerate children."

It's like he's lit a match in my insides. Along with the flames, anger rises. Nico thinks my life is ... fun and games? He thinks I'm a child? What. The. Fuck? I work my ass off every single day of my life and always have. I might be his pretend wife and much younger, but I haven't gotten a lobotomy! Business or no business, I'm not allowing him to be condescending to me and treat me like shit.

I force myself to smile widely, getting into the character of the dutiful wife. Back straight and complete poise. "Of course, baby. Business trips are stressful for you. But no worries." My voice is loud enough for him to hear, but I'm careful to make sure no one else does when I say, "I brought plenty of Viagra. I know what stress does to you, and I made sure you'd be covered." My eyes trail down his pants, stopping at his thick, heavy bulge. I try to ignore the fact that I know how gorgeous his dick is and focus on the task at hand—embarrassing him. "I have it all figured out with one"—pause—"tiny"—pause—"pill." I smile widely.

His eyes flare. Immature of me maybe. But ... score!

Natalie's gaze flits between us, her mouth poised in almost laughter. Luckily, Nico doesn't give it any thought. His face is solely trained on me when he starts to chuckle. Darkly.

"If you insist on this behavior of yours, I'll have to punish you, wife." He says *wife* like a curse.

I squint my eyes. Oh shit.

"You know"—he moves closer, bending his huge body lower—"the thing I did to you on our honeymoon after you flirted with that waiter?" His breath moves to my ear, causing tingles straight down my spine. "Remember, Elira, when I put clamps on your perfect pink nipples. Ate you out until you were coming in my mouth? And then, after taking all that Viagra," he says loudly, raising his brows, "fucked you so hard all night, you could barely walk for the remainder of our trip?"

I'm in a state of shock.

He steps back, smirking, and I swear to all that is holy that I'm more turned on than I ever thought possible. Natalie's face is on fire, and I'm sure mine is burning, too. My breaths are quickening—in anger. In embarrassment. Thank God it doesn't seem like anyone heard. I have never, in all my life, known a man who sparks up this crazy attraction combined with anger like he does.

How am I going to end this thing?

He smiles, waiting patiently for me to respond. But I can't. What am I supposed to say to *that*? I turn my head left and right. Who heard? No one seems to be paying attention to us. But ... *but* ... ugh!

Nico puts his hand out at Natalie. "Hello."

She blushes fiercely, taking it. "Hi, Nico. N-nice to see you again." She smiles like a regular debutante.

I glare at her because what the hell? She's supposed to be my wingwoman, not a fangirl! Knowing her, she's probably picturing herself tied up and at Nico's mercy. With her nipple piercings! Just great.

Nico smirks, like he's happy about the effect he's having on my friend. A burst of jealousy so strong moves through me, making my bones shudder. It's a feeling I'm not used to having, but damn, it's painful. In this moment, I feel like an animal. I want to claw her eyes out and scream that he's mine.

But he isn't, a snarky part of my brain reminds me. *You're only here because he needs you for business*, she says. *When he's done, he'll throw you out of his life, just like he did after Kosovo.*

His smile is charming—for Natalie. "Have you been to St. Barts?"

"No," she purrs. "But I've been to other Caribbean islands."

I can feel the blood in my veins pulsing. She's my friend! How could she?

"Well," he continues, leaning an arm against the wooden overhead bin, "we fly into St. Maarten first and then switch to a much smaller plane to get to St. Barts. It's a tiny airport, you see."

"I bet." Natalie's eyes twinkle.

"Enjoy the flight." He looks between us, slightly amused. Turning around, he sits in his seat before pulling out a silver Mac laptop.

I turn to Natalie, glaring at her.

And she has the audacity to laugh, whispering, "You're insane, friend. You two are electric. Jesus!"

"Electric? He wanted to kill me."

"Oh, no." She shakes her head. "He wants to fuck you. Trust me on this."

"You flirted with him!" I accuse in my quietest voice. "You were fawning and—"

"Oh. My. God. You've got it so bad. Badder than bad." She shakes her head before glancing up, making sure he isn't hearing us.

I do not! I mouth, clutching my purse like a lifeline. I'm lying through my teeth, and it's so obvious.

"I might need to pierce your nips. Stat." She laughs, and I slap her shoulder, holding back my own laughter.

She pulls out a pen from her gigantic purse and writes on the back of her gossip magazine.

He's ridiculously hot! Holy shit! And all yours if you want him!

I take the pen from her, writing beneath it.

Oh, stop. I don't want him. He doesn't want me. This is for Agron.

She pulls the pen back and takes out a second one for me from her purse. Then, she writes, *Stop the lies. Tell him how you feel!*

Are you nuts?

Hook up with him this weekend. For my sake, use the clamps!

I give her a stink-eye.

I can't hook up with him.

He wants you!!!

He's MAFIA!!!

Mafia schMafia. Just focus on him, not what he does.

But ...

Flipping the book to another page, she writes, *No buts! Enjoy this trip, wifey! And if he 50-Shades you, I need every fucking detail.*

Don't flirt with him, Nat.

Ahh, so you DO want him? Otherwise, I'm interested.

I glare at her, and she laughs.

Don't fucking touch him!

Love you.

Love you, too.

I spend the rest of my flight listening to music and reading the newest book by Leigh Ford. I do my best not to lift my head because, when I do, I see Nico. He's so focused on what he's working on. Over six feet of intelligence combined with a body set to kill, he's impossibly sexy. The worst part is, even my mind has found a way to rationalize his Mafia business. He was born in a time and place where this was just the way it was. And he excelled. I'm not a big believer in religion, but I do believe that we have paths that are prescripted. And this is his. Deep in my gut, I don't blame him for the course he's taken.

The moment we're in the air, the girls on the jet unbuckle their seat belts and bring drinks from the bar, handing them to the men. The guys are talking sports, their voices familiar. And, suddenly, it hits me. I know the way they sound, laughing, because I've heard it before. My breathing stalls as my chest tightens. I'm surprised at the feelings bubbling up in my chest, but they're unstoppable.

Nat puts her hand over mine. "You okay?" She squints. "Let me get you a drink."

Before she can move out from her seat, Nico is on his haunches in front of me. His hat is off, black hair straight and smooth. Lips so full. I want to jump into his arms, but I can't. I'm just business to him.

"What's wrong? I was just kidding about the clamps," he jokes, but I can't move.

His face turns truly concerned. I want to reply, but I can't. I didn't think I was this affected or traumatized, but it turns out, delayed reaction is a real thing. He unbuckles my belt and takes my hand, walking me into the room in the back of the plane. It's a bedroom. Under normal circumstances, I'd look around. But I'm trying not to puke. My head spins as he places me on the soft comforter.

"Are you afraid of being in the air?" Again, he drops down to his knees, so we're face-to-face.

A pang of déjà vu moves through me.

"N-no, I—"

He nods, urging me on. When my words still won't come, he steps out and brings me a can of ginger ale with a cup full of ice. He opens and pours before bringing it to my mouth. I sip, the cold, bubbly drink soothing my frayed insides.

"No mint tea here," he whispers with his lips turned down.

And that's when I burst into tears. He wraps me in his arms, and my body curls into his chest, yearning for warmth and comfort.

Into his shirt, I tell him, "I heard your guys talking. And I thought about being taken. I couldn't move my limbs, Nico. I thought I was going to die. What did they give me?" My body trembles, like the aftershocks of an earthquake.

He pulls me closer. The fact that I'm seeking solace within the man who ordered all of this done is fucked up. But I can't seem to help myself.

He rubs my back. "I understand. I'll keep them away from you this trip. Under my protection, you should never worry. They wouldn't have touched a hair on your head. If they said otherwise, it was because some of them are sick fucks who wanted to scare you. And I'll make them pay for that. Trust me."

Holding me into his broad chest, he kisses my hair. It's not fatherly or brotherly. It's more. I let him soothe me in the way only he ever could. His deep voice. The way he shushes me. His warm, thick hands against my back. My entire body heats from his proximity because it knows this man.

Unstoppable words spill from my lips. "I-I didn't touch Jack, I swear. We were drunk and fell asleep. I wouldn't have done it ... I was confused over what was going on between us, and Jack seemed so simple and easy." I continue to cry, my emotions flinging back and forth between Nico, the boss of the Mafia Shqiptare, and Nico, my childhood friend. "I never would have—"

"Calm down," he whispers, his thumb brushing against my forehead before wiping my tears away.

"But I need you to hear me. I wouldn't have. I was drunk, but when push came to shove, I couldn't. Didn't."

I blink, lost in his stare. His dark eyes zero in on me like he found something he'd been missing. A mixture of relief and thankfulness. My head has no idea what to make of this.

"Alek let me know you'd slept with your clothes on. You didn't have sex with him." His jaw slightly clenches.

"You knew?"

He nods.

"Are you ... mad?" My eyes widen in worry.

His jaw clenches. "I'm not a child who needs to yell and scream for your attention. And, Elira, for your information"—he bends his head lower—"when I'm with a woman, there can be no man other than me in her life. I don't share. You walk around, telling people you're my wife? I expect decency from you. Maybe I didn't make myself clear enough before, but I demand it." His eyes flash.

"Decency? I don't even know what's happening between—"

"You know what's happening." He swallows hard, and my head turns to clouds.

"Nico," I whisper, trying to backtrack, "I've respected you as a man for as long as I can remember. You were my life when I was a child. You became my savior when you got us out of Kosovo. I owe you for the friendship you showed me and for saving us from what surely would have been death. Forget the other guy. Just forget him. It was nothing. He was nothing. Right now, I'm yours. Okay? I gave you my word, and I meant it."

He gives me a small nod. For a second, I imagine myself next to the man I grew up loving. The one who owned every piece of his own life and mine. Is that the man I'm looking at now?

Another few minutes pass, but neither of us speaks.

Eventually, I calm down. He stands up, bringing me another cup of ginger ale.

When I'm done, he tells me, "Wash your face. There's a private bathroom here."

I use the bathroom. Blow my nose. Get a grip. That was intense. God.

When I leave the bathroom, Nico is lying down on the large bed with his legs crossed in front of him, a laptop on his lap.

"Come," he tells me, looking at the empty spot next to him.

Slowly, I make my way there. My stuff is here, too.

I touch my earbuds, and he asks, "What are you listening to?"

"Rage Against the Machine. I love it. But you know that already from your super-stalker skills." My voice is all sass.

He nods. "Yes, I do know that. I prefer alternative rock. The hard shit gives me a headache."

"Old man," I taunt. "Who do you listen to?"

"I love Dave Matthews. Coldplay. U2."

"That's cool. Jack plays—" I stop. Oh shit. I didn't mean that. I seriously didn't mean to drop his name!

A million apologies are on my lips when his face hardens, radiating anger.

He moves his laptop to a table beside the bed.

If I run, where would I go? Should I scream?

In a flash, he's above me, hovering. My breaths shorten. For a moment, he shuts his eyes. But then they're open again—and gleaming.

In a swift move, my wrists are held above my head. A dark menace. He can hurt me. And yet, I still want him.

As I struggle against his hands, he tells me, "Just slow down. Stop trying to win a battle you can't win."

I imagine him from a few weeks ago. Naked and sweating, gripping me to his huge, muscular chest. I wanted to touch him, but he didn't allow it. And now, he's got me back within his control. I shudder, a moan boiling from my mouth as I imagine him doing all the things he's never done. Kissing my lips and down my neck. Licking me between my thighs.

"I want you to let me go." Lie.

"Is that right?" He cocks his gorgeous head to the side, calling bullshit with his smirk.

"Y-yes." I'm shaking. His proximity has me mindless. With all the strength I can muster, I tell him, "Get. Off. Me." Lie.

"I can smell you from here. How badly you want me. You think you can hide your feelings with your attitude? You think I can't see straight through that smart mouth of yours? You're soaked. You're panting. And it's for me."

Am I panting? I'm panting. Shame fills me. But it's undeniable that my whole body is on fire, just as he said. I want to defy him because anger is better than this.

"I said, get off!" I whisper-yell through my teeth.

He shakes his head. "When the time is right, you'll see what comes of this between us." He lowers his face, inhaling the scent from my neck.

Oh God.

"No other men, Elira. None. You were a child when I knew you, but you're a woman now. Men like me don't play silly games. What I want, I take. What I hate, I kill. And what's mine, I protect." With his free hand, he moves the hair out of my face. "You asked if I was angry. The answer is yes. I'm still fuming. With me in your life, there is no room for anyone else. Don't drag other men in my line of sight, thinking it'll bring me closer to you. It won't ever work. Do you understand?"

"Yes, Nico. I—"

"For this trip, you're mine, twenty-four/seven. Don't fucking forget who you're dealing with. I'm not some college idiot trailing behind you like a lovesick puppy. Your brother is on the hook here. You'd do well to remember that."

"But—"

"This conversation is over now." And then he's off me.

Off me!

What in the fuck?

And then ... he leaves the room. I'm left soaked, wanting, and angry as hell.

When I get back to my seat with my bags in hand, Natalie is concerned. I shake my head, letting her know not to ask me now. She gets the point and puts her earplugs back in.

The girls on the flight are all still giggling, enjoying themselves. Meanwhile, my panties are soaked, and my hands are clammy. This is bullshit.

Am I mad over what he did to me? Yes, I'm fucking mad!

A card game is happening alongside a game of backgammon. I hear ambient sounds of different conversations flowing around the plane. One of the women is dying to get an appointment at Millenial Plastic Surgery. Someone mentions a gas leak in their garage and a wife who can't stop spending money. A male voice mentions he needs a blow job. It might be a trip for business, but clearly, pleasure is on the menu. For them, not for me.

Nico, however, is completely unaffected. It's almost as though he has a fence around him, topped with barbed wire. No one comes near unless he calls for them. I want to cut that fence with a chain saw before punching him in the face. The fact that he's not distressed like I am or suffering from a case of blue balls is infuriating.

I reach for my travel bag and root around for my Kindle. I put earbuds in my ears, trying to calm down. Limp Bizkit's "Break Stuff" is the first song that comes on, telling me how it's one of those days when you don't wanna wake up because everything is fucked and everybody sucks. I huff, letting Fred Durst's anger fuel mine. Before I know it, I'm clenching my fists. If I were in a cartoon, steam would be billowing out from my ears. I turn off the music, stuffing it back into my bag. This is hitting too close to home.

In my defense, I didn't mean to mention Jack. It was a stupid mistake. I drop my head, pissed off. What can I do?

At some point during the flight, Elena comes to say hello. I would have gone to her first, but I wasn't sure what to say. Something tells me that starting a conversation with, *Thanks for taking care of me while I was drugged and kidnapped*, wouldn't have been a good icebreaker. Regardless, she comes, says hi, meets Natalie, and is totally cool.

She's a dermatologist and married to one of Nico's guys, Mat. They both lived in Brooklyn and fell in love during high school regardless of the fact that his Albanian family was mortified when he introduced his beautiful blonde girlfriend to them. Splitting up so that she could go off to school to study medicine, he began working for the family. When she moved back to New York for her residency, they rekindled their romance.

She also confirms that, other than the three of us, the rest of the girls are here for "fun." And by fun, she means to party, screw, and do whatever else—for money. Not that I'm judging. I mean, these girls are living their best life. They're on a private jet, for free, ready to party in St. Barts, keeping company with rich and powerful men who aren't exactly hard on the eyes. And they get paid, in cash, for it! I'm not blind. I see how good they look and how happy they are. All of them in Chanel bags. The fact that I have one of my own now, courtesy of the boss himself, isn't lost on me. All of them are in beautiful clothes and jewelry. I'm sure some of them even have mortgage-free apartments in Manhattan. Is this what Nico is expecting from me? No. It can't be. We haven't even had sex! And our two sexual exchanges, if you could call them that, were more like erotic experiences than anything else. I don't think watching the man you love getting his dick sucked or having him touch himself while you touched yourself counts. *God, I'm screwed.*

When Elena goes back to her seat, Nico nods at me, as though he approves of our conversation. I can't hold his eyes. Not because he was right, but because, somehow, he reads me too well. With Nico, there's no hiding. And still, I wish he'd come near me or talk to me. For all my bravado, I feel completely shaken inside. The walls I've worked so hard to build feel unstable. I want him to be the Nico I know, not the Mafia kingpin. I also just want to apologize. Tell him I'm sorry about Jack. I have never in my life wanted to apologize to a man before. But Nico brings that out of me because he demands it. I hate him for making me feel this way.

The captain goes on the loudspeaker and tells everyone to sit down, as the flight is about to land. Natalie does a little shimmy in her seat. I don't want to smile and laugh, but I do.

9

THE LAST LEG OF OUR TRIP HAPPENS FASTER THAN I THOUGHT POSSIBLE.
After getting off the flight, four tiny planes, seating eight each, are
ready for us. I get on and buckle up before I realize that this jet is
smaller than small. It's a bird, and I don't mean that in a good way. I
find myself praying for my life when Nico puts his large hand on my
thigh, as if to say he's got me.

"I'm scared," I whisper.

"Don't worry. It's noisy and shaky but quick."

After landing, we're whisked to huge black SUVs, lined up and
waiting for us on the tarmac. In the car I'm in is Nico, Alek, me, and
Natalie.

Alek pulls out waters from a small cooler in the back, handing
one to me. I'm exhausted, and I feel so dry. I open the cap and drink,
immediately feeling better.

"So, where are we going?" I ask.

"The mansion sits on St. Jean Bay on the island's northern shore.
We'll have access to the best sand and a coral reef. Just wait until the
morning, when the sun rises. It's heaven." Alek turns his attention
back to Natalie, giving her details about restaurants and beaches we'll
visit.

Nico sits in the front seat, discussing something with the driver. His voice is low, and I can't make out what he's saying. After a few minutes of trying to hear—and failing, no thanks to Alek and Natalie —I zone out. I wish we'd landed in the daytime, so I could see the world around, but it's dark. The car takes us up and down what feels like millions of rolling hills.

Finally, we pull into a large driveway. The car door is opened, and an ocean breeze wafts up around me. I step out, looking up. The night sky is littered in twinkling stars.

There is unimaginable beauty in this world, I think, eyes glancing around a magnificent white stucco mansion, complete with a beautiful orange roof.

The entire place is lit up in lights. It's breathtaking. Stuck in my own head, I finally turn around to see Nico intently staring at me. The look on his face is thoughtful.

I let out a small smile. "Thank you for bringing us. It's so beautiful," I tell him honestly.

"Just wait till morning. There's nothing like it." He puts his hands into the back of his pants pockets. In this moment, he's just a man.

Suddenly, what looks like two dozen men and women in crisp white uniforms come running out of the house. Some are taking luggage from the trunks of the cars, and others are offering cold towels and drinks. Natalie easily takes a glass of what looks like champagne and follows Alek into the home. I guess the entourage is sharing a house.

One of the ladies welcomes me. "*Bonsoir.* I'm Yvette. Welcome home. Your name?"

When I tell her Elira, she motions for me to follow her. She's similar in height to myself with light-brown hair tied tightly in a bun. We walk past a huge pool, bright with lighting; beyond it is nothing but dark ocean.

"There is the outdoor kitchen." She points to the right where I see large, round set tables. "We will serve breakfast there every morning. We can also bring food to you in your room, if you'd like. And over there"—she points to the opposite end of the house—"is the outdoor bar."

The bartender, a tall man with a shaved head, waves to us.

"If you'd like a nightcap this evening, Jean is ready."

She walks me up a flight of outdoor steps and finally into a small, long corridor. "This is your room. The Queen Suite. The King's Suite is next door."

The white door opens, and I pause, almost afraid to follow her inside. I grip my purse and force my legs forward. Beauty like this is once in a lifetime. I want to enjoy it.

"Your room faces the ocean. The most beautiful one here, I think." She continues to show me the room's amenities, from the magnificent pink-and-white marble bath to the huge closet that is filled to the brim with clothes.

I even have a huge white four-poster bed with crisp white sheets and a fluffy pink comforter. I wish I could have brought my mom here with me. She deserves a vacation more than I do.

Before leaving, Yvette hands me her card and the Wi-Fi password. "If you need something, call me."

"Um, Yvette?"

She turns around, pausing at the door. "Yes?"

There are so many questions I have, and there's no way I'm losing the opportunity to ask her. "Is this a hotel or someone's private residence?"

"This is a boutique hotel. But your group has rented the entire mansion for the long weekend. We're all at your service."

"I see. And do you know Nico?"

Her mouth immediately straightens out. She doesn't reply, but I can't help but notice how her face tightens up. Nerves? I wait another second or two, but she doesn't reply. I guess I've hit a dead end on that one.

I need to try another route. "Has this group been here before?"

"Oh, yes." She seems relieved. "Every year, they come."

"And who usually takes this room?" Seriously, if finance doesn't work out, I need to be a lawyer.

"I have been working here for three years. This room has always stayed empty. Until now."

I tilt my head to the side, confused. Maybe there was an issue with the plumbing or something. Huh. "Thank you," I tell her, not unkindly.

And with a final small nod of her head, she's gone.

Playing around with the room's lights, I see there's a balcony outside my room, facing the ocean. I slide open the door and find a small, round table and two chairs. The moon shines brightly, and the ocean adds a briny chill to the air. I take a seat and a deep breath when I hear music wafting around me. The party must be underway. I inhale and exhale the ocean air. I would sleep out here if I could.

Does Nico expect me to stay in my room? Go down to the party? I check my phone and input the password for Wi-Fi. No new text messages.

I guess I'll just wash my face and go see what's happening outside.

There's a DJ. Two bartenders behind the bar. Girls scantily clad. And then the men. Everyone is washed up, changed, and ready to party. The weather is incredible, too. Meanwhile, I'm still in my travel clothes. How was I supposed to know this was going to be all fancy?

I turn around to go back to my room to change when Elena calls out, "Elira, hi!"

She hugs me like we're old friends, smelling like fresh soap and expensive perfume. Her happiness radiates. Her husband, Mat, steps over to us at the same time Natalie comes over. We talk as a group, his hands always on one part of Elena's body. We chat about Green, and they tell us about their new apartment in the West Village. What they have together looks pretty amazing. He even beams with pride when Natalie asks Elena about certain dermal fillers, and she discusses them like a doctor. Because, well, she's a doctor. The fact that she's a full-fledged physician and married to this man is both surprising and ... not. Nico is offering me a taste of this life that Elena seems to be okay with. More than okay. How does she do it?

A strong arm wraps around my waist. "Hey." His eyes are warm.

I can feel a number of looks move to our direction.

Suddenly, I don't feel like a stranger in the party. I'm with *him*. My stomach flutters. I want to say that I'm sorry about the flight. I don't want games. I don't like drama. I know he said the conversation was over, but I still feel guilty. He looks back at me, reading the remorse in my features. He nods his acceptance, and I want to sag with relief. Moments later, drinks are pushed our way.

Nico hands me a glass. "Tequila soda with lime."

Under my breath, I say, "What a stalker." I can't help the smile on my face.

In my ear, he whispers, "You know it." He takes a sip. "Having fun?"

"It's beautiful." I look around, remembering that I'm still icky from the flight. "I think I should go back to the room to change."

"Stay." He takes another long sip of his drink.

I look around, noticing Natalie, Mat, and Elena are suddenly no longer near us. "Um"—I lick my lips—"there's something I want to mention."

He quirks an eyebrow.

"I heard what you said about other men, and I want to know if it applies to you."

"No men for me either."

I stand straighter, wanting him to know that I'm serious. "I can't feel comfortable if you're fucking other women, Nico. I know that the power here is yours. But I'm asking you."

"What does it matter to you if I fuck other women?" he challenges.

"It matters to me. You talked about respect. Well, I want it back. I'm doing you a favor. Sure, you're promising to protect my brother. But I could have said no. And then you'd be stuck with one of them." I nod my head toward one of the girls. The truth is, there is nothing at all wrong with these women. They seem perfectly nice and beautiful and ready to have fun. "Not exactly wife material," I point out, hoping I don't sound as jealous as I feel.

"You want respect, too." The look on his face is satisfied, like I asked for something he had been waiting to hear.

"That's right," I reply defiantly. "If I'm committing myself, you should, too."

He wraps his free arm around my waist, bringing me flush against him. "Only you, Elira," he whispers in my ear. "I wouldn't dare touch another woman." He's so earnest that it takes my breath.

My flow of relief is palpable. Knowing that Nico and I are exclusive for this time makes me feel so much more secure.

We spend the rest of the night talking. And once I relax, I'm laughing! Reminiscing about people we used to know and the crazy shit we thought was normal back in Kosovo but realize now that it just wasn't. Not in a bad way. More in a *we just didn't know better* way. When I remind him of Bardha, he actually laughs out loud.

"Believe it or not, she runs one of my stores."

"You're kidding!" I exclaim. "She once told me you were good in bed, and I thought, *Who isn't good when they're sleeping?*" I wheeze with laughter. I look at my drink, now empty, and wonder just how much tequila was poured into the cup. I love this place! "Those boobs though."

"Gigantic." He laughs. "Seriously. They used to scare the shit out of me."

"Don't think about her anymore," I squeal, unable to stop laughing.

"Why not?" He licks his full lips, and I stop laughing. Stop thinking. All of my attention focused on his perfect mouth.

Before I can think it through, I tell him, "Because I loved you then. It hurt me to know she had any part of you." The alcohol has clearly severed any thought before speech.

"I'm sorry," he whispers in sincerity. "You were a baby, and I was a man. Or did you forget?" He's smiling sadly.

"I didn't even understand what I wanted from you." I roll my eyes as a waiter walks over and takes my empty glass before handing me another full cup. I murmur, "Thank you."

"Oh, you understood. You didn't know the names for what you felt. But you wanted me for yourself."

"Oh, come on. You were a man-whore. Every single woman was dying to get into your pants."

He leans forward, body language serious. "My parents were dead. I was fighting constantly. Rising up within the Liberation Army. Women were falling at my feet, begging for it. I'd go out to the bar, and they all knew who I was and wanted a piece. I gave in. I was angry with God for taking my family. Spilling blood of the enemy in retaliation. And woman after woman would come and go. It was fucking in its most desperate form. But then I'd come see you. A little girl. The sweetest. You loved me for reasons no one else did. I was addicted to it. Needed that love like I needed my next breath."

"I'm not a baby anymore." My voice is throaty.

I'm in his arms now. He smells so. Fucking. Good. I could sleep here for eternity. I sway, but he keeps me on my feet.

"No, you're not." He walks me to a small outdoor seating area.

People are there at first, but upon seeing Nico, they stand and disperse. He sits on the couch, and I drop myself down, putting my head in his lap. Giggling. Drunk. So fucking happy that I could die right now, and it would be cool with me.

The topic changes. He tells me about the places he's been since Kosovo and the friends he's made. About the men running the Colombian cartels and how he managed to befriend them.

"*Those* guys?"

"Yes. You see"—he brushes my hair to the side—"my business model is simple but managed to change the existing order. Before, there were cocaine importers, and then there were Dutch wholesalers. I cut out the Dutch middlemen and began negotiating directly with the Colombian cartels. I've always thought brokers were useless. Without them taking a cut, we were able to charge less money for our product."

"Margins. You got better ones. And how could rival gangs compete when you have cheaper product?"

"That's right. They couldn't." His hand strokes up and down my back. "So smart."

"You're telling me about your business." The realization is a revelation. He's letting me in.

"Yes."

"You trust me?" I manage to sit up.

He's smiling. I jump onto his lap, straddling him so our chests are
facing each other, and drop my head on his massive shoulder. I can
feel the outline of his dick. I try not to moan. It's a combination of lust
and pleasure and, frankly, comfort. I want him to fuck me right here
and now, and then I want to fall asleep, just like this. How strong was
this tequila? Not that I'm complaining, but I'm shit-faced from barely
two drinks.

"I trust you." His voice is gravelly.

I grumble like a petulant child as he lifts me off his lap and places
me beside him.

He laughs at me. "No drinking without me anymore. I see what it
does to you. Time for bed."

"Bed? What? No. Why?"

He lifts me in his arms. Could I walk? Maybe. But I like being
carried. I wrap my arms around his neck and legs around his waist.

"Where is everyone?" I croak.

He moves swiftly up the stairs and down the corridor. "Fucking or
sleeping. It's close to three in the morning." After bringing me into
my room, he places me down on the bed. "I'll see you in the
morning."

"Stay?"

"Not tonight." He kisses my forehead, and in usual Nico fashion,
he walks out the door.

10

I check the bedside clock. It's eight thirty a.m. I step out of bed, stretching my arms up and feeling pretty darn good, considering the night I had.

I wash myself up before putting on one of the new bikinis hanging in the closet. It's sexy but nothing too revealing. It's a beautiful tan color with painted red flowers. The coverup goes on next, a cream netted sarong. There's even a beautiful wide-brimmed white hat and a woven beach bag. It's all classy and beautiful. Whoever does my shopping needs to win an award. I'm still sort of uncomfortable with taking these clothes. Then again, I'm not keeping them. It's just to borrow for this trip. Feeling better about my newest rationalization, I slide on a pair of Jimmy Choo wedges. I can't imagine they're waterproof, but there are no plain flip-flops, so I'm going to assume these are the ones for the beach and pool. Throwing sunscreen, my Kindle, phone, and wallet into the bag, I make my way out of the room.

Pausing for a moment, I check my phone. A text.

Agron: He'd better not touch you.

My brother is seriously losing it.

I look around, nothing but silence and sunshine greets me. Boy, I could get used to this. I walk back down the beautiful white corridor and down the steps to the pool, bar, and breakfast area. The house is even more incredible in the daylight. The outdoor kitchen table is devoid of any people, other than Nico. He's having a smoke and reading a newspaper, his seat facing the ocean. Seeing Nico, the boss of the Shqipe and the man I used to love, relaxing and acting normal is just ... too much. It's so much more than simply attraction. I've been attracted to men before. And I've gotten the butterflies, and I've swooned and all that from an amazing kiss. But seeing Nico here has me frozen.

He drops his paper and calls out, "Get over here, Elira. I see you."

I grumble but walk over to him.

"Sit. Coffee and bread are on the table. Someone will come out to take your order now." He puts out his cigarette in a small green ashtray but continues to read intently.

"So ..." I start, picking up a slice of the crusty baguette. It's sweet, crispy, and freakin' amazing. "What's the plan?"

He pushes a second newspaper my way. "Read a bit, and let's eat. Then, we'll figure it out."

I lift the paper and begin skimming headlines until I find an article of interest. I normally read every morning over breakfast, so this is a welcome surprise.

A few minutes later, he says, "You look very serious. What has your eye?"

"Hamas. So desperate to win world sympathy, they use Palestinian kids as shields. Hiding weapons and mortars beneath United Nations schools and firing rockets from there. I swear, it turns my stomach to shreds, reading this."

"We're not the only ones who've suffered. Helps put things in perspective." He presses his lips together firmly. "I was in Israel a few years ago. Incredible country. They're similar to us Albanians. Strong work ethic. Love of family. Never back down from a fight. They're forced to live in constant war with neighbors who refuse to recognize their existence. Something else we know about, eh?"

"I guess everyone suffers to an extent. Some more and some less. Makes it annoying though when I'm in school, learning with these entitled assholes. They just ... don't get it. They have this naiveté. Hard to look at when I've seen so much."

"There's a difference between us and them. But why fight it? Why not just appreciate the fact that you're not the same as them, and that's okay?"

We stare at each other then. Moments pass. I can't help but notice little details about Nico I must have missed. A small scar on his chin. A black rope bracelet on his left wrist. I look up into his face, losing myself in his dark, soulful eyes.

Get a grip, my head reminds me.

And then I say, "I heard the beaches are beautiful here." My voice comes out in a whisper.

"The most beautiful." The way he's staring at me, it's as though he isn't talking about the beaches at all. I watch his throat as he swallows.

"I want to tell you"—he moves closer to where I sit—"I know you like your sarcasm and you don't like it when other people tell you what to do. But you've got to trust me." His thumb slides across my hand. It's warm, dry, and rough. Awareness bursts through my veins. While it's soothing, the look on his face is anything but. "Trust that I'd never let anyone hurt you. Trust that when I say to do something, it's for your own good."

"W-why are you saying this?" I stumble on my words, confused. It feels like a warning.

"Because other people are coming on this trip, too, who we will hopefully be meeting here. There are some big mergers in the works. But even while we're all partying and having fun, business will be conducted. There are also some small factions of different crews who might decide to show up. I'll need you by my side—unless I tell you to go. And I need you to do as I say."

My head manages to nod, agreeing before my mind can chime in that this sounds scary.

"Good girl," he whispers, moving an errant hair from my face.

"*Bonjour*, madame," a sweet voice interrupts us.

I turn my head to find a waitress smiling at me. She's tan and golden blonde, and she has that natural beachy look that I'd give my right arm for.

"*Bonjour*," I reply, taking a look at Nico.

He pays no attention to her and is instead staring at me.

"Eggs? Waffles? Pancakes? We can make anything you like." That beautiful French accent. *God.*

I look to Nico, who has nothing but coffee in front of him. He lifts his newspaper back up.

"I'll have an omelet with spinach and tomatoes. Do you have whole wheat toast? Butter and jam?"

"Yes, of course. Any juice? We have fresh orange."

"Sure. I'd love that."

After she walks away, I rummage through my purse and find my Kindle. Sometimes, current events are just too depressing to read about.

Just as I'm about to power it up, Nico clears his throat. "No one will be waking up for a while. After you eat, let's go to the beach."

"Yeah?" I can't stop the excitement in my voice. No, I can't swim. But who cares? I can dip my toes in and enjoy.

I can see his lip quirk up in a small smile, but he doesn't speak after that. I'm sipping my coffee when the juice is brought and placed in front of me.

After thanking the waitress, I ask Nico, "Any idea which room Natalie is staying in?"

"Yes. She's directly across from yours, facing the garden. How is your room? Are you comfortable?"

"No. The mattress was hell, and the view sickened me." I look up at the sky, exclaiming, "He asks if I'm comfortable!" I pull out a cigarette from his pack, and he lights me up.

"Funny girl." The smile reaches his eyes.

I guess last night broke the ice because I feel like we're friends now. There's an easiness between us.

The food comes, and I barely touch it. Just kidding! I inhale.

When I'm done, Nico tells me to get whatever I need and meet him in front of the house in twenty minutes. I want to take this time to visit Nat. I easily find her room and knock. It only takes her a few seconds to open the door, and she ushers me in. The room is small, charming, and positively beautiful. Natalie jumps back into her large white bed, scrolling through her phone, a huge smile on her face.

"Let me guess," she starts, dropping her phone to her side. "You've been up for over an hour and already had breakfast?"

"Maybe," I reply, laughing.

She knows me too well.

"Spill. Were you with Nico just now? The two of you have been attached at the hip. His hand was always on you. You guys were literally in your own little orbit." She hugs me close. "He loves you."

I blush up to my roots. "Stop it, Nat. We had a really good time. And this morning, we had breakfast. I ate; he had coffee. Nothing sexual."

"Well, it's a good thing I'll be right here when the time finally comes." She twists onto her side before standing up. She's in a sexy, silky, short white nightgown. It's gorgeous.

"Since when do you sleep in such fantastic stuff?"

"I bought it for the trip, just in case I got lucky."

I laugh as she stands up, stretching her arms up high before entering her bathroom. I follow her and watch as she throws her long hair in a super-high ponytail and spreads toothpaste on her toothbrush.

"So," I start, interrupting her routine, "he wants to take me out this morning. We're supposed to meet up soon in front of the house."

"Aha!" she says before spitting and rinsing. "Listen." She grabs the small white hand towel by the sink and dries her mouth. "Take advantage of this time you have together. Try to relax and have fun. I know you harbor a lot of pain from leaving Kosovo. Maybe he can help you through some of that. I know he's tough and Mafia and all that. But he's also human. And from the things you've told me, he's a decent man."

"You're right."

"I'm right?" She squints her eyes. "I love hearing that word from you! Have fun. I'm going to tan on the beach today and drink wine. Be all classy 'n' shit." She chuckles.

I smile as I leave her room and head back up to the front of the hotel. I find Nico standing against a stone wall at the top of the driveway, staring at the crystal-blue ocean.

"Hey."

He turns around, flashing me a smile that I can feel straight down to my toes.

He grabs my hand, and we walk to a red Jeep, engine already on. The top is off.

"Two beach chairs and towels are in the back, *monsieur*." One of the staff opens the door for me as another opens the door for Nico.

We both get in at the same time and buckle up. And we're off, wind blowing around us.

The car is stick shift. Why it's sexy to watch him drive, I can't say. But it is. From his thick, corded forearm, down to his heavy hand gripping the shift, I can barely focus on anything outside of this car.

I want to know more about him. I've gathered bits and pieces from others, but I want to know from his own lips. As he drives, I let myself come to terms with the fact that Nico is in front of me. Here, by my side. Part of me can't believe he's really real. I idolized him as a child. Dreamed of him on a nightly basis through my teenage years. I could barely have a decent relationship with any boyfriend I ever had, and the reason is obvious. It was because Nico was always the one I compared them to. And truly, there was never any comparison. And Nico's here. *Here.* As my friend maybe? Spending time with me definitely.

I can't stop the smile on my face as he turns on the radio.

Ten minutes later, I start to notice a large black SUV is on our tail, changing lanes each time we do.

"Uh, Nico?" I ask.

"Yeah." He turns to me before gazing back at the road.

"Looks like someone's following us." I swallow hard, gripping the edge of my seat.

"Yeah," he says nonchalantly. "Alek. He always follows my car. Someone is ahead of us, too. And someone will be at the restaurant we eat dinner in. And someone else will watch the chef as well. In this world, Elira, I never, ever travel alone. I'm also always carrying weapons."

I shake my head, my eyes moving to his body. I can't see anything. Clearly, that doesn't mean it isn't there. Anyway, it is what it is. This is the life.

"We're going to St. Jean Bay." He easily changes the subject. "The waters are calm. There's a great restaurant there on the beach, too."

"What about everyone else? Are they going to meet us later or—"

"They'll meet us for lunch, and we'll party at the restaurant through the night."

"Oh, okay."

Nico parks the car in a small, sandy parking lot, and I adjust my hat. Stepping out, he lifts both beach chairs from the trunk into his arms. In an effort to be helpful, I take the blue-and-white-striped towels. It seems that while St. Barts is really upscale, it's also very laid-back. All of the cars here are Jeeps, like ours.

Standing on the beach, I feel unstable in my wedge heels. I pull them off as I follow Nico, and the white sand feels amazing beneath my bare feet. Pausing at the beauty before me, I can't believe these stunning waters. I've been out to Jones Beach on Long Island, New York, before. But it doesn't even hold a candle to this. Other people are here, but everyone seems to be scattered about so as to give each other privacy.

Nico sets us up close to the ocean before pulling off his shirt.

Holy hell. I swallow the saliva in my mouth and try not to gawk at the huge Albanian eagle tattoo on his shoulder and pec, along with the small scars scattered around his back. My stupid, poor heart thumps as I force myself to turn around and remove my sarong.

"Let's go see if my boat is ready."

"Sure!" I say a little too excitedly, my traitorous voice squeaking.

Suddenly, his eyes move to my pale, slightly freckled chest. And that's where they stop. His face is serious. *Intense.* I worriedly look down at myself. Is something wrong? Nothing seems to be out of place; my boobs are nicely tucked into the bikini top. When I look back up, his jaw is tight, eyes on the ocean. Self-consciousness overwhelms me. I'm sure he's seen the hottest girls on the planet naked. And me? I don't even go to the gym. My stomach is flat but soft, not rock hard. My thighs are on the fuller side. This is me though. I'm not some girl who subscribes to the idea that ultra-thin and rock-hard muscles are synonymous with health and happiness. Sometimes, I need to eat more. Other times, less. And what is wrong with that?

For a few years in high school, I went through phases of yo-yo dieting. I wanted a waist as small as this model or that actress. The result was, the thinner and more enviable I was to others, the more miserable I felt inside. Well, screw that shit. I'm not letting myself feel insecure right now.

I stand taller, telling my inner confidence to stop hiding. My boobs are real. This is what I've been given, and I'm proud—white pasty skin and all.

I lift my bag, and he stops me. "No need to bring anything."

"Are you sure? It's my phone, sunscreen, and a Kindle."

"Leave it all. We've got people here, watching our stuff."

I look left and right, trying to see whom he's talking about. Before I can spot them, he takes my hand, and we walk off to the end of the beach, where there's a section full of water sports.

As we stroll along the beautiful shoreline, he begins to talk about the different beaches on the island and how he has made it a yearly excursion for himself and his closest crew to come down here. I listen and nod, enjoying the cadence of his voice. It turns out that Alek has become a right-hand man for him. When I ask about the few guys who frankly scare the shit out of me, he laughs, saying that that's exactly what they're meant for.

"Each person has a place in this family. For example, if you were trying to create the best baseball team, would you want it to be comprised entirely of pitchers?"

I shake my head, the warm sun heating me from the inside out.

"You need a well-rounded group, including pitchers and first basemen and catchers. Think of the Shqipe like a sports team. I need different men for different positions. Otherwise, it wouldn't run smoothly. I wouldn't have what I needed."

"As for their similarities?" I ask curiously, the blue ocean sparkling wildly beside us.

"There are many."

I can feel him beside me. His heavy steps. His perfectly measured breaths.

"A deep reliance on honor, loyalty, and family. The old Italian families and even Russians have lost those qualities. But not us."

We find ourselves in a small spot at the end of the beach, facing a dock. There are five small boats and then a yacht at the end. It's enormous with what looks like three levels.

"Ours is at the end. I'm driving today."

Before I know it, he's holding my hand to step on. I'm shaking inside.

"Just relax. I got you."

I finally walk on, following him up an unbelievably narrow staircase to the top of the boat. He sits behind the wheel, and I take a seat beside him. With expert ease, he drives us off into the ocean. The wind is blowing my hair wild, but I'm loving it. When we're sufficiently far enough at sea, he pauses. The breeze. The man. Everything about this moment is heavenly. In the ocean, away from all the drama and headaches, I feel free. I pull my knees up to my chest while his are lying out before him, crossed at the ankles. I guess we're stopping here for a while.

"It's been a long time, Nico. I missed you." I exhale, surprised at my honesty. But hey, why not?

"When I first got to London, I tried to bury myself within the crowds. Walked around aimlessly for hours. I had this shitty apartment over a pizza shop"—he chuckles—"with nothing in it, except a mattress on a floor and a crappy wooden table with two chairs left from the tenant before me. There was even one of those hanging lights. A bulb dangling from the ceiling." His eyes glaze over as he thinks back on his time.

I wouldn't dare speak or ask a question, lest I interrupt his flow. He's finally opening up, and I want to hear every. Single. Word.

"I had a veil over my eyes, blurring everything around me. Everyone I knew was dead or gone. Alek came, too. He was a kid himself, but he had no one and nothing in Kosovo. He followed me like a shadow. Slept in a corner of my shitty room with the roaches. I was twenty years old."

His feet slide up in a slow motion as he pulls out a pack of cigarettes along with a fancy looking silver lighter from his pocket. Sliding one out, he lights himself up. I wait patiently for him to continue. I'm barely breathing because I don't want him to stop.

"I would drink myself into a stupor most nights." He lets out a long exhale. "Got as fucked up as I could get in the pubs. During the day though, I had a job at the pizza shop below my apartment. Washing dishes. Honest work, you know?"

He turns to me, taking another deep inhale. "You remember Jakup, right?"

I see his eyes squint before smoke moves around us like a cloud. The sun is getting hotter, and I can feel perspiration beading between my breasts and on my forehead. His chest looks impossibly tan and damp. I turn my head toward the water. Eye contact with Nico is somehow too intense. I'm also worried that if he sees anything in my eyes that he doesn't want to see, he'll stop talking.

I reply to the waves, "Of course I remember him. Jakup and my father originally led the Kosovo Liberation Army." The ocean rolls back and forth, a steady beat. "They died together."

He waits in silence for what feels like an eternity before continuing, "Behar was Jakup's brother. He was the one who got me to London and hooked me up with work. It was his pizza shop and his building, too, that I lived in. He saw I was falling into a fog. Fucked up from all the shit I'd seen and done. I guess he heard a lot about me from Jakup because he knew what I was made of regardless of the fact that I was fucked in the head at the time. Started having me do some small-time stuff for cash." He licks his full lips, ashing his cigarette into a small tray by the wheel.

"One night, I drank myself into oblivion. Came in and out of consciousness in the doorway of my apartment building. At one point, I woke up and saw a man in uniform." He takes a long, hard drag, the tip flaring red. "I got angry, thinking he was someone he wasn't. A Serb." He blows out a cloud of smoke. "Someone who'd hurt my family maybe. I grabbed his throat. Slit it with a knife I kept in my boot."

I blink, unable to take my eyes off his face. His features perfectly match the rest of him. Dangerous. This is the man who has killed hundreds of men with his hands. This is the man who runs the entire Mafia with the absolute threat of violence.

"As fate would have it"—he drops his butt into the water —"Behar went to check on the pizza shop late that night. He found me in an alley with blood like tar all over my hands and a man slumped in front of me, dead. It didn't take long for him to hide the body. See, he was already heavy with the underground and knew the owners of a garbage disposal company. Convenient, right? He took care of the problem before cleaning me up. And then he brought me into his fold. I already had all the connections from when I was in Kosovo. Lots of my friends were now scattered around the globe— and this turned out to be a very good thing. Behar already had a network in the UK. Together, we began to build the Mafia Shqiptare."

I slowly nod my head. It feels like he's telling me something no one else knows. Trusting me with his secrets. It makes me want to open up, too. But the truth is, I'm still sore over the fact that he never reached out to me. I know I was a kid. But, eventually, I grew up. And didn't I deserve ... something?

My emotions start to run, and so I go with my usual MO when I'm insecure—sarcasm. "I was just a kid in the States, wearing pink Chucks on my feet, and there you were, growing a massive empire.

No wonder you cast me aside so easily." My words come out angrier than I intended them to.

His mouth sets in a grim line. "You were safe and sound in America. You were learning in school with a good mother by your side and a brother who loved you. I had been through a lot, Elira. So had you. You deserved to start fresh."

I challenge, "How did you know I was safe and sound? For all you knew, I was suffering. There is no such thing as a fresh start in this life. We all carry our past with us, wherever we go."

He looks up at the clear sky, exasperated, before bringing his gaze back down to mine. "You weren't suffering, Elira. You were a regular kid, dealing with typical American problems. Which is exactly what you should have been doing." He speaks like he knows.

And, sure, maybe I wasn't exactly having a rough go. But how would he know how I fared?

I open my mouth to ask, but he speaks first, "I knew you were all right because you wrote letters to me, remember? Sent them to my home in Albania. A neighbor who checked my mail forwarded them to London."

My stomach dips down to my toes. What? "I-I ..." I turn my head sideways toward the ocean, avoiding his face. I thought he never got them. And right now, I'm wishing he hadn't.

For the first year or two after coming to America, everything I wrote was innocent. I was just waiting—no, praying for him to reply and to contact me. After a few years, I overheard my mom on the phone, mentioning to someone that Nico no longer lived in Albania. Still, I continued writing. I poured my heart out on the page—to Nico. I gave him everything about my life. I told him how much I missed him. Weekly, I wrote to him all the intimate details of my life. It was a strange and cathartic habit. A form of therapy for me. Good news. Bad news. Boyfriends. Friend drama. Agron. Virginity lost. College applications. My mother. Her back problems, for God's sake! I told Nico. Always Nico. Well, until I began college, when I decided it was time to move on from that fantasy. It wasn't easy to stop, but I knew that if I ever wanted to really move on, I would have to stop harboring hope. It's been three years since I wrote him.

He whispers, "You loved me for a very long time." He doesn't ask. He *knows*.

My lips part. "You read ... all of them?" My voice is strangled.

He nods his head, and I feel the urge to jump off this boat and swim back to shore. No, I can't swim. But anything is better than this, even drowning. I gulp, my mouth desert dry.

From my periphery, I can see his solemn nod. "All of them."

I mean, yes, the letters were technically sent to him. But he had to have realized at a certain point that he wasn't actually meant to read them. They were essentially diary entries!

I look up at the sky. *Why, God?*

What on earth am I supposed to say? What do I say to someone who has read my innermost thoughts, especially when so much of my life was consumed by the reader himself? I swallow hard and finally look at his handsome, hard face.

"I loved your letters." His voice turns impossibly gentle. "Loved hearing about you from your own hand and heart. There were times when they kept me going. Gave me hope for something more than the hard life I was living. I was in the process of growing the Shqipe. I took down anyone who stepped in my way. But then, at night, before I slept"—he pauses, taking a hard swallow—"I'd read your words." He shifts, as though opening up in this way is uncomfortable for him. "I have them all still. I've kept them."

"You read everything. And yet, you never even reached out?"

He cocks his head to the side, confused. He leans back into the boat before sitting back up and pushing back his dark hair. "Elira," he states my name aggressively. "I wasn't going to write back until you were old enough. It wouldn't have been right. When you began college, you stopped sending letters. That's when I decided to come see you." He opens his hands to me, as though I'm supposed to connect some sort of dots.

"Wait," I say. "You came to see me?" Now, it's my turn to be confused.

"Yes. I came to see you in Tobeho. I saw your mother. She told me you hated me. Wanted nothing to do with me. Me!" He points to his thick chest. "The man who had smuggled you into freedom. The man who always put you first. I was fuckin' insulted, Elira. Livid that she'd told you such a lie that you so easily believed."

"Nico," I start, shaking my head, "what lie? I don't understand this. I stopped writing to you because I hadn't heard back in so many years. I never knew you'd even gotten those letters. I was trying to give myself a shot at moving on." Complete panic rolls through my belly. What is he saying?

"She told me you thought ..." He pauses, taking my head between his callous hands. "She told me you thought I'd orchestrated the death of your father and Jakup that night. So that I could take over the KLA."

Devastation has my head feeling light. "She thinks you aligned with the Serbs?" I repeat. I think I'm in shock. "To kill my father?"

"Yes. And she told me that you thought so as well."

"Why would she say that?"

"I have no idea. I have asked myself a million times, *Why?* But the truth is, she always hated me. Never thought I was good enough to be where I was."

"That's ridiculous."

He cocks his head to the side. "Is it?"

"But then you set up this entire thing with Agron. Why?"

"Why?" He laughs, squinting his eyes. "To bring you back to me, Elira. Why else? I paid ten grand to settle his debts. You think I gave a fuck about that money or even cared if he paid me back? That amount means almost nothing to me. It was just the way to get you through my door.

"After all those years and letters you wrote to me, I wanted to find a way to tell you the truth. I hated thinking you thought so low of me, that I'd killed your father. I couldn't give a fuck what anyone else thought of me—never have. But you? I couldn't let you believe that lie. Never in a million years would I have had your father killed.

Never. If only because he was yours. I didn't think you'd hear me unless I locked you in."

If I wasn't sitting, I'd collapse.

"My mom thinks you killed him." I look back out to the water. Thinking out loud, I say, "That's why she was always trying to pull you away from me. She never told me that. Just always, 'Stay away from Nico.'" My breaths quicken. "There must be some sort of explanation. I'll call her. I'll find out why. There has to be some mistake. It's fixable. I'm sure of it." My voice trembles.

How could she have kept this theory to herself? How could she possibly think this about the man who helped us to escape? I'm not sure if I should scream or cry.

He shakes his head, jaw clenching. "I thought ... if that's what you were told and that's the reason you stopped writing to me"—he exhales—"then nothing short of kidnapping you would bring you back to me. How else could I show you my innocence? Agron being a moron and coming to me to pay his debt was just the spark I needed." He scoots closer to me. "Let's just put your mother aside for now. You believe me, don't you? That I never killed your father?"

I look at him. I trust Nico. I always have. Slowly, I nod. When I close my eyes, a tear leaks through.

"No more forcing. That ring?" He lifts up my left hand, the enormous diamond glittering in the sunlight. "I hate seeing it on you because it's essentially a handcuff. I never want you to be with me under force, and I hate feeling like you are. If you stay with me now, it must be of your true free will. You know the truth. No more lies. If you stay, I don't want it to be because you're afraid for your brother's life. I'll protect him within the Shqipe. Stay here with me because ... you want me."

I shiver, still unable to turn my head.

"Look at me, Elira. I can't read what you're feeling if you don't let me see your face."

The ugly cry wells from my toes up into my sinuses. My lip quivers, and my eyes fill. *Why wouldn't she have shared this theory with me?*

With all my strength, I open my eyes. Let him in. For the first time in all my life, I allow myself to be open for another. His eyes flash with emotion.

"There you are." He lifts me up, bringing me down between his legs and holding me tightly to his body.

I put my head in the crook of his neck. In his arms, I feel precious.

But I can't shake the fact that since we've reconnected, it's been mentally exhausting. He hasn't been consistent. Can I trust that now that he will be?

"The first time I saw you again after all these years was when you stole me. And then you were cold but then hot and then cold. Is all of that back and forth done?" I press my lips together, wanting to hear that, yes, it is.

"I wasn't cold, Elira. I was careful. Last night and today, I've been speaking about my past with you. Do you think I do that normally?" His voice is measured, like he wants to make sure I catch each word. "And what would you have done had I told you my intentions from the first time we saw each other?"

"Intentions?"

"I thought you believed I'd killed your father. You despised me. I needed to be able to change your mind. Because ..." He exhales. "You're meant to be mine, Elira. It has always been so. From your birth, I held you, and it was written for us. Beyond that, you have always been the most loyal, honest, and loving girl. Did you think I didn't see it then, even when you were a baby, looking at me with love in your eyes? It was all there for me to see. You had been born for me. Made for me.

"I didn't know how to bring you back into my life after the lies you were told. I tried to shake you off. But your letters were still in my closet. Burning a hole into my psyche. I had to drag you back to me. Could I have done it another way? I had to have you." Something like worry flashes in his face.

Does he think I'll walk away?

My heart pounds. I'm with Nico, the man I looked up to and loved for so long. And he's telling me these things that I've dreamed of.

My mom is clearly misinformed. When I get back to the room, I'm going to call her.

Tears drip down my face, but he doesn't pull me into his chest and hug me. He doesn't kiss me passionately either. He continues to sit so close to me, his body so large and strong. My head spins.

"You've dated other men. Like Jack, that musician."

I try to find anger in his face, but surprisingly, there is none. I swallow hard.

"He was a nice guy, but there was always something missing with him. You thought maybe it was because he wasn't Albanian. But that's not the whole truth. It's because he wasn't me."

I should explain better. I don't want him thinking that Jack means anything more to me than a friend. Yes, he is a nice guy. But the men just don't compare—at least, not for me. My heart could never belong to anyone else, and that's the truth.

"Nico, I—"

"It is the same for me," he interrupts. "Many women have come and gone in my life. Many have wanted to be my wife. But the spot I reserved for you can never be filled by another. Never. When you were a baby, it was a simple spot. A sweet one. And, now, as an adult, it's much, much more than that."

In Albanian, he tells me, "I will wait until the time is right to touch and kiss you the way you're meant to be held and loved. Let me show you who I am and the man I will be—for you alone. Let me earn the right to love you. I know that my life is filled with danger and blood. But I know you can handle it. And I want you by my side as my queen."

Chills run through my body. And the fact that he spoke to me in our native tongue? My emotions are so high that I can't reply. Albanian is the language I still dream in; it's the language of my thoughts when I'm in deep. It's the language of who I am, and I never realized how much weight it has in my life. And yet, I have no idea what to think of his comments. Am I really going to just fall into his arms and let myself enter his world, which I've never had any intention of joining? My mother, for reasons unimaginable to me, thinks that Nico killed my father. Why would she think that? I'm on a shade-free path right now. A regular college girl with dreams of a big career in a big city. Coming together with Nico would mean I'd be setting myself up within a world of violence and crime.

He puts the boat back in drive as waves ripple heavily around us. Regardless of the torrent in my heart, nothing has ever felt more natural.

11

AFTER PARKING AT THE DOCK, NICO TAKES MY HAND AND HELPS ME OFF his yacht. "Ready for lunch?"

It seems our conversation is put on hold, and I couldn't be happier about that. He said a lot of things, and it'll take time for me to process.

"Yeah," I tell him, my feet sinking into sand and cool ocean water.

Just feeling him close to me like this gives me a sense of security I haven't felt since I was a child. I was always an independent kid, never asking my mom to walk me into school or my brother to sit with me at lunch. In fact, I've always been a loner. Being with Nico and wanting his company is a revelation.

A few minutes' walk up the shore, and I see the restaurant. We're still in bathing suits, but Nico doesn't seem to care. Round white tables are set in the cream sand. Above the restaurant looms a blue-and-white-striped awning, shading the patrons from the sun. I can hear the music, too. It's a steady, sexy beat that has me itching to dance.

Nico squeezes my hand. "The food is great. And this place is the best day party you can find in St. Barts."

He steps ahead of me as we walk up to the wooden hostess desk;

his eyes scanning the crowd. I do the same, immediately spotting Natalie at a large table in the center of the restaurant, laughing with a few of the guys. She waves to me, her smile shining. Before I can tell Nico where they are, I see an emotion passing through the hostess's model-like face as she stares at Nico—lust.

"Do you have a reservation?" She stares at him, spellbound, as he gives his name. "Follow me," she purrs.

The restaurant seems to be full to the brim with important people. They all look like celebrities or athletes. The waiters and waitresses are all wearing white, walking around with trays filled with what looks like glasses of champagne. There's a long bar in the back, too, packed with people who all look incredibly happy and ... tan.

Mat is the first one to notice we're almost at the table. Within a millisecond, he and the entire Shqipe rise with the women following suit. Eight imposing men and the women who accompany them wait for Nico to reach them. The entire restaurant suddenly quiets, watching as we walk. Nico is so striking, huge, and serious. I can feel the growing number of eyes around the restaurant taking peeks in our direction, people wondering, *Who is he?*

We stride forward, the hostess falling behind us. I do my best to match Nico's quick pace, happy to ditch her. When we reach the table, he pulls me into his side, bringing me in front of each man and introducing me. Standing beside him has me half-thrilled, half-petrified.

Despite the fact that the men make no eye contact with me, only slightly bowing their heads and saying hello, I can tell by the way they hang on Nico's every move that they all want his undivided attention. And although none of them have said a word to me until right now, I can sense their interest in what I must mean to him. I'm not sure who does what for the Shqiptare, but clearly, this is his closest circle. Even the ones I recognize from my abduction are almost reverent in the way they say hello. When we reach Mat and Alek, they are completely deferent. While the women remain standing, Nico passes over them as though they're of no consequence. Only to Natalie, he nods.

After we make the round, Nico gestures for me to take a seat to his right. The table is a large rectangle. He is now at the head of the table with me at his side. Once I'm seated, he lowers himself into the chair. Finally, the rest of the table takes their seats.

I know that the men respect and fear him. But it isn't until now that I see their devout loyalty. These guys haven't even ordered food or drinks yet, and it's because they were waiting on Nico. He's their king.

The table finally breaks into chatter; it's a mixture of Albanian and English, and the blend of languages is soothing.

Nico takes a sip of his water, bending toward me. "Just so we're clear, each one of these men now knows what you mean to me. They'd kill for you and die for you."

I let my gaze move around the table. Seeing as this crew abducted me, it's hard to imagine ever feeling safe or secure.

He lifts my left hand and turns it around, kissing the center of my palm. His eyes flash with an emotion I can't place, but it makes my heart pound. This is real. It's happening.

A waiter interrupts us, asking if I'd like wine or champagne. When I look up to reply, his eyes noticeably flare. I awkwardly turn away to find Nico, his demeanor turned to granite. *Oh shit.*

"Apologize." He cracks his knuckles, his voice so quiet. The waiter's face turns red as Nico continues, "You make a habit of staring at another man's wife like you want to fuck her?"

"No-no, sir." He shakes his head side to side, all traces of cockiness gone.

Nico growls, "Get the fuck out of my sight. Next time you see my wife, you put your fucking head down."

He runs off, and I turn to Nico, my jaw practically on the floor. A new waitress immediately takes his place. With a big smile, she asks if I'd like wine or champagne.

I tell her I'll have the champagne. After she pours, I'm surprised to see it's pink.

"Rosé," Nico tells me, earlier anger apparently vanished. "You'll love it."

The waitress pours a glass for Nico as well.

Who knew it would be so easy to get spoiled? When I finally have my own job, I'm buying myself a big bottle of rosé to celebrate.

Is this how most of the students at Green live? Fancy trips on gorgeous beaches?

I look around, wondering if there are any familiar faces here. Taking another sip of my rosé, I feel a bit like an imposter. I'm not usually the one being served; I'm the one doing the serving. But here I am, drinking champagne and enjoying the party like all the other people here. It's strangely unnerving.

"Elira!" Natalie calls out. She's across the table from me, a few seats to the right.

Alek is beside her, his arm wrapped behind the back of her seat.

I lift my glass, trying to shake off my melancholy. "The champagne is amazing."

She nods her head. "The best. Oh, and Janice texted me. She's like, *Where the hell are you guys?* I told her we were here. She is totally going to kill us for not bringing her along."

I bite my lip. "You're right." I feel bad for not getting her invited, too. But it all happened so quickly.

Nico lights up a cigarette, inhaling. He exhales as his free hand grips my thigh, fingers spanning from inner to outer. Nothing is indecent, but it could be. I have to will my body not to shudder.

The corner of his mouth kicks up, like he's happy to have this effect on me. The man to his right—I think his name is Darius— turns to Nico. They begin to talk, but still, his grip keeps me close.

I didn't notice Darius last night or on the jet, which is surprising, considering how imposing he looks. Maybe he just got here today. Even though they're seated, it seems he's at least as tall as Nico, if not taller, with long black hair and a deep scar down the side of his face. He's definitely scary-looking. For a moment, our gazes cross. His eyes are hard and dark.

A silver platter of giant raw fish is brought out by a waiter who, by looks alone, seems like he played in the NBA.

Nico stops speaking and inspects the fish before nodding to the waiter. "It'll do."

That's when the song "We No Speak Americano" begins to blast through the speakers. It's a song Agron used to love. My brother was always into electronic house music, the stuff that doesn't make you want to mosh but begs you to dance in a club with friends.

The tables on either side of us begin to cheer and dance, getting rowdy. Clearly, the song is a fan favorite. One of the men at the table to my right shakes up a champagne bottle before popping it. Suddenly, it's spraying everywhere, and then I'm drenched! My jaw drops.

Nico notices I'm soaked. He pushes back his seat, face hard. He looks mad. Like, really fucking mad. I put my hand up to him, my laughter bubbling up from my belly. I'm giggling, drying my hands on my napkin as the ends of my hair drip with champagne.

"It's fine," I tell him, my smile unstoppable.

"I can get them thrown out if you'd like."

"No. They're having fun. Look!" I point to the couples who are laughing and dancing, also soaked.

"Wanna do it back to them?" He lifts a brow.

"Oh, no." I shake my head. "What a waste. How could you buy an expensive bottle and just empty it like it was tap water?"

He licks his lips. "Let's do it."

I grip his muscular forearm. "What? No!" As if my hand could ever physically stop him.

"Yes. It's fun. I'll show you." He signals to the waitress, who stops taking a table's order and runs over to where we sit. "Twelve bottles of Veuve Clicquot, please."

"Yes, sir." She nods before scurrying away.

"Twelve?" My eyes widen.

"Yes. We live hard, so we should party hard, too, right? It's a short trip. Let's live a little."

Moments later, she's back with the bottles on ice.

Nico hands one to me before taking one for himself. "You shake it up like this." He smirks, standing.

I can't take my eyes off him.

I follow his lead, rising out of my chair and shaking the champagne. I know I should try to act calm and cool, but I can't! Because who actually does something like this? Rappers and rich people—not me. But then, here I am. Life is crazy.

He pops the cork, and it sprays in all directions, soaking our table and me. The group erupts in laughter and cheers, shouting. Some of the other guys take bottles, too, and spray them at everyone. I see Natalie from the corner of my eye, soaked and giggling.

The waitress brings over a platter of shots. "Tequila," she tells me.

Nico takes one, and so do I. Together, we drink. It turns out, the family isn't just for protection and illegal business. They have a shitload of fun, too.

Three drinks later, my arms are wrapped around Nico's neck. My body sways as I close any distance between us. The sun sets, and the party continues. He turns me around so that my back falls into his chest. I grind into him, dancing, as his hands splay across my stomach. He bites down on my shoulder, and I shudder in his possession. He's hard, and I'm dying for it.

Curiosity gnaws at me. How would it be, with Nico? A man who I'm crazy attracted to in mind and body. A man who ... cares for me. My brain asks me if this is something I'm going to regret. I want him, but am I really ready to make this real? I'm terrified of the prospect but so turned on that I can barely see straight.

I push back against him again, moaning at the feel of his cock against my ass.

In my ear, he whispers, "Fuck, Elira. You're making this difficult." His voice is a low, deep rumble.

I turn to him, feeling powerful. I stroke his heavily muscled shoulders, wanting his lips on mine. This man. He just does it for me like no one else ever could. The music blasts around us, but we stop moving, completely in tune to each other. His head dips low. I can feel his breaths against my damp neck, sweet from wine and smoke. The temperature is cooling off, but my insides burn. He stares down at me, deep into my eyes.

Love me, I think.

As if in slow motion, his lips lower to meet mine. And then he kisses me. It's deep. I moan into his mouth as my hands tug on his shirt.

Oh ...

He pulls away, leaning his forehead against mine.

What to do?

I remember his earlier comments—he wants to earn this. And as badly as I want him, I need him to prove himself, too. I need to know who he is now.

You know who he is, my mind chides.

But do I?

This man wants me. He told me so. The magnitude of what he shared on the boat slowly seeps into my insides. I hug him tightly.

I want this, my heart pounds.

He holds me, one hand behind my head and the other around my waist, as though I'm something precious.

Don't let go.

He loosens his hold on me, stepping back. Lifting his drink off the table, he takes a nice swallow.

I take a moment to look around. The women we're with are dancing on our table. No striptease because, out in public, these men expect a modicum of class. But they're dancing in G-string bikini bottoms and tops that barely cover their nipples, drinking champagne and living their best life. Even Natalie is up there, shaking her ass.

The party settles, and we finally eat. Salads and fish and plates of fruit all at once. And then we're all back to dancing again.

By the time we return to the mansion, it's close to two in the morning.

"I can't believe how long we were there for." I stretch my arms over my head, entering my room. "You coming in?" I'm not even sure what I'm asking for. We're no longer drunk, so any excuse I could have had is gone. I don't want to let him go though.

"Let me wash up. I'll come back." He pushes his hair back. It's windblown and wavy. He's so big. Utterly gorgeous.

"Okay," I whisper, trying not to melt.

Entering my room, I go straight into the shower. I shave, scrub, and pluck every errant hair I can find. I'm so tired, but if there's a chance we're hooking up, I want to be as clean as possible. When I'm done, I wrap a white towel around me and pull out a set of beautiful pajamas from the closet. They're pink satin shorts and a matching lace cami. After I'm changed, I look in the mirror. My white skin is lightly bronzed, some new freckles peppering my chest. I can't believe I'm here. Oh, who am I kidding? I can't believe I tanned! I should take a picture for Natalie.

Before I can get my phone, my room door opens and shuts.

It's Nico.

He leans against the wall, sexy as hell in black jersey sleep pants and no shirt. I open and shut my mouth. Is this it?

My body hums, *I want him.*

I step up to him. "I'm happy to be here with you. On this trip, I mean."

"Yeah?"

"Yeah." I nod. "I thought maybe there'd be more ... drama."

"Gun fights?" He smirks.

"Something like that." I shrug. "Maybe some drug deals or a dead body in the ocean."

"The trip isn't over. Anything can happen," he jokes.

"Way to keep a girl guessing."

He laughs before sobering, eyes turning serious. "My world is dangerous. You know this. But most of the danger is on the bosses below me and their underlings. Those are the guys on the streets, doing the dirty work. I've done it all, but my feet are no longer on the ground. How could they be? If I'm going to lead everyone, then I need to stay safe. Are there constant threats to my life and the lives of the Shqipe? Yes. That's why I always have security with me. Are there times when things are on higher alert because of trouble? Yes. But you should know, I'm a businessman first."

"I'm in danger when I'm near you."

"That's right. That's why I have protection for you, too."

"Alek and I had dinner," I blurt.

"I know."

I lean into his arms, and my fingers trail down his bare, muscular back. I want to know him in every way there is to know a man.

"Nico." My eyes roam across his chest.

He may be the biggest mistake I'll ever make. But I want him now, more than I've ever wanted anything. I move away from him, taking a seat on the bed and pulling the pajama shirt off my body.

He groans. In a nanosecond, he's beside me on the bed, huge hands cupping my breasts, thumbs rubbing against my pebbled nipples. He doesn't kiss me. He just touches. Strokes. Feels my skin.

I lean my head back. "I want you."

"I'll take everything—eventually. You know that, don't you?" His thumbs move back and forth, my nipples turning so hard that it's almost painful. "Once we fuck, I won't be able to back off. Not from you. Not ever."

"God," I mutter, feeling drunk from his hands and his words.

"That's why we aren't having sex tonight. Not yet. Not until you're absolutely ready to commit to me."

He pushes off his pants and mine, lifting me up and above him, nudging his erection between my thighs and pressing it against my ass. I have no idea what's happening, but I'm his for the taking. He's so powerful. So ... in control. My body trembles with the thought.

His hand slips inside my folds, stealing my breaths. When he presses his fingers inside my mound, I buck. Suddenly, he twists us around, so I'm in a seated position with my legs wrapped around his waist. His lips are finally on my lips. Heaven. I'm gasping against his mouth, shaking, as he begins a torturous, slow burn ... his enormous cock dragging back and forth against me. It's the most hellishly amazing torture.

"So responsive," he murmurs. "All for me."

I can feel my wetness leaking on his dick. My heart hammers. Is he going to fuck me? Fear hangs onto the heels of want. Would it hurt? He's so big, and while I'm not a virgin, I'm not experienced.

All thoughts cease to exist when he pulls his fingers out from my body. He stills, and I stop breathing. Slowly, he puts his fingers into his own mouth. My eyes widen.

"You taste perfect."

My entire body is focused on him, every cell tuned into this moment. His gorgeous face, pulsing with arousal. His eyes, open and glossy. He brings me back to that position, rubbing me up and down against himself. My clit tightens. I swear, I can feel his cock pulsing. I might die from this pleasure. He keeps rocking me as hot sweat beads on my forehead.

"I'm going to make you come." It's a threat. A promise.

I'm throbbing. His mouth moves to my nipple, and he bites down, almost viciously, before sucking the pain away. Holy hell.

He grunts, pushing me down harder. Harder. HARDER.

Oh my God. "What—I can't. I can't." Am I begging him to stop? To keep going? I'm out of my mind.

"I can feel your heat. Soaking me. When you give yourself to me, I'm going to own you. I'm going to have you on your knees, begging for it. I can't wait to see that."

I want to beg him now, but my mouth can't seem to form words. His fingers move back to my clit. A punishing rhythm. My whole body is damp. I look down. His strong chest glistens. I want him to claim me. I try to move myself to catch his cock, but he won't budge. His pace gets more frantic until every nerve in my body is coiled. I can feel the edge of him against my ass. Holy fuck. It's coming.

He grunts, long and hard, as his cock keeps moving between my thighs, wreaking havoc.

"More. More. More," I'm chanting.

Adjusting my hips, so my thighs close in better around his shaft. He rears back, gripping my neck, forcing our eyes together.

I love you, they say. *You belong to me. Mine.*

Those eyes. I know them. I know this man. My body quivers, the orgasm boiling through me like a thunderbolt. His hands move to my waist, letting me ride out my pleasure. I'm done, muttering and moaning, sweat dripping. He grabs my hand, forcing it around his cock. I pump up and down only once, and he shouts, hot cum filling my palm. My body crumbles on top of his, and he holds me to him, gripping the back of my head. Nico is safety and warmth.

I blink, staring at his full lips and straight jawbone. Eyes so dark, staring at me with a strange kind of wonder.

It's minutes before he turns to the side table, picking up a small towel and wiping my hands and inner thighs with a gentleness I didn't think possible. My body shudders as he cares for me. When he's finished, I move to stand. Body swaying, I use the bathroom. I return to find Nico lying on his back beneath the white sheet, a strong arm behind his head.

Moving next to him, I lie on my stomach, tracing the Albanian eagle tattoo on his shoulder. "I love this." My voice is hoarse.

"Respect for the motherland." He rolls his eyes, and I laugh. Almost all Albanian men have this same tattoo somewhere on their body. It's tacky but awesome. Our form of pride.

"When did you get it?" I whisper, although there is no need to.

"Back in Kosovo."

I press my nose against his chest and breathe in. It soothes me.

"Come on, baby. Let's sleep."

I turn around, and he pulls me into him, creating a man-made cocoon. He could have ravaged the hell out of me. But he didn't. I exhale, the heaviness in my body taking over. I love him.

12

I WAKE UP AND CHECK THE TIME. STARING AT THE BEDSIDE CLOCK, I RUB
my eyes. No. It couldn't be. I look again. It's almost noon! I pop up,
confused and exhausted. I haven't slept that late since ... well, ever.
The bed is also empty. Where's Nico? He must be outside already.

I brush my teeth before stepping into the shower, which is still
amazing. After stepping out and wrapping myself in a towel, I go to
the closet.

I slide on a beautiful black triangle string bikini. It's sexy, not
trashy, with just the perfect amount of coverage. I tie a gauzy black
sarong around my waist and put on a pair of silver wedges on my feet.
On the right side of the closet, purses stand. I spot a silver netted bag.
It looks like it'll work for the day. I take it off the shelf and remove the
paper stuffing. Inside goes my wallet, phone, Kindle, and sunscreen.
Perfect. I wonder if there are sunglasses in here. I open the drawers,
and in the third one, I find four pairs. Chloe. Gucci. Oliver Peoples.
Saint Laurent. I open each one and go with the round black Gucci
frames. They're gorgeous. Very Audrey Hepburn.

Before leaving, I look at myself in the floor-length mirror. I'm glad
to say that I'm still me, even with all the designer duds. Have I been

feeling better or more confident in these fancy things? I guess they look pretty good on me. And it does feel nice, getting the extra attention for looking so good. Exciting even. Like I'm acting in a movie where I get to be the girl everyone wants to be. On the other hand, it's annoying. I didn't earn the right to wear these things. Well, whatever. One day, I will. And I know when that day comes, I'll feel like a million bucks, wearing clothes I earned. I'll see this as a little test run. Regardless, I'm still me with or without these things. Still the girl from Tobeho, studying at Green.

I catch movement from the corner of my eye. Nico comes walking through the balcony door, looking so gorgeous that it's almost too much. Dark aviator sunglasses, blue bathing suit, and a navy shirt.

"There you are," he tells me with me a soft kiss to my lips.

"What were you doing out there?" I gesture to the balcony.

"Reading the paper. Smoking. Drinking coffee and waiting for you to finish up."

"You could have told me you were waiting—"

"No." He shakes his head. "You don't need to rush on vacation. Do you want to eat here or upstairs?"

"Here's good." I smile.

He picks up the room phone and tells whoever is on the line to bring breakfast right away. Twenty minutes later, a feast is brought to the balcony. Nico and I eat together and talk. I listen as he tells me about upgrades he's considering for his pizza shops. From what I'm gathering, it seems like Nico does a blend of illegal and legal businesses. He gives so much thought to everything he does.

He asks me about my life, too, but I know it's only for my benefit because he knows everything there is to tell. I'm glad he's letting me talk though. When I mention my upcoming interviews, his eyes light up.

"You'll get whatever job you want. Always so bright and hardworking."

His compliment fills me up to the brim. The fact that he's supportive of my dreams intensifies the way I already feel about him.

I think about Elena and Mat and how accepting he is of her vocation. Is that how it could be with me and Nico?

When we're done chatting, he drags me back into the bed, ruining me with his mouth. Both of us are naked. I can hear the ocean waves crashing. His head moves into my lap, and my fingers rake through his thick hair. I'm happy to see he likes this, being taken care of by me.

"It's amazing here."

He makes an agreeable sound, like he's too tired to speak.

I smile, kissing his forehead. "What is it going to be like when we leave?"

In what feels like a ninja move, he switches our positions, so I'm pinned beneath him. His strong, tanned chest looming above me. "When we leave here"—he brings himself down like a push-up, kissing my neck—"we're going to keep going just like this. Until you're done with school. Until we're together the way we should be."

"School is annoying," I whisper, wishing I could fast-forward time.

"Next semester, make sure you have no classes on Mondays or Fridays. Spend Thursday night through Monday night with me."

"Tell me more about London. I've never been."

He shifts himself, so my head is nestled on his shoulder. "London is pretty incredible—when you've got money. I made a lot of close friends there. The Italians control the ports in mainland Europe. 'Ndrangheta is the most powerful Italian Mafia. And because of our friendship, I was able to expand our operations. Together, we employ about three hundred thousand at the Dutch ports. I convinced 'Ndrangheta to outsource their smuggling to us."

"Albanians have always been good at moving things. Remember how we'd move things around to confuse the Serbs?"

He chuckles.

I press my lips together. "You're telling me secrets. The FBI could force me to speak, you know."

He moves himself above me, a sparkle in his eye. "I know what you'd say to them."

"Do you?"

"You'd say Nico Shihu has the biggest dick and the best—"

I grip his head and force him down to me, kissing him through our laughter.

He moves back up again, and my eyes rove over his face. He's all hard lines, full lips, and warm, glazed eyes. He loves me.

~

WHEN WE LEAVE THE ROOM, it seems all hell has broken loose; any semblance of remotely clean fun is gone, done, finished. Girls are dancing everywhere. And it isn't a dozen anymore. There might be twenty extra women here now who weren't here before. I keep my head down as we walk toward the pool bar, hand in hand. Holy shit, this is awkward. Adding insult to injury, it's that slow rap music that's probably on a playlist titled Stripper Pole Hits.

Nico's arm around me tightens. "You're here with me. Don't let a little skin freak you out."

I stop walking, forcing him to pause. "You didn't want to warn me? Like, *Hey, just so you know, there's gonna be some craziness going on outside. Some orgies.*"

He laughs. "Don't be squeamish now. This is just part of my world."

We stop at the edge of the bar and are offered sangria and mimosas. Nico takes two glasses of sangria, handing one to me. I do my best to keep my eyes averted, avoiding the nude girls dancing on top of the bar. The last thing I want to see is some girl's cooch. I stay close to Nico, not letting him away from me. This place pulls on a completely different set of emotions than I normally use, jealousy being one of them. I wonder what other elements of my personality being with Nico will summon.

I brush some of his hair back with my hands, hoping every single woman here sees that he is off-limits. *Hear that, bitches? Mine!*

Sunlight plays off his tanned skin, his navy T-shirt tight enough to show he's jacked, but not so tight that it's suffocating. He's so physically and emotionally strong.

A woman struts over to us, wearing a white bikini, if you could call a set of strings with teeny pieces of cloth a bikini. A smile fills her face. It's the kind that makes me want to slap it off. I've never seen her before. Long black hair and brown eyes, like a doe.

"Hello." She has a beautiful French accent.

When she licks her lips, I notice a silver tongue piercing peeking from inside her mouth.

I shoot her a look of, *And you are?*

She looks up at Nico, and he stares down at her.

"Hi, Colette."

They know each other.

She smells like dark fruit, and my stomach twists.

"Darius," Nico calls out.

A few seconds later, the man appears. He's gigantic. Maybe close to six-five. Black hair braided down his back like a rope. And that scar …

Colette appreciatively cocks her head to the side before Darius slides his gigantic hands up and down her bronzed shoulders. She looks back at us, beckoning. "The two of you will join us, *oui?*"

She looks directly at Nico, and I instinctively squeeze his hand, signaling no.

Nico chuckles, lowering himself to my ear. "I will never share you. And Darius won't touch her either. He'll find someone who will."

My curiosity rises, but we walk away. I turn back to see Darius lifting her onto a barstool. He doesn't seem to mind that we've left.

When we're a few feet away, I can feel my face turning red. Nico pulls me to him, kissing me until I relax.

"I didn't like that," I admit.

"They're here for a little fun. Nothing more. Come." He starts to walk, dismissing my nerves. "Let's go in the hot tub."

I take off my little coverup dress, leaving it on a blue-and-white-striped lounge chair. Nico must say something to the people inside because, in a matter of seconds, the tub is emptied of guests. He steps in, the steam billowing around him. I step inside after he's sitting comfortably.

The rest of our afternoon, we talk and kiss and focus on nothing other than ourselves until I can barely make out the rap music playing in the background.

13

I WAKE UP, GROGGY AND CONFUSED. I HEAR A SHOWER RUNNING. Rubbing my eyes, I grab my phone off the side table, wanting to check the time. I have a text message from Agron. *Check your e-mail*, it says.

Elira,
How is St. Barts? I hope you've had your fun. Has Nico taken advantage of you? Hurt you? We'll make him pay.
Now, listen, something is going down soon. I can't give details, but I need you to stay calm, no matter what. Remember I'm your brother. I'd never hurt you.
I will no longer be working for the Mafia Shqiptare and Nico.
The Albanian Men is what we call ourselves.
Soon, you'll be free of him.

Oh shit. Fuck, shit, fuck, fuck, fuck. Agron.

I drop my head in my hands, not sure what the hell to do. What is he thinking? His e-mail is too cryptic. He'd never hurt me? Stay calm, no matter what? This is bad. Really fucking bad. Should I tell Nico about this? No way. That might earn my brother a one-way ticket to the graveyard. I have to just stall him. Wait it out. We go back home tonight. I'll speak to Agron then.

Nico steps out of my bathroom, steam rolling behind him and a white towel around his trim waist. My heart sinks. Agron is making a liar out of me.

He seems to notice my mood because he asks, "Hey, are you all right?"

"Fine!" I plaster a smile on my face. "Just a headache."

"I didn't think you had too much to drink." He takes a seat next to me. He's worried.

"No. Not at all. I'm not sure what it's from. Once I get moving, I'll feel better."

I stand up and walk to the closet, doing anything I can to avoid his knowing eyes. If he sees my face, he'll be able to tell something is wrong. He's always been so good at that.

"Let me get you something."

I hear rustling in the bathroom but refuse to turn my head. I'm moving dresses from left to right and sifting through sets of plain T-shirts that are as soft as my old ones but miraculously new.

I hear him behind me when he says, "Aleve. I had them stock up on everything in here."

I look at the tag on a simple V-neck blue T-shirt, keeping myself busy. James Perse.

I murmur, "You really set up the entire room. Clothes. Everything."

"For you." He wraps his arms around my body and kisses the side of my neck before handing me the pills with a cup of water.

I quickly swallow them down.

"You like everything in here?" Kiss.

With my eyes shut, I tell him, "Of course."

My brother's face flashes in front of my mind's eye. What will become of him?

"Nico," I ask, my back still pressed against his chest, "you'll always be honest, right?"

He hums his assent, lips against my bare shoulder.

"Why did you choose me to be your pretend wife?"

"I told you already." His lips tease kisses in a line down my shoulder, voice so gentle.

I shut my eyes, leaning my head back. Despite my inner turmoil, I love the feel of him.

"I wanted you back in my life." Each consecutive kiss is slower and longer than the last.

My legs weaken.

"I needed to make sure you'd come to me. After what your mom said, I thought I needed to use more extreme measures." Kiss.

"What we have is real, r-right?"

Suddenly, he stops moving. I can feel the heavy beats of my heart as he says, "What is it that's making you nervous?" His voice is deceptively calm.

Even though we're no longer touching, I can feel his energy. Coolness radiates where warmth used to be. I wouldn't dare turn around, not now.

"Did something happen between last night and now?" he whispers, so dark, so carnal.

Oh shit.

"Nothing." The lie burns like sour acid.

"Are you sure?" His voice is slow and steady. Scary as fuck.

When I don't reply, his hands twist me around to face him. I tightly shut my eyes.

With his index finger, he lifts my face to his. "Open," he commands.

Slowly, he comes back into view.

"I don't know what you're hiding. But you'd better figure out how to tell me whatever it is and come clean. I'm not a patient man, Elira."

Before I can think about his words, his lips are on mine, soft and gentle. He's tasting me, warm tongue sweeping through my mouth. And then harder, his hands grip my body like he owns it. I want his body warmth against mine, but I wouldn't dare move.

Please believe me, my kiss begs.

His hands tangle into my hair, slightly pulling. My head spins off into space.

Oh ...

And then he stops, his lips turning dead cold over mine. He tightens his grip on my hair, tilting my head to the side. His breaths are short and choppy. My body knows in this instant that everything is about to change.

In my ear, he whispers, "The truth. I'll be waiting for it."

He lets go of me, straight mouth on his gorgeous, hard face, and turns away. It's worse than if he screamed. Where is he going? When he drops his towel to the floor, all I see is his perfectly hard and tight ass strutting into the bathroom. How badly did I just fuck up? I need to fix this!

While he's in the other room, I pace. My brother on one side, Nico on the other.

Agron, Agron, Agron. Why?

He steps out of the bathroom in a white bathrobe, walking directly to the door. I swallow hard, waiting for him to speak. His hand touches the knob. Opens it. And out he goes, taking all the warmth from the room with him.

I re-read the e-mail from Agron before hitting Reply. My hands shake almost uncontrollably.

Agron,

What are you doing? Are you insane? Nico is so good to me. He has treated me like a queen. I think you have the completely wrong idea. He isn't trying to steal my virtue or ruin me. I know I never wanted to be part of this life before, but it seems to have chosen me. And just as you said all those months ago, we aren't strangers to this world. It isn't what I would have chosen necessarily, but Nico has always been my soul mate. I'll take him however he is.

Agron, you CANNOT try to hurt the Shqipe or Nico. They are very power-ful. Nico never travels alone. They won't hesitate to kill you.

Whatever plan you have, STOP.

Elira

I go into the bathroom, washing my face and brushing my teeth. I'm trembling as I use the towel to dry my face. Back in the room, I check my phone. Another e-mail from Agron.

Elira,

He's brainwashed you. The man is psychotic. I used to think he was amazing, too, because of what we knew from the old days. But we had it wrong. He is extremely dangerous, and he's willing to do anything to get what he wants.

I spoke to Mom.

Did you know that Nico orchestrated the death of Jakup and Papa? He wanted to be in power and knew that they had to be taken down in order for him to rise. He worked with the Serbs! He's a traitor of the worst kind. Mom explained it all to me. I could never take orders from a man like him. Just stay calm, no matter what. Act as you normally would.

Agron

I shut my phone, shock initially putting my entire body on pause. No. I'm not going to sit here, frozen. I gotta figure this out. I have to speak to my mother.

I pick up the phone, and with a shaking hand, I dial her number. She answers on the second ring.

"Mama?"

In a rush, she asks, "Are you all right? I'm just about to leave for work—"

"Why do you think Nico killed Papa?" I cut directly to the chase.

"Elira ..." Her voice trails off.

"I need to know. This is important. Agron is trying to avenge Papa because he thinks that Nico orchestrated his death. You told him this. Tell me why."

I can hear her breaths over the phone. A chair pulling out. I can imagine her taking a seat. "Remember I told you how Nico threatened your father for slapping you?"

"Yes. And?"

"He always had his evil eye on Papa after that. I think he was always jealous of him. Jealous that he ran the KLA. Nico was also extremely possessive of you."

"He was my father." I frown, unable to understand where she's coming from.

"Yes, but Nico always wanted to be the only man in your life. He never touched you inappropriately, but he had this need for your utter allegiance to him. At the same time, he continued to grow within the Kosovo Liberation Army. Each month, he grew stronger. The people ... they were all flocking to him. They loved him.

"A week before he died, Papa told me he was worried Nico was getting too powerful. '*What's to stop him from getting rid of me and Jakup, so he can run the KLA?*' he asked. Papa was nervous it would come to that. He and Jakup were running everything at the time. Nico was always on their heels. Learning from them. Taking their ideas and making them better."

"But maybe Papa was wrong. You're connecting things that aren't there. Just because Papa was worried about Nico's strength doesn't mean Nico killed him."

"So, it's just a coincidence that after Papa voices these concerns to me, Jakup and he were killed? And then Nico comes flying into the dining room at that exact moment and manages to save you?"

"Why didn't you tell me this before?" My entire body shakes like a leaf, doubt creeping around my insides like a shroud.

"Because I didn't think it mattered. Nico has nothing to do with your life, and you promised me that he never would. He does have nothing to do with your life, right?"

I blink. Swallow hard. "Agron wants to avenge Papa's death. W-why did you tell him then?"

"Because I wanted to stop him from trying to join the Mafia Shqiptare! He admitted to me that he was joining. He had this idea that Nico would bring him under his wing. If Agron wants to avenge his own father, that's his right as his firstborn son."

"Oh God." I sit down on the bed, gripping the sheet. "Mom, you're wrong. You have never been more wrong about something. I gotta go."

"Elira," she snaps. "Tell me you haven't connected with that monster!"

"I'll talk to you later, Mom." I hang up the phone, my body trembling.

What is going on in my life? I have to calm myself down and think about all of this rationally. I shrug the self-doubt off my shoulders, needing to clear my head so I can think.

First off, why would Nico lie to me? I have nothing to offer other than myself. He dragged me back to him and used my brother because he thought there wasn't another way to get to me. Even in using my brother, he still helped Agron by paying his debts and offering protection. Not least, how many times could Nico have easily taken advantage of me? Had sex with me? He has had so many opportunities. But he didn't take them. Everything Nico has done since he dragged me back into his life has been decent. And if he were as deranged or obsessed with me as my mother claims, then he would have written back to me when I was a child. But he didn't. In that regard, I'm the one who couldn't let go.

On the other hand, I have to think about my mom's theory. I can see why she'd think that Nico had my father killed. The timing of my father's murder, coinciding with Nico's arrival, is definitely suspicious. But the truth is, Nico was the better leader and the better option for commanding the KLA. It was war. My father and Jakup were more like pillars in the community. Wealthy, well-respected men who had good educations and the money for warfare. Sure, they fought. But Nico had that ... grit. That youthful energy that magnetized people to him. He still has it. His rise up the ranks didn't have to be off my father's blood. It could have been because my father was shot, and Nico was the one who deserved to rise.

I look at the floor, picturing Nico all those years ago. Giving me his food. Carrying me in his arms. And then him as an adult. His absolute loyalty for the family he's built and the empire he's grown. His openness with me despite the fact that he's a completely closed book to everyone else.

My mother has it wrong. I know Nico. He wouldn't have killed my father.

"If only because he was yours," he said on the boat.

Okay, that's settled. I have to think about Agron now. I'm not sure I can convince him of Nico's innocence. At least, not via e-mail. He's hardheaded and clearly already in deep with this other gang. I'll get home tonight and see him first thing.

I walk over to the closet. Choosing a flowing black dress, I slide it on over a forest-green bikini. A pair of strappy gold wedge sandals slide easily onto my feet. Oh shit. I haven't even showered. Whatever. Fuck the shower. I put my hair back in a bun and tinted ChapStick on my lips. This will have to do.

Nico sits at the outdoor dining table with a steaming cup of coffee in front of him, chatting with Alek. The moment they see me, their conversation stops. All I hear is Dennis Lloyd's "Nevermind" playing around us.

I'm an outsider.

All of Nico's warmth is gone. We had a fire raging between us, and there's nothing left of it. Not even smoke. Is he going to kick me out? My heart slams into my rib cage.

"Nico." I smile, taking a seat beside him, and try to calm my insides. "Hi, Alek."

Alek looks at me, his face no longer bright.

Did Nico already tell him that he thinks I'm lying about something?

Alek turns away from me, completely dismissive. God, it burns. I look at Nico, hoping he'll say something. Do something. But he doesn't. Just lights up a cigarette like he couldn't give a fuck that I'm here. That connection we always had together is strained. Damaged even. I need him to turn to me, but he won't. If he looked at me, he'd know that I love him. I could make a scene or insist, but my pride won't allow it. He should acknowledge me.

The men continue to speak, like I'm not even there.

"Yeah, those motherfuckers don't know who they're dealing with.

After all this time, they only learn when the absolute threat of violence is force-fed into their mouths." Alek shakes his head.

"Get Darius over there right away. He'll handle it. He's good at rat-crushing." Nico's eyes look at mine, glaring, before turning back away.

He thinks I'm a rat? My stomach dips.

Alek grunts. I look around, noticing no one's here but us. Even the pool is completely still, not even a ripple in its heated skin.

"We're leaving in about an hour. Get your stuff together."

The men stand.

"Natalie is still sleeping. Wake her up." Nico's voice is curt.

Alek leaves, but Nico stands there and waits. He wants me to tell him. But I can't. At least, not yet. I can get through to my brother, but I need to see him first. Once we talk, this drama will be behind us. The best thing I can do right now is just shut up and act calm. If Nico knew about the e-mail, he might act and do something rash that could be avoided. It's a misunderstanding.

"Want a water?" I stand up, telling my restless legs to calm down.

Moving behind the circular bar, I pull out a bottle of Poland Spring from the mini refrigerator nestled below bottles of vodka. There's a gun beside the Grey Goose. Just another day in this life. I open the water's cap, feeling the sun beating over me as I drink. I open up another bottle, handing it to him. The move feels desperate.

He doesn't take it from my hands. With one more long look, he leaves.

BOTH FLIGHTS ARE ESSENTIALLY SILENT. Natalie is so tired and hungover that she sleeps the entire time on one of the couches in the front of the plane. Nico and I are right beside each other, and yet it feels like we're oceans apart. His head focused completely on his laptop. I want to get his attention, but I know he won't take it until I give him what he wants. Tough for him, he's going to have to wait. I'm not selling out my brother because Nico needs everything right when he wants it. The stewardesses walk by us, asking if we'd like anything to eat or drink. We both say no, and she leaves us alone.

I put my headphones on, the rock music riling me up more than I want to admit. And anyway, how can Nico just expect me to be an open book at all times? I have my own life. No matter how much I might love him, I can't just keep my mind open, so he can look inside. That's fucked up, too.

His hands are typing away at an Excel spreadsheet, focused on the task at hand. Meanwhile, I'm freaking out inside. I just need to get to my brother.

I raise my hand to the stewardess, who struts over to me. "Can I help you?"

I pull my headphones off. "How much longer is the flight?"

"We'll be on the ground in under twenty minutes."

"Thank you."

She nods before leaving. I put my earbuds back on and hear Foo Fighters' "Walking After You." I swallow hard, listening to the lyrics. They're soothing and so sad. Is it possible that I could lose Nico over this?

"You haven't stopped shifting since you got on the flight." His brows are furrowed, annoyed.

"What's it to you?"

He squints. "To me? It's annoying and distracting. If you have to move around like a child who can't sit still, take yourself to the back. I'm trying to focus on work right now."

"You're a real asshole," I yell under my breath. I'm mad and upset over what's happening now with my brother, and for whatever fucked up reason, I'm taking it out on Nico.

"Is that right?" He folds his computer. "How about you end this shit and fucking talk to me? Tell me what got you so upset. I wasn't even sure at first, but the moment I asked you what you were hiding, your entire body froze. You're a shit liar."

"I'm not hiding anything! I'm allowed to have my thoughts. And my thoughts are my own, not yours."

"It's about trust. You're hiding something that has to do with me. I feel it." He grits his teeth.

The plane shakes as it sets down on the ground. All I can do is thank God that I made it back before Agron did something he'd regret. I need to find my brother right now. The doors of the jet open, and the entire Shqipe, plus all the girls, stand up, pulling their sunglasses back on. They're all hungover and unhurried. Each moment that goes by, I feel my desperation grow. I need to get to Agron before his plan goes into play.

"I gotta go." I practically jog to the front of the plane, stepping out first.

Nico calls out my name, but I ignore him.

There are five identical SUVs parked here. A window pulls down, and a driver waves to me. I'm jogging to his car when I hear someone call out my name again, louder. I can't listen. I need to go. It'll all be okay. I jump into the car, slamming the door shut.

Oh shit. Natalie!

I sit up, telling the driver, "Just a moment. My friend is coming back to Tobeho also."

He hits the gas, turning the car around and speeding away.

"Hello? Wait!"

"Call your brother," is all he says.

"My brother? Wait. Who are you?"

"I'm with the Albanian Men. Consider yourself in our custody."

I pull the phone from my purse, hands shaking. "Agron?"

"I'm so glad you made it! We weren't sure it would happen this easily. We found the Shqipe's drivers having coffee at Starbucks near the airport. Talked with them for a few minutes. When one said he was taking his car to Tobeho, we killed him in the parking lot. Needed you to come with us, and here you are!"

Holy shit. "Where are you taking me?"

"To my place. It isn't much. Just a starting off point. Nico will come find you, and then I'll have him," he speaks like it's just another day.

"Are you insane? Agron, you can't use me as bait!"

"Don't worry." He's so nonchalant that it's shocking. "No one is going to hurt you or take advantage of you. Unlike that motherfucker! I'll kill him with my own hands!"

"You can't do this. Listen, just listen, Agron—"

He hangs up the phone just as the car stops at a red light. I try to open the doors, but they're all locked.

"If you can't stay calm, I'll have to sedate you. Give me your phone."

"No." I press my lips together defiantly.

"If you don't give me the phone right now…"

He turns his head, and I get a good look at his horrible face. A chill runs through me as sweat breaks out on my forehead. With shaking hands, I do as he said.

HE BRINGS me to an apartment building in Belmont. We're in the Bronx. We walk up four flights of creaky steps. It's a shitty building, even for my own standards. Crust peels off the walls. Dingy everything.

Brown wooden door. Apartment 4F. He opens it with a silver key.

Agron is on his knees, snorting something off the coffee table. Shock hits me upside the head.

"You're here." My brother stands up, wiping his nose with his forearm before hugging me. "Thanks, man." He pounds fists with the psycho who drove me.

"Agron, you gotta get it together. Is there somewhere we can talk?"

He laughs loudly. "Talk? Anything you say to me, you can say in front of my brothers."

I look around at the losers surrounding us. Two scrawny guys who look like they do drugs for breakfast, lunch, and dinner and the driver, who resembles an undertaker.

"Take me back," I demand.

"You're asking to return to the Shqipe? How fucked in the head is your sister, man?"

Agron turns around, growling, "Don't talk shit, motherfucker!" His eyes are erratic, hands shaking.

I cross my arms over my chest. "I need privacy with you."

He drags me into a bedroom in the back. It smells like shit in here, like there's an animal farm somewhere. I see a metal cage filled with rats, and my stomach rolls. "What is that?"

He smiles. "Oh, they're cool. We found them in the kitchen."

An air mattress sits on the floor alongside a wooden cabinet that looks like it was picked up off the street. "You can use my bed. I doubt you'll need it for long. Nico should be here soon enough."

"I'm your sister. I'd never lie to you. I need you to listen to me."

He crosses his thin arms over his chest.

"You're wrong. Nico never killed Papa. And now, you're trying to fight a man who will have you dead and buried. Why? End this, so you can live."

I can smell his sweat intensifying. It's the fear.

He grabs my head to face him, and I tell him again, "I swear, Agron. Nico didn't kill Papa."

His eyes move from pale green to completely dilated. He knows I'm telling the truth.

"Fuck!" He lets me go, cursing. Kicks the wall. "Look, it is what it is."

"You're not making sense, Agron!"

My brother has a terrible drug problem. It's so obvious that I can barely believe how blind I've been.

"You need to let me go," I beg. "We can pretend this never happened. Just stop and let it be over."

"The Shqipe isn't the place for me. There's no room to grow. I have plans for myself, Elira. Big ones. I can't just be an underling. But I can't make it happen if Nico is in the picture. Even if he didn't kill Papa, he still needs to die."

"It's called working. Have you heard of it? No one just wakes up a billionaire. No one just wakes up and says, *I'd like to be Nico's right hand*. It takes time and energy."

"Well, I don't want to wait. And now, I don't have to. Those guys follow me. They love me. With their support, I'll rise."

My mouth drops open. He's being genuine, believing his own words.

"Nico is crazy about you," he continues. "He'll come find you. And when he does, I'll end him. And then I'll be the one everyone's bowing to. Our father had the strength, and so do I."

I stare at his scrawny body and gaunt face. "You've lost it," I screech. "Look in the mirror! You're doing drugs. You're out of control. Lead? You look like you haven't even showered in weeks!"

"Don't fucking lecture me!" he yells. "In here, I'm the one in charge. I'm the king."

"Here?" I look around. "This place is infested. It's disgusting."

His hand wraps around my neck, gripping me. "Don't talk shit about the life I've built, you disrespectful bitch."

His eyes are now black. I can see the pulse beating in his neck.

I blink. Agron. Is this really my brother?

"You'll stay here until he comes." He lets go, and I step back. He averts his eyes. To the door, he says, "No phone in here. Windows are barred. Once Nico's dead, we'll let you go."

"How are you so sure he'll be here?"

"Oh, he'll be here. Nico has loved you all his life. He'll come."

"Mom expects me back. Natalie, too."

"Don't worry about them." His hand touches the knob. "First things first." He steps out, and I hear him turn the key.

I SIT on the gray-carpeted floor in shock. That doesn't last though. It doesn't take long for me to scream, "Motherfucker! You pieces of shit!" I slam my hand against the door over and over. "Get me out of here!"

I feel RAGE!

Over the next twelve hours, Agron walks in this room a total of two times. Each time he visits, he brings me a McDonald's Happy Meal and then immediately scurries out, head down, ignoring my shouts to let me go. Not least, he looks like absolute shit. Shaky and physically unstable.

The next time he comes in here, I'm going to jump him and fight my way out. I've had enough. I won't let him keep me here like a prisoner. I'd scream and shout again, but I know it's no use. My voice is already hoarse. I've scoured the entire room for ways of escape. Nothing in here but a pair of ratty old boxers and a few broken bongs. There's a shitty bathroom with a cracked mirror, too. I tried to pull the glass off the wall, but it's not budging.

Surprisingly, I don't simply feel anger toward Agron. I also feel resentful of him. What I work for, he takes. The man I've fallen in love with, he's trying to destroy. Am I supposed to forgive him all of this because he's my brother? Or forgive him everything because he has an addiction? Maybe I should. But I don't. I won't.

I can't do this anymore! He's a grown man who needs to take responsibility for himself and his actions. Frankly, I'm sick of rationalizing everything he does. I'm loyal, but I'm not stupid. Agron is a druggie and lazy to boot. I can't be the one he hangs on to any longer. If anything, my loyalty and love for him have become what enables him to continue his downward spiral, and at this point, he's surely dragging me down with him. If I want to help him, it's time to let him find his own way. If he finds a way to kill Nico—

NO. No. I will not think that.

I hear the front door open, and my heart stops as I hear a man squeal, "I got him! I got him!"

There's a shuffle. Furniture moving?

"I saw him at McDonald's!" the squealer says excitedly. "I told him I knew where his girlfriend was. He came with me willingly. And then I cuffed him before he could react."

What in the fuck? It couldn't be Nico.

"Let me see her first. Before you kill me." It's his voice. Firm and calm.

Holy shit!

"Should we wait for Agron?" the squealer asks again.

A deep voice says, "Nah. I'll kill Nico myself. Fuck Agron."

I step back, and the bedroom door opens. It's Nico, hands cuffed behind his back. He is literally twice the size of the men around him. Healthy and shining, he makes them look like sidewalk grime. The men look up to him like he's a god who randomly showed up on their doorstep. It's a mixture of awe, fear, and complete adoration.

Nico takes a quick glance at me, and I nod that I'm fine.

"Elira, come closer." Nico looks left and right. "They don't mind."

"Yeah," the driver says, "don't see the problem in that."

Even though Nico is in cuffs, he still commands the entire room.

I hug him as he leans down, whispering, "Stall," into my ear.

I've got a job to do.

Letting go, I ask the squealer, "When is my brother coming back?"

"We don't know." He shrugs. "Left two hours ago to get you McDonald's. Then, he called me. Said he had a meeting to make and asked me to pick up the food instead. He owes me five bucks, by the way." He points to me, like I'd better cough up the money. "Lucky for me, I found Nico in line!" He's excited when he adds, "God must want you dead, man."

I clear my throat. "I can pay you back. My bag is in the living room. I've got some cash there."

"Not anymore you don't." The driver snaps a piece of gum into his mouth, laughing. "Took it when you came in."

A chill moves down my spine. I look up. Darius is looming in the doorway, a gun in his hands, looking like the Grim Reaper himself. He's dressed in black, long hair unbraided and straight down his huge shoulders. That brutal face, complete with a scar from his eye to his chin, is eerily calm. I realize he's on my side, but a scream bubbles up my throat. Three bullets are fired, and each man drops to the floor. Squealer is hit directly in the back of his head. He splatters. I zero in on the bones and brain matter spread on the ground.

Nico's laugh breaks my freeze. "When you think people can't get any dumber, they do."

Darius walks toward us, putting his hands in the squealer's pockets. He pulls out a key and immediately undoes Nico's cuffs. I stand there, frozen in place while the room spins. I might have seen lots of death in my past, but it's been a long time, I guess.

"Nico?" I'm nearing hysteria, breaths coming out short and choppy. "H-how did you find me?"

He shakes out his hands and cracks his knuckles. "The moment you were taken, I had Darius find your brother. I figured whatever you were hiding had something to do with him. Turns out, he was coming into McDonald's during meal times, buying two Happy Meals before leaving back to this shithole."

He crouches down to the driver's body and checks inside his pockets, pulling out my phone and handing it to me.

"Darius, get this shit cleaned up."

Bodies.

Dead bodies.

The smell of dirty rodents.

My knees shake. I need someone to hold on to. Oh shit.

Nico grabs me by the shoulders, keeping me upright. Lifting me in his arms, he carries me outside where a black Mercedes awaits.

14

AFTER A HOT SHOWER, I'M ON NICO'S BED, WEARING ONE OF HIS BLACK T-shirts and a pair of his boxer briefs.

He steps over to me, his face flashing with anger. "You stood in front of me and lied! Tell me everything right now, Elira."

He might have saved me, but that doesn't mean we're okay.

"P-please, Nico, I swear, I was about to tell you everything. Everything happened so fast—"

"You were going to tell me?" He laughs darkly. "The moment you knew, you should have spoken!" he yells.

"No, you have it wrong!" I beg. And in that instant, I know—just know—that he's done with me. The thought of losing him. Losing what we have. All of it, it's too much.

"Tell me," he screams.

"I got an e-mail right before we left St. Barts." My hands shake. Pulse rising. "The Albanian Men. Agron connected with them because he believed you'd killed our father, and he wanted r-revenge." My words come out so fast, I'm tripping over them. My insides twist. Absolute panic rolls through my blood.

"Why wouldn't you talk to me?"

"I thought you'd have Agron killed. I figured I could stop him first."

He shakes his head but sits beside me. "Stop him? Did you even know how many people he was working with? You could have walked into a situation that resulted in your death!"

I grip the back of his neck. "I'm sorry I didn't tell you right away. He's my brother. My blood. I know it was dumb of me. It's hard for me to see what he's become ..." My voice trails off, the image of a skinny, drugged-up Agron sitting front and center in my mind's eye.

"Elira," he whispers my name, pressing his lips together before shaking his head from side to side. "He meant to kill me. What would you do in my position?"

"Y-you told me you wouldn't have ever killed my father, if only because he was mine. Say the same for my brother. I know Agron is a lot of things. But he's still mine," I plead. I might be furious with Agron, but I'm not heartless.

On his shoulder, I burst into tears. I keep thinking about me and Agron as kids, like when I popped my bike's tire and he brought me home on his handlebars. All the times he'd flush the toilet when I was showering, just to make me scream. I'd get him back by dumping ice water on his head during his own shower. He's crazy, and he fucked up. He's also a druggie who took advantage of my kindness and loyalty. It *hurts*.

Nico rubs my back, letting me unravel. I'm devastated, shaking so hard that if he wasn't holding on to me, it feels as though my bones would crumble.

He grips the back of my head, pressing me to his chest. "I heard the underlings of the Albanian Men had some plans. Their boss called me. Said a few of his guys went rogue, and they'd probably do something dumb."

Hiccuping, I look up at him. The noise in my ears comes to a full stop. "What?"

"Yes. The moment we landed in St. Barts, I was told."

I blink.

"We're good with the Albanian Men. They do the work the Shqipe would never touch. Our scraps. I don't allow human trafficking within my crew, no matter how profitable. That's the kind of shit the Albanian Men like to handle. They buy product from us, too. And those guys Agron linked up with? They're shrimp, eating the trash on the bottom of the ocean floor to survive."

"What now?"

He looks at me closely, shaking his head from side to side. "It's not your business."

"My brother is not my business?" I fume. "How fucking DARE YOU!" I stand up, wanting to shriek. All my pain and anger boils up.

He doesn't reply. Just watches me, in full control over himself while I erupt.

I heave, "What the fuck? And now, what? You just kill him? Put a gun to his head and then tell me, *Oh, sorry, your brother isn't your business?*"

He stands up, straightening out to his full, enormous height. "When it comes to this part of my business, it's not your fucking concern. But you'd better hear me, Elira. I won't tolerate you keeping things from me or lying. I have to come before your brother." He points to his chest. "Your mother, too. I need your complete trust. I've always expected loyalty from those who surround me, and while you don't work for me, you aren't an exception to that. If anything, I need it *more* from you. You aren't allowed to hold information like that to yourself. Never! You put yourself in danger. You should know I would never hurt you. Trust me to do right by you."

"But my brother ..." Tears fall, and my body weakens.

"Trust me, Elira," he murmurs, taking me into his arms. "I'm not always a good man, but for you, I won't do wrong. I didn't kill your brother. In fact, hours ago, I met with him at that same McDonald's he was bringing you food from. He was the one who broke down crying. Came clean with the truth while he was coming down from a high. He's a loser, but he does love you. Even sent that pissant to come so that I could get to you. I had a plan in place."

My eyes widen. "Okay." And just as quickly as my anger fired up, it disappears.

I lean against him, moving to my tiptoes to wrap my arms around his neck. He turns his face from mine, still angry. I kiss his cheek until he turns just enough for me to catch his full lips. He doesn't move his mouth but lets me press mine against his. I'll take what I can get.

He lifts me up, and I wrap my legs around his waist as he sits back on the bed. He presses his hardness against me, dragging his nose across my neck and quietly, chastely loving every inch of my body until my anxiety, anger, and sorrow quiet down.

"I need the same in return." I exhale, my head slightly clearing. "You scared me earlier. Made me think you'd leave me. I didn't tell you right away about Agron because I needed some time to speak with him. I thought I'd get off the flight and convince him that he was going the wrong way." I'm gulping in air, my ugly cry back in full swing. "It was my mistake. But I need to know that you trust me, too. That I wouldn't ever knowingly hurt you."

He grips my head, forcing me to look into his face. "I need to come first. I need you to swear your life to me. Maybe it's extreme, but this is how it must be. For a man like me. I would do the same for you."

The iron around my will melts. "I'm yours. I always have been. I love you, Nico. I always have. All my life, it's been you."

He nods.

I look around his bedroom. It's decorated just like I'd imagine it to be. Sexy and masculine. Blues, blacks, and whites. The furniture heavy wood and commanding.

"Text your mom and Natalie. Let them know you got held up with some stuff for Agron, and you'll call them in the morning." He sets me aside and pulls off his shirt. Heavy muscles, tanned. Eyes black, like the ocean at night.

I tremble in his presence. He nods to my phone, already charged. I send them the texts, just like he said.

He climbs over me, pulling up my shirt. He slides my shorts down. I'm nothing but a quivering body, flesh bared to him.

"The most beautiful," he whispers over my skin, hands wrapping around my waist. "Mine forever."

"Tell me, Nico."

A knowing look passes through his eyes; he knows what I'm asking for.

"I love you, Elira. When you were a baby, I loved you as a baby. Now, as an adult, I love you like a woman should be loved. I pledge"—his lips trail a path down my stomach—"that you will always come first to me. You will always come before the Shqipe. Before my own life. I love you like I love myself because you are part of me."

I still, putting a hand over his back. "Wait."

He looks up, a small smile on his lips.

"I know that line. I've said something similar before."

I was at the diner. I told Natalie, "My brother is part of me. Helping him is the same thing as helping myself."

"You don't remember?" he asks, his mouth sucking a path down my stomach.

I shake my head, and he pauses.

"There was a doll you loved, but it was dirty. Your mom forced you to throw it away. You told me, getting rid of it made you feel like you were missing something within yourself. And I told you—"

"You told me," I state, the memory rushing back, "when you love something deeply, it becomes woven in your fabric. Disrespecting that thing is like disrespecting yourself."

"That's right." He nods, smiling.

"Nico," I gasp. "So much of me was made by you. That's how it feels."

He holds my stare. "In the ways we are alike, we are perfect matches. And the ways we are different, we complete each other's lacks. You were made for me."

"Kiss me," I whisper.

He exhales, almost like relief. He licks his full lips, heavy fingers stroking my cheek. He watches me like he can't wait to finally take what's meant to be his. There is no other man for me. I kiss the coarse stubble on the contours of his face. I feel the scars marring his skin. Some, he got while protecting our country. I can feel his heat, smell his scent. Oh God.

He murmurs something like, "Tell me this is it." Desperation lines his voice.

"Please."

The look in his eyes moves from reverent to starving. His mouth finds mine. Curiosity is gone. He's in it to take. My core tightens like a bowstring. His hands move so quickly across my body; it's like he's everywhere at once. Hot. He's so hot.

"Oh ..." My breasts feel heavy in his hands.

His mouth covers my nipple, tonguing me. I ache for him. My legs wrap around his, the only thing I can do to lock him to my body. A sheen rises above my skin as he lowers himself to the bottom of the bed, dropping to his knees, spreading my thighs, and taking, taking, taking, like he's parched and I'm the well. My heart trips over its own beat, his mouth marking my pussy as he incinerates me with his tongue. I'm burning to ash, screaming and moaning who the hell even knows what. My hips lift as I explode, and he holds me down, mouth sucking as my fingers grip his hair.

Licking a path up my body, he finds my lips, and I'm dazed. The sheet beneath me is soaked. I should be embarrassed, but I don't give a shit. I want this man. His thumbs stroke my jaw. I memorize the small discolorations on his face, which must be traces of scars.

"I'm ready," I whisper.

He grunts, reaching to the drawer on the bedside table and pulling out a condom. "You're getting on the pill. No barrier for us."

I can only nod as he gently skims his fingers up and down my thighs. I feel so delicate beneath his rough hands.

His eyes light up. "I love you." He licks his lips. "But you need to tell me, fast or slow? How's it going to be?"

My heart kicks up. Suddenly, I remember my inexperience. "I-I don't know. Whatever you want, I guess."

He moves his head to the side. "Don't tell me you're going to be shy. After you saw my cock getting sucked, I thought for sure you'd be more open." His eyes flash. He's teasing!

I grab the pillow and throw it over my head, laughing and dying at the same time. "Jerk! Will you ever let me live that down?" I squeal as he pulls it off of me, laughing out loud.

"When I saw you there, deer in fucking headlights, my cock got a hundred times harder. You were practically perfuming up the room. That's how hot you got."

"I don't do—no, I didn't!" My face? It's burning. BURNING. "And how could you?"

"I didn't even know your brother had brought you. Trust me, I was shocked." He chuckles playfully.

"Yeah, real shocked. The way you ordered me around with another girl on her knees." I'm jealous. Snarky. Mad.

"Tell me how turned on you were." He kisses my neck before taking a small bite.

I yelp. "You know."

"I want to hear it." Another kiss, bite, and then suck.

"Your body," I tell him.

"My body?" He sucks my neck.

"Yes. I couldn't see your face too well, but I loved your body. Happy now?"

He kisses a trail between my breasts. "You have an entire life of sex you haven't explored. I'm going to do it with you. Show you every damn thing I've got and then some. You sucking my dick is definitely top priority." He blows on my nipples. "God, you're hot."

He slides two fingers inside me, curling upward. I groan, throbbing.

"So ready."

He tears the condom open. I watch as he slides it over his thick, heavy length. I lick my lips as he lowers himself.

Inch by inch, he enters me. My eyes roll back into my head as he fully sets himself inside me. I'm panting, and he hasn't even moved. Suddenly, he sits up to his knees, spreading my legs apart. The muscles in his abdomen flex, the visual so crazy hot that I can barely believe it's real.

"You're gorgeous," he whispers, gripping my calves.

My heart leaps into my throat as he raises my legs up higher, over his thick, strong shoulders. He thrusts in and out while his hands work my nipples.

"Oh fuck!" I scream, crying out. What is this? The pleasure is peaking, but release isn't coming. Higher and higher. Holy hell.

Our bodies meet again and again, slamming, his hips swirling and pressing upward, a rhythm forcing my mind to shreds. His sweat drips down to my chest as my pussy tightens, climax building and sharpening. He curses, gritting his teeth.

He pulls out, flipping me onto my stomach like I'm a rag doll. "Get on your knees." He lifts my hips, helping me move.

Mouth dry, I push my ass out to him. He takes hold of me, slamming so hard and deep that my entire body weeps in pleasure. I take him in until his punishing cock hits that last spot. I'm over the edge, yelling his name like a prayer. Seconds later, he comes with a roar. I can feel his cock throbbing within me.

We're both breathing so hard. Not one coherent thought crosses through my head as he gently pulls out. He strokes my damp body, kissing me everywhere. I need to cry, but I don't want to. I'm not comfortable feeling like this—so emotionally vulnerable. He pulls me even closer to his body, and I whimper.

"You good?"

"Mmhmm." I inhale and exhale, trying to get a grip.

"Did I hurt you?"

"No. I'm just sensitive, I guess. Everywhere. It's a lot." I throw a leg over his stomach, wanting to keep him near me. I know he has to take care of the condom, but I really don't want him to leave just yet.

In my ear, he whispers, "It's okay to get emotional after sex." He puts his nose in my hair, inhaling. "Especially with the way I worked you over."

I throw my hand to the right, slapping him on the arm. He laughs.

Finally, I relax. We lie together quietly, so sated, until he rises. He looks too good, walking away from me. I prop myself up, wondering how wild life is to have landed me in this position. Being with Nico feels so natural that it's almost strange. How can one man burst into my life the way he did and yet make me feel so at ease by his side? In his arms is a safe haven—not to hide, but to flourish. With him, I'm the most me I've ever been.

15

THE NEXT MORNING, THE MERCEDES PULLS UP TO MY HOME IN TOBEHO.
Green University still shines from the hilltop while city streets are full
of grime and destitution. I wonder if the gap will ever close.

Nico wanted to come in the car with me, but I insisted he stay
home. It's time I speak with my mother face-to-face. I've been with-
holding this whole Nico thing for too long. Plus, there's a long conversation about Agron waiting to be had. It's time.

"Mom," I call out from the door, still unlocked. Pulling off my
shoes and dropping my purse, I'm in my home. Same smells. Same
everything—but me. I feel completely different than I did before I
left.

She's sitting at the kitchen table. Her body language isn't angry.
More like resigned. "You're tan!" she exclaims, looking me up and
down.

I laugh. "Yeah. Turns out, it's possible." I take a seat beside her.

"Let me get you some coffee. I picked up the kind you like, Koffee
Kult." She stands, brushing the back of her skirt. "Just ground the
beans this morning."

I raise my brows. Clearly, we have a lot to talk about. She pours
my coffee into a white mug that says, *I'm not always sarcastic. Some-*

times, I'm sleeping. Agron bought it for me for Christmas last year, and it's been my favorite since.

"I spoke with your brother yesterday. Turns out, he's on his way to rehab." She pauses, like it's hard for her to get the words out. "He told me Nico is sending him. Is this true?" She takes milk from the refrigerator and pours some inside my mug, just how I like it.

I clear my throat, in utter shock. Nico is ... helping Agron? He did say he had a plan, but this?

"He told me," my mother continues, "he's had a substance abuse issue for a long time. He'd been stealing and skimming other gangs for years. Nico insisted he get help. Afterward, Nico is going to place him in a regular, run-of-the-mill job."

It seems that Agron's punishment is living the straight life. The fact that Nico is supporting him means he's supporting me. A warmth fills my veins.

After cleaning off the counter with a small towel and putting the milk back in the refrigerator, she brings my coffee to the table, setting it with two perfectly brown dates. "I lived life with a man just like Nico. Even though I loved your father with all my heart, it wasn't easy." She points to her own chest, lips quaking. "I had to raise you guys all on my own. He insisted to be on the front lines of the resistance. He wanted to organize and fight. This isn't who I ever wanted for you." Her voice increases in its desperation. "We're here in America now. You can choose any man. Why go backward—"

"He isn't backward," I interrupt. "Nico, for better or for worse, is the man for me. I love him, Mom. And I love you, too. But I'm definitely angry over how you dealt with this. Nico could have died. Agron, too."

"Well, they didn't." She shakes her head. "And what about your career and the life you've been planning?"

"Nico and I discussed it."

"Oooohhh," she says exaggeratedly. "You and Nico discussed it, did you?" Her attitude feels like a slap in the face.

I blink, and her face softens, as though she feels bad.

I take a deep breath, doing my best to stay calm. "I'm going to

continue my life, but he'll be with me. I can still do what I want." My
heart squeezes.

I want to make her proud, not disappointed. And yet, here we are.

"Elira," she whispers, "I don't want to fight. I just want you happy,
and I want your dreams to come true."

"But Nico is part of my dream. You have to come to terms with
that."

Her gaze moves to the dining room window. "Agron told me I was
wrong about Nico. He told me how Nico could have killed him in that
McDonald's, but he didn't. For you." Guilt is written on her face. "Elira," she sighs, "I never meant to hurt you. I only want—"

"I know." I put my hand on hers, and she looks back at me.
"Things could have gone wrong, but everyone is okay. Better than
okay. If not for your bad judgment, Agron might have never gotten
the help he needs." I smile, my backhanded joke lightening the
mood.

"How did we not see the signs?" She lifts her hands in question.

"I guess we just didn't want to. He came in through my window
once. Asked for money. Looked like shit and smelled like it, too. I
didn't know what to think, so I didn't. Or maybe it's just denial. Too
much love. Who knows?" I look down, pressing my lips together. "But
he'll be okay now."

"I love you. You know that, right? I am so proud of the woman you
are. I am so in awe of who you managed to become. You were always
strong and decisive. Your father's daughter."

"I'm still her. And I'm still going to continue working, and I'm
going to get that amazing job and move us into Manhattan."

She looks down. "I can't go there, Elira."

"What do you mean? We always said, once I got my job, you'd
come with me."

"This is where my life is. My friends. Even my cleaning job. And
by the way"—she clears her throat—"there's something else I think
you should know."

I tilt my head to the side.

"After the plant shut down, The Campus Cleaning Company was

bought out by Besa International. I never thought much of the fact that Besa means trust in Albanian. But after this whole fiasco, I began wondering. I've never been fired despite the days off I've had to take because of my back. So, I made some calls."

"And?"

"It's impossible to know for sure, but I'm almost positive that Besa International is one of Nico's companies. They do commercial cleaning all across the country."

My jaw drops. "Wow."

"You know, I never applied for the job. After the plant shut down, Besa called me for an interview. I hadn't even filled out an application! I thought maybe one of the girls had filled it out for me. You know how close we all are. The moment I walked in, they made me an offer. Nothing crazy, but better than the factory job and more than enough to continue giving you and Agron a good life. We always had everything we needed. Home. Food. Vacation time. Clothes."

Tears well up in my eyes. We sit quietly together, sipping our coffees. I only just left Nico, and already, I miss him.

"Have you thought about what would happen if he knocked you up?"

I spit my coffee out, laughing. "It's called birth control. No babies till marriage."

"I taught you well, eh?"

"The best."

EPILOGUE

New York City, New York
Twelve Months Later

THE CUBICLE I WORK IN ISN'T MUCH. FOUR SCREENS, THREE OF WHICH are showing me what's happening within the global markets. When I got this job as a stock analyst at Goldman Sachs, I was screaming for joy. It's extremely high stress, but I love it. I get to learn all about publicly traded retail businesses and decide if I believe, based on their numbers, if the stock will rise or fall. The salary doesn't hurt either. For a first-year analyst, I'm kicking ass. My boss can be a dick. But he's also brilliant, and I'm learning a shitload from him. Overall, I'm happy.

My line rings, and I answer, "Hello?"

"Tell me you brought your clothes to work."

I glance at the bottom drawer of my desk. "Yep. I got my backpack filled with everything I need. Jeans. Black tank. Chain belt. Platform boots. Happy?"

"Hell yes!" Natalie exclaims. "I can't wait for this."

She's taking me to see a new band she's been following on the scene. As a music journalist, her career takes off between midnight and five a.m. It works perfect for me because my hours are usually eight in the morning until about nine at night.

"Are we having dinner and a drink first?" I look to my left and right, relieved that my colleagues are glued to their screens.

"Yep. There's a small Italian restaurant in Alphabet City, next door to Plan B, where they're playing. How does nine sound?"

"Perfect. Text me the address."

"Is Nico, the sexiest Mafia boss of all time, coming?" I can feel her smile on the line.

"I don't think so. He's in London for business and getting back tonight." I bite my lip, missing him more than I have a right to.

He's only been gone a week, but I guess I've gotten used to having him with me every night.

"There's someone I need him to threaten, by the way." She huffs. "Remember that guy Sam I was telling you about?"

"The real estate guy?"

"Yeah."

"I thought you really liked him."

"I did. What I didn't like was finding out about his pregnant wife and three-year-old daughter!"

"Oh shit."

"New York City has the worst men. I'll feel better if Nico or one of his friends pulls a gun on him. If you can make it happen, I'll love you forever."

I laugh. "Consider it done."

After telling me about a new thrift shop down in SoHo that she's dying to check out, we hang up the phone. I lift up a photograph of me and Nico, framed on my desk. We're at one of his nightclubs in Paris, kissing on the dance floor. Over the last year, we've visited most of Europe together and stayed at the best hotels, eating at the most incredible restaurants.

After Nico and I decided to make a go of our relationship, I stopped working at the diner. My focus became school, finding a good job after graduation, and spending any remaining time with him. My mom still had her job that made enough money to cover bills, and I no longer needed the extra cash. I was worried when I first quit, but the truth is, I've loved being at Nico's side and enjoyed every minute of our time and travels.

Despite all of the incredible things Nico and I have done together, it's nights like tonight that I've really been missing. Just time getting into the crowd, listening to great live music, and getting drunk with Natalie. I do wish Nico would join me though. The experience of listening to a rock band is incredible. I wish I could share it with him.

I put my earbuds back in my ears, listening to the new Heretic Pope album. It's flying up the Billboard music charts while Jack graces almost every magazine cover these days as The Hottest Guy in Rock. I'm not surprised in the least. Actually, I'm really proud to have known him and the band. Jack was never for me, but he's still an incredible guy.

A message flashes on my screen from a hedge fund analyst I've been dying to reach. I reply, asking if he's available for lunch next week to discuss a stock I've got my eye on. My ring sparkles on my left hand as I type. No, it's not The Rock. That baby is sitting pretty in Nico's safe. I've nicknamed this one The Pebble. A beautiful two-carat emerald cut with two smaller emerald-cut side stones. It's so classically beautiful, and it was given to me with Nico down on one knee. We were on his yacht with Alek, my mom, and one healthy Agron. The sun was setting. He catered the entire evening by our favorite Albanian chef. When I said yes, fireworks went off. It was pure magic.

When I'm finally done with work, I shut down my computer, change out of my skirt suit, and leave the building. I spot Nico leaning against his black Range Rover. As usual, two huge SUVs are in front and behind his car. Nico's waiting for me!

I run straight into his arms, having learned a while ago to ignore the bodyguards who are surely nearby. He's wearing jeans and a white T-shirt. Nico looks sexy as hell in a suit, but I must say, I love him casual like this, too. It looks like he hasn't shaved in days, and I wrap my arms around his waist, rubbing my nose into his chest. He smells delicious.

He groans, kissing my head. "You look gorgeous." Eyes roaming up and down my body, he takes note of my low-slung jeans and cropped shirt.

"You coming to the concert, or is this just a hello? You must be tired from your trip."

"You changed at the office?" He squints his eyes in that way I've come to know so well.

"I used the lobby restroom. Don't need them seeing me dressed like this." I roll my eyes. The people at work are cool, but they'd probably pass out if they saw this side of me. "You going to drive me downtown?"

"Even better. I'm going to come with you to the show. Jump up and down like you crazy fucking kids. What is it you call it? Moshing?"

My heart soars from excitement, but I bite my cheek, not wanting him to know just how happy I am. A girl has gotta keep some distance every now and again. "Just don't throw out your back. I know how hard it is for you to move at your old age."

He brings his lips down, kissing me hard. "You." Pulling back, he leans his forehead against mine.

"Was it a good trip?"

"Yeah. Things are pretty calm right now. Everyone is doing what they're supposed to do. But those are usually the famous last words before hell breaks loose."

"Well, hell hasn't broken just yet. So, let's enjoy the peace."

"Wedding next week. You ready?"

I stare into his face, and my heart pounds. Even exhausted from an eight-hour flight, he looks fucking amazing.

"I've packed."

And by packed, I mean, I dumped all of my clothes from my small studio in Murray Hill into huge, odorless trash bags. Nothing I own is too important that it can't be fixed with a good ironing job. The furniture is all IKEA, and I'm planning on donating it all to Goodwill. Other than that, it's just me.

When I moved into my own place, Nico wanted to have his decorator fix the apartment up for me, but of course, I refused. The reason

I wouldn't take it? Because I'm not charity. I'm proud of the things I'm able to afford. He was pissed at what he called my "hardheadedness" but relented when I promised to sleep at his place all weekend, every weekend.

"Now, let's go get shit-faced and party." He opens my car door, but I pause before getting in.

He questioningly looks at me.

"You own my heart."

"I love you, Elira. As long as I have breath in my lungs. And maybe even beyond that." He pulls me around by my waist, and his mouth is instantly on mine, hot, seeking me out. His hands slide up over my hips. "After the show, I'm going to fuck you so hard ..." He pulls back, my lips feeling bruised and my panties wet.

I give him a broad smile before getting into the beautiful car and settling in. The best with Nico hasn't even begun.

CONNECT WITH JESSICA RUBEN

Already wondering what's in store for the rest of the crew? You can catch Nico, Elira, and the rest of the Mafia Shqiptare in my next standalone book in the Sex Rock Mafia series —coming soon!

Make sure to follow me on Amazon, sign up for my newsletter, or join my Facebook group Jessica's Jet Setters to stay in the know!

Check out my Amazon author page, where you can find all of my books:
https://amzn.to/2MwV7eF

Sign up for my newsletter to get all the info about upcoming releases, bonus content, and sales!
http://jessicarubenauthor.com/newsletter/

Interested in hanging out with me and chatting all-things bookish? Join my Facebook group, Jessica's Jet Setters!
https://bit.ly/2PdyXnE

ALSO BY JESSICA RUBEN

Vincent and Eve series

Rising (Vincent and Eve Book 1)

Reckoning (Vincent and Eve Book 2)

Redemption (Vincent and Eve Book 3)

Vincent and Eve, The Complete Series

Standalone:

Warrior Undone

Sex. Rock. Mafia. (All interconnected standalones):

Light My Fire

Untitled 2

Untitled 3

ACKNOWLEDGMENTS

There are so many people to thank for making Light My Fire possible. By far, it was the most fun book I've had the pleasure of writing.

Firstly, I must thank my husband and children. They are the light in my life and the breath in my prayers. I write romance because I know true love exists.

I must thank Autumn Ganz at Wordsmith Publicity, who is not merely a publicist but is also my sista from another mista.

Leigh, my master beta reader, who holds my hand while always pushing me forward. Jana, Roxy, Ronna, Jayme, Jana, Keeana, Caitlin, and Candice for cheering me on and giving me feedback I couldn't live without.

Nicole Bailey for asking just the right questions to bring my book to the next level, and Jovana Shirley, whose attention to detail is second to none. Sarah P, your proofing skills are unmatched.

Sarah Hansen at Okay Creations for the BOMB cover.

Thank you so much to Jessica's Jet Setters Facebook group for your love and support of my books! Love you ladies.

Special extra thanks to all the bloggers who shout books from the rooftops of social media! You guys are The Shit and I'm blessed to have you in my corner. You've made my dreams come true.

Lastly, to the READERS! Yes, you! Thank you so much for reading and I truly hope you enjoyed the story. If you have the time, please leave a brief review of this book. It would mean the world.

With love,
Jessica

PREVIEW OF RISING (VINCENT AND EVE BOOK 1)

Before you go, make sure to read the first chapter of Rising (Vincent and Eve Book 1), the start of my Amazon Bestselling series!

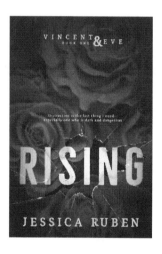

Chapter 1

Oak desks, scuffed from years of abuse and handy knife work, stand single file in the back of the dingy public library. Curled up in a dark wooden chair, with elbows resting on the etched wood, I read the newest novel recommended by my teacher, Ms. Levine. I lift my head for a moment when my gaze lands on the nearly opaque second-story window, grimy from New York City pollution.

My eyes widen. "Oh shit," I say out loud, my voice ringing through the empty room. Eyes registering the darkness outside, my stomach liquefies with dread. I check my cell to confirm the time— it's ten fifteen.

Grabbing my ratty backpack off the floor, I slide the book inside and zip it closed as quickly as my shaking hands allow. Throwing it over my shoulder, I rush out the front door and make it to the dimly lit bus stop, just as the M-6 pulls in. I walk up the steps and swipe my metro card at the kiosk by the driver.

Noticing an empty seat by the window in the second row, I walk over, squeezing my small five-foot-one frame past the woman sitting in the aisle seat. She sighs as if annoyed, leaning back in an attempt to maintain distance. Wearing green scrubs, she has exhaustion written all over her drawn face. I take my seat and lick my dry lips, turning my gaze to the window.

As the bus approaches my stop on the Lower East Side, I raise the hood of my black sweatshirt. Anonymity is key in my neighborhood— particularly as a lone female walking at night. I live in the Blue Houses, a New York City housing project recently dubbed by the *Post* as "the hellhole houses." The nickname came as no surprise, as the complex is dilapidated and crime-ridden. It's common knowledge that cops always enter the building with their guns drawn, assuming that all tenants are packing weapons. To make matters worse, two gangs, the Snakes and the Cartel, are in a turf war for rights to push crack, the preferred pastime for many Blue House residents. The gutters run blood daily. Although I'm born and raised here, my time spent with my head inside the books has left me with street smarts that are at best decent, and at worst delinquent. My older sister Janelle reminds me of this constantly, and in this moment, I'm proving her right.

I'm so close to the building now, only about nine hundred feet away from the front yard. My eyes scan the eerily empty streets that, during daylight hours, are full of commotion. I force myself to stay calm by focusing on this morning when my sister's friends chatted about who's banging who, while old-school Tupac blasted on someone's iPhone speakers. I pull the hoodie closer to my head as my mind revists to the scene.

~

"Jem got pregnant—"

"Ohhhhh shit! No way! No fuckin' way! That poor mama of hers—"

"—I heard that Mark is gonna kick Sean's ass. He owes him money, but who's gonna pay that debt? Everyone knows he spends all his money on his—"

I shift my focus from the gossip mill to the girls jumping rope in front of me, crisscrossing and jumping with ease.

"Yo Eve, you listenin'?" I turn my head to Vania, one perfectly plucked eyebrow raised in frustration.

I plaster a smile on my face. "Sorry, what?"

She rolls her dark brown eyes. "Girl, you've got to get your head outta la-la land!" I flush with embarrassment; this isn't the first time I've been accused of spacing out. "I asked you if you saw Jason. He told Jennifer that he thinks you're: Hot. As. Fuck."

I shrug my shoulders. "Nah. I'm not really interested." She looks at me like I've got a screw loose in my head, and I immediately wish I said something other than the truth. Jason is tall with jet-black hair, blue eyes, and totally tatted from his head to his ankles. Most girls would give almost anything to be with a man like that. And while my eyes recognize his relative attractiveness, he doesn't affect me the way he does everyone else.

"I love your shade of lipstick!" My voice is full of forced enthusiasm, but I'm hoping to divert the conversation.

"It's called Honey Love. It's MAC." She purses her lips together, showing off the creamy nude shade.

I nod my head, relieved that the conversation of Jason is now behind us. "That's cool. I gotta tell Janelle to try it on me sometime."

Warmth fills her face. "Yeah, baby girl. And with your tan skin, pouty lips, and huge brown eyes...shiiiit. You'll have guys lining up." I blush, uncomfortable with the praise.

I turn to my sister, who is all long blond hair and legs for miles. While I share her small nose and bow-shaped lips, our physical similarities are minimal. Janelle is five-foot-seven and statuesque, whereas I'm short and curvy.

Vania clears her throat, rummaging through her purse. "Here. Let me put some on you." She takes out a lipstick and lipliner from her huge black tote bag that looks more like a suitcase than a purse, and gets to work on my lips. When she's finished, she leans back, seemingly pleased.

"Yo, Janelle. Take a look at baby sister over here." Janelle turns her head, smiling as she takes me in.

"You're smokin'. Je-sus!" She winks at me before turning back to Vania. "What color is that? Honey Love?"

"Of course, you know, you bitch!" They laugh together, Vania turning her attention back to Janelle. "I read that Mario uses this new color mix on Kim Kardashian—"

I slide up closer to them, trying to listen to their conversation, but everything they say goes in one ear and out the other. I'm the listener. The dreamer. The girl with her head in a book at all times. But even I know that in order to survive here, I've got to belong. Loners get picked on and picked off. But Janelle? She's the social butterfly. The girl everyone loves. And if not for her, I'd probably be floating in the Hudson by now. I move my body closer to the group, doing my best to fit in.

I stumble on a hard piece of trash on the sidewalk, bringing my focus back to the present. The unnaturally silent air has alarm bells ringing in my head. I wonder if the gangs are roaming hard tonight. I look to the park adjacent to the Blue Houses, trying to find the regular late-night junkies. It's the most secure place for people to do drugs, as the cops never make regular patrols; apparently, they're too busy answering 911 calls. I take a sharp breath; the entire park is seemingly abandoned.

I tighten my hold on the straps of my backpack and quicken my pace, focusing on making it to the front door of my building. My heart rate increases as my imagination spirals. Maybe someone was shot earlier, and now everyone is home scared? Did someone die? Someone must have died. Is there blood on the sidewalk? There's blood. I know it. Fear takes hold, choking me. For all the laughter and friendly neighborhood vibes during the day, the reality is the Blue Houses are a deadly place to live.

When I hear the telltale *hiss* of the Snakes, the blood in my veins turns cold. I run as fast as I can, but the *hissing* only increases in volume. Risking a glance over my shoulder, I see a group close behind me. Janelle's voice enters my mind, *"If you run, you'll look scared. And looking scared makes you more vulnerable."* Even though my heart is pounding like a steel drum into my rib cage, I force myself to slow down. My legs beg to sprint forward, but showing fear isn't an option.

I make it a few more feet when they circle me, blocking any path of escape. My mouth opens, poised to scream, but my throat locks shut. It's so dark, but the shadows of the streetlamps bring their red and black colors into focus. My body quakes from my fingertips down into my toes. Dropping my head, I stare at the ground as the lieutenant of the Snakes moves in front of me. Focusing on his black steel-toe boots, a cold sweat breaks out on my forehead.

It's Carlos. As a kid, he used to torture and kill mice in the stairwell and leave them as threats for people by their front doors. He's been in and out of prison more times than I can count. In my mind's eye, I can see the blue teardrops tatted under his left eye down to the corner of his thin lips, each oval bead signifying a kill.

"Take that hood off. I wanna get a good look at you." His voice is low and menacing. I move to lift my head, pausing at his muscular bare chest. I shudder, making eye contact with his black-and-red snake tattoo. It peeks over his right shoulder, tongue hissing between two pointy white fangs like a beast from hell.

When Carlos sees I'm not doing as he demanded, he throws off my hood, roughly grabbing my chin and forcing my head straight. I can smell his rancid breath as he fists my hair in his hand. Staring at my face, he nods with what looks like appreciation.

"We found something good tonight, boys," he chuckles as if he's found a new toy he can't wait to play with. Bile rises up my throat as his smile widens.

My eyes dart from side to side as my breathing turns erratic. I'm fresh meat, and these animals are in it for the kill. Screaming won't make a difference. How many times have I heard yelling outside my bedroom window, but never thought to help the victim? Countless. Maybe it's karma. Maybe I deserve this for all the times I dropped my head and tried not to get involved. If I only listened to Janelle and made sure not to be alone on the streets at night—

Carlos steps back, pulling a cigarette from behind his ear and placing it between his lips. Taking a black lighter from his front pocket, he flicks it on and off, letting the fire burn at his will. Bringing the flame to the end of his cigarette, he takes a hard pull, turning the tip into a shining ember. With an exhale, smoke wafts around his face and blends into the night. He stands silently, assessing every detail of my trembling body.

"Looks like we're gonna have some fun," he laughs as his boys cackle in delight. My jaw slackens as my mind searches for an escape. If I can't physically get out of this, maybe I can force my mind to move elsewhere.

He grabs my upper arm. I can feel the bruising take shape as he turns me around forcefully, dragging me like a rag doll toward the Blue Houses. The others trail behind us, reminding me with every step that I have nowhere to go. Nowhere to hide. Nowhere to run.

Pushing through the front door of the building, we stop in front of what I always thought was a storage room. Carlos stuffs his hand in his pocket, removing a key. Shoving it inside the keyhole, he throws the door open, using his free hand to push me into the room. I trip over my own feet, the cement greeting me as I fall to my hands and knees. He flips a switch and the light casts a shadow below me. I lift my head and see a tiny barred window above a small bed. I look to my right, only to see a kitchenette with a round table surrounded by plastic chairs. Carlos bends down, grabbing me by the neck and pulling me up to face him. I want to scream, but my throat is closed. I see the exhilaration in his eyes and briefly wonder if death isn't the better option.

He loosens his hold on my neck, and I take deep, but shaky, inhales. The moment I catch my breath, he slaps me hard across the face. My body gets the message—he's the one in control. I open and close my mouth, shutting my eyes and willing my brain to tune out and turn off.

He grabs my chin. "I've been seeing you around. And get this? You're just the one we need for tonight. You see, we've got lots of energy we need to burn off after where we've been." He licks his lips and I can see the dull yellow of his teeth. "I know you like to hide in those baggy clothes with those books in your hands, but I think it's about time you show us what you've got goin' on underneath all that shit." He laughs, pulling out a fresh cigarette and lighting it up. "Take your clothes off for us, and do it niiiice and slow. I think we're all in the mood for a little live show tonight."

A chair is pulled out and I lift my head to the sound. I make eye contact with one of the guys and his head snaps back in recognition. "Oh shit, Carlos, that's Janelle's little sister." It's Jason. His hair is styled in an undercut, buzzed on the sides and long on top. I'm shaking so badly it takes me a second to realize he's staring right at me, waiting for a reply.

"Y-Yeah," I stammer. "I'm J-J-Janelle's sister."

He shrugs casually at the guys. "Let's get rid of her. She's harmless. You know Janelle; she's the one who does all the old ladies' hair for free, and—"

Carlos throws a hand up in the air, silencing him. "Rid of her? Like, shoot her in the head?" He cocks his head to the side in question and the blood drains from my face. "Nah. I don't think I want to kill her just yet. Fuck her virgin brains out, yeah. Let all you guys take a turn when I'm done, hell yeah. Afterwards, you can kill her if you still want." He smiles and grabs my hand, lifting it above my head. I shut my eyes as he twirls me in a slow circle, showing me off to his crew. I hear wolf whistles and try to turn my thoughts into white noise.

A scratchy voice from the side of the room starts up. "Don't rough her up too much at first. I want her to have some fight left when I get my turn."

Tears drip from my eyes, burning as they fall down the sides of my face. "I'll d-d-do anything. Just let me go. Please..." I beg, dropping down to my knees and lifting my hands in prayer. "I'll do anything you want, but I don't want to die."

"Anything, huh? Get up," he commands. I stand on wobbly feet as Carlos grins maliciously. "Ah, you take directions. That's good. Very good." He lifts his steel toe boot, kicking me in the stomach. I double over.

Carlos bends low, grabbing my hair to lift my head and bringing his lips to my ear, his voice a dark growl. "Let me give you a piece of advice. Shut the FUCK up and take what we're all about to give you. You may even enjoy it after the first few times." He puts his nose to my neck, smelling me deeply as he presses a sharp object against my side. My eyes widen; I feel the cold sharp edge of a blade drifting from my ribs up to my chest.

"Listen to what I tell you. Don't want to mess up that gorgeous face. But..." My breathing stops. "I will, IF you don't do as I say. You want to live? Shut up and take it." He moves his knife back to his pocket. "Strip."

He chuckles.

I oblige.

I remove every layer of clothing and stand crumpled. My shoulders are curled down and my arms cover my bare breasts. He thrusts my arms away.

His dirty fingertips grope my intimate parts as if he owns them.

The body I thought belonged to me is now on loan. Finally, my mind separates from my body and floats away. But Carlos, unwilling to let me go in body or mind, pulls the cigarette out of his mouth and presses it against my shoulder.

I let out a scream from the burn.

He laughs.

Carlos turns to his boys, rubbing his hands together in eagerness. "I'm gonna make sure she's good enough for you all, first." They all chuckle at the joke, while one of them stares at me with rapt attention and a look of utter excitement.

"Poker—"

A cabinet opens and shuts.

The smell of old and wet laundry.

I close my eyes.

"Open your eyes and look at me!" Yelling, he grabs my neck to face him, forcing me to watch his ministrations.

My eyes connect with his, nothing but evil lurks in his depths.

I'm thrust forward, face down on the bed. I hear pants unzipping and falling to the floor. I hold my breath. If I hold it long enough, will I die?

"Yo, snake charmers! Cartel is In. The. Housssssse!" Voices and laughter radiate straight through the barred window and into the room. Carlos pauses, turning toward the glass and screaming, "We're coming MOTHERFUCKERS!"

My body shakes uncontrollably. I can hear him pull his pants back up, heaving. "The FUCK? If the Cartel is looking for a fight tonight, we'll give em' one!"

I dare to crack my eyes open, watching as they nod to each other. The rivalry between the Snakes and the Cartel is vicious. While the Cartel has fewer members, they make up for less manpower with intense and frequent bloodshed.

I'm in a state of shock, watching them pull weapons from their pants. Am I going to die? I shut my eyes again, moaning.

"Yo!" Carlos slaps my ass so hard I bite my lip, tasting copper. "Don't think you're off the hook, bitch. I got a glimpse, and now I want in. I'm coming back for you." He raises his gun and thrusts it into my mouth. I choke as he pushes it deeper down. Tearing it out, he nods—his version of a guarantee.

Seconds later, I feel warm hands on my naked back. "Open your eyes and get up." The voice is soft but urgent. Jason is on his knees by the bed, my clothes in his hands. "Put your clothes on, and get out of here!" he whispers loudly.

Somehow, I stand. I'm a machine, clothing myself like I've done millions of times before. He has the decency to turn his head as I put one foot and then the other into my underwear. As I slide my T-shirt and sweatshirt over my head, I realize I am no longer the priority to these criminals. If there is a time to run, it's now.

I take my bag and run out of the room with a speed I didn't know I was capable of. Opening the heavy stairwell door and running up the steps, I take two at a time as sweat pours down my temples. Are they after me? Are they coming? I want to turn my head back to see if they're behind me, but my fear won't let me turn around.

I hear cursing and some screams, but all the sounds are muffled by the whooshing sound in my ears. The stairs seem to vibrate with the sound of gunshots. Have I been shot? Adrenalin mixed with confusion pumps through my veins as I jet up the darkened stairwell; the lights are all out on the third floor, and it feels like I'm running through a black hole. My heart pounds into my throat.

In a blink, I'm back inside my empty apartment, staring in a trance at my gray threadbare living-room couch. I look at my feet and realize I'm barefoot. Oh shit, I'm going to need to buy a new pair of sneakers. I wonder if there's any in my size at the thrift store.

Turning toward my bedroom door, my mind registers the crack down the center. I briefly remember one of my mom's old boyfriends throwing a vase against it, splitting the wood. I walk into my room like a zombie and complete my nightly routine of brushing my teeth, washing my face with soap and scalding hot water, and changing into a clean pair of pajamas. In the recesses of my mind, I know what just happened to me is horrifying, but I keep telling myself if I just act normal, maybe it'll all just go away.

Before getting into my bed, I kneel on the floor, fisting my worn-out navy comforter in my hands. Prayers tumble out of my mouth to God, begging him to get me out of here before Carlos finds me. All at once, I feel punched in the gut. I run to the toilet, dropping my head into the bowl and emptying all the contents of my stomach.

Are they going to come for me tonight? Should I hide? I shut the bathroom door and curl up in the fetal position by the toilet, too afraid to go back into my bedroom where there's a window.

What feels like seconds later, I hear the front door open and close. As footfalls get closer to the bathroom door, my chest constricts, my mouth gaping open and poised to scream.

"Eve, are you in the bathroom? Get out, I need to wash up!" Janelle throws the door open and looks down at me on the floor, momentarily confused.

She gives me a once over. "You look like shit, girl." Her voice is quiet and laced with concern. "What are you doing in the bathroom? Are you sick?" I hear her, but can't manage a reply. She squats down, placing the back of her hand on my forehead.

"Holy shit, Eve, you're burning up! And your face is pale as hell. You think it's food poisoning or something? Let me get you some meds." She helps me up off the floor and walks me to my bed, letting me lean on her as we walk. A few minutes later, she drops two pills into my hand. I put them on my tongue when she hands me a glass of water. I swallow the medicine and a few minutes later, I'm plunged into sleep.

Buy Rising (Vincent and Eve Book 1) now!

Printed in Poland
by Amazon Fulfillment
Poland Sp. z o.o., Wrocław

54478734R00163